Appetite for Death

Janet Laurence began her career as a cookery writer, producing a weekly column for the *Daily Telegraph*. She has written four cookery books, contributed articles to a number of publications, including a series on historical cooking for *Country Life*, and is the author of *The Craft of Food and Cookery Writing*. Under a pseudonym she also writes contemporary women's fiction.

Appetite for Death is the ninth novel in her culinary mystery series featuring Darina Lisle, following most recently *Death a la Provençale* and *Diet for Death*.

She is also the author of an historical crime series featuring the eighteenth-century Italian artist Canaletto.

Also by Janet Laurence in Pan Books

Janet Laurence

Appetite for Death

A Darina Lisle Mystery

PAN BOOKS

First published 1998 by Macmillan

This edition published 1999 by Pan Books
an imprint of Macmillan Publishers Ltd
25 Eccleston Place, London SW1W 9NF
Basingstoke and Oxford
Associated companies throughout the world
www.macmillan.co.uk

ISBN 0 330 37154 1

1 3 5 7 9 8 6 4 2

A CIP catalogue record for this book is available from
the British Library.

Typeset by Intype London Ltd
Printed and bound in Great Britain by
Mackays of Chatham plc, Chatham, Kent

To Ben,
who inspired Rory,
and Alfie,
who appeared halfway through the writing

Acknowledgements

Many thanks to the following who provided much necessary information: Michelle Berriedale-Johnson, for details on running a specialist food production company and also on food intolerances; Richard Anderson of Puddings and Pies, for showing me round his food company and sharing his experiences; Dr Christina Scott-Moncrieff and Dr Yvonne Greenish for medical details. Any errors in this book are mine, not theirs.

Heartfelt thanks also to Tessa Warburg, Shelley Bovey, Maggie Makepeace, Brigid McConville and Lizzie Pewsey (The Group) for invaluable advice, understanding and support.

Finally, as always, my deepest thanks to my long-suffering husband, Keith, who puts up with scratch meals, untidy house and monosyllabic wife until the current opus is finished.

Chapter One

Darina Lisle raised a silver spoon loaded with mashed fish finger and potato. A pair of eyes so blue they made sapphires look overrated gazed into hers, their concentration absolute. Then the food vanished into an eager mouth, a look of bliss came over the small face and a fat fist banged down in ecstasy. It caught the edge of the plastic bowl with its prettily patterned rim and the contents shot out, splattering the kitchen wall and the tray of the high chair.

The blue eyes grew round in wonder and a gurgle of appreciative noises were almost intelligible as two chubby fingers dabbled experimentally in the splodges then picked up a fragment of fish and carefully conveyed it to their owner's mouth.

'What a greedy guts,' said Jemima Ealham. She was sitting comfortably in a cushioned kitchen chair nursing a glass of white wine and made no attempt to help.

'I'd call him a keen trencherman,' laughed Darina, rescuing bits of food from the tray of the high chair. 'Rory is the sort of man I like to cook for.' Some of the depression that had crept over her during the last few weeks, like fog infiltrating a sunny stretch of water, dampening all sparkle and muffling thought, lifted.

'Don't worry about that,' Jemima said idly as Darina

went over to the sink for a cloth. 'Mrs Starr will be in soon, she can clear up.'

'Haven't changed your habits since school, I see. Still get everyone else to do your dirty work.' It was said with a lightness that removed any possible sting from the words and Jemima didn't appear to take offence. She was a tall girl, not as tall as Darina, but well over medium height; thin rather than slim, with a restless energy that kept her shifting in her chair, reaching for the plate of cheese straws, pouring more wine, fiddling with the buttons on the jacket of her shocking-pink tailored suit, worn, it seemed, without any form of blouse underneath. The sharp knees revealed by the short skirt made her oddly vulnerable, an impression heightened by the short brown hair and too big nose that dominated an elfish face. Large blue eyes reflected emotions that changed too rapidly to be identified.

'Never do anything you can get someone else to do for you is one of Dad's maxims, and look where it's got him.' Jemima grinned at Darina.

Darina finished the wiping up and returned to feeding the small child. 'If you're still hungry when you've finished that, I'll grill you another fish finger,' she told Rory, for once abandoning her long held principle of not cooking in other people's houses unless she was paid for it. Feeding people was Darina's business. Before she'd turned into a writer and television demonstrator, she'd been a caterer, but babies were a novelty. She intended them to stay that way, at least for the immediate future, but it was impossible not to succumb to the charm of his big, wondering eyes.

'I've seen fillet of beef attacked with less gusto,' Darina commented as Rory cleaned off the spoon with

enthusiasm. 'Perhaps it's time you offered him something more challenging than fish fingers?'

'Don't you start! Dad's trying to get his latest girlfriend to start a line of gourmet baby foods, says kids like
Rory need educating.'

'Really? Sounds great. What sort of line is she in?'

Jemima lost her animation. 'Val Douglas? Not sure
exactly, she has this company that's something to do
with foods for people who can't eat certain things. She
and Dad are pretty chummy at the moment. And, well,
you know Dad, always thinks he knows best for other
people.'

What Darina remembered best about Basil Ealham
were his absences. Jemima's father had rarely made an
appearance at their school. Once, however, he'd landed
on the hockey pitch in a helicopter, leaving Jemima
covered with glory and for once not having to explain
that her father was far too important running his business empire to attend founder's or sports' day. More
recently, on the rare occasions she glanced at the financial pages, she'd seen his name mentioned in take-overs,
always on the winning side.

'Did you say Val Douglas? I've met her. She used to
write cookery articles for one of the women's magazines
but I haven't seen her around at press do's or the Guild
of Food Writers for some time.'

Jemima appeared uninterested in this piece of information. 'Well, Dad thinks the time's ripe to launch a
gourmet baby food and that Val should do it.'

'Is she going to?'

Jemima gave a hoarse little laugh. 'If she wants
to keep in Dad's good books, she will. They fight enough
as it is.'

'Fight?' Darina found it hard to imagine the controlled and pleasant Val Douglas fighting with anyone. 'What about?'

'Oh, I don't know, whether streamlining production would affect quality, that sort of thing, Val gets quite heated.'

Darina could remember Val sounding off about commercial production methods that reduced the best of ingredients to anonymity.

'At the moment,' Jemima continued, 'they're on about what privileged babies need for their daily diet. I can't see why they bother. Why not fish fingers? After all, they've got protein and everything, haven't they?'

'Nutritionally, they're excellent,' Darina agreed. 'But they're not much of a culinary experience. Why not challenge a baby's taste buds? Stimulate their palates? After all, early habits shape the rest of our lives.'

'I suppose your mother was a marvellous cook,' Jemima said idly.

Darina laughed. 'Ma hates cooking! But a gastronomic cousin used to stay with us and he was always experimenting in the kitchen. I grew up waiting for the next meal.'

'And now you're taking over from Delia Smith.' Jemima sounded genuinely impressed.

Darina gave a derisive snort. 'Wish I was! You see before you a struggling food writer. I lost my regular column recently and still haven't found another.'

'But you're on television! I saw one of the programmes, what was it, a year ago?'

'Over a year, and nothing since,' Darina said gloomily, feeling more and more depressed. 'I haven't even got a book commission at the moment. Since I got married, nothing seems to have gone right.' She hadn't meant to say that, somehow it had slipped out.

Jemima sat up a little, a wicked light in her eyes. 'Darina the great optimist in the dumps? I don't believe it. Mind you, I've never thought marriage had much going for it. Love 'em and leave 'em, that's my motto.' Her air of bravado suggested otherwise.

'I'd hate to leave William,' Darina said simply.

'How long have you been married?'

'Eighteen months.' It had been a cold March day, blustery, the wind had whipped her veil across her face as they stood outside the church for the wedding photographs. Finally the photographer had asked for a volunteer to stand behind her and hold the fine tulle in place. With Darina's height, it hadn't been difficult to find a girlfriend who would be swallowed up and not intrude in the family grouping.

'Practically still a bride! You wait!'

'You haven't had a go yourself?'

'Far too canny,' Jemima said positively.

Darina laid down the spoon and wiped excess food off Rory's mouth with the side of her finger. He gave her an enormous grin that lit up his face like northern lights on a winter's night, uttered another mouthful of almost intelligible phrases and picked up the spoon.

Again the load of depression shifted from Darina as she smiled at him and reached for the implement.

He screamed with outrage and waved the spoon possessively. It caught her eye and the momentary maternal impulse vanished. 'Ouch! Don't do that!'

'He hates giving anything up,' Jemima said laconically, sipping her wine. 'Just like his grandfather. He's going to be such a handful.'

'Can you really feed yourself?' Darina asked Rory. He gave her another big grin, said, 'Da,' dug the spoon clumsily into the bowl and raised some food to his mouth. With an enormous effort he managed to eat most of it.

'I can see why you're all dotty about him.'

'I'm not dotty about him,' Jemima declared. 'I find it quite easy to resist the charms of nappy-changing, screams in the middle of the night, toys scattered everywhere and Rory relentless in the pursuit of what he wants. As I said, he reminds me too much of Dad.' Then she spoilt the impact of this by popping a kiss on the baby's head as she brought a glass of wine over to Darina.

'Isn't he like your sister at all?' Darina asked as she watched, fascinated, the baby's struggles to eat his lunch. Such determination, such greed!

Jemima shrugged her narrow shoulders. 'Can you see any resemblance?'

'I never really knew Sophie,' Darina said apologetically. 'She was so much younger than us, ten years, wasn't it? I only met her when she was a little girl, that time I went on holiday with you all.' From some deep recess of memory she dragged out a picture of a small child hugging an enormous teddy bear that had taken up much too much room on the journey out to Italy, sucking her thumb and surveying her big sister's friend with large brown eyes. 'When did she die?'

'When Rory was born.' Jemima circled her glass of wine on the table.

'How dreadful! Why? I thought childbirth was pretty safe these days.'

'I wasn't there at the time but Dad said it was toxaemia.'

'It sounds as though she didn't have proper care,' Darina suggested doubtfully. It was difficult to imagine a child of the well-heeled Ealham family not being given the best of medical attention under any circumstances, let alone a pregnancy.

Jemima sighed. 'She'd run away from home. Just dropped out of sight. We didn't know where she was or what she was doing until the hospital called Dad and said she'd had a child and was dying.'

Darina tried to imagine losing sight of a sister like that and failed. 'How dreadful! Your father must have been out of his mind with worry!'

Jemima was silent.

'Why did she leave home?'

Jemima shrugged again. 'I don't know. I was living in town when she left, running my fashion boutique.' She looked at Darina. 'Since Mother died, I haven't spent much time at home. I tried to keep in touch with Sophie, I really did, but it was difficult.'

Rory banged at the table with his spoon and shouted for attention. His plate was empty.

'Shall I do another fish finger or is there pudding?'

Jemima caught her underlip with her upper teeth as she thought. She looked like a hamster dressed by Dolce e Gabbana. 'What did Maeve say he was to have afterwards?' she addressed the air. 'Oh, I know, one of those fruit fromage things and I think she said grapes or a clementine.' She gave a flashing grin, 'That's it, she had the cheek to tell me they had to be peeled! The girl seems to think I'm an idiot. The fridge is over there,' she added, smiling charmingly.

Darina stayed where she was and after a moment Jemima gave her another grin that suggested anything was worth a try, and went and fetched her nephew's dessert.

At school Jemima had been the leader, issuing orders, expecting them to be obeyed. Darina had been one of the few girls who hadn't done her bidding. They'd made friends on a school trip to Paris. Jemima, at thirteen, had met a young man and slipped away from a visit to some Russian folk dancing to meet him for dinner in a fashionable restaurant. It had been Darina who'd covered up when Jemima's absence had been noted. Large, conscientious and law abiding, if Darina said someone was there who wasn't, authority believed her. Receiving Jemima's thanks, Darina had said bluntly that she was an idiot but she wouldn't mind hearing what they'd had to eat. A somewhat spiky friendship had flourished from that point, Jemima seemingly charmed by someone who didn't jump to do her bidding, Darina fascinated by her irreverent approach to life.

Rory's arms waved happily as Darina spooned raspberry fromage frais into his rosebud mouth and watched him concentrate on the new taste. 'Maeve's his nanny?'

' "Nanny" is going a bit far for an Irish girl whose only qualifications, as far as I can find out, are the bringing up of umpteen brothers and sisters. Still, Rory likes her and I don't know how we'd manage if she left.' She topped up her glass of wine. 'Dad seems to think she's a good thing as well,' she added in a colourless voice.

There was silence for a while. When, Darina wondered, would this child realize that he was motherless? What would it mean to him? He wouldn't lack for the material things of life. The kitchen looked as if it had come straight out of a glossy designer magazine but there was no friendly clutter of utensils and odd impedimenta on any of the granite worksurfaces; no board stuffed with messages, shopping lists and postcards, everything was pristine and soulless. Did Rory have a nursery with fantasy painted walls and a rocking horse? Were there toys scattered around or was everything there as well ordered as here? Was this Maeve girl mother as far as he was concerned? It certainly didn't seem as though Jemima was making much of an effort to take her sister's place. 'My rescuer,' she'd greeted Darina as she'd opened the door of Blackboys, the Ealham mansion, half an hour earlier, the boy clutching at her legs. 'It's time for Rory's lunch and I'm useless with him.' Then she'd kissed Darina warmly and taken them all through to the kitchen.

Jemima's call had come out of the blue. They hadn't met since they'd left school and how she'd got hold of Darina's number was a puzzle. Despite the gap of so many years, Jemima had sounded really delighted to have made contact with her again. So much so that Darina had found herself accepting an invitation to lunch, 'to discuss,' Jemima had said, 'a small matter I need help with'.

Darina had put down the phone wondering, in an amused way, what it could be; Jemima had been well known for taking advantage of friends at school. Then she'd chided herself. Hadn't Jemima given her that Italian holiday when she was fifteen? There were many schoolgirls in their house who'd have helped Jemima with homework, lent her clothes or done any number of favours to have gone with her to the lush villa in the

Tuscan hills equipped with swimming pool and daily maid. But she'd asked Darina, whose Latin and maths were worse than her own and whose clothes wouldn't fit even if Jemima had liked their style.

As Darina offered Rory the last spoon of fromage frais, there was the insistent beep of a mobile phone.

Jemima snatched up the instrument from the table. 'Dominic, hi!' she said eagerly. 'Great to hear you, how are things?' Holding the phone, she rose and walked over to the other side of the kitchen.

Darina tried to concentrate on Rory but it was impossible to turn her ears off. 'No, sorry, Dom, Dad's back tonight and I want to be here. No, look, I've said I'm sorry,' she pleaded. 'It's, like, really difficult. He'll want to talk about the negotiations and everything. It's not often I get him without Val around.' Pause. 'Of course I'll miss you.' Her voice was soft. 'Can't wait to see you. Tomorrow then? I'll ring you.' Jemima clicked her phone shut and came back to the table without comment.

'So,' said Darina, scraping out the pot for still greedy Rory, 'what's this matter you need help with?' Please let it not be cooking, she prayed to herself. The days were gone when she was grateful for any sort of catering that came her way.

Jemima looked across at Darina, her gaze open and direct. 'I want you to find out who Rory's father is.'

'You don't know?' Darina was astonished.

Jemima shook her head. 'By the time Dad reached hospital, Sophie was in a coma; she never regained consciousness.'

'But someone must know,' Darina protested. 'What about her friends?'

'She didn't tell anyone,' Jemima said with a note of finality.

'Hasn't your father tried to find out?' Darina couldn't imagine the mighty Basil Ealham not motivating an army of private detectives into discovering who was responsible for his daughter's pregnancy.

Jemima looked exasperated. 'He says it doesn't matter, that Rory is Rory. He's besotted with him.' She made it sound a dangerous perversion.

'But you think it's important?' Darina separated out several clementine segments and handed one to the child, who took and examined it closely before placing it in his mouth with a grunt of approval. She put several more segments on the tray in front of him. He obviously liked having control over his food.

'Don't you?' Jemima sounded amazed at the question.

'Well, yes, but why have you waited so long?' Darina considered the child now picking up the next piece of fruit with a fat finger and thumb. 'I mean, Rory's what, fifteen months old?'

Jemima thought for a moment. 'Seventeen months.'

'Shouldn't you have tried to find out who his father was when he was born?'

'Yah, well, we didn't,' Jemima said stubbornly.

'And no one contacted you?'

Jemima shook her head. 'As I said, we don't know anything about where she was living, what she was doing, or who her friends were.'

There was something very odd here. 'I'm not a private detective,' Darina said repressively, not at all certain she wanted anything to do with this curious task. 'I wouldn't know where to start.'

11

'Nonsense, you've solved any number of crimes if half of what I hear is true. It was when I met Esther Symes and she told me how well you'd been doing that I got the idea.'

So that was who must have given Jemima her number. 'You know how Esther always loves to exaggerate everything. Remember when we were in the fourth form and she told us her uncle was President of the USA?'

Jemima gurgled with laughter. 'Weren't we all impressed? Until we found out he was really just president of some American corporation.' She looked closely at Darina. 'Are you saying you haven't solved any murders?'

'Well, not exactly,' Darina prevaricated. 'But it was just luck, a matter of being in the right place at the right time.'

'You always were a modest soul. But you can't deny that you're married to a policeman, a detective inspector no less. He can tell you exactly how to go about things.'

'Actually, he's just been promoted, he's Detective Chief Inspector William Pigram now, with the Thames Valley Police. That's why we've moved up from Somerset.'

'I want to hear more about him,' Jemima commanded. 'Esther says he's dreamy.'

Darina smiled. 'I didn't think tall, dark and handsome men were in fashion these days.'

'Ooh, he sounds delicious! A sort of Mr Darcy?'

'Well, yes,' Darina acknowledged, thinking that William wrestled with difficult emotions just as hard as Jane Austen's hero.

'Oh, heaven! I get so bored with wimps. That's all I

seem to meet these days, wimps or macho men bent on proving they don't need women.' Darina wondered which Dominic was. But a macho man would surely have insisted on Jemima going out with him that evening. 'I bet you can twist William round your little finger and get him to help you in any way you want.'

'He's working his way into his new job. It's an important move and I wouldn't want to bother him with this sort of thing,' Darina said repressively, knowing all too well that giving her advice on how to investigate anything was the last thing William would do.

'Come on, if you're not writing books or doing television programmes, surely you can spare a little time to do some sleuthing?' Jemima looked pleadingly at Darina. 'It would mean so much to me. And I'll pay you, of course.'

Which was more than anybody else had done! But, 'I don't do it for money,' Darina said.

'Well, you ought to. Come on, please, it's so important.' Her eyes were luminous, her body tense.

When Jemima let down her defences, she was difficult to resist. And it was true, Darina didn't have any deadlines at the moment. But trying to fight for a regular place in the media market was time consuming and there was William to consider. The last thing he needed at the moment was her irritating him by invading his work space.

But surely investigating Rory's fatherhood wouldn't count as police work? After all, it wasn't as though any crime had been committed. There was something here though that Darina didn't understand. 'Just why are you so keen, Jemima? If your father's happy not to know, why aren't you?'

Jemima ran a hand through her short fair hair and looked exasperated, as though the answer should have been perfectly plain. 'Heavens, Darina, you know what a time I and my brothers had growing up, don't you think Rory ought to be saved from all that?' Jemima's expression was fierce. 'If only I'd realized how completely Dad was going to take him over, I'd have come back sooner. He's ruined my life, I'm not going to have the same thing happen to Rory. If you think food's important for a child, how much more so are proper parents!'

'He might be someone totally unsuitable.'

'Or someone who'd give him a decent upbringing and not insist on the importance of possessions and status,' Jemima insisted.

How well would Jemima manage without the money that bought her expensive clothes and provided this luxurious home? Darina wondered, then went after a different angle. 'Don't you have any idea who Rory's father is?'

Jemima shook her head. 'Apparently she didn't have any boyfriends, or girlfriends come to that. Sophie, well, Sophie found people a bit threatening.'

Jemima had never been particularly perspicacious and Darina realized Sophie must have lacked social skills to a high degree for her sister to have noticed this much.

'Dad says Rory was several weeks premature, you can't imagine how tiny he was when I first saw him,' Jemima looked at the sturdy infant banging the high-chair tray and her gaze softened for a moment before she switched her attention back to Darina. 'Sophie had been missing for seven and a half months when Rory was born. So if he was six weeks' premature, it must have been someone she met after she disappeared from my brother and sister-in-law's, mustn't it?'

Darina didn't see that it necessarily followed but decided not to pursue it for the moment.

'But if you don't know where Sophie was living or what she was doing when she became pregnant, how can anyone even start an investigation?'

Relief bloomed on Jemima's face. 'I knew you'd do it! And I know exactly where you can begin, with my brother.'

Rory banged imperiously on his tray.

'What does he want now?' asked Darina. 'More food?'

Jemima rose and found a baby's mug. 'Orange juice to finish off the feast.'

Rory grabbed the mug with both hands and started sucking. How simple life was at that age!

'Which brother?' Darina asked. There had been two on that Italian holiday: Job, an introverted under-graduate who had made a point of avoiding any contact with the rest of his family and Jasper, a ten-year-old boy who'd kept them in fits of laughter.

'My dearly beloved elder brother, Job,' Jemima said wryly. 'When Sophie left here she went to him and Nicola. Did you know he'd married?'

Darina shook her head. 'I haven't heard anything of you or your family for years. There's a limit to the number of Christmas cards you send without getting one back,' she added severely.

Jemima gave a shamefaced smile. 'Well, I was sort of involved with other things. Everything's so exciting when you first leave school,' she added as though that explained matters. 'When I bumped into Esther the

15

other day, it was the first time I'd seen any of our lot since we all left.'

'What's Job doing these days? Did he do anything with his writing? I remember he was always scribbling in a notebook.' Which he'd taken enormous pains to make sure nobody could read. Jasper had managed to get hold of it one day. Darina could see him now, dancing around the swimming pool, holding it up in the air, evading a vengeful Job, for once jerked out of his moody melancholy. Both brothers and the notebook had ended up in the water. Jasper had had the grace to apologize and offered to try and rescue the soggy pages but Job had stalked off, blind with rage, and it had been days before he'd brought himself to speak to any of them.

'He edits the city pages of a weekly magazine.'

'But surely if Job knew anything, he'd have told your father?'

'He hates Dad, he's always trying to do him down in his column. He says he has no idea where she went but I'm sure he knows something.'

'Why don't you ask him?' It all seemed odder and odder to Darina.

Jemima sighed. 'We've never really got on and ever since I started to work for Dad, Job won't have anything more to do with me. It's as though I've gone over to the enemy.'

'You're working for your father? I thought you hated him?'

'That was when I was growing up. I can hold my own now and I thought it was time I worked myself into the firm. So I suggested he took me on as an assistant.' Jemima refilled her glass. 'By the time he retires, I'll be able to take over the company.'

The thought of Jemima, who had always had trouble concentrating on anything longer than it took a flea to jump the width of a bed, at the head of an international organization was, if not exactly laughable, difficult to take seriously. Had she changed in the last twelve years or was she kidding herself?

'Anyway, all you have to do is tell Job Dad doesn't want Rory's parentage investigated and he'll spill all.' Jemima took a piece of paper out of her pocket and handed it to Darina. 'I've written down his details for you.'

So, she'd been all prepared, maybe she had changed!

Darina quickly scanned the details. Job and Nicola Ealham lived in Battersea, just over the river from her house in Chelsea. Quite convenient, as Jemima must realize. Without quite knowing why, she folded up the slip of paper and put it carefully in her handbag. 'I'll think about it,' she said. 'I'm not going to promise anything.'

'Just talk to Job,' Jemima urged. She leaned forward. 'It's important, Darina, really important.'

Somewhere a door slammed and a distant voice shouted, 'Jemima? Where the hell are you?'

'Dad! He's not supposed to be back until this evening!'

Heavy footsteps could be heard approaching the kitchen door.

Jemima stretched a hand across the table to Darina and squeezed her wrist painfully hard. 'Don't breathe a word, promise?'

Darina nodded. Once she and Jemima had sworn eternal friendship and never to rat on the other.

The kitchen door was flung open and Basil Ealham

stood there. 'How's my boy?' he shouted. Rory dropped his piece of fruit and flung his arms in the air, his face beaming as he shouted delightedly at his grandfather.

Jemima's face as she watched her father scoop up the little boy was impossible to read.

Chapter Two

Basil Ealham lifted a delighted Rory up high.

'He's only just had his lunch,' Darina warned.

'Hmm, perhaps you're right.' The strong hands lowered Rory and Basil sat himself down on one of the kitchen chairs with the child on his knee. Rory reached for the last of the cheese straws. Jemima whipped the plate away.

'Spoil sport,' said her father.

Deprived of his titbit, Rory turned his attention to the glasses that were in his grandfather's top pocket, plucking them out and opening a sidepiece. 'This is Darina Lisle, Dad,' said Jemima, waving a negligent hand towards her guest. 'You remember she came to Italy with us that time?'

Darina found herself being assessed by a pair of eyes as blue as Rory's but a great deal keener. 'You had to return to England after a couple of days on business,' she murmured. 'I'd be surprised if you remember me.'

'Not at all,' Basil said crisply. 'You produced a great meal for us the first night, tagliatelle with prosciutto, tomato and basil, and a marvellous salad. I was most impressed.'

So was Darina with his feat of memory. She'd forgotten all about that arrival. The plane had been late,

Mrs Ealham had drunk whisky throughout the flight and gone to bed as soon as they reached their destination. Everyone else had been hungry and the villa, set high up in the Tuscan hills, seemed miles from any habitation but on the table had been a collection of food supplied for their arrival.

Rory tried to put the glasses on. They fell to the floor.

'Hey!' objected Basil. 'None of that, now.' He rescued the spectacles and returned them to his pocket. Rory's face puckered.

Jemima scooped the baby up. 'Time for your rest,' she said.

'Just a minute, young lady,' Basil said sharply. 'Why aren't you at the office?'

'I'm looking after Rory. It's Maeve's day off, remember?'

'So where's Mrs Starr?'

'She had to go to the dentist,' Jemima said smoothly.

Darina remembered that tone from their schooldays. She wondered what Jemima had told Mrs Starr to stop her coming in that morning.

'So I rang Darina and suggested we had lunch here rather than in town.'

'What about Jasper, couldn't he have looked after him?'

'In town, said he had to see his agent.'

'Jasper's making a name for himself as a novelist,' Basil said to Darina. 'Too experimental for me but apparently he's well thought of,' he continued expressionlessly. Then he turned back to his daughter. 'Presumably everything's up to date in the office?'

'Of course, Dad, you know you can rely on me!' Jemima said in injured tones. 'Have you had anything to eat? I can lay an extra place, there's plenty of lobster salad.'

'No thanks, I was fed on the plane.'

'What happened to this morning's meeting?'

'The Italians wouldn't play ball last night so I walked out on them.' Delight filled his face. 'They must be mad as all hell. They were sure I'd compromise.'

'More fool them.' Jemima hoisted Rory on to her hip. 'They'll regret not being more co-operative.'

'You better believe it!' Basil said ominously. 'I thought I'd call in and see Rory before the office. I couldn't believe it when I saw your car outside.'

Jemima tightened her hold on the child. 'Entertain Darina for me whilst I put Rory down, will you?' Her tone was imperious enough for Basil Ealham himself.

His right eyebrow raised itself fractionally. Then, 'I'll be delighted,' he said and gave Darina a grin astonishingly like his daughter's. 'Let's go somewhere more comfortable, shall we?'

Darina allowed herself to be led into a vast drawing room furnished with deeply cushioned sofas and chairs, their pale upholstery set off by the deep polish of antique occasional tables.

'What will you have to drink?' Basil opened a door in the corner of the room and Darina caught a glimpse of a well stocked bar.

'Thanks, but Jemima gave me some wine.' Darina held up the glass she'd brought with her. 'And I'm driving so this will do me fine.'

'Good girl! Tonic water with a dash of Angostura Bitters is my tipple.' He emerged with a large glass of pink liquid and took a seat on the opposite sofa.

Basil Ealham was every bit as impressive a figure as

Darina remembered. A shade under six foot, he had a powerful body downplayed by the cut of his well tailored suit. His fine head was held slightly in advance of the rest of him, his beak-like nose, so unfortunately inherited by Jemima, carved the air as though to cut a path for his figure to follow. There was about him the same restless energy that inhabited his daughter and Darina wouldn't be at all surprised if it wasn't in Rory's genes as well.

Basil leaned forward, his legs slightly apart, his whole attention focused on her. 'Nice to see you again. I always thought you'd turn out to be a stunner.' He managed to make that sound both sincere and unhackneyed. His eyes were admiring but kept a slight distance. 'What are you doing with yourself these days? No, don't tell me.' He surveyed her even more closely and Darina felt like a mouse being inspected by a python with lunch on its mind. 'I'm sure you must have put that cookery talent to good use but I don't see you as just a cook. I know, you run your own catering company.'

'I'm impressed,' Darina said calmly, wondering if this was a genuine guess or whether he knew something about her. 'I did at one time. These days, though, I earn my living writing about food rather than cooking it. Oh, and I do the odd television spot – demonstrating,' she couldn't resist adding.

'Now it's my turn to be impressed,' Basil said jovially, not relaxing the intensity of his gaze for a moment. 'I shall have to tell my friend Val I've met you, I'm sure she'll recognize your name.'

Which suggested that he hadn't. Well, no reason why an industrialist should know a humble cookery writer.

Still, Darina's depression intensified. 'Jemima mentioned Val Douglas's name. I know her slightly, we used to meet at press receptions but I haven't seen her around for some time.'

'She concentrates on manufacturing food these days. Is doing extremely well. I've been helping her, with procedures, management, that sort of thing.' He didn't even try to sound modest.

Darina remembered Val very well. In her own way she was as commanding a figure as Basil, tall and attractive but Darina would have expected Basil Ealham to go for someone less brisk, more sensual. Then she chided herself. She'd only seen Val in business mode, perhaps socially she softened and opened herself up, like an aubergine melting into sweet flavoursomeness under the influence of heat. She restrained an involuntary gurgle of laughter at the ridiculous image and concentrated on what Basil was saying.

'Val saw the potential of the market supplying people with food intolerances and went for it. She's even in supermarkets these days. Really impressive! But it's small stuff, she needs to get more commercial and introduce a new line that can command more sales. Gourmet baby food, I've told her, that's what she needs to work on. It's a market worth one hundred and twenty million pounds, even one per cent of that is ten times more than she's making at the moment and with her talents she could easily grab much more.' He smiled at her. 'When she's got her range together, you must come and sample it, we'll be planning a big press launch.'

'I'd be very interested.'

'Talking of Val, would you mind if I gave her a quick call?' Darina had to admire the way he actually waited for her demur before plucking a mobile phone out of an inside pocket.

'Val?' Basil leant back into the corner of the sofa, his gaze fixed somewhere on the ceiling. 'I'm back. Yes, got in this morning, tried to ring you on my way from the airport but you weren't at your desk.' Slight pause while Basil listened to whatever explanation Val had for not being glued to the end of a telephone waiting for a call he might just make. 'OK. Now, look, come over this evening and we'll go through those projections you've been working on.' Another pause.

Darina rose and walked over to the french windows. The garden blazed with autumnal colours. Well ordered herbaceous beds surrounded smooth green lawn with a small, ornamental fountain in the centre. Beyond, she could glimpse the edge of a swimming pool.

'Well, I can see you weren't expecting me back so soon. All right, then, we'll just have dinner tonight and go over the figures tomorrow evening as originally planned.' There was an edge to Basil's voice. Unused to people not being ready with whatever he wanted when he wanted it, obviously. But Val was holding her own, thought Darina with some amusement as it became clear that she had other plans for this evening.

Not for long, though.

'Cancel,' Basil said calmly. 'I want you here.' There was no mistaking the note of possessiveness in his voice. 'Shall I send a car? No? Well, I'll expect you by eight.' More protests from the other end of the phone. 'No,' he said with a slight edge to his voice, 'it'll just be you and me. You know Jasper never eats with us and Jemima is going out.' Darina remembered Dominic, now Jemima would be able to see him after all – but at the cost of the quiet evening with her father she had looked forward to. 'You know,' Basil's voice changed, 'I've missed you. Can't wait for this evening, bye.' There was the sharp click of a mobile's cover being snapped back into place. 'Sorry about that.'

Darina returned to her seat as Basil slipped his phone back inside his jacket.

'Now, where were we?' he asked complacently. Darina decided he was as pleased to have been able to demonstrate his power to her as he had to Val.

Basil relaxed back and said with a new, boyish charm, 'I'm so glad Jemima is looking up some of her old friends. She needs some outside contacts. I think sometimes she's too involved with the family.'

This was not a side of Jemima that Darina recognized. At school, she had always had masses of friends, she'd spread her favours as liberally as strawberry jam on clotted cream scones. Her quick wits, irreverent attitude and attractive appearance had made her an icon.

Perhaps, though, she'd never actually made a real friend. Since school Darina had occasionally seen her name in gossip columns, linked to a wide variety of young men, all rich or famous.

'She says she's enjoying working with you,' she murmured.

'Ah, yes, my right-hand girl! Well, it keeps her out of trouble and, who knows, she may be of use one of these days.'

Darina didn't like the dismissive way he said that. 'She's always been very enterprising,' she said firmly, 'and she's really interested in your business.'

'Yes.' Basil drew the word out as though Jemima's

attitude was somehow suspect. The old sensation of being girls together against authority filled Darina.

'We all voted Jemima girl most likely to succeed in any field she chose,' she said, her manner openly provocative.

'She's always known how to put herself over,' Jemima's father agreed with a silky smoothness. 'It's a valuable asset – as long as it's backed by genuine commitment.'

All at once Darina lost the impulse to fight Jemima's corner. They weren't schoolgirls any longer and what, after all, did she know of Jemima's doings since they'd thrown away their panama hats?

'Isn't your grandson great?'

Basil's face lit up, rather like Rory's had when she fed him. 'Little monster,' he said fondly, one hand negligently playing with the edge of a cushion. 'Chip off the old block! I can see him running the empire when I finally decide to retire.'

How old was Basil? wondered Darina. He looked around fifty but the evidence suggested he was nearer sixty, after all, Jemina's elder brother must now be about thirty-five. But Darina had read somewhere that Basil Ealham had never been to university, he'd clawed his way up from humble beginnings, so he might have married early. Even so, he must be at least fifty-five. Did he really see himself controlling his empire until his grandson was ready to take over? Was that what was worrying Jemima? Nothing to do with her father dominating Rory's life as he grew older?

Darina was by no means sure she wanted to accept Jemima's commission but she thought she might as well take advantage of a Basil relaxed and complacent after his little victory over Val. 'I was sorry to hear about poor Sophie. It must have been devastating. To have been worried for so long and then to have your worst fears confirmed like that . . .' Darina let the end of the sentence die away as Basil's face darkened, literally. Blood suffused his face and his eyes sparked dangerously.

'What has Jemima been saying?' His voice was harsh.

The change in him was more than disconcerting, Darina found herself repelled by his sudden animosity. 'I was interested in Rory,' she said stiffly, trying not to feel she had to justify herself. 'Sophie was such a little girl when I last saw her. It was hard to realize she'd grown up, let alone given birth to such a big boy.' Basil's eyes closed as if he couldn't bear the memory. 'Her death must have been dreadful,' she added gently.

He opened pain-filled eyes. 'I've never felt so helpless in my life,' he said simply. 'Here I was, able to command anything money could buy and there was nothing I could do to save her life. She looked just so small, so shrunken.' He sounded exhausted. 'I couldn't believe it, nobody dies of childbirth these days. The doctors said it was pre-eclampsia, and that if she'd only had proper attention earlier, it could all have been brought under control, she needn't have died at all. God knows where or how she'd been living.' As though he couldn't bear to sit still any longer he got up and went over to a table loaded with photographs in silver frames. He picked one up and held it out to Darina. 'That was Sophie before she left home.'

It was a posed, studio shot, the sort that would once have graced the front page of *Country Life*. The girl who wore a single string of pearls and matching stud earrings looked about seventeen. Brown hair was held back with a velvet alice band from a shy, trusting face with brown eyes full of sweet innocence. Darina was struck by how much she resembled her mother.

'I'm sorry, I probably shouldn't ask you this but I can't help wondering, why did she leave home?'

She'd feared a return of his antagonism. Instead, Basil shrugged his big shoulders in a helpless gesture. 'If only I knew! You can't imagine how many times I've asked myself that question. You know what youngsters are, so mixed up they hardly know themselves why they do things.' It was hard to tell whether he was being genuine or not.

'And you don't know who Rory's father is?'

The blood flooded back into Basil's face. 'Jemima told you that, too, did she?'

Darina said nothing.

'If I could get my hands on the man who abandoned her like that, I'd lynch him,' Basil ground out.

Why hadn't he tried to find out who the man was? If he had been that vengeful, surely he would have employed every aid his money could enlist? Then it suddenly occurred to Darina that perhaps he had tried – and failed. Perhaps he didn't want to admit there was something else his money couldn't buy. In which case, what chance had she got?

'So Rory will grow up not knowing who his father is,' Darina persisted.

'Won't hurt him,' Basil insisted, taking the photograph back. 'Better that than to have the burden of a useless failure hanging round your neck as you grow up.'

'That's what you think the man must have been, a useless failure?'

Basil's eyes narrowed. 'You're very interested,' he said in a voice that was suddenly cold.

This wasn't a man it was safe to cross, Darina decided. 'Having met Rory, I can't help but be interested.'

Once again his grandson proved the key to softening Basil Ealham's attitude.

'Look,' he said as he put the photograph back on the table, 'aren't we all bowed down with the weight of our parents? What about yours? Hasn't your father affected your approach to life? What was he? Ah, I remember, a doctor.'

What a memory the man had.

'So, he will have imposed standards of caring on you, and of duty. Without his influence, you might have turned out very differently.'

Darina didn't want to consider the influences that had shaped her. 'And are you going to mastermind Rory's upbringing?'

'You bet I am! A great deal better than the sort of chap that loves and leaves without a second thought.'

Was that how it had been? Darina remembered the sweet, trusting face of Sophie Ealham. Sweet faces sometimes hid complex characters with less attractive attributes. Basil wouldn't be the first father to have blinded himself to the truth where a daughter was concerned. Darina found herself being drawn into the mystery of Rory's birth as question after question occurred to her. It was like being presented with an unexpected set of ingredients and wondering how to assemble a satisfactory dish.

'Jemima's taking a long time to settle Rory,' she commented.

29

Jemima entered. 'Rory's down at last,' she said, running a hand through her hair as though the task of settling him down had been exhausting. 'Shall we eat?'

Chapter Three

After lunch Jemima saw Darina off with regret. She'd brought back so many good memories.

Sometimes Jemima thought that school days really had been the happiest of her life. Her mother had been alive, life seemed to be under a certain control – there'd been hope things would get better. Then school had finished and soon afterwards Jemima had come home after a long session shopping in the new car that had been her eighteenth birthday present. Her mother hadn't been able to come with her, a bad headache, she'd said. So Jemima had carried in glossy bags filled with terrific clothes and dashed upstairs to show them off, hoping the headache was better.

Jemima had entered that bedroom an eager adolescent and emerged an embittered adult. She'd known immediately she'd seen the still figure, it hadn't been necessary to read the note propped up against the empty pill bottle. For a little while she'd sat on the bed, held the cold hand and remembered her mother's last words. 'It won't be nearly as much fun without you, Mum,' Jemima had said. And Julie Ealham had sighed, 'I hope life will always be fun for you, darling.' And Jemima had flounced out of the room, angry because her mother seemed to have given up on life when there was just so much there for her if only she'd take it.

But Jemima, her two brothers and her sister hadn't been enough for Julie Ealham. Not enough to compensate for their father and his behaviour.

Jemima had looked at the cold, rigid face and felt something inside her shrivel up, like a sea anemone curling in its fronds. Then she'd rung Basil and the doctor and the house where Sophie had been sent that morning. Having done what had seemed necessary, she'd methodically hung up the new clothes.

As Jemima drove her Mercedes coupe fast along the narrow roads, she was deeply conscious of her father sitting in his office like an over-active spider in the centre of a pulsating web. She'd told Darina she wanted to take over the company when Basil retired. What a laugh. Jemima Ealham in charge of a multi-million corporation!

Why hadn't she told her old friend the truth? That her boutique had gone bust because Basil had refused further funds, that she couldn't find anyone to give her an interesting job and the only sort of flat she could afford on the salary she could command was too poky and too far out of the centre of things to be considered for a moment. Everyone she'd known at school seemed to have gone on to interesting careers or had got married to upwardly mobile men. Why was she, the girl they'd voted most likely to succeed, the only failure?

Then she thought of what she'd asked Darina to do and for a moment fought panic. What had she started? Could Darina discover the truth? Esther had said how clever she was. 'The thing is, sweetie, she never gives up, just keeps going at it until she's got an answer. It's nothing to do with fingerprints and all that, I think it's because she works out the human factor.' And Jemima had had this sudden impulse.

Now she wondered if the truth mightn't be something best not discovered. Perhaps it wouldn't mean a better upbringing for Rory than hers. And what would her father do? The thought of a Basil threatened with Rory's removal from his control was suddenly so terrifying, Jemima almost called Darina there and then to cancel the investigation. Then she pushed the thought away as the complex mix of emotions that had decided her to ring her old friend returned in full force. Her father had to learn other people had rights as well.

Clinging to that thought, Jemima parked her car behind Ealham House, an aggressive looking red-brick building that had won some award for progressive architecture, and walked inside with quick steps. If you looked purposeful, people thought you were someone important.

Rosie Cringle looked up as she entered the office. 'Mr Ealham wants you in his office. He said as soon as you got back.' Jemima's secretary was a mouselike but immensely efficient girl.

Jemima gave an unconscious tug to the bottom of her jacket, picked up the file that was sitting ready on her desk, tapped on the communicating door between her and the Chairman and Managing Director's office and entered without waiting for a response.

Basil was on the telephone. He waved her to a chair in front of his enormous, bare desk. Behind him she could see he already had up the latest production figures for the most troublesome company in the conglomerate. 'Right, you do that,' Basil said unemotionally into the telephone. 'Just remember your job depends on it and there are no second chances,' he added pleasantly before putting the receiver down. 'Ah, Jemima. Good lunch, was it? Nice girl that. Now, here are the notes I made in the plane coming back. Get them printed out.' He handed her a floppy disc. 'You'll note several action points for you, don't hang around on them. When's that meeting I asked you to arrange?'

'Tomorrow at ten,' Jemima said smoothly, rather pleased with herself. Basil had wanted her to get hold of an elusive industrialist with a deep distrust of the Ealham corporation. It had taken a good deal of persistence first to track him down and then to persuade him it would be a mistake not at least to meet.

'Good work,' said Basil absently. Coming from him this was high praise and Jemima felt a fizz of achievement.

'And those projections I asked for?'

She handed over the file, blessing Rosie for pressuring her to complete it the previous day. It made her feel efficient. This job was proving a success. Producing projections was boring but she loved sitting in on meetings, watching her father run rings around captains of industry as he produced ideas that sounded off the wall then made you see were just a revolutionary way of dealing with a problem that had defeated everyone else. Sometimes the ideas were so simple you knew they couldn't work – until he insisted you tried, when they did. She was really looking forward to hearing him talk about what had happened in Milan this evening. She'd got one or two ideas of her own that she wanted to tell him about.

'You've only got half the figures here,' Basil said,

throwing the projections on the desk. 'What's wrong with you, your mind on that wimp Dominic?' He sounded bored rather than irritated and Jemima suddenly saw a similar looking document already on the desk.

'By the way, Val's coming over this evening. I take it you've got plans?' Basil swung round to his computer screen and Jemima knew their time together was over.

'Yah,' she said quickly. 'Dominic's taking me out.'

Basil grunted, his attention already given to the figures he was playing with.

That evening Jemima drove up to London with Oasis blaring out of the car stereo. She sang along at the top of her voice, refusing to think of anything but the frustratingly heavy traffic. She had to get there early because otherwise Dominic might decide to go out for a drink and there was no way she was going to chase him round the various watering holes he could choose from.

Parking for Dominic's flat was always a problem if you didn't have a resident's permit. Jemima left her car perched on a corner, picked up her long-handled Prada bag and swung it over her shoulder. Her stiletto heels clicked decisively as her legs flashed along in tight, wetlook trousers. She had the key to Dominic's flat all ready in her pocket. As she let herself in she called out, 'Surprise!' And it was.

Had she been an idiot or had she actually wanted to catch him in the act? Jemima only knew she didn't feel taken aback as she walked into the bedroom and found the two of them at it like ferrets up a trouser leg.

The girl had seen her first. Her startled eyes locked

on to Jemima's furious ones then her green enamelled
nails dug into Dominic's back so that he arched away
from her, cried out, then collapsed, his sweat-licked skin
gleaming in the low light.

Jemima marched out of the bedroom and helped
herself to a large whisky from the collection of drinks
Dominic kept on the glass and chrome side table. She'd
helped him furnish this flat, had chosen the silver and
white decor. 'Too thirties, angel, but it suits the architecture,' she'd said, giggling, as they drank champagne to
celebrate the decorators' departure.

'So now you know,' Dominic said, coming up behind
her, tieing the sash of his kimono. He poured himself an
equally large glass of The Macallan. His breathing had
returned to normal, his dark hair was slicked back, his
tone conversational. 'Sorry you had to find out this way.
You should have told me you'd changed your mind
about this evening.'

Jemima shrugged and moved away; he needed a
shower.

He sat down in one of the square armchairs. The
kimono opened itself revealing his smooth knees and
hairy legs. 'Like a bear,' she'd used to say, running her
fingers gently over the dark fuzz, feeling its softness
send sensual little messages along her nerve ends.

'Who is she?' Jemima leant against the chrome
shelving unit that ran along one wall.

'No one you know.' Half Dominic's whisky had gone
but he seemed totally calm, even bored. How could she
ever have found this well bred but pompous fool entertaining?

The ache that ever since her mother's death had

never been far away filled her gut. Why did the people she loved disappear?

'She's a sweet little girl,' Dominic added idly.

'Sweet . . . little . . . girl,' Jemima repeated through her teeth. Suddenly she lifted the heavy cut glass tumbler and threw it hard and accurately across the room.

Dominic ducked and the tumbler smashed against the wall, shattering the glass of the modern etching that had been her house-warming present.

'You bastard,' she screamed and flung herself at him, her nails just managing to draw blood before, with surprising strength, he grabbed her wrists and forced her to the ground. She fought back, rage, humiliation and a host of less identifiable emotions giving her a power she hadn't known she possessed. It wasn't enough, though, and at the end she collapsed into a heap on the carpet, sobbing as though her heart would break.

Dominic helped himself to more whisky. 'Don't pretend you really care,' he said, breathing fast. 'The only person who matters to you is you. Oh, and your father,' he added.

'I hate my father!' Jemima flung at him, with a hiccuping catch to her voice.

'So you always say. You never lose an opportunity to lay into him yet you take his money. You're spoilt, immature and self-centred,' he continued dispassionately, 'and it's time you got a grip. You're a good lay but there's more to life than sex.'

The effrontery of it made her breathless. When she thought of how he'd begged her to make love. The way he'd whimpered under her caresses.

She got herself to her feet and found her bag. 'You'll

be lucky if she gives you half as good a time,' she told him coldly. 'You don't deserve someone like me.'

His eyes narrowed unappealingly. 'Any man who deserves you needs to be removed from society.'

She laughed unsteadily. 'Have fun with your bimbo, I don't suppose she knows any better than you, poor cow.'

Halfway down the corridor, she heard him calling her. 'Leave the key, you bitch.'

She flung it at him, her aim so bad the metal pinged off the wall and lay shining on the carpet as she swayed out of the block.

Her car had been clamped. It had only been there half an hour and it had been clamped!

Well, might as well make the fine worthwhile. Jemima walked to a local pub where she was reasonably certain of finding someone she knew.

Much, much later, escorted by a beefy twenty-something who'd been touchingly grateful for her sudden appearance in his life, she paid her outrageous fine. 'There you go,' the young bull said, after the clamp had been removed, and opened her car door. She got in, he slammed it and stood back.

Then she realized he hadn't asked for her phone number. After all the expertise she'd lavished on him, he hadn't even wanted to see her again.

She gunned the engine. Chaps like him were ten a penny, she could have as many as she wanted – any time. She roared away, not even looking in the rear view mirror as she left him behind.

After their excessive activity, she felt completely sober but she drove home with unaccustomed carefulness. While she drove she wallowed in self-pity. A cruel fate was against her. If only she'd been able to spend the evening with her father, everything would have been all right. She wouldn't have known about Dominic's two-timing, nor been treated as a one-night stand by that callow sod.

By the time she reached Blackboys it was the early hours of the morning and Jemima had decided that the person to blame for everything that was wrong with her life was Val Douglas.

Chapter Four

Darina had gone home from Blackboys to several hours of housework, the pristine standard of the Ealham household having made her horribly conscious of her shortcomings in this area. As usual her husband, Detective Chief Inspector William Pigram, was late. So it was nearly nine o'clock before she cooked them both a stir-fried dish of chicken and fine shreds of vegetables zested with fresh ginger and lemon grass. Minimum cooking, maximum flavour, she'd thought.

'I'm sorry, I'm not very hungry,' William said, laying down his fork. 'I was so starving in the office, I got myself some sandwiches.'

Darina sighed and pushed the remains of her meal away. 'My lunch was very filling,' she said.

William picked up both plates and dumped the remains in the bin. 'How did your reunion with your old friend go? Lots of giggles over the doings of the lower fourth?'

'Darling, those leftovers could have done lunch tomorrow!' Darina protested. Then thought how unlike William to sound sour. She looked carefully at her husband. Little of Mr Darcy about him today, unless you counted the gloomy lines of his clean cut face. Very unheroic were the dark smudges under his grey eyes while the puffiness around them and the network of minute red lines on the whites themselves were positively worrying. As was the depth of the vertical crease between his brows. And the way he placed hands either side of his forehead and squeezed, as though trying to relieve a headache.

Then Darina was shocked to notice several strands of silver in the curly darkness of his hair.

Ever since William had been promoted to take charge of the CID of a small police force in the Thames valley, it had been a case of hallo and goodbye. Hallo late each evening, if, that is, Darina wasn't already asleep when he returned home, goodbye in the early morning when William often left the house before Darina was up. Their relationship these days seemed full of tension. When was the last time they'd had a relaxed evening together, or had friends round, or even made love?

'Any chance of us enjoying a quiet weekend?' she asked as he started filling the kettle for coffee. 'We could go for a walk somewhere. You look as though you could do with some fresh air and exercise.'

'Tell me about it! But it's no go. I'm buried in paperwork and this evening Roger rang. He's appropriating Terry Pitman, my inspector, and another officer for what looks like several days. Division are mounting an operation to clear up the gang of high-class burglars that's been stripping all our patches.' He put the kettle down with an angry thump.

'No! But that's good news, isn't it?'

'Good news that hardened criminals are to be removed from our patch and life made safe for valuable antiques. Bad news that while it's all going on my lot will be too thin on the ground to check the nefarious activities of less hardened criminals; every little weed will grow into a bloody great thistle.' William sat and knocked back the rest of his whisky.

'How long is this going to go on?' she asked, trying to sound sympathetic and understanding and hearing it come out irritable instead. She reached out and placed her hand against his cheek, hoping touch would get through to him. 'Unremitting work is no good for anyone. You need to take a break.'

William managed a brief smile, kissed her hand, then sank back against the banquette. 'I need to get on top of things first,' he sighed.

'Bloody Roger,' Darina said savagely. Superintendent Marks was no friend of hers, she found it difficult to understand why William was such close friends with the over-large, overbearing and charmless – as far as she was concerned – officer.

It had been Roger who'd persuaded William that moving to a home counties' constabulary would be good for his career pattern. The promotion to chief inspector had been welcome but this unrelenting pressure was not. 'Superintendent Marks,' she continued through her teeth, 'is using you to save his skin. These staff shortages are threatening the success of his division and he knows he can bully you into working twice as hard as anyone clsc.'

'We're all suffering,' William said quietly. 'Roger has promised me a new sergeant and that should make life easier.'

'As long as he isn't anything like Detective Inspector Terry Pitman,' Darina said caustically.

'Terry's a good officer,' William protested. 'And he

expected to be promoted into my position, it's no wonder he slightly resents my presence.'

'Slightly!' Darina hooted. 'If thought transference worked, you'd be in some rat-infested hole in the outer Hebrides by now. Face it, darling, as far as Terry's concerned, you're a networking country toff who can't tell a local villain from a Victorian lamp-post and he's just waiting for you to make the mistake that will see you back in Somerset.'

'Thanks for the vote of confidence,' William said quietly and leant back, closing his eyes.

'Darling, don't be like that. I'm just saying that's what Terry thinks. I know and you know that you thoroughly deserve your promotion, that you're one of the brightest detectives in the entire country.'

'Perhaps you'll suggest, then, how I get that over to Terry Pitman?' He kept his eyes closed.

The kettle boiled. Darina rose, rubbing her forehead where depression threatened to turn into a raging headache. She had to tiptoe round William in velvet slippers these days.

Perhaps she had been wrong to persuade him they should live in Chelsea rather than renting somewhere close to his new station.

But when they'd gone to look at the house he'd found, it had seemed so small and, well, *mean*, compared to the spaciousness of the house between the Thames and the King's Road that she'd inherited from her cousin. 'Would it really be so difficult to commute?' she'd asked, pushing vainly at the patio window that should have opened on to a minute, overgrown lawn. The terrace outside her Chelsea drawing room wasn't any larger but it was surrounded with mature old-fashioned roses, wisteria climbed the mellow brick and small shrubs provided an ever varying pattern of greens and golds that constantly refreshed the eye.

The size of the main bedroom in the house for rent was no larger than the boxroom at the top of the Chelsea house. 'Wouldn't you like to be at the centre of everything?' she'd asked, running a finger over the back of a mock leather settee and looking at the dirt. 'On the doorstep of theatres and exhibitions, not to mention restaurants?' William liked his food. What she hadn't said was that she felt it would kill any creative instinct she had if she was forced to live in this graceless, poky house. Not because of its size, their cottage in Somerset hadn't been any larger, but because it had no character, was a mere collection of boxes that would close oppressively round her, leeching out her spirit.

William hadn't put up any arguments and she'd thought he'd been relieved to settle into the space of her Chelsea home, now vacant after a long let to tenants who had paid a pittance and left its previous elegance looking worn and down at heel. Now, though, she realized that commuting nearly an hour to and from Weybridge each day was yet another pressure on him.

'Anyway,' said William, opening his eyes, 'it'll please Terry he's going to be part of Operation Chippendale.'

'Operation Chippendale!' Darina hooted.

William gave her a tired grin. 'Some sort of *double entendre*, you think?'

'I think Roger fancies his muscles! Heaven protect me from the vanity of macho policemen.' Darina poured hot water on to coffee grounds then set cheese and fruit on the table. On her way home that afternoon, she'd visited an excellent delicatessen and bought some of the

Vignotte William loved for its creamy yet firm texture, plus a piece of the traditional farmhouse Cheddar that was so difficult to find. She added a selection of the savoury biscuits she'd prepared for a piece she was working on. Not that it had a home yet, she was still trying to interest editors in an article on superior accessories for simple meals. But who had the time today to prepare such delicious titbits?

She brought the cafetiere to the table, pushed down the plunger then tried to amuse William with a description of the Ealham household. 'You must meet Jemima, one day when you're not so busy,' she finished. 'She's a real character.'

He roused himself, cut a large piece of the Vignotte and transferred it to his plate with three of the homemade biscuits. 'I like the sound of Rory better.' William looked at Darina. 'Isn't it time we started our own family, darling?'

She bit back a flip remark about chance being a fine thing and fought panic. 'You know we decided it would be better to wait a bit. Until you're settled and my career's on a steadier path. When at the moment would you have time to see a child, let alone play with him, or her?'

William started to slip slivers of cheese into his mouth, biting neat little bits out of a biscuit between each piece. 'This pace isn't continuing for ever,' there was a hint of steel in his voice. 'This is just a bad patch, a few weeks and I should be through the worst. But what about you?'

'Me?'

'When do you think you will have your career on track?'

She looked down at the steam gently rising from her cup of coffee, wisping around as though starring in some television commercial. Hopelessness filled her. 'You know how difficult it is, how much competition there is.'

'So why don't you give it a break and start a family instead? After all, it's not as though we're that desperate for money.' At least he hadn't said the loss of the money she was earning at the moment wasn't going to make a whole lot of difference to their lifestyle.

'You don't understand, I've got something of a name at the moment, if I don't try and capitalize on that now, I'll never make it.' Darina looked with pleading eyes at her husband.

'No, I don't understand,' he said roughly, as though patience was something he no longer had the energy for. 'There's more to it than you wanting to write about food or do some television programmes. Why don't you tell me, why don't you say it – you just don't want children!'

'That's not true,' Darina burst out, then stopped, wondering. Was she fooling herself? Trying to put off the decision until her biological clock said, now you don't have to worry because it's too late? But she was only in her early thirties, that time was far off. And these days you could have children even if you were past the menopause. Her mother's voice saying it was against nature sang in her head. Her mother who was so sure of her opinions on everything, who agreed with William that she should be getting on with starting a family, and who had needed quite a different daughter from the one she'd got. 'Darling, this isn't the time for discussions of this sort, we're both too tired,' she prevaricated.

'Jemima made a suggestion today,' she continued,

determined to deflect him from what was beginning to seem like an obsession. If she gave him the opportunity to be dismissive about the idea of her searching for Rory's father, surely that would make him better tempered? For that she was prepared to sacrifice her dignity.

'Do you know, I don't think I want to hear about Jemima,' he said, rising. 'I can hardly keep my eyes open.' He finished off his cup of coffee, cut a thick finger of Cheddar and left the room.

Darina felt first lost, then angry. She'd been left with all the clearing up and William was turning into someone she wasn't sure how to deal with. What had happened to the delightful husband she'd married?

As she wrapped the remains of the cheese with exasperated efficiency, the thought came that for someone who wasn't hungry enough to eat what had been a delicious stir fry, William had consumed an amazing amount of cheese. Then she dismissed it. Tomorrow she was going to give Job Ealham a ring.

Next morning Darina rang the number Jemima had given her. Job answered the phone, his voice edgy and impatient. In the background she could hear children arguing.

'I'm sorry if this is an inconvenient time, my name's Darina Lisle. Jemima suggested I rang, it's to do with your nephew, Rory.'

'Rory?' Anxiety replaced intemperance. 'Nothing's wrong, is there?'

'No, not at all,' Darina soothed, wondering how to approach what had initially seemed a relatively simple matter. She decided to go for plain truth without a garnish. 'Jemima wants me to find out who his father is.'

'For God's sake!' Impatience was back. 'How on earth does she think you're going to do that? None of us knows a thing.'

'Apparently your father is dead against the idea.' Darina followed Jemima's scenario. 'He won't co-operate in any way. I agree with you,' she added quickly. 'The chances of picking up any leads at this stage are remote but if I could have a few words with you? I'm only just across the river, I could come straight over.'

There was silence from the other end of the tele-phone. Then Job said, but not to her, 'Dinosaurs didn't eat their cereals, that's why they're extinct.' Muffled screeches suggested his children weren't going to buy that but it had amused them. 'If you're that keen, you'd better come over,' he said in a resigned tone. 'Jemima can be remorseless in pursuing her crazy ideas. I shan't be able to give you long, though,' he added curtly, 'I have to leave for my office soon.'

'No, that's fine, I'll be with you in about twenty minutes,' Darina said hastily.

She grabbed the bag she'd prepared the night before, picked up her car keys, gave one last glance to the A-Z and set off for the Albert Bridge. As she passed almost static queues of cars and lorries trying to get into central London, she was heartily glad she was going against the traffic.

Job Ealham lived in a tangle of streets around the back of Clapham Junction. Darina found the address without much trouble, more difficult was somewhere to park. She had to walk a little way back to the house, past rows of small, Victorian cottages, no doubt originally destined for labourers, now a mixture of well painted, gentrified dwellings and untidy buildings in need of a face lift. Job's was one of the latter, its tiny front garden decorated with weeds and a leggy climbing rose, the front door's paintwork peeling, the windows dusty and smeared. Darina moved a battered scooter and pressed the bell. She failed to hear it ring so banged a knocker that would require painstaking polishing to restore its brass finish.

The man who opened the door was as lanky and dour looking as she remembered. Even the jeans could have been the ones he'd worn on the Italian holiday. But instead of a dark T-shirt, he sported a faded blue formal shirt, neatly buttoned and worn with a thin, bright red tie. He'd filled out a bit but his eyes were just as wary. Then they suddenly lightened and a brief smile lit his face. 'Yes, it *is* the girl who cooked us those great meals at that god-awful villa. I knew your name rang bells.'

Darina was used to having both a name and an appearance that people remembered. A height a shade under six foot, a frame that was always fighting fat and long blonde hair meant you could never hide in a crowd. But every now and then it had its advantages. She gave him a big grin. 'Nice to see you again, Job. I'd have sworn nothing about that holiday made enough of an impression for you to have remembered anyone there beside yourself.'

His mouth lengthened derisively. 'No doubt I deserved that. Come in and tell me what you've been up to since then.'

The door opened directly into a living area that had obviously once been two rooms. Toys littered the floor. The furniture looked battered and a sofa and chairs had the worst of their drawbacks hidden underneath Indian throws that had needed a better aim, the material was scrunched untidily around the lumps and sags.

'Do you want a coffee?' Job asked as Darina let herself down gingerly into one of the armchairs and felt a spring give.

'No, thanks, I've just had breakfast.'

'Wish I had. You don't mind if I eat as we talk do you? It's more than I can manage when I'm monitoring the children.' He threw himself in a highly dangerous manner into another rickety armchair and picked up a plate loaded with two thick pieces of attractive-looking bread generously spread with butter and marmalade.

'Please, carry on. That bread looks wonderful, do you get it locally?' Darina rootled around in her leather shoulder bag thinking she'd be prepared to drive across the bridge regularly if there was a baker here supplying real loaves.

Job stopped eating and grinned at her. 'Nicola makes it. In between organizing a local play group, bringing up the kids and running a home-based computer business. She's a fanatic on good eating, makes the muesli, buys organic meat and vegetables, the lot.'

'My word!' Darina marvelled. 'It sounds as though you got yourself a bargain in the wife department.' The whole set-up here couldn't have been farther from the Ealham mansion less than thirty miles away in the Thames valley. Only the computer business suggested these Ealhams had even a nodding acquaintance with commercialism.

Job gave her a lopsided smile as he picked up his mug of coffee from a table any self-respecting junk shop wouldn't give floor room to. 'Nicola says I'm her mission, the reason she was born. She says she's never met anyone with less natural born talent for living.' He looked down into his coffee and his smile faded. 'That was before she met Sophie.' He glanced at his watch and spoke briskly. 'It's Nicola's turn to take the kids to school today. Someone's supposed to be coming to look at the washing machine so I said I'd be here until she got back. I'd say you've got about twenty-five minutes. Which should be more than enough time to convince you I know nothing new about Sophie that'll be of any use in finding out where she went to from here.'

Darina at last located her notebook and brought it out with a pencil.

'Good lord, you are being serious! But you're wasting your time.' He picked up the second piece of bread. 'What's got into Jemima anyway?' All at once he looked very like his father.

'I think she's worried about his grandfather's influence on Rory. She says if only we can locate his father, Rory will have a better chance at life than you all had.'

'Ah!'

'You sound as though you don't agree.'

Job shifted in his chair. 'I yield to no one in my contempt for my father.' His voice was bitter. 'He's a bully and he tried to force his twisted values on us. I escaped as soon as I could. Jemima, well, Jemima is more ambivalent.' His tone grew detached. 'She believes she hates him but she crawled back to him when her business failed.'

Darina thought of Jemima's clothes and of Blackboys, Basil Ealham's luxurious house. No doubt the new job carried a powerful car with it as well. She remembered how Jemima would describe the delights of her holidays when term started. Delights that had always involved considerable expense. 'She mentioned something about a fashion boutique.'

'Yeah,' Job's lip curled distastefully. 'Jemima persuaded the father she despises to invest in a shop she said she'd make the success of London.'

'I'd say she had quite an eye for fashion.'

'No doubt about that. But no talent for hard work. Running your own business takes hard graft. Jemima only knows how to enjoy herself. It wasn't much more than a year before the enterprise went bust.' He thought for a moment while Darina silently acknowledged that what he'd said was probably true.

'My own bet is that Jemima thinks if she can find out who Rory's father is, he'll make trouble with Dad. Either he'll demand money or Rory. Whichever it is, Dad'll hate it.'

'Your father says he'd like to get his hands on whoever it is.'

'He's not the only one,' Job was suddenly grim.

Was that why Sophie had disappeared, because she knew her family wouldn't accept whoever it was she'd fallen for? It sounded a good reason but why, in that case, hadn't Rory's father come forward when Sophie collapsed? How could he let her disappear without contacting the police or the hospitals?

'You think it's a good idea to try and find him, then?'

Job shrugged his shoulders, 'I don't think you're going to get anywhere,' he said, his voice losing its sudden force.

'You think it doesn't matter if Rory is brought up by his grandfather? Is it what Sophie would have wanted?' Darina found herself intrigued by Job's mixture of passion and detachment. He sounded as though it had been a considerable struggle to come to any sort of terms with his upbringing, yet he could still be dismissive about how Rory was to be raised.

Job finished his last bit of bread and marmalade and brushed crumbs off his fingers. 'Look, Sophie and Jasper are different from Jemima and me. After Mum died they could see Dad as the all powerful giver of good things, they didn't have to endure the fighting or Mum's misery. Sophie adored him and I think, yes, that she would be very happy to know he was looking after her son.' He sounded controlled, almost academic, as if his brother and sister's lives had little to do with him.

'And Jasper seems content to live with his father,' Darina commented, now totally intrigued by these new insights into life with Basil. 'I gather he's writing a novel.'

'So he says,' again that little curl of the lip. Darina remembered the notebook that Jasper had stolen from his big brother and Job's desperate struggle to get it back.

'It must be great for him to have you to come to for advice,' she said, deliberately disingenuous.

'Jasper knows better than that!' The curl became more pronounced. 'My business is reporting the financial scene; I'm not a creative writer, I discovered that a long time ago.'

Darina wondered how much agony it had caused him.

'Anyway, what's your part in all this?' Job asked.

What indeed? 'I'm married to a detective,' she said cautiously. 'I've been involved in the odd case so Jemima asked if I could help.' It was more or less the truth. 'Why don't we start by you telling me exactly when Sophie came here to stay and why,' she suggested, fixing him with a frank stare.

Job's face re-acquired its earlier shuttered expression. For a few moments there, he'd opened up and talked like a normal human being. Now it was as though the wary, suspicious undergraduate she'd met all those years ago, who'd acted as though he was living under some sort of totalitarian regime, was back.

Was he going to change his mind about talking to her? 'I promise none of what you say will get back to your father, at least not through me,' she added hastily.

He gave a great sigh and some of the suspicion left his face. 'Can't do any harm, I suppose, certainly not as far as poor Sophie is concerned. All right, then. I'll have to think, though, we're going back aways here.'

Darina watched as he stared at the ceiling.

Then he looked at her. 'OK. Sophie came to us about two and a half years ago.'

'How old was she?'

'Oh, eighteen and a bit? Yes. She left school after two years of having a go at GCSEs, without any success, which didn't please Dad. She just wasn't academic. So Dad sent her to Switzerland, to some finishing school where she was miserable. Then a friend of his suggested she brought Sophie out; you know, cocktail parties, Ascot, Henley, all that, so she could meet lots of young people. Dad even gave a ball for her and his friend's daughter.'

This sounded more promising. Surely Sophie could have met all sorts of young men during her season. 'Who was this friend of your father's?'

'No idea! My father knows any number of socially

adept women, half of whom want to share his bed, the other half rather more.' His voice was caustic. Darina scribbled a reminder to herself to ask Jemima.

'So Sophie came out?' she prompted Job.

'Right.'

'And then?' she asked as he showed no signs of continuing.

'I don't know!' he said in exasperation. 'Jemima's no doubt told you I severed all connection with my father when our mother died.'

'But your sisters and Jasper?'

He gazed out of the back window that gave on to a tiny patio area with a rabbit hutch and a paddling pool covered with dead leaves. 'From time to time one or other of them comes and visits'.

'But you don't make much of an effort to keep in touch?' Darina tried to sound neutral but she found it difficult to understand someone who could ignore family ties so completely. An only child herself, she had longed for a brother who would explain things to her, escort her to parties and introduce her to his friends, and a sister to share clothes and giggle with.

In Italy she and Jemima had giggled together. They'd giggled about the boy who had hung around the walls of the villa, waiting for a sight of them. They'd giggled about Job and his scribbling. They'd giggled about the maid who cleaned the place and washed and ironed their clothes, handling them as though they were studded with diamonds. Once they'd seen her holding up Jemima's striped culottes and gazing at her reflection with awe. For a time Darina had felt she'd almost had a sister. Really, so when she'd suggested at the end of the holiday that Jemima give the maid the culottes Jemima

55

had actually agreed. Afterwards she'd said that the girl's reaction had been well worth the loss of one of her favourite garments.

Job shrugged his thin shoulders. 'The only one who rang regularly and came often was Sophie. So it wasn't really a surprise when she turned up one evening with a small holdall and asked if she could stay.'

'You knew she was unhappy at home?'

'How could she be anything else?' He sounded surprised and his dark eyes sparked at her. 'She had nothing to do. She'd hated all the partying bit, said she couldn't talk to the girls, they were all too snobbish.'

'Didn't she meet any young men she liked?'

'Please! Sophie didn't have party chat and she didn't know how to flirt. She wasn't intelligent enough to distance herself from the world my father thought she should belong to, so she floundered. Worse, she was drowning. By the time she came here she was a nervous wreck.'

'And your father hadn't noticed this?' Darina thought of Basil's bright blue eyes that shone such a searchlight into people. Could he really have failed to see what was happening to his younger daughter?

'Father only notices what he wants to. And Sophie didn't want him to see her unhappy. But when he started suggesting she became his hostess, ran the house, all that sort of thing, she couldn't deal with it.'

'So she came to you.' Darina made it a statement.

Job nodded. 'I was her big brother,' he said bitterly. 'She thought I could make life safe for her. Instead, I must have made it worse.'

Chapter Five

William stood at the window of his office looking down into the police parking lot and waiting for Detective Inspector Terry Pitman to answer his summons. A child was kicking a football. He looked about five, dressed in a too large T-shirt and dirty jeans.

The ball was kicked inexpertly against a wall between two cars emblazoned with police markings. Not the dignified blue and white Avon and Somerset shield and chequered band William had grown so fond of over the past few years; these were more strident.

'You'd have him pick up that ball and run with it, wouldn't you?' Terry Pitman's voice suddenly sneered behind him. 'Tell him to forget Wembley and aim for Twickers,' the last word was given a savagely affected twist. He was short and thin with sharp eyes an unusual shade of light hazel and mid-brown hair slicked back in a way that emphasized both the thinness of his nose and his face's curious lack of contours.

No doubt the man would have resented anyone who had been given the job he obviously thought should have been his but a public school and Oxford educated superior living in Chelsea had seemed to rouse an additional bitterness.

'Close the door and sit down,' William said curtly,

turning and leaning against the windowsill. That way the light fell on the sergeant. 'I had Superintendent Marks on the phone last night,' he started.

'Ah, yes, your mate,' Terry murmured with another little sneer as he subsided on to the chair opposite William's desk.

Would Terry Pitman have gained the promotion he so desperately sought and believed should have been his if his man-management skills had been greater? 'You and DC Hare are to join the super's team for Operation Chippendale. You will both report to Divisional Head-quarters this afternoon to be briefed,' William said.

Terry's sneer vanished. 'That's great,' he said with a rush of unaffected enthusiasm. 'I'll tell Chris.'

'No, don't move,' William said, his voice steely. 'You're a bloody good detective, inspector, but you're not going to get any further in the force unless you change your attitude.' He heard himself with despair. Why couldn't he manage a telling off in the bluff, all boys together way Roger had? 'There's no reason why you should like me,' any more than there was any reason he should like Terry. But, under different circumstances, he thought that he could. Terry had an eagerness, a rat-like determination to get through to the truth of whatever lay behind a particular case, that he approved of. 'But you're lumbered with me as your superior officer. If you can't treat me as such, then get out. Do I make myself clear?'

Terry's face was wiped of all expression; he sat rigidly in his chair. 'Sir!'

With relief, William realized there was no hint of insolence in the way the word was barked out.

'By the time Operation Chippendale is over, I shall

expect you to have recognized that we are all on the same side.' William held his gaze for a long moment and watched Terry, much his own age, struggle to control his feelings. 'That's it, inspector,' he said cheerfully. 'We go forward from here. Oh, one more thing,' he added as Terry rose with the sort of alacrity that suggested springs had been released. 'Go down and check on what that boy's doing in the car park. He's too young to be on his own, even on police premises.'

'I'll get DC Hare to suss it out, sir.' Terry moved rapidly towards the door.

'No, inspector, I told you to do it yourself,' William said pleasantly.

For a split second the other man hesitated. Then, 'Right, guv,' he said smartly and left the office.

William turned to look at the car park, just in time to see a girl emerge from the door below and screech something at the child. The boy picked up his ball and ran towards her, tripped over a loose shoelace and fell. Roars of pain rose.

The girl picked up the boy and cuddled him, the strident ticking off that rose up to William a complete contrast to her body language.

Then Terry Pitman joined the scene. William couldn't make out what he said but she visibly bristled as she held the child to her.

Pitman picked up the ball and handed it back to the mother with a dismissive air. The child leant against her, thumb stuck in mouth, surveying the officer with a resentful stare.

William sighed. Was that a problem teenager in the making? An opportunity to create a sense of trust in the police had been lost. He should have taken a tougher line with Terry Pitman from the moment he realized how the sergeant was reacting to his arrival. He should have realized a conciliatory approach would be taken as a sign of weakness. Was he losing his grip? If only he could get on top of the work on his desk, perhaps he'd manage to beat his constant tiredness and rediscover a sense of vitality. He pulled a bunch of reports towards him and made a mental note to have a word with the desk sergeant to see if anyone had been aware of the child playing alone in the car park.

Later that morning William returned to the station from interviewing the proprietress of a high-class dress shop over a series of thefts. She was convinced a member of her staff was tipping someone off when new stock came in. Normally a detective sergeant and a constable would have conducted the interview but with the loss of two of his staff to Operation Chippendale and the remainder already covering incidents, William had gone himself. It was the sort of job he got too little of these days. Interacting with the public, eliciting details and instigating inquiries he had always found an enjoyable challenge.

The only drawback was the resultant paperwork. On the way back to the station gnawing hunger gripped him. Lunchtime was some way off yet. He bought a couple of chocolate-covered snacks, to hell with conscience and a healthy diet. Appetite had to be fed.

He pushed through the station's swing doors. As he made his way across the entrance hall towards the stairs leading to the CID quarters, he was subconsciously aware of a pleasing and familiar scent that cut through the institutional aroma of dust, disinfectant and silicone polish.

'Sir!' called the desk sergeant, 'there's someone waiting to see you.'

Only then did he identify the scent as Darina's favourite. What on earth had brought her here? he wondered.

A neat, petite figure dressed in a dark brown skirt and jacket that had a certain dash stood up.

He went forward. 'DCI Pigram,' he said helpfully.

The girl raised one eyebrow and gave him an amused smile that managed to suggest intimacy. There was something familiar about her and William trawled his capacious memory. 'I'm probably the last person you expected to see here,' she said with a distinct Somerset burr.

Good heavens! Turn that cap of russet curls into a mid-brown pageboy and a face from the past came into focus. 'Of course, it's Detective Constable Pat James!' William was aware that the ostentatious way the desk sergeant was scanning his incident book masked a deep interest in this unexpected visitor. 'How splendid to see you again. Come upstairs and fill me in on what's been happening to you.' He led the way, relief at being able to postpone the paperwork fighting with despair at losing precious time. But overweighing all that was pleasure. He and Pat had worked well together at one time, her unobtrusive efficiency had helped smooth the path of more than one investigation.

'I understand you're married now,' Pat James said as she followed him up the concrete staircase. 'My congratulations. Darina, wasn't it?'

He nodded. 'We finally made it to the altar about

eighteen months ago. And how about you?' he asked, opening the door into his office.

She shook her head. 'Haven't found anyone I want to settle down with yet.'

'I'm sure you will soon,' he said heartily. 'It's good to see you again, how long ago was it we worked together, three years?'

'Three and a half,' she dimpled at him, settling down in the chair so recently vacated by Terry Pitman. 'And it's Sergeant James now.' She said it with an air of expectancy.

'Congratulations,' he said heartily. 'It's no surprise, though, I knew you'd make it. Tell me what you've been doing since we last met.'

While she told him about her transfer from the Somerset to the Wiltshire Police three and a half years ago, he studied her unobtrusively.

It was no wonder it had taken a moment to recognize her. Pat James had always had an air of composure but now there was a new confidence about her. Her clothes had a chic they'd lacked before, she'd learned how to use make-up and this plus the new hairstyle gave her previous rather ordinary looks immediate impact. In fact, she was now something of a knockout.

'Are you up here on a case or having some time off?' he asked as she finished an account of her sergeant's exam.

Pat gave him a demure smile. 'I've been seconded to you by Superintendent Marks, William.'

He stared at her, as thrown by her use of his full name, hardly ever employed by his colleagues on the force, as by what she had said.

'You mean he hasn't told you?' For the first time

Pat James looked disconcerted. 'Well, I know I'm not supposed to be starting until Monday but he said he was going to let you know.'

'Did he!' William said grimly. He reached for the phone just as it rang.

'Bill? Roger here. Your chaps have just arrived, many thanks. Now, in return, I've arranged an additional sergeant for you. Maybe only temporary but it should help your immediate workload. Nice little piece of goods, name of Pat James, says you were once a team in Somerset. She worked for me when I was in Wiltshire and she's just made sergeant. Know you would have preferred a man but she should be all right, bright enough. She'll be along first thing Monday. Well, say thank you!'

'Ah, yes, thanks, I'm sure she'll work out fine.'

'We must have a pint sometime soon,' Roger added perfunctorily then rang off.

William controlled the urge to slam the receiver down. Why couldn't the man have let him know earlier? 'Well,' he said, sitting back. 'Welcome to the station. I must warn you we were stretched before two of the chaps went off to join Operation Chippendale, now we're elastic that's about to ping.'

She laughed dutifully.

'It was good of you to come straight round, I'm afraid you can't meet what's left of CID until Monday, everyone's out at the moment. But I'll take you downstairs and introduce you to some of the uniformed lot.'

'Could you fill in a bit of the background to this manor? The super said life would be very different from the sticks.'

'Of course.' William sank back into his seat, aware of

how unsettled she made him feel. What was it about her? Her new look or the way she seemed to think they enjoyed a special relationship? Then he told himself not to be ridiculous. They were old colleagues, of course she presumed they would enjoy some sort of friendship. 'We're understaffed with a backlog of cases that could keep you here twenty-four hours a day if you let it.' William refrained from telling Pat that his predecessor had been a sick man who'd been allowed to remain in his position too long.

'Sounds as though there'll be lots for me to do,' Pat said brightly.

William laughed. 'Sergeant, you have no idea how much!' He wondered how she was going to get on with Terry Pitman. The CID room at the moment only had one other woman, a very junior detective constable who came from a high rise in north London and was used to fighting her corner.

'First, there's the obvious, this is a suburban rather than a rural area,' he started but got no further before the phone rang again.

It took a little time for William to get all the details. Then he studied his notes for a few moments, thought about his empty CID room and looked across at Pat. 'How'd you like to start your new job? There's been a fire in a food factory on our patch. Arson is suspected and there's a body.'

Pat rose with alacrity. 'Right, guv, I'm ready, notebook and all.' There was a satisfied smile on her mouth as she picked up her handbag.

*

Eat Well Foods was situated on a trading estate a couple of miles from the police station.

There was a map of the various firms occupying the estate but Eat Well Foods was clearly signalled by fire engines, police cars, a crowd of watchers and a line of blue and white tape sealing off the scene.

The windows of the factory had exploded in the heat of the fire and soot marks licked their way up the outside walls. Pools of water were everywhere and as William drew up, he could smell the fumes. They reminded him of the time his mother's deep-fry pan had spontaneously combusted but with an added bitterness and acridity and a terrible top note of out-of-control barbecue. This was an odour that sank into your consciousness. It was noticeable that every window of every other building in the vicinity was shut.

'Euough,' said Pat James in disgust.

Inside the scene of crime tape stood a group of people: three or four firemen, several uniformed police, a burly man in an anorak and dark trousers, a tall, slim woman in a trench coat and a man in a well cut suit, his fair hair swept back from an attractively open face.

William flashed his warrant card at the officer guarding the taped-off area. 'CID,' he said. 'Where's the fire chief?'

'Over there, sir.' The officer waved at the little group.

Followed by Pat, who carefully picked her way through the puddles with what looked like a new pair of shoes, William approached the burly man in the anorak. 'DCI Pigram, sir,' he introduced himself. 'Chief Shorrocks?'

'Right, Chief Inspector,' he acknowledged. 'Glad you could come so promptly.' He drew William a little apart.

'The fire was reported around four o'clock this morning. It was under control by six but the premises couldn't be properly inspected until a short while ago; the heat, you understand.'

William looked at small tendrils of steam still rising from the inside of the building and could appreciate the difficulty.

'This is Officer Melville,' the chief waved forward one of the firemen. 'It was he who called me in.'

'Can you tell me what you found, officer?' William asked.

The fireman's craggy face was smudged, his eyes reddened and tired. He took off his helmet and ran a hand round the back of his neck. 'It's a one-storey building, as you can see, and the roof held. Both the offices and the factory, though it's more like a huge kitchen than a factory if you ask me, were badly damaged. The body was in the corridor between the two areas.'

Overcome by the fumes? Or was there a more sinister reason for his death? It was unlikely William would be able to determine much from the body, fire would have obliterated all obvious clues. It would be down to forensics and the pathologist to detect the cause of death. Reluctantly, though, he faced the fact that he would have to inspect the charred corpse.

'Any idea who it could be?' Pat asked.

'We gather there was a night security man,' the fire chief interpolated.

'And you suspect arson?' William offered.

The fireman nodded. 'There was broken window glass inside one of the offices, suggesting a break-in. The office was obviously where the conflagration started. I'd say an accelerant was used and it smelt like petrol. Scorch marks up the walls together with the intensity of the fire suggest it was thrown around pretty liberally but your forensic boys will make sure.'

'There's a Scenes of Crime team on their way. Who reported the fire?'

'Someone passing the estate rang in.'

'Did you get a name and address?'

Melville nodded. 'It's all on tape but I reckon it was a kosher call, not one of those pyromaniacs who set the thing off then call the brigade and hang around to watch the fun.'

William looked back at the ruined factory. 'Who's the owner?'

'Place is rented by a Mrs Douglas, that's her, over there.'

'Right, we'll have a word. Thanks, Officer Melville, we'll need a full statement from you.'

The fireman nodded, seemingly resigned to the formalities. 'Any time, sir.'

William went over to the woman. 'I understand you're the proprietor of Eat Well Foods, Mrs Douglas?'

She nodded. Her eyes were shocked, huge and dark. In any other circumstances she would have been beautiful, now strain had hardened the lines of her classically shaped face and the creamy skin had an unnatural pallor. The short, glossy dark hair was dishevelled and she wore no make-up.

'I gather you had a night security officer patrolling your factory?'

Her eyes closed briefly. 'Gerry Aherne,' was all she said.

'When was the last time you saw him?'

'Yesterday evening, as I left, about seven thirty.' It seemed an impossibility but her face grew even paler and her eyes larger.

'Where does he live?'

She pointed to one side of the factory. 'There's a small apartment at the back.'

William looked at a fireman. He shook his head. 'No sign of anyone there, sir,' he said.

'Mrs Douglas, is there anyone you can think of who could have a grievance against you?'

She looked at him, her dark eyes dilated – with fear? Shock? Bewilderment? 'Are you saying the fire wasn't an accident, that someone did this deliberately?' She hunched her shoulders and folded her arms across herself in a gesture of denial.

'I'm afraid it looks as though the fire was started deliberately,' William said expressionlessly, watching her carefully.

The crossed arms tightened and she shook her head vehemently. 'There isn't anyone, I mean, I can't think anyone would do such a thing.'

Her companion placed an arm around her shoulders. 'Do you have to question her now?' he asked William. 'She's in shock, she should be home, in bed.' His voice was angry but also uncertain.

William looked at him politely, 'And you are, sir?'

'Paul Robins,' the man said, his spurt of anger subsiding. 'Public Relations consultant to Eat Well Foods.'

Val Douglas moved away from his arm. 'Paul, I know you're trying to help, but there are things to see to.' She glanced at the crowd on the other side of the blue and white tape. 'I've got to tell them to go home,' she said with a sigh.

'It's the staff,' Paul explained to William. 'They all turned up for work as usual. Well, they would, wouldn't they? I'll talk to them,' he said to the woman.

'No, it's my job.' She advanced towards the crowd. 'Look, I'm sorry, but, as you can see, we won't be able to do any work today. Why don't you all go home and I'll let you know when production can start again.' She scanned their faces.

There must be about thirty there, William reckoned, mainly women. Their expressions were excited, apprehensive, frightened even. He couldn't see any that looked knowing or unsurprised.

Mrs Douglas squared her shoulders, a natural authority begining to emerge. 'Look, Eat Well Foods is going to remain in business. I'll find other premises until we can rebuild here.'

'It had better be near,' someone shouted out.

She nodded. 'Of course, trust me.' At that moment, William thought, even he might have.

A short, sturdy girl rather better dressed than the others came forward. 'What about the records? Have they survived?'

Mrs Douglas saw immediately what she was getting at. 'Thanks, Shaz, I'm not being allowed to check on anything at the moment.' She looked back at the ruined premises. 'But I shouldn't think so.'

'Then I'll make a note of everyone's address and telephone number,' the girl said. She pulled out a small notebook and the others clustered around her.

'The perfect secretary,' Mrs Douglas said and the girl gave her a gratified smile. 'Stay behind when you've finished, Shaz, and I'll see if I can put two thoughts together on where we go from here. And we'll have to tell our regular customers we can't fulfil any orders today.'

'Pretty much in control, isn't she?' murmured Pat to William.

He nodded. It was an impressive performance. Val Douglas had courage, was a woman who wouldn't let go easily. He wondered what the finances of Eat Well Foods were like.

'I appreciate you have a lot to deal with, Mrs Douglas,' he said as she rejoined Paul Robins. 'But we shall need to talk to you.'

She eyed him. 'Talk to me?'

'We need to know about the company, about your nightwatchman and how the fire could have started.'

The slightest of flushes stained the pale cheekbones. 'I can't help you there, I'm afraid. I wish I could.'

'Look,' Paul Robins said aggressively, 'this is a devastating experience for Val, for Mrs Douglas. You suggesting she might have had something to do with the fire is ridiculous.'

'I'm not,' William said mildly.

'Oh, well, that's all right then.' Paul stuck his hands in his pockets and kicked at some loose rubble on the ground.

'Paul, I think we need to draft a statement we can give the press,' Val Douglas said. She sounded as though her stock of energy was exhausted. 'If we don't tell them something, all those reporters who were here earlier are going to print I don't know what. You should call a conference.'

'Of course,' he said eagerly. 'Look, if you won't go home, come to my office.' He put his hand on her back as though to guide her away from the ruined factory.

'Would you mind giving me details of where your office is, please, sir?' Pat asked.

Paul Robins dug out a card and handed it to her. She gave it a glance then handed it to William. Robins Associates it read, with an address in a nearby town.

Just then a Rolls Royce glided up and stopped beside William's old Bentley. Two thoroughbreds but one was at the end of its life and the other had hardly commenced its career. Out stepped a man tailored and groomed to a fine finish. Piercing eyes swept the scene.

'Basil!' Val Douglas breathed with what seemed enormous relief. 'Thanks for coming back.'

He strode possessively over to her, holding up and stepping underneath the blue and white tape as though it was fairground decoration.

'Sir!' expostulated the uniformed constable.

William quietened him with a wave of his hand.

'I've finished my meeting and cleared my diary. Now we can sort you out,' the newcomer said. He put his arm around her shoulders, where Paul Robins's had so lately been, and would have swept her away but William stepped forward.

'If I could have details of where I can contact Mrs Douglas?' he asked amiably.

Cold blue eyes looked into his and he had the impression they weren't pleased to find they were on a level with his own. A man used to dominating others with his size. 'And who are you?'

'Chief Inspector Pigram, sir, CID. I'm investigating the fire.'

'Are you, by God! I would have thought that would be a matter for the fire department.'

'They've found a body, Basil,' Val said and her voice

trembled. Now this man had appeared, it seemed reaction was setting in. 'It looks as though it's our nightwatchman's.'

'Good God!' he said sharply. 'In that case, I understand.' He, too, reached into an inside pocket but his cards were carried in a silver case. He detached and handed one over. 'You can contact Mrs Douglas through my office.' The full name was Basil Ealham, Chairman and Managing Director of Ealham Industries with another local address.

'Will you be taking Mrs Douglas there, sir?' Pat asked.

Basil looked down at her. 'I've said you can contact her through my office,' he repeated with a touch of pomposity.

'Thank you, sir,' William said quietly. There was no point in antagonizing the man unnecessarily; William thought he'd be very surprised if obstacles were placed in the way of an interview with Val Douglas. When the investigation started to uncover sensitive material, if it did, that was the point when Ealham would try to take control.

'But, the press statement?' Paul Robins said helplessly as he watched his client being taken over.

'We'll ring later,' Basil Ealham said curtly.

Paul Robins looked pleadingly at Val but William doubted she even realized he was still there.

It was only as the car purred away that William remembered that his wife's old school friend, the one she'd lunched with yesterday, apparently in some style and not far from the address he'd just been given, was called Ealham. Why hadn't he paid more attention to what she'd said?

Chapter Six

Nicola Ealham took her two children to the school gate and gave them a gentle push in the direction of the classrooms. 'See you at four o'clock,' she called as they gathered speed, melting into the flow of children. Kinsey looked back over her shoulder and waved, the fat pigtails with their blue butterfly bows bouncing on her eight-year-old shoulders, but seven-year-old Arthur was too busy punching the arm of his best friend to be concerned with saying goodbye.

Nicola grinned to herself as she turned to walk back home. There wasn't much wrong with her little world. As long as the washing-machine man came and didn't extract Danegeld for fixing the darned thing. But she'd just got paid for that programming job she'd done for a local estate agents and she could probably cope with the damage.

Anyway, she wasn't going to worry. A warm September sun was shining and back home Nicola had plans for making a batch of oat bread and trying out a new recipe for soya pancakes which she planned to serve with maple syrup for supper. If they were a success, she'd make some more and stuff them with organic mushrooms for a meal over the weekend. Nicola believed what you fed people was important, especially children. After all you didn't expect a Rolls Royce to run on poor petrol, did you?

She let herself into the house. 'I'm back,' she called cheerfully then realized that Job was sitting in the living room talking to a very tall, blonde girl.

'Hi, darling.' Job smiled up at her. 'Meet Darina Lisle. She went to school with Jemima and she's trying to find out who Rory's father is.'

'Good heavens, lost cause that.' Poor little Sophie, every time Nicola thought about her she felt sad. Nobody had been able to help her, not Job, not herself. 'Why now? I thought your father wasn't going to bother. Mind you, I always did think that was odd, his not wanting to know, I mean.' She sat down on a large bean bag and gazed with open curiosity at the girl, who smiled back with easy friendliness.

'It's Jemima,' said Darina. 'She's the one who's so concerned.' She hesitated a moment then added, 'Something to do with balancing the effect Rory's grandfather will have on his upbringing, I think.'

'I quite understand,' said Nicola cheerfully. Basil represented so much that she was anti – possessions, ostentation and disregard for other people, particularly people who depended on you like your wife and children. 'We've been worried about that ourselves. My suggestion he lived with us was as popular as raw steak to a vegetarian.'

'I've got to go,' Job said, unwinding his long body. 'Why don't you talk to Darina, darling, after all, you saw much more of Sophie than I.'

Nicola caught Darina's hopeful look and decided that, after all, oat bread could wait for another half hour or so. 'The man hasn't turned up for the washing machine?' she asked, looking up for Job's parting kiss.

'Yup, he's in the kitchen.'

'Why on earth didn't you say!' Nicola was up in an instant. On the kitchen table, in between dirty cereal bowls and half-drunk mugs of milk (trust Job not to insist the kids finished them), were oily lumps of machinery. Carefully inspecting one of them was a spotty youth, his overalls looking as though they'd never seen the inside of one of the machines he spent most of his life communing with.

'Well?' she demanded.

'Wouldn't have a coffee going, would you, miss? My old lady wouldn't get up this morning.'

Nicola put the kettle on. 'Right, now tell me about my machine.'

Ten minutes later, blinded by his combination of engineering expertise and inability to communicate it to her, she'd agreed to the replacement of a highly expensive part on the understanding he'd have the machine working by the end of the day. Carrying two fresh cups of coffee, she returned to the living room.

'I sometimes think I should take evening classes on the maintenance of kitchen machinery.' Nicola handed over one of the coffees and sank down on the bean bag again.

'I'm useless. Can just about fix a plug – and William's not much better. We reckon it's cheaper in the long run to give DIY jobs to a professional first time around.'

Nicola inspected the girl more closely. About five years younger than herself, she reckoned, and someone she felt an immediate liking for. Nicola usually made up her mind instantly about people. When she'd met Job, they'd both been reaching for the same Thurber book in the university library. She'd looked at his reserved face and lanky body, added a liking for surrealistic humour and decided. She'd suggested they went and had tea in a nearby cafe. He'd hesitated, looking agonized, and she could see he was torn between wanting to accept her invitation and dreading it would develop into a relationship he couldn't sustain. 'One exchange of a library book is what I'm talking about, not a commitment for life,' she'd said, grinning at him, knowing that her freckles, short ginger hair and the impertinent tilt to her nose would be immensely reassuring. It had almost reconciled her to the fact her looks were so unprepossessing.

The girl sitting opposite her was no classic beauty either, too big boned. But she had an openness about her, a warmth in the eyes that were neither grey nor quite hazel, that was more attractive than model-girl looks. 'I can't imagine how you and Jemima became friends,' Nicola said suddenly. Jemima was one of the few people she had never been able to make up her mind about. Sometimes she despised the way she snatched at what she wanted out of life, other times she liked her zest and thought with a bit of hard work they could have a good relationship. But Jemima regarded her with the wariness of a cat assessing hostile territory and hid behind a finishing-school drawl until Nicola could have shaken her.

'Not much alike, are we?' Darina sounded amused. 'Perhaps that's why we got on. Jemima was always so much fun. She did and said the most dreadful things but made you laugh.' She fell silent for a moment then added, 'Yesterday was the first time we'd met since school.'

'Good heavens, that must be, what, thirteen years ago? But, then, Jemima doesn't really know much about friendship. Lives in a little world of her own. Her father has a lot to answer for.'

'Job says she's dependent on him.'

'He buggered up all his children's lives.' Nicola spoke with quiet passion.

Darina leaned forward. 'Tell me about it.'

Nicola was more than happy. It was a long time since she'd had an opportunity to exorcize some of the anger she felt against Basil Ealham. 'To start with he turned their mother into an alcoholic.'

'Ah!' A small sigh that said a lot. 'When Jemima and I were about fifteen, I spent a holiday with the Ealhams in Italy and afterwards I wondered. Jemima would never talk about it though. Did Job?'

'Yeah. I'd guessed actually. I reckoned there had to be major damage in his background, he was so withdrawn and he'd never talk about his family. I didn't even realize he had a brother and two sisters until he suggested we got married. I told him I wouldn't begin to think about it until I'd met his relations. I had to get him to confront his problems somehow!'

'I often wondered why Job came on that holiday. After all, he was at university, most undergraduates I've known would die rather than go abroad with their family. Not that Basil stayed more than a few days with us. Business, we were told.'

'Always business,' Nicola agreed. She crossed her legs yoga style on the bean bag. 'Job probably went because he adored his mother. I wish I'd met her, she died just before we got together – I only found that out later, too. When I think of all Job bottled up . . .' For a moment Nicola felt the suffocation that came whenever she confronted how badly damaged Job had been. She took several deep breaths and reminded herself how successful she'd been in coaxing him into something approaching the sort of normal human being who could ask for help.

'You're the first person I've met I can talk to about Job's mother. What was she like?'

Darina thought for a moment. 'Very unpretentious. Almost aggressively so. I admired a skirt she had on once, it was long, pleated, in navy, just the sort of thing that would look good with my hips,' she glanced wryly at herself. 'She told me it came from Marks and Spencer's and made it sound as though she'd gone somewhere forbidden and that it was some sort of victory. Jemima was always telling her she should get some decent clothes and that their house needed redecorating.' Darina gave a short laugh. 'She thought the villa we were staying in was marvellous. Apparently it belonged to some business friend of her father's and it was full of the most beautiful furniture, a lot of it modern, very expensive I should think.'

'Jemima likes expensive things,' Nicola murmured. 'Did you visit Blackboys while her mother was alive?'

Darina nodded. 'Several times. My mother said it looked as though it had been furnished by a second-rate department store with no expense spared. Everything colour co-ordinated with no taste.' She laughed again, 'She'd love it now.'

'I hate it,' Nicola said repressively. 'Talk about pretentious! Come on, tell me more about Julie. Did she seem happy?'

'Heavens, no. I used to wonder why she stayed with her husband. He'd make awful, snide remarks to her and she'd just sit there and say nothing. The night after we arrived we heard them shouting at each other. I remember Sophie coming into our bedroom, crying. Then Basil left and Sophie was even more upset. Jasper didn't like it either.' She smiled at Nicola. 'Jasper was such a clown. That second night he walked on his hands all the way down the table in the middle of the meal, glasses and plates everywhere, with Basil shouting at him to stop being such a fool. He didn't disturb a thing, then leaped off like an acrobat and said with an enormous grin, "For my next trick, walking on water!" And Basil just creased. Jasper was over the moon. After his father left, he was really depressed for several days. Jemima and Job were relieved.'

'What about their mother?'

'She was certainly less tense but she drank as much if not more.'

'How did she manage the cooking? Or was there a cook laid on?'

'No, I did most of the cooking.' Darina's face suddenly lit up. 'I loved it, all those marvellous vegetables and I'd brought Elizabeth David's *Italian Cooking* with me. I think that's when I decided food was going to be my life.'

'I wonder what the Ealhams thought of it all! According to Job, his mother was a terrible cook. She and his father both came from very poor backgrounds and her idea of a really good meal never progressed beyond steak and chips.'

'They should never have married,' Darina said sadly.

'Old story, he got her in the family way, then felt he had to marry her.'

'Well, something to be said for him, then.'

'Thought he'd make sure of his home comforts so he could concentrate on making his fortune,' Nicola said caustically. 'The women came later. That's when Julie's drinking started, apparently. Then everything was downhill.'

'Why didn't she leave him, has Job told you that?'

Nicola thought about the way Job used to close up like a hedgehog rolling itself into a ball, all prickles, and the long, slow process of getting him to open up and unburden himself. 'He thinks she really loved his father and couldn't bear the thought of life without him. More interesting is why he didn't leave her. My theory is that he liked playing around and didn't want to commit himself to anyone else. After all, he's never married again. Julie was one of life's victims. She ended up taking an overdose of sleeping tablets. Job has never forgiven his father.'

'That's why he won't have anything to do with him?'

Nicola nodded. 'Wouldn't even invite him to the wedding. Not that I think it worried Basil, he'd made it clear he didn't think I was up to much; no background, no connections, no money.'

Darina shook her head. 'What an arrogant bastard.'

'In spades,' Nicola said levelly.

'Jemima says that since she started working for Basil, Job won't speak to her.'

Nicola pulled at her short, ginger hair with both hands. 'Aaargh! He can be such an idiot! He's lost one sister and now he's doing all he can to lose the other.'

'Tell me about Sophie.'

Nicola leant back against the bookshelves. 'I think she was her mother all over again. Frailty thy name is Sophie, was what I always thought.'

'Job says he doesn't know why she left you, do you?' Darina's gaze was very level and Nicola thought how difficult it would be to hide something from those eyes.

Nicola looked down at the freckles on the backs of her hands. Freckles like brown sugar, Sophie had said. They'd been sitting at the kitchen table. It had been a lovely May day with the sun shining and they'd been enjoying the wild cherry tea Sophie liked so much, not really talking, just appreciating the warmth and the feeling that conversation wasn't necessary. Sophie had run her finger over Nicola's hand, then put her mouth down and licked it. 'You taste sweet,' she'd said. 'Like sugar.'

Nicola had grinned at her. 'You better not eat me, you know sugar isn't good for you.'

Nicola dragged her mind back to the present. 'Sophie was so hungry for love. But I think she was afraid of it, too. Her mother died when she was eight and she'd grown up with a series of housekeepers and a father who was hardly ever there but demanded everything from her when he was. He wanted too much. He wanted her to be intelligent and bright and ambitious.'

'Like Jemima,' murmured Darina.

'Yeah, like Jemima.' Nicola said sourly. 'But Basil was always on at Jemima, too; about her men, her clothes, her failure to stick at anything. Basil always wants to make people into his idea of what they should be. It wound Sophie into knots. She was in a terrible state when she arrived here, bursting into tears at nothing at all, you had to handle her as though she was made of incredibly short pastry.'

Darina smiled at the metaphor.

'But being with Kinsey and Arthur, our children, was just what she needed. She loved them and they adored her. They couldn't believe it when she went off like that.' Nicola paused then added, 'Neither could I.'

'Not so trusting, after all, then?' Darina said gently.

Nicola shook her head sadly. 'I'd thought we were friends. I really thought she'd be able to tell me anything.'

'Can you tell me exactly what happened?'

Nicola had been over the events of that week so often she was able to rattle them off without thinking. The routine had become familiar over the couple of months Sophie had been with them. Sophie had taken the children to school and collected them as usual. Nicola had taken her turn in running the play group on the Tuesday and the Thursday mornings while Sophie did some housework. On the Tuesday afternoon they'd cooked together because Martin Price was coming to supper.

'Who is Martin?' Darina interrupted. 'A boyfriend of Sophie's?'

Nicola laughed. 'Heavens, no. Martin was at university with Job. He runs a financial company in the city now. He married about the same time we did and he and his wife, Eleanor, are great friends.'

'But Eleanor didn't come to supper that night?'

'No,' Nicola said more slowly, thinking about that for the first time. 'Eleanor was in Cornwall, looking after her mother, I think she'd broken her arm. Eleanor had rung me before she left and I promised her we'd look after Martin. He came round for supper several times. He was sweet with Sophie, didn't make her feel an idiot, you know?' She thought about that for a moment. 'Anyway, Martin came to supper that night. And the next night he took her out to the cinema.' She felt the quality of Darina's attention alter. 'But there was nothing like that about it,' she protested. 'He was just being friendly.' She looked down at her hands, lying between her crossed legs. 'Perhaps I should tell you a little more about Martin. He was very upset at that time. His son, Charlie, had been killed in a traffic accident and he thought Eleanor blamed him for his death. Martin's the type who always feels guilty, whatever happens. Whatever the truth, he was really worried Eleanor wasn't going to come back to him from her mother's.' Nicola looked at Darina and added quickly, 'But she did and they're fine now. So you see that there couldn't have been anything between Martin and Sophie. He took her out to give Job and me an evening to ourselves. However much you like someone, you need a little time out every now and then.'

Darina made a note, it was impossible for Nicola to tell what she was thinking. 'So that brings us to Thursday, what happened then?'

Nicola realized she'd stopped talking, caught up in remembering that last week. Nothing was what had happened then. Nothing out of the ordinary, anyway. Except, 'She did seem a bit quiet,' Nicola said. 'But she was never exactly noisy. Sometimes you hardly noticed she was there.' She could see Sophie now, sitting in the corner of that ratty old sofa as relaxed as a cat.

'I've never known anyone who seemed so happy doing nothing. Not reading, not sewing, not listening to music, not watching the television, just doing absolutely nothing at all. And all over that weekend she seemed to be getting quieter and quieter. The only time I heard her laugh was when she played with the children. Martin came round for Sunday lunch and he managed to raise a smile or two from her but apart from that, it was like living with someone who was turning into a ghost.' Nicola gave a small shiver, she wasn't normally that imaginative.

'Did you ask if anything was worrying her?'

Nicola screwed up her face. 'It was difficult with Sophie. If she thought you were getting at her, she dissolved into floods of tears. Sure, I asked her if everything was all right and she said it was. After she disappeared, I asked Martin if anything had happened the night they'd gone to the cinema but he said nothing, she'd been sweet and he couldn't think of anything strange.'

'She left, when?'

'Monday. I had to go out on a job. Mostly I work from home, I've got a work station in our bedroom. But Monday I had to visit a small company down the high street. When I got back at lunchtime, Sophie had gone. Packed a small bag, left us a note – and vanished.'

Nicola felt tears pricking at the back of her eyes. She'd never manage to get over the way Sophie had disappeared or the tragedy of her death. She went to a desk in the corner of the room, found a piece of paper and handed it to Darina. 'You'd better see it, I suppose.'

As Darina unfolded the note, Nicola could see again the large, unformed letters that said, 'Thanks for everything. I've got to go now. See you soon, lots of love, Soph.'

'And she never contacted you?'

Nicola shook her head, trying to swallow the lump in her throat. After all this time, she should be able to handle the fact of Sophie's disappearance better.

'Did she have any money?'

'That's one of the first things we thought of. She'd drawn thirty pounds out from her bank account a few days before and, as far as we could find out, that was all she had.'

'She didn't draw any more?'

'No, nor use her credit cards. It was as though she realized they could give away where she was.' Nicola didn't add that when Basil had first found that out, they'd all thought it meant Sophie was dead. The news of her actual death had been doubly tragic. She'd been alive for all that time and they hadn't known.

'It's Job's theory that Sophie ran away not from us but from Basil.'

'What does he mean? Was Basil threatening to take her home? Presumably he knew she was staying with you?'

'Oh, yes. But after she arrived here, Job went over to Blackboys, it was one of the few times he's been there since his mother died, and told Basil that if he didn't leave Sophie alone, she'd have a nervous breakdown. Eventually his father agreed that he wouldn't contact her for at least three months. I think Job said the words Basil used were, "I'll let the girl get herself together." But she used to ring him up every weekend, tell him what she'd been doing, ask him how he was, all that sort of thing.'

'It didn't worry her to talk to him?'

'No, really, she adored him. It was just too much for her being with him, trying to fulfil his demands.'

'Did Sophie talk to her father that last weekend?'

Nicola thought for a moment. 'No,' she said at last. 'I remember now, he was abroad. She tried to get him at some hotel but he wasn't there. She left a message for him to ring her but he didn't.'

'Was she upset at that?'

'Didn't seem to be. But, as I said, she was so quiet, it was difficult to know what she was thinking. Just like a ghost.' It was an image that kept coming back to Nicola, like a haunting.

'So after you left her in the house on the Monday morning, you never saw or heard from her again.' It was a statement and all Nicola had to do was nod.

Darina frowned and looked at her notes. 'Can you give me your friend Martin's address and telephone number?' she asked finally.

'But he doesn't know anything,' Nicola protested. 'After she disappeared, we really grilled him. We thought if anybody knew where she'd gone, it'd be him. After all, he was the only person outside the family she'd seen while she was here. Oh, just a minute, there was someone else. He worked for a friend of Basil's, she was in food. I remember Sophie telling me she produced dishes for people with food intolerances and I thought it sounded really interesting.'

'Val Douglas,' Darina contributed.

'I've got it, Paul Robins, that was the name.'

Darina wrote it down. 'You met him?'

'Yup, he just rang the doorbell one afternoon not long after Sophie arrived. Said he was in the area, knew she was staying with us and thought he'd drop in. Quite attractive, if you like that rather smooth, nothing under the surface type.'

'Was Sophie pleased to see him?'

Nicola tried to think back. She couldn't believe that she had so completely forgotten all about this visit. 'It was difficult to tell with Sophie, she talked to everyone as though they were the most important person in the world.'

'Captivating,' was Darina's comment.

'Yes, it was,' Nicola acknowledged. She supposed she would always miss Sophie.

'But you didn't see this Paul Robins again?'

Nicola shook her head.

'He couldn't have called round when you weren't here?'

'Well, yes, I suppose so,' Nicola acknowledged. 'But Sophie would have told me. I'm sure it was just that one time.'

What was this investigation going to drag up? Nicola hoped it wasn't going to upset Job. 'Look,' she said to Darina, 'I'm sure it's a good idea to try and find out who Rory's father is and I'll give you Martin's details if you think it'll help, but please don't talk again to my husband.'

'The Ealhams aren't an easy family to be involved with, are they?' Darina said.

Chapter Seven

Darina left Job and Nicola's house wondering about Sophie.

Had she been as lacking in intelligence as Nicola seemed to suggest? She certainly seemed incapable of surviving on her own. Someone who had lived all her life surrounded by love in a completely protected environment. Yet she'd disappeared and managed to live nearly eight months without contact with anyone she'd known up until then. How?

When she'd disappeared, the Ealhams had contacted the police but, because Sophie was over eighteen, there'd been little they could do. However, a sympathetic officer had unofficially checked with social services and then told them that Sophie had not applied for any benefits. At that point, the family had feared she must be dead.

Darina had gathered a few more details from Jemima. Basil had disappeared to his office before they'd had lunch, brusquely instructing Jemima to follow as soon as Mrs Starr appeared.

Over lobster salad Jemima had told Darina about the boutique she'd been running in London at the time of Sophie's death, and the man she'd been involved with. 'One of those real shits who give less than nothing but take everything and do it with so much charm and style, you'd be happy to go on giving to them until hallelujah day.' Her face had had an unfamiliar, yearning expression. 'He had those dark eyes that seem to look right down to your fanny, and what a body! Some Sundays we'd never get out of the sack. Mondays I could hardly crawl to the shop. Oh, it was wonderful!' She'd glowed as she talked.

'What happened?'

'What always happens to my men, he found something else.' Not somebody, Darina noticed. 'In Titus's case it was rafting down the Colorado River. He said it was no place for a girl and it would only be for three weeks. That was fifteen months ago. I hear the Colorado River is drying up so maybe I'll see him again one of these days.'

'You haven't had a boyfriend since?' Darina was sceptical.

'Good heavens, darling, what do you take me for, a nun?' Jemima placed a bowl of fruit and a cheese platter on the table. 'There was Mike, he was a journalist, always dashing off on some story or other. Never had any money. "Waiting for my expenses, sweetie," was his excuse every time the bill came round. I gave him the boot when I met James.' She cut into a golden peach. 'James was a financial consultant, fearfully rich. He took me to all the best places, and was almost as good in bed as Titus.'

'So what went wrong with him?'

'His mother! Practising to be the mother-in-law from hell. James adored her and she was always round at our place. Mummy dear had nothing else to do but involve herself in our activities. Just when I couldn't stand it any more, I met Dominic. That was about six months ago.'

'And what's he like?' a bemused Darina asked, thinking that Jemima had always seemed to need men. On the Italian holiday, it hadn't been long before she'd made contact with Claudio, the youngster who'd hung around the villa. After that, there was rarely a day she hadn't gone off with him somewhere. Once Claudio had produced a friend and they'd made up a foursome but all the boys had been interested in was removing the small amount of clothes the girls were wearing. Jemima hadn't seemed to mind but Darina had. 'Honestly,' she'd told her friend afterwards, 'you want to watch it. It's not that I'm a prude but haven't these lads heard about chatting a girl up?'

'Oh, you!' had been Jemima's only comment. Next time she'd suggested they make a foursome, Darina had said she preferred to enjoy the pool at the villa. She'd wondered that Jemima's mother hadn't protested at her daughter's behaviour but Mrs Ealham spent every day sitting beside a long drink that rapidly grew shorter until it was replenished. Her only comment ever seemed to be to tell Sophie to keep her sunhat on. It had been Darina who applied the suntan lotion to the little body and Jasper who kept her amused. Job had been as elusive as Jemima.

'Dominic? Raaather tasty!' Jemima drawled. 'Unfortunately he's in television. What with his hours and the way Dad's such a bear if I take time off, I don't see nearly enough of him. Anyway, compared with Titus, he's not so great!' For a fleeting instant her mouth drooped.

'I'm not surprised you didn't have any spare time to

look for a missing sister.' Darina said crisply. 'I'm just amazed you manage to combine your social life with working for your father.'

Jemima suddenly looked vulnerable. 'Don't say things like that, please! Nobody really understands; I need men, it's like a sort of hunger. It's not just sex, though that's part of it, I need to have someone I can connect with, you know? Someone who cares. But that doesn't mean I can't work as well. And I did care about Sophie, really I did.' She sat holding half a peach, ripe juices slowly dripping on to her plate. 'It was just that there was too big an age gap between us. It was me and Job, and her and Jasper.' She gazed at Darina, her mobile face despondent. 'As I told you, she wasn't the brightest of kids. Dad never seemed to realize it but holding a conversation with her was like trying to talk to someone who didn't know what time of day it was. She had no idea of the sort of life I led and wasn't interested in hearing about it. But her small brain didn't seem to matter to Dad.' She put the piece of peach down on her plate and sat looking at it as though a scorpion might crawl out.

She was jealous of her sister, Darina suddenly realized. All those years Basil hadn't turned up at school, had abandoned her on holiday, she'd been desperate for his attention. Instead, he seemed to have given it to her baby sister. 'Perhaps he was trying to make up for the fact she didn't have a mother,' she suggested.

'Guilt, more like,' Jemima said bitterly. 'How Mum put up with him all those years, I'll never know. Marriage, huh! Who needs it!'

Darina had no wish to explore that argument. 'But

didn't you say he'd backed your boutique? And now he's given you a job you seem to enjoy.'

'Only so he can demonstrate his power,' Jemima said bitterly. 'He's never given any of us any real independence. Jasper gets an allowance so he can write but it's not enough for him to have his own place.'

Darina thought that Jasper was lucky not to have to combine his writing with a daytime job.

'And my salary isn't anywhere near enough for me to live on my own any more. The trouble is, we're too used to this sort of lifestyle.' Jemima gave an all-encompassing glance to the beautifully furnished room, the silver and crystal on the table, the perfectly ripe fruit and cheese. 'But I can't bear it if Rory has to go through what we did, all the bullying, the shouting and Dad never being there when he's needed.' There was a note of genuine desperation in her voice.

Darina had been working herself up to say that she couldn't take on what seemed to her a hopeless task but she found herself unexpectedly moved. 'Tell me more about this hospital business,' she suggested. 'Did someone take her there, or did she go by ambulance? Either way, there must have been a name or a record of some address?'

Jemima shook her head. 'If only it had been that simple! Apparently she collapsed in the street and a shopkeeper sent for an ambulance.'

'And how did the hospital know who to call? Did she tell them?'

'No, I think she was in a coma when she arrived. Dad said they'd found her driving licence with this address and got the telephone number from directory enquiries.'

'Driving licence? In her handbag?'

Jemima nodded.

'Wasn't there anything else in there that would help to trace her?'

'Look, I've told you, there was no way we could find out where she'd been living.'

'Exactly where did she collapse?'

Jemima grinned suddenly. 'I knew I was right to ask you for help, you don't let up on the questions.'

'What did you expect? That I'd conjure information out of nowhere? So, where did the ambulance pick her up? I can't imagine your father didn't ask.'

'Oh, yeah! He interrogated everyone he could get hold of. She was in the Portobello Road when she collapsed. And it's no use asking me what she was doing there.'

'Did she have a shopping bag with her?'

'There was a sort of string bag in her coat pocket.'

Had she been just about to start shopping when she collapsed? 'And what time of the day was it?'

'One p.m.'

'Lunchtime,' said Darina thoughtfully. 'What else do you know?'

'Well,' Jemima put both her elbows on the table and fiddled with a ring while she talked. 'As you can imagine, Dad went into the whole thing pretty thoroughly. Apparently the ambulance men said that by the time they got to her, Sophie had just come round. Someone had put a folded coat under her head and was holding her hand. She told the ambulance man that her head ached and it felt as if someone had hit her. He asked the crowd if anyone had seen anything but various people said she'd just collapsed. The paramedic couldn't find anything wrong except that her hands, legs and feet were all

93

terribly swollen. Sophie said she felt awful and he decided to take her to the hospital. On the way Sophie was sick and by the time they arrived she was in a coma.' Jemima ducked her head and ran her thumb along her forehead. 'I hate thinking of her like that, all on her own.' She seemed genuinely moved. If she had been jealous of Sophie's hold on their father, it didn't seem to have affected her love for her sister.

'And she didn't tell them anything about herself?' asked Darina gently.

Jemima shook her head. 'As I said, they found this address on her driving licence. Mrs Starr gave them Dad's office number. He said their first diagnosis was that Sophie had had a stroke.'

'A stroke?' A nineteen-year-old? Darina couldn't believe it.

'I know,' Jemima said sadly. 'But apparently it's not unknown. It wasn't until she was examined that they realized she was pregnant.'

'Good heavens!'

'She didn't look it, you see. She was wearing a loose dress and the baby was so small. Then they realized she was suffering from pre-eclampsia, that's a form of toxaemia,' she added kindly. 'That was when they brought in an obstetrics team, who said the baby was in difficulties and they performed a caesarean. Result, one minute little Rory but Sophie never regained consciousness. Apparently it was an aneurysm in the brain, a weakness in a blood vessel which burst.'

Darina could think of nothing useful to say.

'They also said she was half starved,' Jemima added after a moment.

'Half starved?' Darina repeated in astonishment

'Well, malnourished was what Dad actually said.'

'And how long after Sophie disappeared was that?'

'Eight months.'

'So she could have been pregnant when she left. Perhaps that was why she went!'

Jemima bent to eat the rest of her peach, the juice dripping down her chin. 'Dad says Rory was about six weeks premature. He was tiny at birth. So Dad says it's impossible to find out who Sophie had been sleeping with because it had to be someone she'd met after she left Job and Nicola and we know nothing about where she went.'

And that had been all Jemima could tell her.

It wasn't a lot to go on. There were, though, a couple of leads Darina could follow up.

Once back in her house, after talking to Job and Nicola, Darina firmly put the problem of Sophie to one side. If Rory's parentage had waited seventeen months, a few more hours or even days were not going to make much difference. It was three weeks since Darina had delivered her last cookery article and so far she'd drawn a blank on the next commission. Oh for the days when she had had a regular column and the only worry was what she was going to put in it!

Darina drew out her file of notes. She flicked through several ideas: Ten ten-minute pasta sauces; seven variations on a basic bread dough; a Scandinavian buffet for thirty; summer picnics. None of them excited her and what on earth was the use of ideas for summer picnics in September? Especially for magazines that would be thinking of their Christmas issues.

Christmas! Of course! She'd given no thought to the great eat-in, when magazine after magazine would be producing supplements to guide the desperate cook over a holiday season that seemed to grow longer every year. Christmas was almost back to the time when the festivities had lasted twelve days.

Darina brightened. A series of recipes for the Twelve Days of Christmas? Bringing in festive dishes from all round the world plus some of the history of Christmas eating. It was probably too late to interest a magazine but maybe one of the broadsheet newspapers?

Her imagination fired at last, Darina switched on her computer and started making notes, consulting books from her extensive library.

Deep in the mysteries of Christmas porridge, mince pies made with rump steak, a rotting fish dish from Sweden and any number of variations on ham, Darina lost track of time. In the afternoon she went off to Westminster library for more research and spent the evening working on recipe ideas. William rang to say something had come up and he'd be late. 'Is it something exciting?' she asked. But he'd already gone and he was so late she was asleep by the time he arrived home.

When she awoke, it was to an empty bed and the sound of the front door closing.

Knowing by now that William would tell her what he was involved with in his own good time, Darina went back to her article idea and sent it off to someone who she thought might be a receptive editor.

The phone was ringing as she came back from the post.

'Have you found out anything yet?' It was Jemima.

'Heavens, give me a chance!'

'But have you been in touch with Job?'

'Yes, I went and talked to him and Nicola yesterday morning.'

'And?'

'And not very much,' Darina said repressively. 'But do you know someone called Paul Robins? I think he works for Val Douglas.'

'Paul? Of course I know him. He's a bit of a creep, does Val's PR. Where does he come in?'

'Apparently he visited Sophie while she was staying with Job and Nicola.'

'Paul did? No one told me that!'

'Do you have his phone number?'

'I can get it. In fact, Val appears to be staying with us at the moment. Her factory burned down the night before last.'

'Good heavens! What happened, dodgy electrics or overdone cakes?'

'Police seem to think it's arson,' said Jemima carelessly. 'They're coming to interview her this afternoon and Dad's doing the big protector bit, insists she can't be on her own.'

'Doesn't she have family? I seem to remember at least a couple of children.'

'They're both grown up, flown the nest,' Jemima said blithely. 'I don't think Dad would have got involved with her else. Can you come over tomorrow? It's Saturday and no work! You can see a bit more of Rory and bring me up to date with what you've found out. We haven't discussed what your services cost yet, either.'

Darina was about to say Jemima needn't worry about that when she thought, no, sod it, doing this investigating was taking up valuable time, it should be paid for. 'OK, I'll see you tomorrow morning.'

Darina investigated the fridge for lunch, finally found some cold pasta with pesto lurking at the back, decided the flavour was worth the slightly dried edges and took it out into the garden with her notes on Sophie.

The timing of Rory's birth seemed to her critical. According to what Jemima had said, he must have been conceived soon after Sophie left Job and Nicola's.

Darina looked at the two names she'd ringed in her notebook. One of them must know more than he'd told so far. In fact, Paul Robins hadn't told anything to date. Well, he would have to wait until Jemima produced his telephone number. But Nicola had given her Martin Price's office number. Why not his home number? Did that suggest she knew, even if only subconsciously, that Martin had become involved with Sophie in some way.

Darina looked at her watch. Just after two. No one had long business lunches these days. She reached for the telephone and was put through by an efficient sounding switchboard girl.

'Martin Price,' said a composed voice.

Darina introduced herself then, 'Nicola Ealham has given me your name,' she began.

'Yes,' the voice said in a comforting way, as though she had established her right to contact.

'I'm looking into the last months of Sophie Ealham's life.' Darina paused as she heard a distinct intake of breath. 'Nicola said you had been to the cinema with Sophie a few days before she left their house and I wondered if you would be willing to talk to me about that evening.'

After the slightest of hesitations Martin Price said,

'As Nicola must have told you, I don't know anything about what happened to Sophie.'

The disadvantage of talking to someone on the telephone was that you couldn't see the other person's face, particularly their eyes. The advantage was that you concentrated entirely on their voice and voices could give away as much as eyes, sometimes more. The comfortable confidence of Martin's voice had vanished.

'So I gather, but I need to talk to someone other than the family, you see.'

He refused to be disarmed. 'It was so long ago, I don't think it would be any use.'

'It's amazing what comes back when you start to talk about it,' Darina said persuasively. 'I know it's a long shot but, well, it's like laying ghosts.' The word had come from Nicola's description of Sophie and it seemed as though it rang bells with Martin Price as well for the faintest of sighs came down the line.

'I suppose if you feel it would help, I can't refuse.'

'That's very generous of you, Mr Price. Could I come to your office or would you prefer me to visit you at your home?'

'No, no!' he said quickly. 'My office would be best. Have you a time in mind?'

'In about an hour?' Darina suggested.

There was a pause. Martin Price was obviously weighing up various pros and cons. 'I'm rather busy this afternoon. Look,' he said with sudden purpose, 'why don't we meet for a drink somewhere?'

He wanted neutral ground, wasn't keen on her invading his territory. Darina grew more and more interested. 'Great, where do you suggest?'

'Why not the Savoy? I could be there,' he paused and

Darina imagined him looking at first his watch and then his desk, 'say six o'clock?'

'Fine,' she said swiftly, before he could change his mind. 'In the Grill Bar?'

'Right!' he said heartily. 'How will I know you?'

'Tall, big and blonde,' she said.

He responded admirably. 'I can't wait! See you then.'

Darina recognized him as soon as she entered the busy bar. Not by his solitary state but by his expression. This was a worried man. His eyes glanced round the bar and one hand tapped at the arm of the chair restlessly, the other held what looked like a gin and tonic which he sipped at nervously.

She went up to him. 'Martin Price?'

He started and spilt some drink as he scrambled to his feet. 'Darina Lisle?'

'It's very nice of you to meet me like this.' She smiled at him, sat down, took a very small notebook out of her bag and placed it on her knee.

Martin Price eyed it as though it might contain semtex.

She gave him another of her reassuring smiles. 'I have such a dreadful memory but if it worries you, I'll put it away.'

'No, not at all,' he said quickly and managed to attract the attention of a waiter. 'What will you have to drink?'

'A dry white wine would be lovely.'

He had a distinct look of a bloodhound, with a creased face and deep pouches under eyes that were a washed-out blue half hidden by tortoiseshell framed glasses. He looked about medium height with narrow shoulders and was dressed in a well cut suit.

The waiter vanished and Martin made a visible effort to appear helpful and unconcerned. 'Now, let's see what I can tell you. I'm afraid it isn't much. Poor Sophie, I was really very upset, first when I heard she'd disappeared and then, of course, to learn that she was dead.' He took off his glasses, whipped out a handkerchief and rubbed them hard while blinking rapidly.

'It must have been a great shock,' Darina said gently. 'And you really had no idea she was planning to leave her brother and sister-in-law?'

He replaced his glasses, pushed the handkerchief back in his pocket and shook his head decisively. 'None at all. As I told Job and Nicola at the time, I was as shocked as they.'

'And you know of no reason why she should want to leave them?'

Again that positive shake of his head. 'I only wish I did, as I told them at the time.' It was like a stuck record that could only keep repeating one phrase.

Her glass of white wine arrived and Darina raised it to him. 'Thank you for this,' she said.

He blinked nervously at her.

She put down the glass. 'Now, can you remember what the film was you went to see?'

His face lightened, obviously they were on safer ground here. 'Certainly. It was *Sleepless in Seattle*. Sophie hadn't seen it and it was showing in some sort of rerun season near where the Ealhams live.'

'Where do you live?' Darina asked artlessly.

'Just off Ladbroke Grove,' he said automatically.

The noise of the bar faded into the background.

Ladbroke Grove was only a few streets away from the Portobello Road, which was where Sophie had collapsed. Had no one made this connection before? But Jemima perhaps didn't know the Prices and maybe Job and Nicola didn't know where the ambulance had picked up Sophie.

'I believe your wife was away at the time?' Darina said, writing the name of the film in her little notebook. She didn't need to make a note of where he lived.

'That's right.' The worried look was back. 'Eleanor had to go to Cornwall, to look after her mother,' he added quickly.

'Nice for Sophie to have someone to take her out,' Darina continued easily. 'Nicola said she didn't seem to have any boyfriends.'

'No.' Martin fiddled with his glass. 'She said she found men difficult to talk to.'

'But she didn't find you difficult?' Darina suggested.

He turned an intense gaze on to her. 'She said she could relax with me, I didn't frighten her.'

'Frighten?' Darina repeated the word with a delicate emphasis. 'Had she had bad experiences then?'

'I don't know, she wouldn't say.' Martin leaned forward and spoke earnestly. 'You have to understand, Sophie was someone very, well, fragile. If she wasn't happy with a subject, you didn't talk about it. She was,' he paused as though searching for the right words, 'she was like a wild anemone, blow on her too hard and she'd sink to the ground.' He smiled self-deprecatingly. 'I'm not usually poetic but that was the effect Sophie had on you.'

Once again Darina thought back to the little five-year-old girl in Italy. Even then she'd been shy and sensitive. If anyone came to the villa, she melted away or clung to her mother. Julie Ealham's death must have been a devastating blow to her.

'She was a sweet little girl,' Darina said.

No wonder, then, that she'd clung to her father. Darina looked at Martin and decided to ask him a question that had been forcing itself upon her. 'Was Sophie, well, slightly retarded, mentally, I mean?' Then wished she hadn't as Martin's eyes bulged and his face grew red.

'Retarded? Of course not! She was absolutely normal. Look, who have you been talking to?' He sounded very angry and people looked round them.

'It was just an idea,' Darina said hastily. 'Her family have been so insistent she wasn't very intelligent.'

Some of Martin's anger faded and he looked sad. 'I know her father was upset she didn't pass any of her exams but I thought Nicola and Job valued her other qualities.'

'It was just me picking up the wrong message,' Darina insisted. She tried to move the conversation where she needed it to go. 'Tell me more about that last night,' she suggested. 'You picked her up from the Ealhams?' Witnesses had to be taken step by step through events, William had told her once. If possible, they should be led to relive each minute. Only that way would the telling little details come out.

Martin shook his head. 'No, I didn't think I had time to pick her up so we met at the cinema.'

'What sort of night was it? The weather, I mean. Was it hot, cool, rainy?'

Gradually, amidst the busy, bustling, noisy bar and after a stumbling start, Darina got Martin to go back to the evening he'd taken Sophie to see *Sleepless in Seattle*.

Just as the memories started to come more fluently, a large party came into the bar.

Darina finished her wine and said, 'Look, it's mayhem in here. Why don't we go outside? It's a lovely evening.'

He had no fault to find with this suggestion, called for the bill and gave the waiter a note. 'Keep the change,' he said, slipping his hand underneath Darina's elbow to steer her out of the bar. He was shorter than she was, perhaps five foot nine, but he managed to give her the impression she was being protected. It was a good feeling.

As they walked towards the River Entrance, Darina thought how reassuring Sophie must have found Martin.

Once outside, they wandered into the small garden that ran between the hotel and the embankment. The sun was still shining and the air was soft but with a hint of autumn. They found an empty bench and sat down.

'So,' said Darina. 'Sophie turned up on time, seemed pleased to see you, asked for popcorn to eat during the film, then afterwards you went to a restaurant.' That bald account left out the impression he had given of a mature man flattered and grateful to have the opportunity of taking out a young, very pretty and very innocent girl, one who seemed younger than her nineteen years. He'd been on his own for three weeks by then, aching with the loss of his son, worried that his wife wasn't going to return to him. Had he been susceptible to the charms of those large brown eyes gazing trustingly into his?

Martin seemed relieved to have the evening reduced to such mundane phrases. 'Yes, that's how it was. As I've said, there wasn't any suggestion she was thinking of disappearing.'

'Did she say anything about the film?' Darina asked, flicking the collar of her jacket up; the evening was cooling now, a light breeze stirring the yellowing leaves that had gathered at the edges of the path.

Martin gazed over to where a young man and a girl were standing close together, his arms around her waist, pulling her towards him. They seemed oblivious of anyone else's existence. It was an intensely private moment and Darina looked away but Martin didn't.

'Did she say anything about the film?' Darina repeated patiently.

Martin dragged his attention back. 'The film? Let me see.' He put clasped hands between his knees, looked down at his well polished shoes and gave every appearance of thinking hard. 'She said it was so strange, two people falling in love without ever having met each other.'

'And what did you say?' Darina prompted.

'What?' He turned towards her and she could see he'd been far, far away somewhere. 'Oh, I said something about sometimes it only took a moment to fall in love and it was very natural to recognize a soul mate through letters.'

'What did she say to that?'

She had Martin's full attention now. 'You know, I'd forgotten all about this bit. Strange how things can come back to you, like finding them at the back of a forgotten cupboard. She said but how if you'd made a mistake and they weren't a soul mate after all?'

'Did that mean she'd had a failed relationship?'

'Maybe,' Martin sounded doubtful. 'But Nicola said she hadn't had any boyfriends.' Was this a man who accepted everything he was told?

'While I was talking to Nicola, she remembered someone called Paul Robins had called on Sophie. Did Sophie mention the name to you?'

Martin shook his head. 'No, she never mentioned any men, apart from her brothers and her father, of course.'

'How did you think she got on with her father?'

Martin studied his fingers, weaving them in and out of each other. 'I sensed that their relationship was complicated.'

'How do you mean?'

'She told me once she loved him but she'd had to leave home because she needed control of her life.' Well, that didn't sound the comment of someone mentally challenged.

'You mean her father was pressuring her in some way?'

He shrugged his shoulders and didn't say anything.

'You saw her for lunch on the Sunday. Did she seem any different from usual?'

He thought carefully. 'She never said much when there were other people around, even her family, but I did think she was even quieter than usual that day.'

That agreed with what Nicola had said. Had something happened between the Wednesday night and the Sunday? If so, Martin didn't know. Darina changed direction. 'Do you have any idea where she could have gone?'

A vigorous shake of his head. 'Do you think I wouldn't have told Job and Nicola if I had?'

'And, later, you didn't see her around the Portobello Road?'

She'd caught him unprepared. For a fleeting second something flickered behind his eyes. 'No, of course not,' he said.

And she knew he was lying.

Chapter Eight

Pat James managed the unfamiliar police car with skill and efficiency. She'd carefully worked out the route before they set off so that DCI William Pigram could concentrate on his thoughts rather than telling her where to go.

As they moved smoothly through the undistinguished streets, Pat decided that this weekend she'd take out her own little Ford Escort and familiarize herself with the area. She'd already found somewhere to live. That was something she'd got sorted out before calling at the station.

The small flat she'd found was on top of a greengrocer's. It was supposed to be furnished and it did have a bed, two armchairs and a much too large mock-leather settee. A couple of badly made occasional tables, a hanging cupboard with a door you could hardly open the wood had warped so much, an equally badly made chest of drawers, and that was about it. But it was reasonably clean, had a kitchenette and tiny bathroom and was five minutes' walk from the police station. She'd handed over one month's rent in advance and promised herself she'd look to find somewhere to buy as soon as she knew the new job wouldn't be temporary.

Her new job! Excitement fizzed in her and her foot

automatically pressed on the accelerator. She forced herself to slow down. This assignment was going to be different from Somerset and Wiltshire! Not perhaps inner city stuff yet but more exciting than rural crime. And she was working with William Pigram again.

She had, Pat cheerfully acknowledged to herself, lost her heart to the tall detective the first time they'd worked together. She'd begun to think men like him didn't exist. Acne, haircuts from hell, slouched shoulders, beer bellies, she'd met them all. Arrogant attitudes from macho marvels or wimps who needed nannying, there seemed little in between.

Until she'd partnered William Pigram in a murder inquiry in Somerset. The tall detective had been a revelation to Pat James. Always courteous, always willing to explain anything that puzzled her, the only fault she had had to find with him had been his invariably gentlemanly attitude. Refreshing at first and then frustrating. Finally, she had met Darina Lisle and gradually recognized that the tall, blonde cook had captured the detective's heart and she herself couldn't hope to aspire to more than colleague status.

That was when she had organized a transfer to Wiltshire and tried to forget William in working for promotion and a move to something more exciting. But when Superintendent Roger Marks had called her along to his new division and casually held out the prospect of working with the newly promoted Chief Inspector Pigram, she'd known instantly that she had to find out if he was as exciting as she remembered. 'It's not promotion,' the super had said. 'But the station's desperate for another sergeant and I remembered how keen you were to get closer to the action.' His small eyes had glinted at her out of his large face.

She hadn't realized the superintendent had even noticed her when she'd worked under him in the Wiltshire force. Total chauvinist, she'd marked him as. One of those officers who felt women were all right in their place and their place was not commanding men. Sergeant status was acceptable, inspector maybe, but anything higher than that and you were flying in the face of nature.

Now she was actually in the same car with William. Already she'd been working with him for over twenty-four hours. How fortunate she'd decided to call into the station after she'd fixed up her accommodation.

The road Pat was driving down was a nondescript assembly of high-street multiples interspersed with antique shops and up-market fashion boutiques. They passed a library and then the town hall. There was no sense of a unifying style, no local identity. Pat thought back to the grey-stoned country towns she had worked in before and felt a twinge of nostaglia, quickly forgotten. William still appeared lost in his thoughts.

He'd seemed really glad to see her. Had he noticed her new hairstyle, though? And the way she'd sharpened up her image?

Pat sneaked a sideways look at her companion as they waited at traffic lights. For a second when he'd turned to her in the station, she'd been, well, not exactly disappointed, but it was as though he'd lost a little of his gloss. Perhaps it was because he looked so tired. He was puffy round the eyes and his sparkle had gone. But he was just as handsome as ever, still a rival for Cary Grant or Greg Peck. There was a dark fleck in his grey eyes that was totally mesmerizing – once you forgot about the puffiness. He'd always made the other men he worked with look ordinary. Whoever saw a policeman in a three-piece suit today? Or with such shiny shoes? But that was typical of the attention he gave to detail. If Pat had learned one thing above all else, it was that patient investigation and the amassing of tiny details led to successful crime busting. Leave inspired hunches to crime novels!

As the lights changed and traffic began to move again, she couldn't resist asking him, 'Do you think Mrs Douglas set fire to her own factory, guv?'

'Suggesting I theorize ahead of data, sergeant?' The voice was reproving but the glance he gave her was teasing.

Pat felt her heart turn over and she grasped the wheel more tightly.

'The only thing I'm certain of at present,' he continued, 'is that that fire was started deliberately and that we have a corpse.'

'So we're dealing with murder!'

'Well, he may have been overcome by fumes but the preliminary report says there's a dent in his head that doesn't look accidental.'

Pat couldn't help feeling excited. The early stages when you knew nothing about the victim or anybody else concerned with the case, were, in her opinion, the most interesting.

'We're not going to Mr Ealham's office?' The question had been occupying her mind ever since William had tossed an address on to her desk and told her to organize a car for them both. She slowed the car then swung across a convenient gap in the traffic and turned right.

'No, apparently Mrs Douglas is at Mr Ealham's private residence.'

'Very protective, isn't he? I wonder if he's banned that PR chap who was so keen to get together with her.' Much as she liked her independence, Pat thought she wouldn't mind having someone being so protective of her every once in a while. 'You said he was an industrialist?'

'His corporation is up there in the top-twenty biggest companies in the UK.'

'Good heavens! No wonder he acted as though he owned everything in sight,' Pat said, impressed. 'Including Mrs Douglas.'

'Quite!' William's voice was dry.

'And we're going to interview her on his territory?'

'Initially, yes. I'd have preferred to see her at her own home but talking to her at Ealham's house will certainly prove interesting.'

'Right!' said Pat.

'As to her possible involvement, I have a completely open mind,' William said. 'We turn left here,' he suddenly added.

'Ooops, sorry,' Pat apologized as she swung the car into a quiet lane. They had left the built-up area behind and were in lush farmland, inhabited by neat cows, well-tended buildings, scenic hedges and trees. It was all subtly different from the agricultural country Pat was used to. The difference, she thought suddenly, was quite simple – money.

Money was even more evident on their arrival at Basil Ealham's residence. The gravel drive that swept up to the mellow frontage looked as though it had been freshly raked, the lawns as though they had just been mown, the flowers arranged in their beds that morning. There was no crack in the paintwork, no flaw in stone or tile, it could all have fitted into some upmarket TV mini-series without the property department having to spend a penny.

The door was opened by a middle-aged woman dressed in a white blouse and dark skirt. Not a uniform but pretty close.

'I'll see if Mrs Douglas is available,' she said pleasantly. 'Will you wait in here?' She ushered them into a library, its shelves filled with books, its furniture leather, a bowl of attractively arranged flowers on the corner of a large, well polished desk. It all smelt like the interior of a very expensive car with just a hint of old books. Pat ran an envious finger over the desk's surface. All of a sudden she hated the thought of the flat she'd just rented. What sort of a home was William and Darina's, she wondered? He was inspecting their surroundings with interest but nothing in his attention suggested they were unfamiliar, indeed, he looked supremely at ease as he noted titles on one of the shelves, assessed the porcelain figures on the mantelpiece, murmured, 'Chelsea', then went and stood at the window, looking out at the garden.

That was the moment when Pat decided that she was going to make every effort to attract her superior officer. Something was wrong with him and she suspected it had to be his marriage. After all, he was obviously doing well in his career, he'd just been promoted. Pat remembered one of her mother's maxims, 'If you want something, go for it.' Well, her mum had achieved her own hairdressing salon, was doing very nicely, thank you. All because she hadn't let anything stand in her way. Her father had left when Pat was four. She remembered nothing of him.

Pat's self-reliance had done her well so far, no reason why it shouldn't take her all the way.

She sat herself in the corner of one of the pair of leather sofas and pulled out her notebook. The minutes lengthened. 'She did know we were coming?'

William half turned, 'Oh, yes, she knew. It's all part of the game.'

'Game?'

'Making us wait. It's telling us who's in charge here.'

'Not us, you mean?'

'Quite.'

'So how do we win?'

'By not allowing ourselves to be moved in any way.' He went and sat down in one of the deep, leather armchairs and contemplated the toes of his highly polished shoes.

From somewhere beyond the library door came a wail of despair that turned into loud crying.

William's head came up, then he relaxed back into the chair again.

The crying in the depths of the house died down. Silence again.

Finally, the panelled mahogany door swung open. There stood a small child, dressed in a bright blue T-shirt, socks and a pair of lace-up shoes. Thick fair hair flopped untidily over a wide forehead. Eyes the same colour as the shirt surveyed Pat and the small mouth chewed on a chubby finger. After a moment the finger was taken out of the mouth and pointed at her. 'Da!' said the child then turned his attention to William, gave him a beaming smile and, with a burst of unintelligible chatter, set off across the carpet towards him. 'Duh!' he said and tapped imperiously on his knee. 'Duh?'

William bent down to him. 'Duh, to you too!'

The baby chuckled happily, waving his bare legs about as he was hauled up to sit on William's lap, reaching out with his hands to grab at the gold chain running across the dark waistcoat.

Pat watched William settle him on his knee and take out a gold watch, click open the cover, press the top knob and hold it swinging while a pretty chime echoed round the room.

The child gazed at it in round-eyed wonderment, then grabbed it. William let go of the chain and allowed him to turn the watch around in his hands, inspecting it with the grave air of a master clockmaker, holding it to his ear then looking up at William in enquiry.

William pressed the top knob again and the child stared in fascination as the repeater chimed out four o'clock once more. Pat thought how at ease William seemed with the child, how relaxed his expression as he looked at the small figure, so intent on the new toy. She knew few men who took so easily to babies, particularly when they had none of their own. The awful thought came to her that perhaps Darina was pregnant.

'There you are, Rory!' said an exasperated voice. Unnoticed, Val Douglas had entered the room.

Despite her frustration with the child, she looked considerably better than she had the previous day. The short hair was newly washed and grey eyeshadow, black mascara and a coral lipstick brought the fine features to life. She wore a short jersey skirt, knitted silk top and an animal print overshirt, all in tones of gold and cream. Heavy gold chains round the neck and on her wrist could have been the real thing and an aura of some expensive perfume wafted across the room with her.

'You little scamp,' Val said, picking Rory up off William's lap. 'You know you're not supposed to be in here. I'm so sorry,' she said to William. 'I hope we haven't had an accident. He slipped off while I was changing his nappy, heaven knows what's happened to Maeve.'

'No, he's fine,' William said, rising and running a finger down the back of the child's head. 'Is he yours?'

Val laughed, looking all at once much younger. 'No, Rory's Basil's grandson. I'm sorry I've kept you waiting, things are in a bit of a state today. Let me find Maeve, then I'm all yours.'

But before Val Douglas could reach the door, it flew open and a girl erupted into the room.

'Is it that my father's dead?' she demanded, grabbing at Val's arm and staring into her face.

Black curly hair sprang round her head, her skin was creamy pale and she had widely spaced dark eyes.

Val took a step back. 'Maeve, what are you talking about?'

'My father! Basil says he died last night in your damn factory!'

Pat sat up and William's long figure stiffened to attention.

Val sat down suddenly on the coffee table with her burden. 'My God, Maeve! You mean Gerry was your father?'

'You know he was!'

'I knew nothing of the sort,' Val stated positively.

'Sure you did! It was Basil that recommended him!' The girl flipped a hand across her face, as though to brush away irrelevancies. 'But that doesn't matter. I want to know, is he really dead?'

At the sound of the hysteria in her voice, Rory buried his head in Val's neck and gave a cry. 'Hush,' she soothed him and her hand caressed his back.

William rose. 'The body found in Eat Well Foods has yet to be identified but I'm afraid that everything seems to suggest that it is that of Gerry Aherne.'

The girl gave a great cry and Pat recognized it as being the same one that they'd heard coming from the back of the house earlier. She clutched her arms across her chest, flung back her head and cried, 'No, no!'

William came and took the child. Val rose and went to draw the distressed girl to her.

Rory started crying, leaning forward and stretching his arms out to the weeping girl.

Basil Ealham appeared in the doorway. 'I couldn't stop her,' he said to Val. 'I'm sorry I exposed you to this.'

'Did you know Gerry Aherne was her father?' Val demanded, trying to soothe Maeve, patting her back as though she was Rory. They were much of a height and the gesture looked awkward.

The big man shrugged his shoulders then glanced towards William and Pat. 'This is something we can discuss later. I suppose you'd better answer the police questions now, they won't be satisfied until they've got your story. Will you?' he demanded.

Pat admired the way William managed to look official even while holding a crying child.

'It would greatly help us if Mrs Douglas could answer some questions,' he said quietly.

'I'll take him,' Basil ground out and snatched the boy from the detective. 'Come on, now, Maeve,' he said curtly to the crying girl. 'There's nothing can be done and Rory needs his nappy.'

Pat found Basil Ealham chilling both in the way he dominated everyone else in his vicinity and his total lack of sympathy for the weeping girl. The only touch of humanity he seemed to have was in the way he held young Rory. This large man, immaculately dressed in a well tailored pale grey suit, blue shirt and silk tie, competently hefted the child and managed to seem perfectly natural. 'Maeve,' he repeated, his tone now exasperated.

Maeve swallowed hard and took Rory from Basil's arms. 'You're a bastard, you know that?' she spat at the large man. Then, in a voice creamy with love and concern, 'Come on, darling, let's get your nappy on and make you comfy.' Basil watched her walk across to the door without emotion.

'Excuse me,' William called after the girl. 'Would you mind if we talked to you about your father?'

The girl looked over her shoulder at him, the top half of her body leaning back to balance the weight of the boy. 'Ask him, he's supremo around here,' she said, jerking her head towards Basil, once again spiteful. 'I work for him, it's his time.' She swept out with Rory.

'Now,' said Basil. 'If we all sit down, we can get on. I'm sure it won't take long.' Stay more than ten minutes and I'll have you chucked out was the subtext. He sat down at one end of a large sofa and spread his arm along its back.

Val remained standing. 'I'm sorry, Basil, I'd rather do this on my own.'

He looked up at her, his expression politely questioning, his attitude implacable.

'If I need your support, I'll call you,' Val went on, still standing. She seemed to have grown in stature. 'I'm sure it's only a matter of routine.' It was a cue for him to leave gracefully.

'Routine,' Basil repeated, looking at William. 'Nothing more?'

'Not at the moment, sir,' William said.

It was easy to see Basil Ealham didn't like it, equally that there wasn't much he could do about it. 'If you're sure, darling,' he said and rose from the sofa.

'Quite sure,' Val said firmly. It was obvious that this was a relationship based on equality.

'I'll be in the study, then, I have work to do.' The big man left the room with smooth economy.

Pat wondered just how many rooms this house had. There must be a lounge and a dining room, this was obviously a library and now a study had been mentioned. No doubt somewhere there was a nursery. Was there a morning room also? An afternoon room? How many different living areas were needed by the rich? Did they change their surroundings as often as their clothes?

Chapter Nine

William waved towards one of the chairs. 'Would you like to sit down?' he asked courteously and watched while Val Douglas gracefully lowered herself into its comfortable embrace.

For once he forgot his constant sense of tiredness as a surge of adrenalin energized him.

He sat opposite Val Douglas. He had no notebook. Pat would record the interview details for the record, he himself would have almost total recall of everything that was said. 'Can you start by telling me something about your business?' His tone was carefully designed to be encouraging without establishing sympathy.

Val smoothed down her skirt, thinking, then looked calmly at him. 'I started Eat Well Foods about seven years ago. I discovered my two daughters were suffering from an intolerance to certain ingredients, dairy foods, chocolate and wheat were the main ones. Being a trained cook, I had little difficulty in adapting recipes to cut out what they couldn't eat but it was time consuming and I found there was very little I could buy off the shelves. No biscuits, no baked products, almost no breakfast foods that didn't have either wheat or added sugar. And the number of products that contained whey was mind-boggling. I was also a cookery writer in those days and discovered that there were an increasing number of people who suffered in the same way as my daughters and almost nobody was producing food they could eat. I saw a niche market that offered potential.'

She spoke dispassionately and fluently. This was a story she had told before and the shock she had displayed at the factory had been absorbed.

'I started production in my own kitchen. I was lucky in that it was large and I could enlist help from my neighbours. I sold first to local health-food shops and a few delicatessens. But sales mounted steadily and I soon saw that I would need proper premises. Also the regulations regarding the manufacture of food were becoming more onerous. So I prepared a business plan and approached my local bank. Three banks later I found a manager prepared to back my belief that this was a business with a future.'

For the first time Val Douglas met William's gaze and he was startled by the depths of commitment she displayed.

'That was when you first rented the factory?'

A glint of amusement sparked in her eyes. 'No, first we started production somewhere much smaller. But we soon outgrew that and I went back and said I needed more money for somewhere bigger with more staff. I'd just got a trial order from my first supermarket and I was sure the future was just round the corner. We found our current premises two years ago.'

This was a remarkably determined woman. William reckoned he'd heard only part of the story, the successful part. Skated over were the hiccups and obstacles that had been placed in her way. 'And now?'

The amusement vanished, replaced by a look akin to

despair. 'We supply a health-food chain, three supermarkets and a number of local outlets with a range of items, some of them baked, some ready prepared meals, plus non-dairy ice creams. If we can't find somewhere to continue production, the company will go to the wall.'

'How's the search going?' William asked.

'I'm confident that by the end of the weekend we shall be able to restart production.' She glanced at her watch. 'I am expecting a call in about twenty minutes.'

It was a warning that she had put a limit on the amount of time she was prepared to give them.

'Tell me about your nightwatchman, Gerry Aherne,' William invited.

Again, she hesitated, then spoke more slowly. 'About six months ago we had a minor break-in one night. The police said it was probably youths who were after petty cash. We don't keep much money on the premises but what there was went. Also a transistor radio my secretary kept by her desk. Some damage was done, presumably in a search for something more valuable, but nothing serious.'

'Did you have an alarm system?' asked Pat.

'Oh, yes,' Val sounded bitter. 'And it was activated. But by the time the police responded, the culprits had gone. The investigation got nowhere and I became very worried about the potential for sabotage. There are some weird people out there today prepared to hold food companies to ransom over the possibility of providing the public with poisoned food. I spoke to one or two people and decided that we needed someone permanently on the premises.'

'Would Mr Ealham have been one of the people you spoke to?' William asked.

She nodded. 'Basil's wide business experience makes him a valuable adviser.'

'And did Mr Ealham provide you with Mr Aherne as a nightwatchman?'

A small frown creased the broad forehead. 'No. I advertised and Gerry Aherne was one of the few who applied. He wasn't ideal, I suspected he was more than fond of alcohol, but the others were even less promising. I know I wasn't offering a fortune but with so many unemployed today, you'd have thought a regular job would have been reasonably attractive.'

'A flat went with the job?' William continued.

'Not at the beginning. I thought Gerry should have somewhere to sit and make himself a cup of coffee and offered him the choice of two surplus rooms. He said he had nowhere to live and could he take both. It meant putting in a shower and buying a bed but the cost was minimal and I could see advantages to having him constantly on the premises.'

'You weren't afraid he'd make himself too comfortable?'

She gave him a sharp look. 'Fall asleep, you mean? Yes, at first I was. I took to calling in at odd hours, just to check. I never once found him anything but alert. Twice he was patrolling the factory as I let myself in.'

'Did anyone know you were checking on him?'

There was a wealth of comprehension in her glance. 'On a couple of occasions Mr Ealham knew, other times no one did.'

'Presumably Mr Aherne produced references?'

'He did and I took them up. Nothing was out of order or suspicious in any way.'

'Can you remember who gave the references?'

'No, but they'll be on his file. Oh, I forgot,' she brought a hand up to her mouth.

'Destroyed by the fire?'

She nodded, distressed. 'Oh, so many records will have gone. Recipes, tests, procedures.'

'You didn't keep any records outside the factory? On your own personal computer, for instance?'

Relief suddenly dawned on her face. 'How stupid of me! Yes, most of the recipes I worked out at home. Some were refined at the factory but I'll have the basic information.'

Was she a very good actress or had she genuinely forgotten?

Distress quickly replaced the relief. 'But nothing will bring back Gerry. And I'd far rather have him alive than a record of my recipes.'

'You liked the man?'

'Chief Inspector, I'd not want any man killed in that way,' she chided him gently, 'but, yes, Gerry was a very likeable man. As I said, I suspected he might be too fond of a drop of whisky but he was immensely amiable, everyone got on with him. He helped the company in many ways. After the factory opened at eight o'clock, he'd go to bed but he hardly ever slept beyond two o'clock in the afternoon. Then he'd be available for odd jobs and errands.'

'And you didn't know he was the father of one of Mr Ealham's employees?'

'Maeve? No, I had no idea.' Her eyes were limpidly clear. 'Her name isn't Aherne, it's O'Connor.'

'She said Mr Ealham got him the job.'

'That's not true. As I said, it was advertised.'

'At what time did the factory close the night before last?' William asked.

'Five thirty, as usual. That is to say, all the staff left then. I stayed until just after seven.'

'What is the routine? I mean,' he added as she looked puzzled, 'does the last person lock up or do you inform Mr Aherne and leave him to secure the premises?'

'Oh, I see what you mean. We do, did,' she caught her breath slightly, 'both. That is, tell Gerry the premises were clear and lock up the office side.'

'And how many people have keys to the premises?'

'There's myself, my secretary, Sharon Moore, and Ron Farthing, he's the accountant.'

'Three people, that's all?'

'Well, Gerry had keys of course.' She thought for a moment, nibbling on her first finger, the brownish red of her nail varnish matched her lipstick. 'Oh, and Paul, my PR consultant. He had a key as well.' Her gaze didn't quite meet William's.

'And where did you spend the night before last?' William asked expressionlessly.

'Why should you want to know that? You don't think I could have set fire to my own factory, do you? That would be ridiculous!'

'It's just routine,' he assured her blandly.

Her gaze fell again. 'Well, it's no secret, I was here.'

'With Basil Ealham?'

'Yes, with Basil,' she agreed, her self-possession back in place. 'He will confirm it. His daughter, Jemima, was out all evening but Jasper, his younger son, came in before we went to bed.'

'Who informed you of the factory fire?'

'The police rang me on my mobile phone. The

number's recorded at the station.' Her eyes closed for a moment.

'You went straight to the factory?'

'Yes.'

'What time was this?'

She thought for a moment. 'About five o'clock in the morning.'

'Did you go alone?'

She shook her head. 'No, Basil went with me but he couldn't stay, he had a breakfast meeting. There was nothing he could do in any case. There was nothing any of us could do except watch my business go up in flames,' she added bitterly.

'Did you wonder about Mr Aherne?'

She bowed her head. 'Yes,' she whispered. 'I asked the firemen if he was safe but nobody knew anything. I just hoped that somehow he'd escaped or that he hadn't been in the factory when the fire had started.'

That made her sound either a cock-eyed optimist, disingenuous, or that she had some reason for believing, despite what she'd said earlier, that Gerry Aherne wasn't always the most reliable of nightwatchmen.

'Mrs Douglas, do you know if your nightwatchman had any enemies?'

Her eyes grew larger. 'As I said, he was well liked and, no, I can't think anyone would have had a grudge against him.'

'Or against you?' That suggestion was also a shock.

'No!' she said instantly. Then a slight wariness appeared, her eyes flickered away from his, her hand gripped at the arm of the chair. 'I suppose if you are averagely ambitious, you make the odd enemy along the way but I can't think of anyone who would have burned down my factory.'

'No ex-staff who might bear a grudge? Or even one presently working for you?'

'We are an excellent team,' she said stiffly. 'No one has had to be dismissed. If anyone's left, it's been for personal reasons.'

'We'll need a list of names and addresses,' Pat said.

'Talk to my secretary. She's working in one of Basil's offices, I think he gave you the details?' She rose. 'Now I'm sorry, Chief Inspector, but I do have calls to make. Have you got all the information you need?'

'For the moment,' said William, rising also. Now that the interview had drawn to a close, he was conscious once again of how tired he felt. He squared his shoulders and tried to inject energy into his voice. 'We shall need an official statement at some stage and we will need to talk to your staff. One more thing, do you know where I can find Miss O'Connor?'

'The nursery is on the second floor,' she said and held out her hand. 'I'll do anything I can to help discover who did this dreadful thing.'

'Thank you, Mrs Douglas,' William said as he shook her hand.

She held his for a moment and inspected him closely. 'You look as though you could use some rest,' she said with a concern that left him almost breathless.

'We're used to long hours in the police,' he said woodenly.

'Of course,' she said. 'I'm at your disposal.' She withdrew her hand and left the room.

'At our disposal as long as we don't interfere with her business,' Pat said, a little sourly William thought.

'Shall we try and find the nanny?' he suggested.

The wide staircase took them up past the first landing decorated with highly polished chests, one of which held another elaborate arrangement of flowers, a second a superb bronze head. The walls held a collection of nineteenth-century watercolours. The staircase to the second floor was narrower.

'Servant's and children's quarters,' murmured Pat as they reached the second-floor landing, decorated with nothing more than a set of rose prints mounted on green with gilt frames.

It was refreshing to have Pat James back with him, William reflected. There was none of the lethal tension between them that Terry Pitman generated and seemed to pass on to the other members of the CID. With Pat, William could concentrate on doing the job and not watching his back. He must remember to ring Roger Marks and thank him properly for arranging her arrival.

It wasn't difficult to sort out the nursery door from the several that led off the small landing, it was named with a porcelain rocking horse. William knocked and they went in.

Maeve O'Connor was sitting on the floor with Rory, now with nappy and dark blue shorts on his bottom, building bricks. Rory looked up the moment the door opened. 'Dah!' he said excitedly, clambered up and ran across the room towards William. 'Dah!' he repeated, holding out his arms.

William was only too willing to pick him up. 'Wheigh-hey,' he said, swinging him up high. 'You're a very friendly fellow, aren't you, young Rory?'

'That he is,' agreed Maeve O'Connor, sitting with her legs tucked beneath her. No nanny's uniform for her, she wore jeans that clung tightly to her nicely rounded bottom, and a pink T-shirt that sported a large red elephant. Small breasts stood to attention.

William placed Rory carefully back on the floor, crouched down and, ignoring his shout of protest, picked up a blue brick and placed it on top of three already there. 'Can you put another on top?'

Rory chuckled and with enormous care added a red one.

'Good boy,' said William admiringly.

Rory took a big swipe, knocked the pile over and burst into delighted laughter.

'Oh, it's the destructive creature you are,' Maeve said indulgently and started another pile. Her eyes were pink round the edges and there was a suspicion of a tremble in her voice.

'Miss O'Connor, I'm sorry to trouble you, but I need to speak to you about your father.'

'You do, do you?' she said and her voice was hard. 'And what is it I can tell you?'

'Can we sit over here?' William went to a table with chairs standing beside a low sash window with safety bars.

'Sure, if that's what you want. You build yourself a castle now, Rory,' she told the boy. After a moment's hesitation, he picked up a brick and started using it to bang another.

Pat came and sat down at the table also with her notebook and pencil.

Maeve sat half turned away, her gaze on the boy on the floor.

'Gerry Aherne was your father?' asked William.

'Yes,' she said flatly.

'Your names are not the same? You are called O'Connor?'

'He never married my mother,' she said in the same flat tone. 'None of them did. They'd get her in the family way and then leave.'

'How many children does she have?' asked Pat with what seemed genuine curiosity.

Maeve flashed her long dark eyes. 'Ten, not that it's any of your business.'

'All by different fathers?'

William wondered if Pat realized how horrified she sounded.

Maeve shrugged. 'There's two or three of them have the same.'

'And did Gerry Aherne sire any more apart from you?' William asked.

She shook her head. 'There's only me from him.' Her eyes watered and she brought her arm across her nose in a rough gesture.

'How well did you know him?' he asked gently.

'He'd drop by every once in a while, to see how we did, me mam and me. He'd bring me a gift or two. Not often, usually he'd be up to his neck in something,' she said fiercely. 'Me mam said he was nothing but trouble and she'd never have married him.'

'Did he come here?' William glanced around the room.

'Once or twice.' She placed her arms on the table, laced her fingers together and looked out into the garden. A long way below the window, a half moon of a rose bed could be seen and the flash of a river through trees at the end of a lawn. In repose you could appreciate the fine bone structure of her face, the deliciously straight nose and the curve of her generous mouth. Even without make-up and her hair looking as though she'd cut it with nail scissors, she was extremely attractive.

'Did you tell him about the nightwatchman job?' William asked her.

Her expression closed in on itself. 'I didn't know about no nightwatchman job.'

'But your father was out of work when he called?'

'As usual,' she agreed harshly.

'So how did he get to know about the position at Eat Well Foods?' he persisted.

She looked back at the child, now carefully and precisely placing one brick on top of another and remained silent.

'Did you mention your father to Mr Ealham, was it he who told you about the job?' William persisted.

'He told me about no job,' she said stubbornly.

'But you did tell Mr Ealham your father needed employment.' It was more statement than question.

She picked at a hangnail on her forefinger. It came away leaving a small, livid scar. She lifted the finger to her mouth and sucked at the wound.

'When did your father tell you he'd found a job?'

She shrugged her thin shoulders, still sucking at the finger. 'Two weeks later he comes here and says he's taking me out for a meal,' she said. Then she leaned towards William. 'Well, he'd never taken me out for a meal in his life before! I asked him who he'd robbed and he told me not to be cheeky to me da.' Suddenly her face crumpled and tears started. 'That's when he said he had a job. It didn't mean nothing to me when he said where he worked. I didn't know it were Mrs Douglas's firm.

Stuck-up cow!' she added, her voice virulent. 'Thinks she's got Basil where she wants. Little does she know!' She went and got a tissue from a side table on which were various nursery items.

'Know what?' Pat shot in with.

Maeve wiped her eyes. 'Know what?' she repeated.

'What does Mrs Douglas not know?' Pat asked carefully.

The red-rimmed eyes were cold. 'How should I know?' Maeve said curtly. She went and sat again on the floor with Rory. 'Clever boy! Now, can you manage one more?' She gave another block to the boy. He staggered to his feet and placed it carefully on top of the swaying tower. Then crowed with delight, clapping his hands together as the bricks tumbled on to the floor. 'Grrrr, what a little monster you are,' she said happily, pulling him to her in a quick embrace.

'Where were you the night before last?' William asked.

She looked across at him. 'Why, here, of course.'

'You sleep on this floor?'

'Rory's room's next to this and mine's next to his. We've got our own bathroom,' she said proudly.

William summoned a mental picture of the landing with its doors. That left two unaccounted for. 'What are the other rooms up here used for?'

'One's a boxroom, the other Jasper uses for his writing, when he's not playing with the boy!'

'But at night-time you and Rory are up here on your own?'

She gave them a sly look. 'You could say that, yeah.'

'Did your father make any friends after he moved here?'

She shook her head. 'He never told me he knew anyone.'

'Did he make friends easily?' Pat asked.

'Oh, aye, down at the pub, you know. He'd talk to anyone that one.' Tears once again threatened. Rory looked up from his bricks, staggered to his feet, came over, put his arms around her and pushed his face into the curve of her neck. 'Oh, it's the lovely boy you are,' she said, holding him tightly.

'Would you know if your father went to a dentist, either here or in Ireland?' William asked.

Her face dissolved into laughter. 'Da? Dentist? Sure and they take money, don't they? If he had a tooth that ached, he took it out with a string and a door. He didn't have more than half o' them left.' Well, that gave them something to go on in the difficult process of identifying the burnt corpse.

'Have you a photograph of your father?' William asked.

'And what you'd be wanting a picture for? He's dead, isn't he?' she said belligerently. Then she shifted Rory more comfortably in her arms and seemed to relent. 'Didn't I take a snap that first time he came? Thought I might never have another chance and, well, he was me da.'

'Would you lend it to us?'

She weighed that one up for a moment. How swiftly she could change moods. 'You'd promise me I'd get it back?'

William nodded. 'We'll take a copy,' he said.

She left the room, still holding the boy.

It only took a couple of minutes before she was back, holding some snaps.

Maeve sat at the table and allowed Rory to help her spread out the prints. 'See, that's you,' she told him. William leaned over a whole series of shots of Rory playing in the garden: Rory alone, Rory with an attractive young man, Rory with Basil. The boy picked up that one and waved it at William. 'Dah!' he said excitedly. 'Dah!' He brought it to his mouth and kissed it.

'Here it is,' said Maeve, picking out a snap of a smiling man. She held it for a long moment. 'What a bugger he was. Me mam'll be sorry.' She handed it over slowly.

It was a good shot, half length and full face. Gerry Aherne looked fifty-something, a big man with a crumpled face, large ears and a lopsided smile. A face small children and dogs would trust. An open-necked shirt revealed a creased neck and a suspicion of a hairy chest. A pair of sunglasses hung from a breast pocket by one of their sidepieces.

'You'll have it back in a few days,' William assured her and gave it to Pat, who placed it carefully in her bag. 'Thank you, Miss O'Connor. As soon as we're satisfied we've been able to identify the dead man, I'll be in touch.'

Apprehension crossed her face. She clutched at Rory. 'You'll not be asking me to see him?'

'No,' William reassured her quickly. 'I'm afraid that sort of identification isn't possible.' As comprehension came, she buried her face in Rory's small shoulder. But only for a moment.

'I'll wait for your call, then,' she said with quaint dignity. 'And I'll not call me mam until you're sure.'

'I'm afraid we shall have to take a formal statement

from you at some stage. Detective Sergeant James here will be in touch.'

Maeve nodded her head gravely.

'Don't bother to see us out, we can find our way downstairs,' William said, ignoring the fact that she showed no sign of wanting to show them the way. He had an overwhelming desire to caress Rory's fair head, told himself not to be so stupid, and strode out of the room.

As they started down the stairs, he wondered whether to beard Basil Ealham in his study that afternoon or wait until more of the background had been filled in. Surprise might give an advantage but the man must realize he would be questioned at some time and, on balance, William thought more information could give him an important edge.

But as they started down the last flight of stairs Basil Ealham came up towards them, his face dark with controlled fury. 'You should have asked my permission before interviewing one of my staff,' he said.

William halted. It was symptomatic of the industrialist's ire that he had failed to realize he'd given William the advantage of being able to tower over him. 'I didn't want to disturb you over a matter of routine,' William said easily, looking down at the angry man. 'After all, you knew I wanted to talk to Miss O'Connor. I gather you told her father about the nightwatchman job with Eat Well Foods.'

He watched the man take a deep breath and control his temper. 'Maeve O'Connor is one of my staff, I take an interest in her welfare, which included that of her father,' he said stiffly.

'Exactly,' said William pleasantly. 'We'll need a statement from you, sir, but it can wait for the moment.'

With well concealed delight he saw he had surprised the other man. 'I'll be in touch,' he said. 'Come, sergeant, it's time we talked again with the fire service.'

Basil Ealham stood back to let them pass down the stairs and William didn't like the expression on his face. It was that of a man who had been bested and didn't intend to let it happen again.

Chapter Ten

'You've been at Blackboys?' Darina said, astonished. It was ten o'clock at night and William had come in half an hour earlier, looking exhausted. She'd heated up some soup then sat at the kitchen table, drinking coffee and watching him eat both the soup and half a loaf of bread plus a large hunk of cheese. He hadn't wanted the chop she'd offered him, said he wasn't that hungry!

'Then it must be you who was interviewing Val Douglas!' She couldn't control her dismay.

He looked up at her sharply. 'You mean you know her as well?'

'As well?' She didn't like the tone of his voice.

'As well as the Ealhams.'

What mischievous fortune had decreed William's first major case in his new job should involve people she knew? 'I don't know Val that well,' she said carefully. 'I used to run into her at press shows and things. Jemima told me about her.'

'And Jemima is Basil Ealham's daughter?'

'His elder daughter.'

'How many children does he have?' William sat back, his hand round the stem of his wine glass. His eyes looked at her clinically and she felt excluded from his mind.

'Four. Two boys and two girls,' she said slowly. 'The eldest, Job, is married and living in Battersea. Jemima, the one I was at school with, is next. She works for her father and lives at home. Jasper's about twenty-four and apparently he lives at home as well. Sophie was the youngest but she died giving birth to a son about eighteen months ago.'

'Ah, yes, that must be young Rory.' For a moment his expression lightened.

'You met him?'

'Couldn't seem to get away from him,' he said ruefully.

Darina did not want to get on to the subject of Sophie's son. For a number of reasons. This was a really wretched coincidence. If William knew what Jemima had asked her to do, he'd explode and tell her she couldn't possibly get mixed up in his case. And he might well have a point. 'Tell me about this fire and the dead man.' She poured more wine into his glass and pushed the cheese a little closer.

Whether it was the mention of young Rory or the effect of the wine was impossible to tell but William seemed to loosen up a little.

'So the Ealhams only come into it because Val is having a thing with Basil?' Darina suggested with relief when he'd finished his account. It might be a wretched coincidence but it needn't mean their paths crossing if she decided to continue looking into Rory's parentage.

William cut a bit more off the piece of mature Cheddar that had already been hacked almost to nothing. 'I'm not so sure about that.'

'But you said Val had advertised the job and didn't

know this nightwatchman chap was the nanny's father. Isn't it just coincidence?'

'I don't trust that sort of coincidence. And, anyway, Maeve O'Connor, the nanny, more or less said she'd told Basil Ealham her father was looking for a job.'

'Ah!'

'Did you meet Maeve when you had lunch with, what was her name, Jemima, the other day?'

Darina poured herself a glass of the wine. 'It was her day off, Jemima was looking after Rory.'

'Did you meet Basil?'

'The great industrialist? Yes!'

'What did you think of him?' It was almost like the old days, when William had been happy to discuss case details with her.

'A bully,' she said cheerfully. 'I wouldn't care to work for him.'

'Mmmn,' William sounded as though he agreed with her. 'What do you think about him as a man?'

'Sexually, you mean? Well, he can be very charming when he wants and that kind of power can be a terrific turn-on.'

'But not to you?' William smiled at her and Darina felt something melt deep inside her solar plexus.

'No,' she said softly. 'Not to me.' She cherished the little moment between them. Then added, 'I like my men thoughtful and with give and take.'

He stretched out a hand. 'I haven't been giving you too much recently, have I?'

'With a new job, you've had enough to cope with and I don't think I was exactly helpful suggesting we lived here.' She gave a glance round the kitchen that arranged itself around them with well loved style and comfort.

'If only it was nearer the station,' he said but he sounded resigned.

'Do you want to find somewhere more convenient for the job?' Darina felt she had to ask.

'Not at the moment, no,' he said. The wine bottle was empty. He got up and fetched another.

'Do you suspect Basil of having an affair with the nanny as well as Val Douglas?'

'Not much escapes you, does it?'

'You think he found her father a job because he was sorry for her? It doesn't really sound like Basil.'

'No, it doesn't, does it?'

'You think he had his own reasons for engineering the man into Eat Well Foods? Has he put money into it?'

'It's a distinct possibility. Another factor is that Paul Robins, Mrs Douglas's PR consultant, appears to have a strongly possessive streak about her himself.'

'So you think Basil might have put him in there to spy on them?'

'Another possibility.' William licked his finger and picked up some cheese crumbs.

Darina's mind was busy. Where did Sophie fit in with Paul Robins? Had he been interested in her? If so, what about Val Douglas? She wanted to discuss this with William but she feared to disturb the rapport that had sprung up between them.

'How did Val Douglas strike you?' she asked instead.

'Surprisingly warm and sympathetic.'

'Why surprising?' Darina asked curiously.

'Oh, you know, successful business woman, involved with Basil Ealham, I expected her to be rather hard.'

'Stereotyping, William?' she teased him.

'I hope not! Her warmth, in fact, makes her more

impressive. She appears highly organized, motivated and ambitious. And to be closely involved with Basil Ealham.'

'You're beginning to make her sound calculating as well,' Darina said slowly.

'Arson is often used as a way for failing businesses to recoup losses.'

'So you think Val might have set light to the factory herself? Knocking out her watchman in the process?' She made it sound a ridiculous proposition.

'At this stage, as you well know, we can't afford to ignore any theory. I should perhaps say that Pat agrees with you that it's highly unlikely.'

'Pat?'

'I forgot to tell you. You remember Pat James?'

Yes, Darina did indeed. A small, quiet girl who'd obviously fallen for William in a big way. Obvious to Darina, anyway.

'She's been promoted to sergeant and seconded to my lot. What with Terry Pitman and DC Hare being commandeered for Operation Chippendale, she's a god-send.'

'What a good thing,' Darina said colourlessly.

'Isn't it!' William seemed more lively now. 'Such a relief to have someone around who's a pleasure to work with.'

Darina rose. 'What do you say to a reasonably early night for once? We could take the rest of the bottle up with us?' she suggested, lifting the rather good Cabernet Sauvignon that William had opened.

An unmistakable gleam came into his eyes and for a blissful moment she thought they were on their way. Then he sighed deeply. 'I'm sorry, darling, I really do need to go over some notes. Tell you what, you go up and I'll join you as soon as possible.' He took the bottle from her, refilled his glass and gave it back.

'In that case, I'll probably be asleep before you can drag yourself away.' But William had left, gone to his briefcase and his precious notes.

Clutching glass and bottle, Darina went upstairs deciding two things. First, that there was no way she was going to give up the hunt for Rory's father, not while she had a promising lead to follow, and second, that she was not going to tell William.

Darina never knew what time William came to bed. She woke at six thirty and found him in the hall, about to leave without any breakfast, complaining of a bad headache.

She gave him two aspirin, saying, 'Food is the best cure for a hangover.'

'Hangover? What the hell do you mean by hangover? I only had a couple of glasses of wine, for God's sake.' William gave her a quick kiss on the cheek, grabbed his briefcase and then banged the front door behind him.

No breakfast, and probably just sandwiches for lunch, if that. William wasn't eating properly! Torn between worry and exasperation that he couldn't be more sensible, Darina turned her investigative talents to the fridge. She must find a quick to cook dish that she could set before him whatever time he got home that night.

The fridge yielded only half a packet of old fashioned cured bacon and the end of the Cheddar. But in the freezer she found some large Dublin Bay prawns.

William loved those! She put them in the fridge to defrost slowly then made a gently flavoured mayonnaise to accompany them with *arachide* oil from France, French mustard, wine vinegar, some grated lemon zest and a dash of extra virgin olive oil. What next?

William loved almost anything with pasta. Thanking heaven for Italy, Darina found she had some penne, short, quill shaped pasta. She would buy a few really fresh courgettes, dice them small, fry them with the bacon in more of the olive oil, add chopped basil and chives from the garden, then serve with grated Cheddar and a salad. The whole meal would be ready in the time it took William to relax with a drink.

Darina liked knowing her day's menu was organized, it left her mind free to concentrate on other things, like answering the telephone.

'Darling, it's your mother. You sound as though you've been on the go for hours and it's only eight o'clock. You'll never get pregnant racketing around the way you do.'

'How are you, Ma?'

'Fine, darling. My arthritis is giving a lot of trouble and I think I'm going to have to see someone about my left eye, I'm sure there's a cataract there. But it's nothing. I just thought I'd give you a ring and check you hadn't departed for foreign parts.'

'I'm sorry, I was going to call you this evening,' Darina said feebly, feeling thoroughly put in the wrong.

'Darling, you know mornings are much the best time to catch me. Now, how are you both?'

Darina tried to pull herself together. Why did her mother always manage to wrong foot her? Diminutive, charming, an attractive sixty-something, Lady Stocks always made Darina feel too-large, clumsy and socially inept. She tried to convey how hard William was working and the difficulties she was having without sounding as though she was complaining.

'Need a break, both of you,' came the brisk response.

'Would that we could but William's got to get to grips with his new job.'

'And you need to re-establish yourself,' Darina's mother suddenly sounded sympathetic. 'I know, I'll come up and stay with you and we can do lots of lovely things together. How about towards the end of next week? I could clear my diary for at least five or six days.'

Darina felt her heart sink. 'That sounds lovely, Ma, but can I get back to you on it?'

'I'm not going to let you put me off,' Ann Stocks said blithely.

'Of course not,' Darina said hastily, 'I just want to be free to enjoy your visit.'

'Give me a ring on Monday, darling, I shall need to get my social life sorted out, you know.'

Darina spent a few more minutes emphasizing how pleased she would be to see her mother, replaced the receiver, sank back against her kitchen dresser and tried to recover.

After a few minutes she set out for Blackboys.

It was another golden autumn day and Jemima was sitting on a wide terrace. A white painted wrought-iron table at her elbow held coffee and croissants. She was wearing lime-green shorts with a white T-shirt appliqued with toning green diamonds and a khaki waistcoat with many pockets and military type buttons that looked too large for her. In a chair on the other side of the table sat a young man.

'Darina,' he called as she appeared on the terrace. 'Terrific to see you again.'

Jemima waved a lazy hand. 'Come and have some coffee.'

Darina walked across. 'I'm surprised you remember me,' she said to Jasper.

'He doesn't,' his sister said. 'But he likes to make people feel welcome.'

Jasper pushed his sunglasses up on to his forehead. 'I do so remember Darina. How could I forget such a golden goddess?'

'You were, what, ten years old last time you saw her?' Jemima said sceptically.

'Nearly eleven!' he said amiably.

'Well, I certainly remember you,' Darina told him affectionately. 'Though you've grown a lot since then.'

He was almost as big as his father with longish, sun-bleached hair, a deep tan and Basil's piercing blue eyes. He was reading a copy of a well reviewed recent novel that was remarkable for its avant garde use of language. Darina found it hard to equate this hunk of male machismo with her remembrance of a small, lithe boy full of fun.

'Are you enjoying that?' she asked, sitting down. 'I gather you're a novelist yourself.'

Jasper closed the book, tapped the cover and wrinkled his nose. 'Pretentious is what I'd call it. Yes, the chap knows how to write, some of the imagery is startling, but the premises are contentious and insufficiently developed, the storyline thin to the point of non-existence, the characterization pathetically inadequate.'

He flipped the glasses back down his nose and gave Darina another of his sunny smiles.

She wondered what he meant by premises. 'Have you had any books published?'

Jemima gave a hoot of laughter. 'Jasper published! That'll be the day.'

'My agent says it will only be a matter of time before the publishing world recognizes my worth,' he told her imperturbably.

'In your dreams, bro,' she jeered affectionately at him. 'The day you're top of the bestsellers will be the day I'm Madonna.'

'The work goes forward,' Jasper said calmly but the fingers tapping on the book increased their tempo. 'My agent is pleased with progress and won't Job be as jealous as hell when my novel is published.' He removed his glasses and gave Darina a smile that would have done credit to a cat who'd swallowed a pint of cream. Then he suddenly focused on Jemima. 'Borrowing Dad's clothes? He'll be mad as hell. *Obsession* is just not his taste, too obvious! Anyway, the too-large look isn't you.'

'Arbiter of fashion now, is it?' Jemima didn't sound at all concerned. 'The sun isn't as warm as one thinks and, anyway, I've seen you in it before now.'

Jasper looked as though he was going to argue further and Darina said quickly, 'I remember you reading to Sophie in Italy, Roald Dahl I think it was, *Charlie and the Chocolate Factory*? You acted out all the parts and she couldn't wait for more.'

Jemima felt the coffee pot. 'This is cold, I'll get some more.'

Jasper rubbed a finger over the cover of his book. 'Sophie,' he said quietly.

'Jemima told me what happened, I was so sorry.'

Jasper tried to flash her a smile. 'Yeah!'

'I'm sorry, I didn't mean to upset you.'

He waved a hand as though to say it didn't matter. 'We had fun that holiday, didn't we?' he said after a moment. 'Sometimes I think it was the last time our family did. Mum got weirder and weirder after that, it drove Dad bananas.' He looked across at her, his eyes hidden behind the dark glasses. 'Everyone blames Dad, you know, but Mum was no plaster saint.'

Darina thought it best to say nothing.

Jasper gazed over to the Gothic pool house. 'I saw her once in there with the gardener,' he said.

Darina stared at him. 'How old were you?'

'About five I think. I thought he was hurting her! Mum made me promise not to tell anyone. She said it was a game grown-ups played.'

Darina was shocked. 'Did you ever tell anyone?'

'Dad, years later. He said we all had our appetites and not to worry about it. He didn't seem to care but he must have done, surely?'

Darina eyed Jasper carefully. 'Your parents stayed together.'

'I suppose you could call it that.' He gave her a sudden grin. 'I didn't fall apart then and I'm not going to fall apart now, just because you bring back a few dodgy memories.'

She couldn't see his eyes behind the dark glasses. 'How did Sophie manage growing up without a mother?' she asked.

He removed the glasses and looked at her, his expression frank and open. 'As far as Sophie and I were

147

concerned, Dad was mum as well. Job and Jemima, they were OK, they'd grown up. People say Dad hasn't time for anything but business but they're wrong. He always made time for us. He was gutted when Sophie disappeared like that.' Tiny pause. 'I was too.'

'You must have visited her at your brother's, didn't she say anything about her plans? Weren't there friends she could go to?'

'I never knew she was planning to do a bunk!' He sounded injured. 'I mean, it had been us two against the world for so long and then she was that secretive!' The wide blue eyes looked bewildered. 'I just couldn't believe it!' He replaced his glasses. 'At least we've got Rory.'

'I'm afraid we have,' Jemima said. She arrived holding the boy with one hand and the coffee pot in the other.

Jasper leapt up. 'Hey, careful, you could spill it on him.' He put the pot on the table.

Rory clasped him round the knees and laughed up at him.

'Oh, the divine innocence of youth,' said Jasper and raised his nephew. 'What has heaven's rascal been up to this morning?'

'You can be nanny,' Jemima said dryly. 'Maeve's got to go out. Apparently that poor man that got killed in the fire was wearing a ring and they think if she can identify it, they can be sure it was her father.'

'Has our mighty force insufficient minions to send one here with the item?' Jasper held Rory up high and wiggled him while the boy screeched with delight. 'I told Dad Maeve should have time off, after all, she's lost her father, poor bugger,' he added in a return to his prosaic style.

'She hardly knew him,' Jemima said, pouring out more coffee.

'Sometimes,' Jasper said with a touch of despair, 'I think you have stone where your heart should be. The idea of a father can be creative, reassuring. The absence of even the idea can be as catastrophic as losing someone one knows and loves.'

'You weren't exactly devastated when Mother died,' Jemima said waspishly.

'But then she wasn't an idea,' Jasper said dismissively. 'But back to Maeve. Does Dad know she's gone out? You know what he's like about her leaving Rory.'

'He and Val left just before the police called Maeve.' She passed a coffee over to Darina. 'Val was going spare, marching up and down the hall, looking at her watch every two seconds. Finally she shouted up that if he wasn't ready, she would go without him.' She gave a little giggle.

'Good, I like a woman with sufficient chutzpah not to relinquish her independence,' said Jasper, lowering Rory to the ground. The boy screamed with disappointment, holding up his arms for another go. 'I can see him interfering more and more over this factory business and she'll not be able to take it. It won't be long before Dad's little idyll has reached journey's end.'

'I wouldn't bet on it. She was hanging on his every word last night. I reckon that fire and then being interviewed by the police destroyed any desire for independence. You know, Jaz, this one's lasted longer than I ever remember any of Dad's fancies.'

'Sweet sis, how ephemera do distress you. Our lord

and master reserves his heart for his family. Everyone else only borrows it for a blink of time.'

'Get lost, Jaz,' Jemima said in a bored voice. 'I can't stand it when you talk what you think is novelese.'

'What you mean is you want space for girl chat with Darina,' Jasper said in a normal voice. 'Come on, Rory, we'll go and feed the ducks.' He gave him a croissant. 'Hold that until we get to the river.' The boy clutched it in both hands and set off in his determined, waddling walk, across the sweep of lawn towards the willow trees that hung over the water.

'Does he really have an agent?' Darina asked in a low voice as she watched the two figures slowly move away.

'Lord knows! He disappears up to London at regular intervals but I doubt any agent would want to see an author as struggling as he is,' Jemima sighed. 'But you never know with Jaz. He really can write. He won some sort of competition while he was at school and got a tremendous fuss made of him. Dad was really delighted. He bought him a laptop complete with printer.'

'Does he do anything besides write?'

Jemima gave an elegant little shrug of her narrow shoulders. 'Smokes pot and snorts the odd line of coke every now and then. But I'll say this for him, he's a bit of a poseur but he really does seem to work at his writing.'

Darina watched Jasper leaning down to talk to the boy, the tiny figure looking up at him. All at once Rory stumbled and dropped the croissant. Jasper prevented him from falling, then picked up the bread and handed it back.

'I've got Paul Robins's office number for you.' Jemima produced a piece of paper. 'Now, what else have you found out?'

Darina told her about Martin Price. 'He knows something, I'm sure of it. Look, your sister collapsed in Portobello Road, right?'

Jemima nodded.

'And Martin lives just round the corner. The odds are that at some stage he ran into her, it's like a village there.'

'If he won't tell you, how are you going to find out?' Jemima asked curiously.

'I'll think of something,' said Darina with more confidence than she felt.

Jemima looked sad. 'Dad thinks she shacked up with someone. Typical of his mind,' she added with sudden venom.

'You sound as though you despise him,' Darina said, remembering Job's comment on Jemima's ambivalent attitude to her father.

'I'll never forget what he did to Mum.' Jemima looked away. 'It was all his fault, the way he put her down the whole time, his women, the fact that he was never there for her. I tell you, if Val Douglas really does move in, she's an idiot.'

Jemima didn't seem to know that, according to Jasper, Julie Ealham had sought consolation and found it at least once.

'Why do you work for your father then?'

Darina was shocked by Jemima's look of distress. 'Because I want the sort of power he's got and because I don't know what the hell else I can do.'

'Power needs to be grabbed,' Darina said slowly. 'And then held on to.'

'Oh, I'm ready to grab,' Jemima said fiercely. 'You don't know how ready!'

Could she retain that determination? Jemima's

schoolgirl enthusiasms had had a way of evaporating but maybe she had changed. 'Look,' Darina said, putting down the empty cup. 'I'm prepared to look into where Sophie went. I think she might very well have taken a job. If she'd been shacked up with a sugar daddy, wouldn't he have made enquiries after her collapse? Contacted the police, or something? Just as Job and Nicola did after she disappeared from them? I mean, he must have known she was pregnant.'

'Oh, Darina, of course! Why didn't I think of that? Why didn't Dad?'

Yes, indeed! Was Basil Ealham the sort of man who wasn't surprised if a woman walked out on him and never followed up on her? Darina began to feel sorry for Val Douglas.

'But it could take me a little time, time when I ought to be writing articles and book proposals.'

'I said I'd pay you,' Jemima said eagerly. 'Come on, tell me how much you need and I'll write you a cheque now for a week of your time in advance.'

She really did seem determined! 'I've worked out what I think would be fair.' Darina fished in her bag and brought out a slip of paper which she laid before Jemima.

Jemima merely glanced at the figures. 'That's fine,' she said. 'I'll go and get my cheque book.'

'I need a couple of other things. Do you know who it was who suggested Sophie came out?'

'Oh, that was the Honourable Cynthia Beauchamp. She had a real thing for Dad at one time. The relationship didn't last any longer than the season. But I think she was very kind to Sophie.'

'Would she talk to me, do you think?'

'Don't see why not. I never knew her well, though. Too society for me. Anyway, I'll give you her telephone number and you can try.'

'And I need a good photograph of Sophie, full face.'

'You're going to get somewhere with this, aren't you?' Jemima said in an odd voice.

'That's what you want, isn't it?'

'Of course it is!' Jemima jumped up energetically. 'Come with me, we'll look in the photo album, then I'll write that cheque and find you the Hon. Cynth's details.' She started towards the house. 'I think you've done wonders already, I really didn't think you could get this far – I mean this quickly.'

In the library Jemima dragged out a collection of photograph albums from one of the bookcases and started looking through them. 'How about this one?' She pointed to a shot of Sophie kneeling beside a labrador, smiling up at whoever was taking the photograph. With her brown hair fluffed appealingly around her face, she looked as cuddly as the dog. And you would have recognized her anywhere.

'Perfect.'

Jemima peeled open the protective, transparent covering, levered off the snap and looked at it regretfully. 'I'd like it back when you've finished with it.'

'Of course. I'll see if I can get it copied, then you can have it back immediately.' Darina put the photograph inside the cover of her notebook.

'Here's Cynthia Beauchamp's number.' Jemima opened an address book on the desk. She scribbled it down and handed the piece of paper to Darina. 'OK, that's that organized. Now come up to my room and I'll find my cheque book.'

She led the way up the graceful stairs. 'This is my room. My God!' she said, standing stock still. 'Someone's been in here!'

At first Darina couldn't see anything to suggest an unauthorized visitor.

Jemima's large bedroom had a white muslin hung four-poster bed, a small sofa and two button chairs upholstered in rose-spattered polished chintz, and several side tables bearing books, an untidy pile of letters and other trivia. A sophisticated looking media centre including a television set stood between a tallboy that looked as though it belonged in a museum and an equally attractive secretaire, its writing flap down and one of the small drawers open.

Jemima rushed across the room. 'This was shut!'

'Are you sure?'

'I always keep it closed.'

'Could your Mrs Starr have needed to open it? Or Jasper?'

'Don't be silly,' Jemima snapped. 'Jasper knows my room's private, just as his is. And Mrs Starr doesn't do housework on the weekends.' She looked in the small drawer, gasped and started pulling out the others, searching increasingly frantically. 'They're not here!' she cried. 'They've gone!'

'What are gone?'

'My pearls! Dad gave them to me for my twenty-first birthday, they're worth a fortune!'

Darina came over to the secretaire. Jemima appeared to use the drawers as a jewellery chest. Rings, earrings, bracelets, chains and brooches flashed expensively at her. Any thief would surely have taken those as well. 'Are you sure you didn't put them somewhere else?'

'I couldn't have done!' Jemima cried, then dashed across the room. Darina followed her into a dressing room. More drawers were opened. Undies fluttered out to lie on the floor like large silk butterflies, tights were strewn here and there; sweaters were pulled off shelves, hangers loaded with designer clothes were rattled along rails. Then she moved into a connecting bathroom and searched in a wall cabinet.

Darina followed behind, checking odd corners that might have been missed.

Finally Jemima turned, her face white. 'I told you, they've gone. Someone's taken them!'

Chapter Eleven

Maeve O'Connor entered the police station with her heart fluttering uncontrollably. Officials of any kind were not good news, but police! They could fine you, lock you away, maybe even extradite you back to Ireland.

Of one thing Maeve was absolutely certain, and that was she wasn't going back to Ireland. Back to her mam's? With the screaming kids, the one bathroom with the toilet that was always getting bunged up, the terrible kitchen where the stove never worked properly? To the life with never enough to eat, never new clothes, and her mother always with a new man, always dreaming that this was the love some gypsy had promised her when she was sixteen? No, she'd got away from all that and she wasn't going back, especially with her father dead and never to come bustling in in his noisy way with a present for her and a kiss for her mam.

Maeve couldn't say she'd known her father, half a dozen appearances while she'd been growing up had not been enough for knowing. But he'd been an excitement in her life, like knowing the lottery might bring up your numbers. And when he got the job only twenty miles away from Blackboys, she'd begun to think that they might, after all, have a relationship. All that had now gone up in smoke.

Maeve clutched her bag and looked at the heavy double doors of the police station. What was waiting for her on the other side? They'd said something about a ring on the phone and that they wanted her to make a proper statement. Hadn't what she'd told that policeman been enough? Oh, but that could just be a clever ruse to get her down here. If only Basil had been at home when the call had come. She could have told him and he'd have sorted it.

Through her worry and distress, the thought of Basil was like a rock. No, more like a soft overcoat, made from that fine stuff, not cashmere, alpaca. She'd gone down to the kitchen late at night once, searching for something to snack on before going to bed. He'd opened the front door just as she went back through the hall. She was supposed to take the back stairs but they were no fun. No soft carpet, no shining brass rods that Mrs Starr got Betty in to polish every week, no nice pictures to look at as she climbed up to her lovely room with its own bathroom. An avocado suite, with a toilet that never failed to flush, she still got a thrill every time she entered the room. Anyway, Basil had caught her there in the front hall.

She'd given him a big smile, this huge man who had total power over her, and hoped he wasn't going to chew her up.

'Lovely Maeve,' he'd said as soon as he saw her. 'Come here, lovely Maeve.'

She'd put her plate of cold steak and kidney pie from the previous day on the hall table. She'd been wondering how long before he made a move. Maeve knew all about men, not from personal experience but from watching her mam; Maeve had backhanded the little runts who wanted playtime with her. There was no way she was going to end up like her mother. When she gave up the goods, it was going to be for someone who could offer her something.

Her first job in England had been with a couple who were both doctors. Busy life they led, hardly ever at home. Two lovely little kids, too. Maeve had really enjoyed being with them, the boy had reminded her of her favourite brother when he was that age, full of life and fun. The doctors hadn't given no trouble either, except the mother had all these ideas about how Maeve ought to behave with them, not smacking them, letting them 'create their own environment', whatever that meant. Maeve had listened, nodded and said, 'Yes Emily,' because they'd told her to use their Christian names, then had gone right back to her own methods. Which were to make sure the kids knew what was right and what was wrong.

Anyway, she'd been happy working for the doctors, even though their house was a mess and the car they gave her to drive was pretty beat up. Only they'd got jobs in America and said they couldn't take her. The kids had cried and Maeve had cried too. But she'd been given some really nice references and the agency had sent her for an interview to Blackboys.

There'd been a Norland Nanny there too. They'd both sat in the hall, a hall so palatial Maeve had rubbed her shoes on the mat for nearly five minutes before she dared to step on to the marble floor. Maeve had looked at the other girl's uniform and thought, no point in my staying, not in this place, not when there's a proper professional in for it.

The Norland Nanny had been first and she'd given Maeve a satisfied smile as she left. So she reckoned her interview was only a matter of courtesy. She'd been given Rory to hold. 'He's a year old. His previous nanny only likes babies. On their first birthday, she leaves,' the big man she hardly dared look at told her.

She'd reckoned he told her that so she shouldn't think this was a place people didn't like to stay. Rory patted her cheek and looked at her with gorgeous blue peepers and it had been love at first sight. Then Maeve had looked at the man behind the desk and recognized the same eyes, only full of age and experience. Like an electric shock it had been and from the way he'd looked at her, she'd known he felt something too. Afterwards she couldn't remember what he'd asked or what she'd replied. She only knew she'd got the job.

She'd wondered when he would make his first move. He was nothing like her mother's men. They could never wait for what they wanted.

The waiting stopped that night he came, smelling of whisky, through the front door in a soft, warm, golden coat. He'd pulled her into his arms as though he'd done it a thousand times and for Maeve it was exactly as she'd imagined. Except she'd never realized how soft a coat could be. He'd laughed when she'd said that and told her it was alpaca.

That was how she always thought of him, making her feel soft and warm like pulling on a coat of alpaca. But lately more and more often there'd been Val Douglas. It had been weeks since he'd come up to her bedroom. Maeve was afraid that the other woman was going to move in permanently. Where would she be then?

After the two police had spoken to her yesterday, Maeve realized she knew something that might be important. Something that Basil might be interested in keeping quiet. If he realized what she knew. However, Maeve wasn't going to tell the police. At least, not yet. Not even though it might have had something to do with the fire that had killed her father. For she hoped like anything that it didn't and, after all, Da was gone and she was still here. She didn't want to lose any of her privileges at Blackboys.

Maeve looked again at the big double doors of the police station. If she didn't go in, there'd be a call to ask where she was. Basil would demand to know why she hadn't gone and he wouldn't be like an alpaca overcoat any more.

Maeve was afraid of Basil's temper. It hadn't been turned on her yet but he could bawl out Jemima like nobody's business. Maeve never minded that, sometimes Jemima treated her like a nasty leftover that had been forgotten at the back of the fridge. But when Basil got to sounding off at Jasper for going out instead of working at his writing, Maeve couldn't help but feel sorry for the lad. She and Jasper enjoyed laughs together, playing with Rory when Jasper said he needed a break from creativity, which seemed to be more and more often. Only Rory seemed immune from Basil's temper. He could do what he liked with his grandfather.

Maeve decided anything was better than having to face an angry Basil. After all, why should she be afraid of the police? Maybe the ring they were going to show her wasn't her father's and maybe he wasn't dead after all.

Maeve had no such real hope but dreams were better than fears, weren't they? She took a deep breath and went through the double doors.

It was a severe disappointment to find that she wasn't going to be interviewed by the nice tall policeman who'd talked to her in the nursery but by the girl who'd been with him and a rat-faced man with a nasty gleam in his eye. 'I'm DI Pitman and I believe you've already met DS James,' he said brusquely. Then he explained something about recording the interview and announced who was in the room, as if she didn't already know.

Maeve's nervousness increased. 'If you'll just show me the ring, I'll be identifying it and then I can go.'

The inspector handed over a small plastic envelope, his fingers disdainful. 'You told us on the telephone you'd know if it was your father's or not. For the benefit of the tape,' he added, 'I am handing over police exhibit A.'

Maeve took the envelope as though it might suddenly turn into a jumping bean. Gold shone dully through the transparent plastic. 'I thought it'd be like, sort of melted and dark,' she said.

'He fell with his arm below him,' Sergeant James said quietly. 'So it was protected by his body.'

Maeve didn't want to think about any of the implications of that. She opened the envelope and took out the ring.

She'd only told the detectives half the truth yesterday. Even if her father had wanted to marry her mother, it would have been impossible. He'd married someone else years earlier. 'I was only a slip of a lad,' he'd told her once. 'And when she fell in the family way, it seemed the decent thing to do.' Not when Maeve had been conceived, though. Then he hadn't even tried to hang around. She'd asked where her half-brother or sister was. 'Ah, isn't that the thing! Three days after we were married, she lost the babby.' It seemed he'd left his wife after that. Had she only pretended to be pregnant? Whatever, the marriage had been a fact and he'd continued wearing the ring.

She turned the circle of gold, looking at the scratches on its wide surface, and remembered her father's thick finger.

'Well?' demanded the inspector impatiently.

Slowly Maeve tilted the gold band. Yes, there, inscribed inside, were the inititials G M A I F and a date. Gerry Matthew Aherne and Isabel Fitt.

She'd known it would be so, known her father must be the man who'd perished in the factory fire but even so she wasn't prepared. She sat quite still and tried to accept that he would never breeze into her life again.

'Well?' the inspector repeated. Now there was a man with no understanding.

'It's his,' Maeve said expressionlessly.

'Just so that there'll be no doubt, Miss O'Connor, you are saying that this ring belonged to your father, Gerry Aherne?'

She nodded.

'For the tape, please,' the inspector insisted, crossly.

'Yes, it's my father's can I go now please?' Maeve jerked it out all in one phrase.

'We need to ask you a few questions first, Maeve, and then get you to sign a statement detailing what you told DCI Pigram yesterday.' Sergeant James gave her a smile that Maeve tried to find reassuring. But the policewoman's attitude had altered. The previous day she'd seemed relaxed, now she appeared anxious and harassed. Was it any wonder, when she had to work alongside this toe-rag?

'Did your father have any savings?' the inspector ground out.

Maeve couldn't help smiling. 'My father, savings? You have to be joking, he didn't know what it was not to spend whatever he had to hand.' Oh, he could be generous all right. She fingered the gold cross and chain he'd given her with his first pay packet. Once he'd given her mother a fine rosary. And he'd always brought a bottle of something whenever he came.

'How do you know that?' Pitman leaned forward aggressively. 'I thought you hadn't seen him often.'

'I knew how he was with money,' Maeve said pugnaciously. This inspector was just how she expected the police to be, suspicious and trying to make her say things she didn't want to. Given half a chance, he'd plant something on her. What was a poor Irish girl to do?

'So you say. What if I told you your father had a considerable sum of money?'

'I'd say you were a liar,' Maeve riposted, hardly pausing to think about what he'd said.

'Maeve,' the policewoman interjected her soft voice. 'Maeve, we found a bank statement in your father's room. It showed he had over fifteen hundred pounds.'

'My father? A bank account?' Maeve was bewildered. 'He never told me he had a bank account.'

'See,' jeered the man. 'You didn't know everything about him and money after all.'

'Do you know where he could have got this money from?' Sergeant James asked, her manner pleasant.

'Well, he had a job, didn't he?' Maeve jerked out. 'He'd been there several weeks, he could have saved it, couldn't he?'

'The man you say never saved anything?' Again that jeering tone.

The policewoman shifted in her chair. 'I'm afraid we've checked into how much your father was being paid and there's no possibility he could have saved that much.'

'He won it on horses, then,' Maeve shot back.

For a moment she thought they'd accept that. For a moment even she did, though gambling was one of the few faults her father didn't indulge in. 'I never have the luck,' he'd told her once when she'd shown him her lottery ticket. 'Horses, cards, the dice, even the lottery. I've tried them all and nary a penny have I won. I gave it all up years ago. I'd rather drink my money away, or spend it on a pretty woman, like my girl here,' he'd pulled at a curl of her dark hair, 'or her mother.' Or some other woman, she'd thought without rancour, because that was how men were.

'So your father was a gambler?' the inspector asked her, narrowing his eyes as though that way he could see the truth more clearly.

She nodded, not at all sure why she was lying but certain her father needed his reputation protected. For how would he have come by such a sum unless dishonestly?

A uniformed policeman entered the small room and whispered something in the inspector's ear. He rose and followed the officer out.

It seemed to Maeve that the policewoman felt as easier for his absence as she did herself. She leant back in her chair and looked at the girl. 'You were fond of your father, weren't you?'

Maeve felt tears pricking at the back of her eyes and nodded. Then remembered the tape. 'Yes, I was,' she said strongly.

'And he was obviously fond of you.'

Maeve pulled at a loose thread in her jeans and didn't feel the tape needed anything from her in response.

'And you did him a great favour by telling Mr Ealham he needed a job.'

Tears started to fall. 'And if I hadn't, he'd still be alive today,' Maeve wailed suddenly. The truth of that hit her with terrifying force. You tried to do good and look what happened!

Sergeant James passed a tissue over. 'Life plays some rotten tricks sometimes,' she said. Then added, 'I can understand wanting to protect your father but isn't it more important that we catch whoever killed him?' Maeve dabbed at her eyes and said nothing. 'If he was involved in something, something that was earning him large sums of money outside his nightwatchman's pay, we need to know. Then maybe we can work out why he was hit on the head and who did it.'

Reluctantly Maeve saw the force of this.

'So, I'll ask again, was your father a gambler?'

Maeve hesitated. The sergeant waited patiently.

'No,' Maeve finally whispered.

'Your father never gambled?'

'No,' she said more strongly. 'He never had the luck, you see.'

'What about drugs?'

Drugs! Maeve thought about the little stash of

marijuana hidden in her room. 'He liked a drop of drink, that I know, but nothing about drugs!'

'You don't think he could have been selling them?'

'A dealer you mean?' Maeve began to feel frightened. 'I know nothing about any of that,' she repeated stubbornly.

'Can you suggest, then, where the money could have come from?'

Maeve shook her head, remembered the tape and said, 'No I can't.'

'You have no idea at all?'

'No, none.' She felt exhausted by the strain of trying to work out what it was they wanted.

The inspector came back into the room, sliding round the edge of the door, and there was something in his eyes Maeve didn't like at all.

'We have to take you back to Blackboys,' he said. 'Something's come up.'

Both Maeve and the sergeant looked at him and Maeve knew that whatever had come up, it wasn't going to do her any good at all.

Chapter Twelve

The Eat Well Foods case had everyone in CID at the Thames Valley police station working at full stretch. Earlier that day William had held his morning briefing meeting.

He'd introduced Pat James. The other female officer, DC Rose Armstrong, a quiet girl with short brown hair and a large mole on her prominent cheekbone, had shaken her hand enthusiastically. 'They're a bunch of sods but not bad ones,' she'd said with a cheeky look at the males.

'In your dreams, love,' said one while the others hooted sardonically.

William held up his hand for quiet. Behind him was the start of an incident board. A map of the area had the factory marked, there were photos of the dead man, of the scene of devastation around him, of the factory front. 'The house to house by uniformed branch has yielded nothing,' he had said as they settled to listen with close attention. For the first time he felt they were all with him, working as a team. He blessed Operation Chippendale. Perhaps by the time Terry Pitman returned, this new spirit would be strong enough to withstand his subversive effect. 'Nobody saw anything, nobody heard anything. Forensics are still sifting through evidence. At the moment all they can offer us is that the fire was started deliberately and that the accelerant used was petrol.'

On the board the nightwatchman's name had a question mark beside it. 'However a few useful leads have come up,' William continued, the quality of the room's attention giving him renewed confidence. 'We've found bank statements belonging to the dead man and have spoken to the bank manager. Over the last six weeks, Gerry Aherne deposited between two and four hundred pounds in cash every Thursday or Friday. The account was opened the day after he started work at Eat Well Foods with a payment of two hundred pounds. However, the firm's accountant has confirmed that on Aherne's first day he gave him a wage advance of twenty-five pounds. Either Aherne was not expecting the larger sum or he was trying to give the impression he had no resources.' He paused.

'Any indication where the money came from, guv?' asked one of the younger constables, his quiet face enlivened by keen eyes.

William shook his head. 'I've instigated inquiries with the Irish authorities to see if they know anything of Aherne. Armstrong, I want you to follow up with them.' Rose looked pleased.

'Do you think this is an IRA job?' someone called out.

'There's nothing to suggest they could be involved. More likely is that it's something to do with the Eat Well Foods company. I want every one of the employees contacted, a list of names and addresses is available over there.' He indicated a pile of computer printouts that

Pat had produced after she'd extracted the list from Val Douglas's secretary the previous evening. 'I want to know everything they can tell us about the company, its products and its employees, including the night-watchman. He'd only been there for six weeks but he lived on the premises and must have had contact with at least some of them during the day.

'Look for any suggestion the company is in financial trouble or that any of the present or former employees has a grudge against the management or against the dead man. Lennon,' he looked at Peter Lennon, a long serving detective sergeant in his late thirties. 'You're in charge of the employee side.' The sergeant nodded.

'Keene, you take the accountant and go through the company's financial records. I don't suppose you've got a fine enough comb in your bag for this case so you'll have to make do with your initiative.' There was a general snigger at this but John Keene, a balding con-stable in his late twenties, looked resigned to being a target for hair-challenged jokes.

'Next, the dead man had a ring on his finger which has happily escaped damage by fire. There are initials on the inside and there's just a possibility Aherne's daughter may be able to identify it. Pat, you've already met her, arrange to see her again, show her the ring and take her statement at the same time. At the local police station this time, I want her off her territory. Let's see who can partner you.' As he ignored Pat's look of disap-pointment that clearly signalled she had expected to work with him again, the door opened and his two missing officers entered to a chorus of derision.

'That was a quick cop!' 'Nicked 'em with a nice

Georgian chest, did you?' 'How are the six packs?' 'Show us a leg, Terry!'

Terry Pitman scowled. Dressed in his usual jeans and leather jacket, he looked as though he needed a good night's sleep and his stubble was more than designer.

'Quiet, chaps,' ordered William. 'Do I gather you had a successful time, inspector?'

Chris Hare, the burly youngster who'd accompanied Terry, couldn't hold back. 'It was fantastic, guv. There must have been forty of us, all over the shop. Only thing was, us two didn't get a look at the villains.'

Terry silenced him with a look that said if he uttered another word he'd have his entrails for breakfast. 'The ringleaders have been rounded up and the super has expressed satisfaction over a successful operation,' he grated out.

'Didn't nick 'em yourself, though, Tel,' someone sang out mischievously.

'We all know not everyone on a major exercise actually gets the satisfaction of fingering the villains' collars,' said William repressively. 'I'm sure you have valuable experiences you can share with us all in due course. In the meantime, glad to see you back, you've rejoined us at an interesting time.'

'Yeah,' said Terry. 'We heard.'

Which probably explained the five o'clock shadow and Chris Hare's rumpled look. They must have come straight over from being stood down. Well, he could do with the increased manpower now at his disposal. William thought rapidly. 'Sergeant James, meet DI Terry Pitman and DC Chris Hare. This is Pat James, boys, courtesy of the super. We worked together once in Somerset and I can recommend her tenacity and acumen.'

Chris Hare grinned at Pat in a friendly way. Terry Pitman looked as though she was first cousin to a mangel-wurzel.

'Hare, you work with Keene; if tales of your darts prowess are anything to go by, you know how to add up.' Chris Hare was in fact something of a financial whizz kid. He and Keene had recently uncovered a major fraud by a local solicitor and were a good team. 'Inspector, you take the sergeant here and interview Gerry Aherne's daughter. Sergeant, bring him up to speed on the case.'

'But, guv,' Terry started.

William looked at him. 'Yes, inspector?' he said frostily.

'Nothing, guv,' the other man muttered and gave Pat a brief nod.

'Glad to meet you, inspector,' she said with careful formality.

'Right, that's all organized then. I shall concentrate on Basil Ealham's possible involvement. When big industrialists turn up in connection with arson, no matter how remotely, my nose starts twitching. OK, everyone, meet back here at six o'clock.'

There was general movement.

William gathered together some papers and watched Terry Pitman and Pat James approach each other with the wariness of a pair of alley cats. As he went out of the door, he heard Terry say, 'Well, what are you standing about for? I'm not about to become your nanny.'

'Nor I yours,' Pat riposted swiftly. 'I take it you'll liaise with the local station re interviewing Maeve

O'Connor and I'll organize a car. You can call me Avis, I try harder.'

She'd hold her own, William decided.

Much later that morning, William drove over to Blackboys to meet Basil Ealham. 'Should be able to make it by noon,' the man had said curtly.

The first thing he saw was a police car in the drive then two more, unmarked cars. One was a CID pool car and the other he knew intimately. His heart sank.

A uniformed constable opened the door to him. William showed his warrant card. 'What's up?'

'Your officers have just arrived,' the man said stolidly. 'They're upstairs, on the second floor.'

The nursery floor. 'Nothing wrong with the boy?' William asked anxiously.

'The boy?'

'Never mind.' William took the stairs with controlled speed, reached the second floor and found not the nursery door open but one further on. It led into a generous sized bedroom that seemed full of people.

The room was furnished simply but with a certain style: polished pine bed with matching bedside cabinet and dressing table, and a built-in wardrobe that had its doors open. In front of it, Pat James and Terry Pitman confronted a distraught Maeve O'Connor. Another uniformed officer waited by the bed. Standing by the window, tapping at the glass with an impatient, scarlet painted finger was an unfamiliar girl of thirty-something, and seated in a small armchair in the background, looking profoundly uncomfortable, was Darina.

'Morning,' William said cheerfully. 'DCI Pigram.' He

showed his warrant card and ignored his wife. 'Perhaps you'd like to tell me what's going on, inspector.'

'Yes sir,' Terry said smartly. 'Miss Ealham,' he indicated the girl standing by the window, 'rang the local police to report some missing jewellery. PC Carter,' he nodded towards the uniformed officer, 'arrived with PC Potts, who is currently downstairs. Miss Ealham apparently suggested they search the room of her nephew's nanny.' Maeve O'Connor gave a small moan and brought the back of her hand up to her mouth. Large eyes deeply distressed looked into William's. 'This they did and then phoned the station where James and I were interviewing O'Connor. We brought her here a few moments before you arrived, sir.'

Which didn't explain why his wife was sitting in the corner looking as though she wished she was somewhere else. William looked across at her, and raised an enquiring eyebrow.

'I was visiting Jemima when she found her pearls were missing,' she said, looking wretchedly uncomfortable.

William decided further details could wait. 'And have these pearls been found?'

The uniformed officer came forward and opened the top of a small set of wardrobe drawers. 'This is exactly how it was when we searched, sir.' He picked up a pair of white pants.

'Hey, those are my things!' Maeve shouted. Terry Pitman took hold of her arm as she tried to grab the pants from the constable. 'You've no right to mess with my things.'

She was pulled back and they could all see that nestling amongst a jumble of underwear was a purse of soft grey suede with gold lettering. The constable took it up and shook out a double strand of pearls. Lying across his large, tanned hand, the carefully graded nacreous beads shone with creamy brilliance. Everyone gazed at their iridescent, pink, gold and silver lights with hints of blue and green. The constable upended the pouch and out popped two larger pearls, a perfect colour match, mounted on gold posts.

Maeve's face was chalk white. 'I never,' she whispered. 'I know nothing, nothing!' She swung round to confront Jemima Ealham. 'You put them there! You've never liked me and now you want to be rid of me. It's not enough I lose my father, I have to lose my job as well!'

'It wasn't I who found my pearls in your drawers,' Jemima said in a bored voice.

'But it was you who put them there,' repeated Maeve obdurately, her eyes flickering wildly.

'That's nonsense,' Jemima said dismissively. 'I have nothing against you.'

Cool as she appeared, William could see that the scarlet-painted nails tapped a betraying tattoo on her upper thigh.

'Sure and you haven't liked me from the first day I came here.'

'I've nothing against you,' Jemima repeated impatiently. 'I'm just happy to get my jewellery back.' She held out her hand for the pearls.

The constable returned the string and the earrings to their suede home. 'I'm sorry, miss, but these are evidence.'

'Evidence?' she looked at him as though she couldn't quite understand.

'In the case against O'Connor.'

William thought how the dropping of any courtesy title seemed to strip a person of all their dignity.

'Maeve O'Connor,' said Terry, 'I arrest you . . .'

'Oh, for heaven's sake,' said Jemima, disgusted. 'I don't want her arrested! I've got my pearls back, that's all I was worried about.'

'Then why call us out?' Pat asked.

'If I'd just come charging up here, I should think she would have had something to complain about,' Jemima sounded self-righteous. 'But Darina can confirm I never came near her room after I found the pearls were missing. And that my secretaire was disturbed.'

Attention focused on Darina.

'When we entered Jemima's bedroom, the secretaire was open,' she said, speaking calmly. She looked straight at William. 'She said that she had left it closed and that someone had been in her room. She looked through the drawers and said her pearls were missing. After we'd searched her room, dressing area and bathroom, she called the police.'

It was a neatly succinct account.

'Thank you,' William said in a level tone. Then to Jemima, 'You are sure you do not wish to press charges?'

She shook her head. 'I told you.'

'Then I think we can leave the matter. Thank you, constable.'

The uniformed officer gave him a nod and, looking disappointed, left the room.

'Have you finished interviewing Miss O'Connor?' William asked his inspector and sergeant.

'Yes,' said Terry.

'No,' said Pat.

'Well, which is it?' he asked impatiently. 'Sergeant?' There was a note of appeal in his voice he was unaware of.

Pat smiled at him. 'Actually, we'd more or less finished, guv, except for the statement. But we can contact her later for that.' Her style was soothing and he smiled at her.

'Not here, you can't,' said Jemima. Everybody looked at her. 'You can't expect her to go on working for us, not after what's happened.'

If Maeve's look had been a knife, it would have killed. 'You bitch,' she said.

William wondered what the truth of the matter was. He thought it unlikely the girl had taken the pearls. It would have been a singularly stupid action and he didn't think she was that unintelligent. Nevertheless, 'If you leave here, Miss O'Connor, will you please let my officers know where you will be?'

'I don't know that I'm leaving yet,' she told him bravely. 'It's Mr Ealham who employs me, not Jemima.'

'Well, we'll need to know,' he repeated. 'Inspector, if you have finished with Miss O'Connor for the moment, you and the sergeant can return to the station and take over from Marks.'

Terry Pitman and Pat James nodded and left the room.

Which left the three girls and William.

Jemima shrugged. 'Come on, Darina, let's leave here.'

Darina looked at her husband. 'I don't need you,' he said. 'But won't you introduce me to your friend?'

She looked a little happier. 'Jemima, meet my husband, William.'

'Well, well,' Jemima said. 'Mr Darcy at last?'

'I'm sorry?'

'A private joke,' she told him, her blue eyes sparkling. It was as if she had forgotten the business with the pearls. 'I'm delighted to meet you.' She put a soft hand in his. 'Darina, you didn't tell me the half! William, come and have a drink with us.'

'I have a date with your father,' he said. Despite his reservations over her part in this affair, he could feel the power of her attraction. It was a subtle magnetism, a mixture of her good looks, the warmth of her smile, the neat curves of her body and the total attention she gave him, as though he was the person she was most interested to talk to in the entire world.

'Ah, well, another time.' She gave him another of those special smiles then left the room.

'You can fill me in on all this later,' William said in a low voice to Darina as she followed her friend.

Maeve slowly slid down on to the bed and sat clutching her hands, her head bent, the picture of misery.

'Was it your father's ring?' William asked her gently.

She nodded hopelessly.

'I'm sorry.'

'What can I do?' She looked up at him in appeal.

'Tell Mr Ealham the truth,' he told her. 'Whatever it is.'

As he came down the stairs, he saw Jemima talking to her father in the hall. She must have button-holed him the moment he came in the door. Darina was nowhere to be seen.

'So you see, she's got to go,' he heard Jemima say as he reached the hall.

Basil Ealham glanced towards the detective. 'We'll talk about this later,' he told his daughter curtly. 'Right, inspector, let's get this over with.'

William followed Basil into the library.

Basil waved William to a chair, then sat opposite him with an expression of patient enquiry on his face.

'I'd like to know your exact connection with Eat Well Foods,' William said.

Basil raised an eyebrow but said smoothly, 'I am investigating acquiring the company.'

'So at the moment you have no financial connection with it?'

The very briefest of pauses. 'No, I haven't.' Basil crossed one leg over the other and contemplated his beautifully polished and no doubt custom made shoe.

William wondered just how much money he had loaned Val Douglas and exactly what the arrangement had been. He took time to make a note in his little book. The other man sat quite still and William could feel the ferociousness of his concentration, he was like a predator who is suddenly aware something dangerous was coming through the undergrowth.

'Can I take you back to the night the fire broke out in the Eat Well Foods factory,' he said, aware of every nuance of the industrialist's body language.

Basil shifted the angle of his leg and waited.

'Mrs Douglas came over and spent the evening with you?'

Basil nodded, his eyes never leaving the detective's face.

'You talked about, what?'

'I can't see that it's any of your business,' the words were studiedly casual, 'but there's no reason why I

shouldn't tell you.' Retaining his right to choose what
he disclosed, William decided. 'We chatted about our
respective children's activities. I told her about the negotiations I'd been involved with in Italy. We then ate a
meal my housekeeper had prepared and talked about
plans for a new range for Eat Well Foods.'

'And your possible involvement?' enquired William
pleasantly.

'Yes.' The clipped word was the first slight sign of
impatience. 'I'm interested in the company for its
potential rather than its current performance.' Basil
straightened himself slightly in the chair.

'And does your housekeeper live in?'

The hard blue eyes were startled by this seeming
change of direction. 'Mrs Starr?'

'You said she'd prepared a meal for you. Does she
live in the house?' William repeated patiently.

'Ah, I see what you mean. No, she comes in each
day, except Sundays. She also has every other Saturday
off. Today, for instance, she isn't here.' For the first time
Basil removed his gaze from William's and scrutinized
his well manicured nails. 'Which makes this business of
the nanny and Jemima's pearls devilish awkward.'

'Right,' William acknowledged easily then refused to
be deflected. 'So the night before last she would have left
at what time?'

Basil dropped his hand and looked at William again,
'Oh, about seven, I suppose. We looked after ourselves. I
don't like staff hanging around when it's not necessary.'

'And was either of your children home?'

Basil shook his head. 'Jemima had a date, God knows
what time she came home, and Jasper took himself off

somewhere. I like my privacy when I'm entertaining. We heard him come in about eleven.'

'You didn't see him?'

'We were already in bed.' It was said blandly.

'So you were together from the time Mrs Douglas arrived here until, when?'

'Until we were woken by her telephone ringing at some god-awful hour sometime before dawn.'

'Four fifty-two precisely,' said William, reading from a page of his notebook.

'If you say so. I was in no fit state to check the time.'

'Oh?'

'I'd taken a sleeping pill. I'd had two very tough days and I needed a good night's sleep. Val took one as well,' Basil added. 'Neither of us wished to be disturbed.'

'But you were.'

'God knows how long that bloody phone rang before I heard it.'

'You answered?'

'I did and then had the devil's own job to wake Val, she was right under.'

Was she? Or had it been a carefully calculated simulation of deep sleep? Wittingly or not, what Basil had said meant that either of them could have faked taking a sleeping pill and slipped out of bed without the other realizing. Or both of them could be in on it. But, in that case, why say they'd taken sleeping pills? Surely if they'd conspired together, they'd want to alibi each other?

Of course, both of them could be innocent. 'What happened then?'

'I drove Val to the factory. Hell of a mess it was! I

stayed as long as I could then had to go to the office and reorganize my day.'

Stopping off at the house to change, thought William; he couldn't possibly have dressed so carefully at five o'clock in the morning. 'And then returned just before noon,' he stated, again making a show of consulting his notebook.

Basil looked bored.

William made another note, snapped the book shut and stood up. 'Well, thank you, sir.'

'Finished, have you?' Basil appeared surprised the interview was over so soon.

'For the moment.' William let the qualification hang in the air. 'I'll let you know if we need to speak to you again.'

Basil said nothing but he did not look happy.

Chapter Thirteen

When Jemima had been telling her father what had happened with her pearls, Darina had murmured an excuse and slipped past into the garden, intending to find Jasper and Rory.

What was going to happen to Rory now? Another nanny, another surrogate mother? What effect was this going to have on him?

Darina had tried to persuade Jemima not to bring in the police. If she was convinced the nanny had stolen her pearls, why not wait for her to come home then ask Maeve if she could search her room with her present? No, Jemima insisted that unless the police were called in, the nanny would not believe the pearls hadn't been planted on her.

Darina remembered Maeve's distress and astonishment at the discovery of the pearls. Was the girl a talented actress or had she really not known they were there?

Calling in the police didn't mean the wretched things couldn't have been placed in Maeve's room earlier, before Darina had been taken upstairs by Jemima to discover the open secretaire.

Then Darina wondered at herself for being so suspicious. Was Jemima really capable of such behaviour?

Darina remembered how scathing she'd been about Maeve O'Connor's qualifications and the bitter comment on how her father had seemed to enjoy the nanny's company as much as Rory did. But could she have actually gone to such lengths to get rid of her?

There was no sign of Jasper and Rory in the garden but on the terrace, clearing up abandoned breakfast things, was someone Darina recognized.

Val Douglas looked up and frowned at her. 'Don't I know you?' she enquired in a peremptory manner.

'Darina Lisle, we used to meet at the foodie press do's.'

'Of course!' Val's face relaxed. 'How could I forget, only I didn't expect to see you here. Nor you me, I expect.'

'Well, actually, Jemima told me you and her father were friends.'

'Ah, you're a friend of Jemima's!' A hint of wariness in the voice and eyes.

'We were at school together. I haven't seen her for years,' Darina said casually. 'We ran into each other the other day and it's been great catching up.'

'Where's Jemima now?' Val asked, brushing croissant crumbs off the table.

Darina explained.

'Oh, my goodness!' Val sat down. Her eyes looked strained. 'What on earth is Basil going to do now? And he's got the police coming to interview him as well, what a mess!' She looked up at Darina. 'Has Jemima told you about the fire at my factory?'

Darina joined her at the table. 'Well, actually, William Pigram, the chief inspector who wants to talk to Basil, is my husband.'

'Good lord!' Val said. 'How strange, you being married to a policeman, but I don't know why, after all, it's a job like any other.'

'Not quite like any other,' Darina said in a heartfelt way.

'No, I suppose not,' Val said slowly. She looked at the loaded tray. 'I was going to take this in and start making some lunch. Mrs Starr is off today. Would you like to come and have a cup of coffee in the kitchen? I've love to catch up on your doings since we last met.'

'Love to,' said Darina with alacrity. 'I'd like to hear about Eat Well Foods.' She picked up the cafetiere and the dish that had held the croissants.

In the kitchen Darina started stacking dirty china into the dishwasher while Val put the kettle on then bustled about assembling ingredients on the scrubbed pine table.

'Have you found somewhere else to carry on production?' Darina asked.

Val placed dried mushrooms in a pyrex glass jug. 'I think we might have, actually. All due to Basil. He's found somewhere with excess capacity that is happy to take on our production as an emergency measure. We met their managing director this morning.' The kettle boiled and Val poured some water over her mushrooms then checked her collection of rice, onion, fresh mushrooms and cheese.

'What about your staff?' Darina put the last mug on the top rack and shut the machine.

'Ah, you've hit upon the snag. They won't use any of our employees, they're trying to keep theirs in business. I can't afford to pay mine for doing nothing but if I don't, they won't be there when we get our premises up and running again. It looks as though it's going to take several weeks at the very least.' She sounded enormously frustrated. 'The other thing is, the production methods of this company are much more mechanized than ours. I've always worked on the "made by hand" principle, it's the only way you can get quality. Basil says it's time-consuming and expensive and I need to look towards expansion and that means using more machines, not people.' She ran a hand through her short hair. 'He's going to be badgering me to use this fire to change all my methods.'

'Why don't I make the coffee?' Darina suggested, filling the kettle again and putting it on.

'Thanks. I must go and find some white wine,' she said abruptly and left the room.

By the time Val returned, carrying a bottle, Darina had the coffee ready. 'Is it risotto for lunch?' she asked, looking at the ingredients assembled on the table.

Val nodded. 'With all the hassle going on with the factory, I thought we needed the contentment factor of carbohydrates and they're much better not mixed with protein.' She looked sweetly serious as she said this. She opened the wine, poured some into a saucepan and put it on the stove to heat.

Though not a follower, Darina was well aware of the theory behind the various combining diets. But, 'Contentment factor?' she asked.

'Carbohydrates raise the spirits, make you happy,' Val said. 'I don't know why it's such a dirty word with so many people.' She started rapidly slicing the mushrooms, the knife flashing with the speed of her attack. 'And a couple of days on rice and lentils does wonders for purging the body of toxins.'

Darina made a mental note to try this one day – but not yet. She pushed the plunger down on the cafetiere and poured out a couple of mugs. 'Won't you have to give your staff redundancy if you have to let them go? Couldn't that be as expensive as continuing to pay them even if they aren't working?'

Val shrugged. 'It shouldn't be much, the company hasn't been going long enough. I just hope our insurance will cover the cost. Thanks for this,' she raised the mug of coffee, then started on the last of the mushrooms.

'You should have got Basil to check it out,' Darina said. 'I bet he's a whizz on comparative costs and benefits. Shall I do the onions?'

'Would you? I only wish I'd known Basil when I was getting going,' Val sighed. Then said, 'Except we would probably have argued so much about production methods we would never have got together.'

'How did you meet?' Darina found a sharp knife, rapidly removed the onions' outer skin then cut them in half through the root.

'Oh, some local charity function we were both involved in. It was deadly boring and we couldn't wait to escape. Basil took me to dinner at a wonderful restaurant not far from here and after that, well, one thing led to another.'

Darina could see that with Basil it would. If he was interested, he'd be remorseless in pursuit. But Val didn't sound as though she'd put up much resistance. Had it been a nasty shock to realize how different their approaches to her business were? Darina made horizontal and vertical cuts through the onion halves, keeping the roots intact, then sliced down, releasing neat little fragments.

Val finished neatly slicing the mushrooms and poured olive oil into a large pan. Darina remembered concise and well written articles under the Douglas by-line in a number of different publications. 'Was it a wrench to give up writing when your food company got going?' she asked curiously.

Val picked up the chopping board and scraped the onion into her heated oil. 'Do you know,' she said, stirring, 'it was a relief? I'm not creative with words, only food. The recipes were all right, it was the articles that were so difficult.'

'They didn't read that way. Why did you keep at it, if that was the case?' Darina washed the knife and swabbed down the board.

'It was the cooking I really enjoyed and, I don't know, I think I had a mission, to bring healthy cooking to people who needed it.' Val stirred the onions, her movements jerky, as though from an inner turmoil. 'And I needed the money. When my husband and I divorced I got the house and support for the girls. But I knew that would end when they left home. I had to build a career.' She sounded harassed, as though the worry had attacked her nerves, leaving them as susceptible to strain as a tender plant was to frost.

'So you started the food company as a better bet than journalism?'

'Do you want to rinse that rice for me?' Val pointed her wooden spatula at the bowl of rice she'd measured out earlier.

Darina found a sieve and poured the rice in.

'Thanks. No, it wasn't quite like that.' She rubbed a hand over her eyes. 'As I explained to your husband the other day, I saw a market niche.'

Darina rinsed the rice under the tap. 'How did you find out your daughters couldn't cope with certain foods?' she asked curiously.

'They had terrible eczema,' Val said promptly, still stirring the onion. 'The doctors said they'd grow out of it and gave me a cream for them. It wasn't very satisfactory and I hated the thought of them being regularly anointed with cortisones. Then a friend suggested I take them to a homoeopathic doctor and she diagnosed food intolerances. After I removed wheat, dairy foods and chocolate from their diet, the change was dramatic. Not only did the eczema clear up but they just felt generally so much better.' Val added the rice to the now transparent onion and stirred some more. 'Do you want to see if those porcini are soft yet?'

Darina investigated the dried mushrooms. They had reconstituted themselves in a startlingly successful way, their hard chips swollen and softened into thick slices of ceps. She fished them out on to a board. 'Do you want them chopped?'

'Just slice them roughly, please.' Val found a fine sieve and strained the mushroom juices into the hot wine.

'And now your daughters are grown up?'

For a moment Val's strained face relaxed. 'Kate's in Australia and Sally's at university.' She looked at the rice mixture for a moment, then added without expression, 'They keep hoping I'll get together again with their father.'

'What's he like?'

'Digby? Army,' Val said succinctly as though that explained everything. She added some hot liquid to her pan and started stirring again but slowly this time. 'Very charming, very correct, very rigid thinker. Expected me to be there in the background, doing all the right things so he could rise to the top. Was even quite proud when I got articles accepted, as long as the writing of them didn't interfere with what was going on in his life.'

'Sounds a bit like Basil,' Darina said, smiling.

'Heavens, no! Nothing like Basil! Basil is . . .' the spoon stopped stirring.

'Happy to have you run your company as long as you do it his way?' offered Darina.

Val stood with an expression of bewilderment on her face. 'He makes me feel wonderful! All he has to do is put a hand on my arm and I turn to jelly.' She gave an involuntary shiver and started attacking the rice again.

Something about the way she'd said it made Darina feel uncomfortable. She changed the subject. 'Jemima said you might be starting a line of baby foods, would that be for children who are food intolerant? Are there many of those?'

Val shrugged as she added more hot wine, 'I'm not sure of the figures. Certainly wheat and dairy products cause problems for some. But the baby-food idea was Basil's. He suggested there was a need for what you might call gourmet dishes for the just weaned. But we're having arguments about them, too. I say they mustn't have any preservatives or colouring agents in them. Basil says that means distribution will be too expensive. We must spend half of our time together arguing.' She pushed back her hair again in an impatient gesture then added, 'He seems very involved with his grandson.'

'Yes,' Darina agreed. 'Rory does seem to be a very appealing child.'

'Oh, yes,' Val said instantly. 'I love him to bits.' It sounded a little perfunctory.

'Would baby food fit into Eat Well Foods?'

'If it's done my way. There's a fantastic market out there and I'm certainly going to need something to improve the balance sheet after this fire.' She added all the sliced mushrooms to her pan, fresh and dried. 'It couldn't have come at a worse time. I've got to go abroad next Thursday, to attend an international conference on food intolerances and allergies. I'm presenting a paper on the problems of providing ready prepared food for sufferers. I'd thought of cancelling but it means so much in terms of prestige, I really can't afford not to go.' The tension was back. Did prestige matter so much to her? Or was it the other pressures – the trouble with her company and Basil?

Val stopped stirring for a minute and turned to Darina. 'Look, would you be interested in working up some recipes we could test for a gourmet baby-food line? I was a regular reader of your newspaper column and I think we have much the same approach to food. No concessions on flavour but simplicity of style. Say if you're too busy. It would be on a proper commercial basis, of course,' she added perfunctorily.

Too busy? Darina almost laughed. 'I think I could manage to give it some time,' she said carefully. 'We'd need to discuss exactly what sort of foods you are thinking of, costings, and all that.'

'Of course,' Val said impatiently. 'But you'll do it?'

'I'll certainly give it some thought.' The idea of developing food for babies definitely interested her. Put those tiny taste buds on the right road and you might be able to develop a lifelong interest in food. Public schools had a lot to answer for. Shepherd's pie, bubble and squeak, baked beans, jam roly-poly, the list of dire dishes they'd programmed generations of young men into defining as their life's diet went on and on. What William really liked to eat at the end of a hard day was not one of her concoctions, delicious though he always said they were, but what she called nursery food. Maybe if he'd been gastronomically challenged when a baby, he'd be more adventurous.

'But what about production? Are you going to have to move over to more mechanization, as Basil suggests, or can you continue your way?'

Val added more hot liquid to her risotto and continued her vigorous stirring. For a moment she said nothing. Then, 'He's asked me to marry him.'

A number of possible responses ran through Darina's mind. 'That's quite a step,' she managed at last.

Val's short bark of laughter had a touch of hysteria. 'Isn't it! Well, I'm glad you didn't go all sentimental.'

'Sentimental isn't a word I associate with Basil Ealham,' Darina said wryly. 'He's a very, well, exciting man?' She made it a question.

Val wiped sweat from her forehead with the back of her hand. 'That's it!' she said with a note of doubtful triumph. 'Exciting. He gathers you up and it's as though you're travelling on a fast, powerful train, rushing along but with perfect control, not a moment's worry.' More liquid, more stirring. 'Rushing along, never stopping, never being allowed to make your own decisions, saved from yourself, saved from the world!' She sounded as though she was about to lose control. 'Big, brave Basil, the weak and feeble woman's friend,' she said, her voice high and unsteady.

The kitchen door opened and Rory trotted in followed by Jasper.

'Dah, dah, duh,' Rory said, waving his starfish hands in the air as he made for Val.

She turned from the stove. 'Rory I can do without you.'

He laughed and grabbed one of her legs.

'Let me go!' she shouted at him. 'Get out of the kitchen!'

Rory burst into noisy tears.

Jasper came and snatched him up, his face set and angry. 'Bitch,' he said with quiet venom. 'There, there, Rory. Nasty woman didn't mean it and we don't want to be in here anyway. We'll go and find your pushcar, shall we?' He didn't look at either Val or Darina as he carried the boy out.

'Oh, God!' said Val hopelessly as the door closed behind them. 'Now he'll tell Basil!'

Chapter Fourteen

By the time Darina had soothed Val and laid the table for the Ealham lunch, then refused an invitation to join them, William had left Blackboys.

He returned home at half past eleven that evening looking exhausted and saying he'd eaten and all he wanted was a large whisky. But he took the biscuit tin up with the drink and sat in bed watching a late-night movie on the television and showering crumbs around until the biscuits were finished.

'Do you have to go in tomorrow?' Darina asked without much hope they'd have a day together.

'Not unless something unexpected comes up.'

'Thank heavens!' she said gratefully. 'We can have a nice quiet day.'

They started well with breakfast in bed. William brought up a tray with coffee and marmalade-laden toast.

'Oh, this is bliss,' Darina said, lying back on the pillows. Then noticed William scratching at his leg as he sat on the bed beside her. 'What's wrong?'

'Nothing,' he said abruptly, stopping the scratching and reaching for his coffee.

'How did your interview with Basil go?'

He sighed with frustration, 'I suppose there's a

normal human being inside there somewhere but over the years he's built up so many defences, constructed so many public faces, I think it would take Freud to uncover it.'

'So you didn't learn anything useful?'

William reached down absentmindedly to scratch his leg again, realized what he was doing and stopped. 'Look,' he said aggressively. 'I don't want to discuss the case, all right? It's bad enough you being so closely involved with the Ealhams, and I don't really understand how that's happened when you say you only met Jemima the other day after a gap of donkey's years, well, as I say, that's bad enough without you trying to wheedle police business out of me.'

Darina nearly spilt her coffee! 'William! You know I hate invading your territory. And you always used to like discussing your cases.' In fact he'd said it was a help, that he found her intuitive approach could sometimes succeed where basic slogging away at details had failed.

William said nothing, merely sat solidly on the bed and pressed his lips together as though to prevent further hasty words escaping. And he was back to scratching his leg again.

'Let me look at that,' said Darina, putting down her coffee.

Reluctantly he pulled up his pyjama trouser leg and revealed a nasty patch of angry looking flesh. 'What is it?' she asked.

'Nothing, I get it from time to time. If it hasn't disappeared by tomorrow, I'll go and get some ointment from the doctor. It's years since I had anything like it,' he added crossly. 'It was always around when I was a child. The doctor would give me some ointment; he said I'd grow out of it and I did. Until now. Now tell me what you've arranged with your mother.'

'She wants to come up on Thursday but I'm going to try and put her off until next Monday at the earliest, I've got so much to sort out. And it would be nice if you had some time to spend with us. Do you think you'll have cracked this case by then?' she asked hesitantly.

'I damn well hope so! We've got enough people working on it,' he said and for a moment she thought he'd start telling her how it was going. Instead, he went and had a shower, leaving Darina staring after him and remembering the way he'd smiled at Pat James in the nanny's bedroom. She seemed to have the knack of saying the right thing to him!

Though William wouldn't discuss the case with Darina, he seemed to spend a great deal of Sunday thinking about it. Even when they went for a walk along the river, he lapsed into silence. After a little she gave up trying to stimulate lively conversation and left him to his thoughts, concentrating her own on ideas for baby foods. Which wasn't something she wanted to discuss with William. He would only see it as a useful crack in her determination to put off having children that he could use to persuade her now was the time to start a family.

So it wasn't the happiest of Sundays and on Monday for once Darina was happy to see William leave the house early.

Particularly when she had a call from a magazine editor expressing interest in one of her ideas. If, that is, she could produce the finished article by Wednesday.

Darina forgot about tracking down Sophie or working on recipes for gourmet baby food.

It was wonderful to have something positive to work on. Soon she was lost, concentrating on the screen of her computer, trying to capture the spirit of the publication that wanted the article. Aimed at the busy cook without much money, all its recipes had to be short and expressed very simply.

Gradually Darina forgot how unsatisfactory the weekend had been.

After she'd finished her first draft, she rang her mother.

Ann Stocks was not best pleased. 'But, darling, I've rearranged my entire diary so I could come to you on Thursday and stay a week. I haven't seen you since you moved to London and precious little for too long before then.'

Darina felt guilt creeping up on her like dry rot.

'You've no need to think I'll be a nuisance. I have masses of London friends who'll be only too delighted to see me.'

'Don't be like that, of course you're never a nuisance. I just want to have the time to enjoy your visit. I've found a couple of exhibitions you'd like and there's a new restaurant I want your opinion on, I thought we could lunch there.'

'Now, darling, you know I can't tell veal from pork,' Ann Stocks said happily.

'But you can always tell what sort of clientele they're aiming at and exactly who's eating there,' Darina said wickedly, knowing her mother's penchant for style. 'But if you come this week, I'll still be punishing the clock. Make it Monday?'

As she put down the phone on a reconciled Ann Stocks, Darina wondered for the first time whether it was her prickly relationship with her mother that meant she was so reluctant to bear children herself. She would really hate not to have a close relationship with them but what did she know about how to achieve it? 'They fuck you up, your mum and dad,' Philip Larkin had so memorably written. She didn't want to fuck up any child of hers.

That reminded her of little Rory and the problem of who his father was. After the scene in the kitchen with Val, Darina thought this could be another reason why Jemima was so keen to discover his parentage.

But first she had to finish her article on a Valentine's Day meal for two.

Uninterrupted by any husband arriving home until well after ten o'clock, Darina was able to work at reducing the number of words in her recipe method while increasing the clarity of her instructions, then on creating three hundred words on the art of using food to demonstrate love.

When William eventually came in, she offered him her lover's meal: smoked salmon pasta with a sauce of smoked-salmon ribbons and cream with basil leaves, a salad of tender green leaves with a mustard and honey dressing, followed by a small heart-shaped meringue and chocolate gateau.

An almost unintelligible grunt said William wasn't hungry. Then he found some cheese in the fridge, cut off a chunk and took it up with a glass of whisky to bed.

Darina insisted on checking the rash and found it had spread further. In the middle of the night she woke to find William frantically scratching a bleeding leg and complaining of a raging headache.

She found some soothing ointment, gave him a

couple of aspirin and then lay awake worrying about him.

Tuesday she finished the article, e-mailed it through to the magazine in the late afternoon, then prepared an invoice. All very satisfying.

Then she wondered about the empty state of her fridge. Was there any point in preparing yet another meal that was going to be flung back in her face? (She'd eaten the smoked salmon pasta for lunch, hardly tasting the food as she worked on her article.) William's constantly tired face came to mind. How much of his bad temper these days was because he was struggling to cope with the new job? She cursed the fire at Eat Well Foods. It had brought nothing but trouble to them as well as to Val Douglas.

Then she wondered about what might be going on between her husband and his new sergeant and told herself not to be silly.

But she couldn't stop thinking about William. Finally she picked up the phone and tracked down Val at the Ealham headquarters, had a discussion with her about what exactly she needed in the baby-food line, then raised another matter.

After a most helpful conversation, Darina went out and posted her invoice then continued on to the shops and bought some chicken breasts. These she stuffed with prosciutto and mango slices. Perhaps this would hit the spot with William.

He got back before ten and wolfed down the food. 'Didn't have time for any sandwiches today,' he told her, sopping up the last of the wine sauce she'd served with the chicken.

Darina was not going to offer her head for another chewing off. She said nothing.

William grinned shamefacedly at her. 'I can tell you that we seem to be making no progress very rapidly.'

'No progress at all?' she asked, cheering up.

'Well, we're working our way through all the staff at Eat Well Foods, taking statements about the company and, especially, the nightwatchman. So far nothing of interest. But Gerry Aherne appears to have a whole list of minor offences on record in the Irish Republic and it's becoming a bit of a mystery as to how Eat Well Foods took him on as a reliable nightwatchman.'

'Forged references?' suggested Darina.

'More than likely,' agreed William, helping himself to a sliver of cheese and a couple of the Prince of Wales Duchy biscuits. 'Unfortunately, most of the records seem to have disappeared in the fire and we can't check.' He bit into one of the biscuits and gave her a level look. 'I'm also looking into Basil Ealham and his relationship with Val Douglas.'

He seemed to expect her to say something but Darina couldn't think of a comment that wouldn't be taken the wrong way. 'Have you unearthed anything interesting?' she asked at last.

'Only that the man is confoundedly successful, everything he touches seems to turn to gold.'

'Val had better look out then,' Darina said with a gurgle of laughter. 'Too bad if she turned into a statue, even if one worth a large fortune.'

William's expression didn't lighten. 'Yes, Mrs Douglas does seem to be fairly heavily entangled with your friend Ealham.'

'He's not my friend,' Darina protested. 'Jemima's my friend.'

'And he's just her father,' William said sardonically, helping himself to the meringue dessert Darina had once more produced.

His attitude was so different from what it had been on Sunday that Darina almost told him about the search for Rory's father. Then decided she couldn't risk it. Instead she told him about Val asking her for ideas for gourmet baby food. 'She's very keen everything should be as home-made as possible. No preservatives or colourings. All as pure and fresh as if it had been made by a caring parent.'

'Hmm, sounds as though you're getting even more closely involved in this business,' William said a little grimly.

'Does it worry you? Do you want me to cancel?' Darina asked, wondering how she'd react if he said yes.

He said without hesitation, 'No, of course not. I can't see that your talking to Val Douglas about baby food should interfere with our investigation. But, a friendly word of caution, don't get yourself too involved.'

'Ah, you mean Eat Well Foods is in financial trouble?'

'It looks like it. Not only because of the fire, they seem to have had serious cash flow problems for some time. The accountant said they're looking for someone either to take the company over or to provide a major investment of capital.'

'Enter Basil Ealham,' murmured Darina.

'Ealham admitted that he was investigating acquiring the company.'

'Val Douglas appears to be in two minds about it,' Darina contributed.

'Oh?' William looked interested. 'Why? I would have thought it was the answer to her prayers.'

'She doesn't approve of Basil's ideas on the production of convenience foods.'

'Really?' William digested this. 'Anything else you can contribute?'

'Uh huh? You saying that maybe my friendship with the Ealhams could be of use after all?'

'I deserved that, I don't know what gets into me these days, darling, you know I always value your opinions.'

'Do I? Well, Val did tell me quite a lot that was interesting but nothing to do with the case. She and I think your leg rash might have something to do with a food intolerance.'

'What nonsense!' William protested. 'I told you, it's a recurrence of the eczema I used to have as a child. I got the local doc to prescribe me some cream today and it feels better already.'

'But where does the eczema come from? That's the real question. Val says her daughters had bad cases as children and changing their diet cured it.'

'But my eczema disappeared as I grew up,' William said, looking profoundly unconvinced.

'Apparently food intolerances often go that way. They cause trouble when you're small, then your immune system learns to cope but only up to a point. Later on, particularly if you are under stress, the system gets overloaded and you start having trouble again.' Darina went and picked up a piece of paper from the dresser. 'Val gave me the name of a homoeopathic doctor. Why not go and see him? It can't do any harm and it might help.'

William glanced at the paper, 'What on earth will this chap do?'

'Diagnose what foods may be giving you trouble, then we can work out a diet that excludes them.'

William's face was a study. 'One of those cranky regimes that stops you eating everything you like, I know! No, thank you.'

'But what if it made you feel less tired?' Darina suggested hopefully.

William looked again at the piece of paper then stuffed it in his pocket. 'I can't see it'll do any good and with all I've got on at the moment I won't have time.'

Wednesday morning Darina collected the copies she'd ordered of the snapshot of Sophie Jemima had given her. Then found her A-Z of London and took the tube up to Ladbroke Grove. The station sat almost beneath the arterial A40 motorway into central London. To the north was North Kensington, a scruffily residential area served by two busy shopping streets, Ladbroke Grove itself and the Portobello Road, which turned into an open-air market every weekend. To the south was the more prestigious village of Notting Hill, which boasted gracious crescents of porticoed houses and a shopping area offering everything from cookery books to Indian artefacts, including a wide selection of restaurants and dress shops.

Darina had checked Martin Price's address in the telephone book. It didn't take long before she stood outside a well cared for stucco building that suggested money and class. There was no sign of anyone moving inside and after a few moments she walked back under the A40 and found Portobello Road.

Was she pinning too much on the fact that Sophie had collapsed here? Perhaps she'd been visiting, there were a number of specialist shops in the area. But Darina didn't think so. Nothing she'd heard about Sophie suggested a girl who shopped far afield. Much, much more likely was that this was where she'd found somewhere to live.

Had someone taken pity on her and offered her accommodation? Had she really not needed money?

Or had she looked for a job?

The more she thought about Sophie's dilemma, the more convinced Darina was that she must have found a job. But what sort? Martin had been adamant Sophie wasn't retarded but the fact remained she had absolutely no qualifications. She was used to looking after children but would any parent take a girl off the street, without references and only a small bag of clothes? It was surely most unlikely.

One of these small shops or a restaurant, though, might very well be prepared to offer work to a well-spoken and obviously well-bred girl like Sophie, particularly if they didn't have to worry about National Insurance, tax and all the other tedious official bits that went with hiring permanent staff.

Darina looked around her. North Kensington seemed a better bet than the smarter Notting Hill.

Unconsciously, she squared her shoulders, prepared herself for a long slog and walked into the newsagent by the tube station.

It was the first of many calls. The routine was always the same. Darina produced the photograph of Sophie, explained she was trying to trace her and asked if she'd been seen or worked in the shop some eighteen months to two years ago.

The sheer variety of shopkeepers and restaurateurs were what kept Darina going: Cockneys, Liverpudlians, Greeks, Italians, Asians, West Indians; this small area was an ethnic stew pot. Often it was hard to make herself understood and equally often she found it hard to understand what was said to her. Darina decided Ladbroke Grove made Chelsea seem hopelessly rarefied.

As she worked her way along the street, Darina wondered again why Basil hadn't hired someone to do this after Sophie died. Hadn't it occurred to him that this must be where she'd been living, could have been working?

Perhaps it really hadn't mattered to him. Perhaps he really meant it when he said he didn't care who Rory's father was.

Or perhaps he had instigated inquiries which had led nowhere. In which case, what was the point of her continuing?

Lunchtime approached and Darina abandoned her search to attend a launch party for a new line of frozen pizzas. At least she'd get some good conversation there, it was always fun meeting other food writers. Her morning's activities had left her profoundly depressed.

After a lively session tasting frozen pizzas and receiving a report that put forward evidence that they tasted better than fresh pizzas (but not those prepared at home, murmured someone), Darina made her way back to Chelsea thinking about the frustrations of the morning. Maybe she was doing this the wrong way round. She'd talked to Martin Price but what of Cynthia

Beauchamp, who'd sponsored Sophie's season? And there was Paul Robins, the Eat Well Foods' PR man. She hadn't talked to either of them yet.

When she got in, Darina rang Cynthia's number. A blase society voice warmed after Sophie's name was mentioned and the Hon. Cynthia Beauchamp said she would be at home the following morning at eleven o'clock. 'I can't think what I can tell you, though,' she drawled.

No doubt it would be another dead end.

Chapter Fifteen

Jemima pushed several files together on her desk and watched her secretary put on her coat.

'Mind you get that report finished,' Rosie Cringle said. 'Mr Ealham will be wanting it in the morning.'

Jemima stared at her coldly.

Rosie's neat little nose suddenly glowed, she was upset at the implied snub. Then her usual enthusiasm drained out of her face, she shrugged and picked up her bag. 'I've done what I can, now it's up to you, I'm off to see the dentist, you probably don't remember I had an appointment.'

Jemima said nothing, merely watched her leave with only the slightest of flounces, closing the door carefully when no doubt she wanted to slam it. God rot all such efficient, conscientious girls.

She lifted the top file and looked at the one underneath it. Then she shuffled all of them together again, shoved them to one side of the desk and leant back in her chair, gazing out of the window at the car park. Heavens but she was bored! What had ever made her think she could work her way to the top of the pile here when her father got someone else to duplicate all her efforts? He couldn't even rely on her to do the simplest report! All she was doing was drawing a salary just about sufficient to keep her in designer clothes. Was there any point in staying?

But she knew if only her father could bring himself to trust her, she could enjoy working here. Anyway, with her qualifications, what else could she do? Dad had suggested she train as a buyer for a big chain but fashion wasn't nearly as interesting as big business.

She bit on a finger and thought.

It was only gradually she became aware of voices coming through from her father's office. She heard first his tones and then the voice of Val Douglas. She couldn't hear what they were saying but they were plainly arguing. Quietly Jemima rose, found the glass she kept on the side cupboard and went over to the connecting door.

Putting the glass against the wood, she listened.

They were having quite a time of it. Basil was insisting he knew best about production methods, Val was fighting him every inch of the way. Jemima smiled to herself as she took in just how independent the woman could be. So someone dared to stand up to him!

The telephone on her desk rang and she had to abandon her eavesdropping.

It was reception. 'There's a Mr Dominic Masters asking for you,' the bored voice said.

Dominic? Jemima felt a sudden thrill. She hadn't expected this. She almost told the girl to send him up to her floor, then realized that she didn't want to run the danger of her father overhearing them the way she'd been able to listen in on him and Val. 'Tell him to wait in the boardroom, I'll be right down,' she said, put down the phone, looked at the glass she was still holding, then went across and held it once more against the wood.

Silence.

No, not quite. They'd stopped arguing but they were still in there and the few sounds she could pick up were graphic.

Silently she put down the glass on the top of a filing cabinet then, very, very gently, she pulled the door slightly ajar.

Her father was kissing Val, his mouth working possessively on hers. Val was giving tiny, gasping moans, her hands plucking and pulling ecstatically at his jacket.

As Jemima watched, Basil finished the kiss, gazed triumphantly at the closed eyes of the woman he was so tightly clasping, then wrenched open her silk shirt and swooped on her naked breast, sucking the nipple with passionate intensity. Val's hand moved to the back of his head, pressing it against her and arching her back, as though desperate for his caress. But Jemima saw her open her eyes and a curiously detached expression come over her face.

Softly Jemima closed the door and leant against it for a moment. Then remembered that Dominic was waiting for her.

He was studying the larger-than-lifesize portrait of her father when she entered the boardroom, his hands in his pocket, his moody face patently uninterested in Basil's thrusting countenance.

'Hello, Dominic,' Jemima said, closing the door behind her.

He turned and smiled at her. A slightly uncertain smile. 'Jemima, hi! I was passing this place and I thought it was time we met again.' He made as if to move towards her but then thought better of it and remained where he was, one hand on the back of one of the red leather chairs. 'I've missed you.' His voice was low and compelling.

Jemima looked at him. His shoulders were squared, his head held high, as though daring her to question his presence.

Was she supposed to melt at the very idea he could still want her? She was interested to discover that he failed to move her in any way. 'Am I supposed to forget what happened the other night?' she enquired interestedly.

He flushed slightly. 'Come on, you know that was nothing. A diversion, that's all.'

'Diversion? Well, well.' She walked round the table and stood opposite him, the length of polished wood between them. 'Is that what you call it?'

Dominic took an eager step forward, realized he couldn't reach her, gave a quick glance to assess the distance round the table then decided to stay where he was. 'You know I adore you.' He spoke with calculated sincerity.

'That's why you haven't rung or contacted me before this?' Jemima strolled to the top of the table and took her father's chair, lolling back and looking at him, enjoying his discomfiture.

He gestured deprecatingly with his hand. 'I, well, I thought it better to give you a little time to get over what happened.'

'I didn't notice any flowers arriving with your apologies,' she continued blandly.

He moved up to where she was sitting and drew out the chair next to hers, seating himself and leaning forward so that he could take her hand. 'You can't make me feel any worse than I do already.'

Jemima allowed her hand to remain in his. Then realized that his palm was sheened with sweat. She looked at him more carefully. 'Is that so, Dominic?'

More confidently he kissed the tips of her fingers, a move that once had begun a series of increasingly passionate touchings that had reduced her to a quivering mass of expectancy.

Jemima touched his eyebrow lightly, took in the earnest gaze of his eyes. 'Tell, me, Dominic, how's business these days?'

He drew back, disconcerted, but still held on to her hand. 'Business?'

'I remember we once discussed whether my father might be able to help if you needed an extra guarantor for your bank loan.'

'Uh, well, yes, we did, didn't we?'

'So, how's business?' She caressed the side of his thumb with hers and gazed at his face.

He shifted slightly in the chair and glanced down at their entwined hands. 'Well, now you mention it, an extra guarantor wouldn't come amiss actually.'

God, he must think her stupid! Or was it that he was desperate? Jemima looked at him through half-closed eyes. What would he promise her to get her support?

She settled more comfortably into the chair, took his hand to her mouth and gently bit the tip of one of his fingers. Power surged through her. What an aphrodisiac it was! She could have had him on the boardroom table right then and there. Upstairs her father and Val, downstairs she and Dominic?

She bit harder on his finger.

With a quick intake of breath he pulled his hand away. 'That hurt!' he said indignantly.

'Did it?' Jemima enquired sweetly. She felt wonderful. So this was how it was to know you could save someone and have them grateful for ever or condemn them to financial disaster. No wonder her father loved it all. 'Dominic, thank you.'

'Uh?' he stared at her, puzzled and definitely unsettled. 'You mean, you'll speak to him? Get your father on my side?' He gained confidence as he spoke.

Jemima gave a contemptuous flick to his nose. 'You really are the pits, you know?' she said conversationally.

His expression became totally blank.

'How you had the gall to turn up here today I'll never know.' She rose sinuously from the chair. 'I think you know your way out.'

'You mean, you won't speak to him?' He sounded dismayed and as though he could hardly believe it.

'You're even stupider than I thought, Dominic. You should have realized any hope of my father's financial support disappeared when you two-timed me.' Ice laced her voice but inside Jemima was warm and glowing.

'You bitch,' he said bitterly, rising. 'You're just like him. It's not enough to do a chap down, you've got to rub his nose in it.' He advanced towards her, his face contorted with rage. She took an involuntary step back. 'I'll get you for this, see if I don't.'

For a moment she thought he was going to hit her but then he thrust his hands into his pockets and, still breathing heavily, turned and walked out of the room.

He must really be in trouble, she realized. The thought thrilled her, he deserved everything that was coming to him. She refused to worry about his threat, Dominic was all wind and no force. She stretched her hands above her head and felt power run through her.

By the time she walked out to the lift, he'd left the building.

She entered her office and found the door into her father's standing open.

'Come in, Jemima,' called Basil as she stood in the doorway.

He was seated behind his desk, with Val perched on it, her hand in his. 'We've got news for you, Val and I are engaged.'

Jemima looked at them both carefully. Val was smiling graciously, her shirt neatly buttoned, and her father exuded satisfaction.

'Congratulations,' Jemima said without expression.

Basil didn't seem to notice her lack of warmth. 'We're going to have a celebration dinner,' he said exultantly. 'You, us, Jasper and Val's daughter.'

'How nice,' Jemima said politely. 'Have you told Jasper?'

'Just rung him. He's delighted.'

How had he managed to convince Basil of that? Jemima wondered wryly. Or had Basil brought him to realize that his allowance and living space depended on acceptance of Val? Life would no doubt change for both her and Jasper.

Jemima went over to Val and gave her a cool kiss. 'I hope you'll be very, very happy,' she told her. Then flung her arms round her father. 'And you, Dad.'

He hugged her, almost crushing the breath out of her body. 'See you back at the house,' he said as he released her. 'Come on, darling, let's go!' He grabbed Val's hand and pulled her, laughing, off the desk. 'Oh, and Jemima, that new nanny is hopeless. You're going to have to help look after Rory until I get back from my trip.'

Jemima watched them go, then went back to her own office. The information about Rory's nanny had failed to get through to her. Entirely occupying Jemima's mind was the knowledge that Val wasn't at all in love with her father but was marrying him neverthless. Somehow this information was valuable.

Wondering how best to make use of it, she switched off her computer and picked up her bag. Then, just as she was leaving the office, her mobile phone rang.

Chapter Sixteen

Pat James listened to William conducting the late afternoon briefing session with a feeling of deep frustration.

The frustration was twofold. Despite everyone's efforts, this investigation seemed to be getting nowhere and despite her best endeavours, Pat was not getting far in re-establishing her relationship with the DCI. Oh, he seemed to be grateful to have her expertise all right but, after that first, heady day spent together, she hadn't seen any more of him than any other member of his team.

'Let's just run through what evidence we've managed to unearth about the actual fire,' William said. 'Forensics have confirmed that the accelerant used was petrol, leadfree. Any results on inquiries to local petrol stations on anyone filling a petrol can?'

'No, guv,' said Rose. 'But it would be quite easy to fill the car and then a can without the attendant noticing. Or to use a station in some other area.' Her face was earnest, her mid-brown hair beginning to fall out of the bun she'd lately taken to wearing it in to keep it off her collar.

'How about if it had been waiting around to be used in a lawn mower?' suggested someone else.

'Mine uses leaded,' Chris said dolefully. 'I have to keep special cans.'

'Fires are the very devil,' William continued. 'They destroy so many clues. The post-mortem has, as we know, established that Gerry Aherne was hit on the back of the head with the proverbial blunt instrument but forensics have found no trace of a possible weapon.'

'How about a rolling pin?' Pat suggested suddenly. 'If it was a food factory, there could have been one lying around and it might have burned in the fire.'

'Good thinking, sergeant,' William rewarded Pat with a quick smile. 'As soon as we've finished here, get on to forensics and see if they can identify a possible rolling pin amongst the debris. And check with that secretary to see whether it's likely one could have been lying around in the office. After all, it's not something you use for filing.'

Pat glowed and made a note in her book.

'Nor are there any footprints,' William continued. 'Forensics say the clothes the arsonist was wearing could be contaminated with both petrol and smoke but until we have a suspect we can't examine his garments.'

'What about the Douglas woman?' someone asked.

'Not enough evidence to ask for a search warrant and I can't see Ealham allowing us to turn over either his lover's wardrobe or his own.

'Now, turning to the location of the business park, the house-to-house inquiries have unearthed someone in this street here,' William turned to the map on the incident board and pointed to a residential road running alongside the industrial park, 'who might have heard the arsonist leaving. A Mike Jones was sleeping on his sister's sofa in her front room, he'd been thrown out by his girlfriend.' There was a snigger from some of the men. Pat sighed at their juvenile approach.

William continued unperturbed. 'Mike got up around one o'clock to have a pee and heard a car coming out of the park. His sister's house isn't far from the entrance and he says it sounded like someone going very fast, then changing gear to go round a corner, skidding, then roaring off down the road. He says he remembers it because it was such an expensive sound, like a BMW or a Mercedes.'

'Audi?' suggested someone.

'Roller?' came from someone else.

'Porsche?'

'Quite,' said William. 'The timing fits in with the fire service's estimate of when the fire was started.'

'What about the chap who reported the fire?' Rose asked.

'Youngster coming home from a late date and his story checks out. Now how are we doing with the reports from the Eat Well Foods staff? Peter?'

'Just finishing, guv,' Peter Lennon said with quiet satisfaction.

'Good work,' said William. 'OK, everyone, we'll have a look at what they can tell us tomorrow. And I want an investigation into Basil Ealham's background.'

'If he's proposing to invest money in the company, would he set fire to its premises?' Terry Pitman asked, sounding sceptical.

'He would if he wanted to clear it of bad debts,' Pat shot in and thought she saw William give her a grateful look, but it was so fleeting she could easily have been mistaken.

'Ealham's a self-made man, comes from a deprived background. We need to look at any contacts he's kept up from those times.'

'Someone shady he could have used to set fire to the place?' Chris Hare suggested.

William nodded. 'And anything else that could have a bearing on this case. Terry, I want you to take charge of that aspect.' Terry Pitman looked far from pleased but said nothing.

'OK, troops, for today, that's it.'

There was a general exodus.

But Pat stayed behind to catch up on the latest reports.

An hour later William came into the incident room. 'Good heavens,' he said. 'You still at it?'

'Nearly finished, guv.'

He lingered by her side, making her very conscious of his presence. She wondered if he was going to suggest they went for a drink together, now that there were none of the others around to see him ask her. Keeping her eyes on the report she was reading, she willed him to do so.

'See you tomorrow then,' he said abruptly. 'Don't work too hard.'

Pat watched his tall figure leave disconsolately. There was something wrong with him, she knew it. Was it this case or his marriage?

She worked on, hoping against hope that William would return and suggest that drink.

Instead Terry Pitman suddenly appeared in the incident room. 'Sucking up to the boss, are we? Showing how hard we can work?' he said in his snide way, coming up behind her.

She shut down the computer she'd been working on and swung round in the chair. 'What's your problem?' she shot at him.

'I don't have a problem, if there is one, it's yours,' he said calmly, leaning against the edge of a table, watching her.

'I know your sort, you believe a woman's place is in the kitchen or working a keyboard. And you always feel everybody else gets a better chance at the top than you,' she added. This was a shot in the dark, stimulated by the resentment of William he so clearly displayed. 'You can't accept that just maybe someone is more intelligent and harder working than you.'

He flushed, the betraying colour surging into his cheeks. 'Quite the little psychologist, aren't you?' he sneered. 'Always think you have the answer to everything.'

She looked at him, leaning against the desk, muscles tensed, and reckoned he was longing for a scrap, dying to work out his frustrations on her. 'So what brings you back? Wanting to suck up to the boss?' she riposted.

'Just needed to pick up one or two things,' he thrust his hands into his trouser pockets and continued staring at her with challenge in his eyes. 'If you ask me, it's going to be a waste of time, going after this Ealham chap,' he said abruptly. 'It's a really long shot.'

Instantly Pat felt resentment at his questioning of William's handling of the case. 'Where would you look instead?' she asked in a way that made it plain what she thought about the matter.

'Quite the loyal little lieutenant, aren't we?' he said softly. 'But how closely are we looking at Val Douglas, eh? If being in bed together doesn't mean Basil Ealham is out of the frame, couldn't the same apply to her? After all, it's equal opportunity these days, isn't it?'

What a prickly, unpleasant person he was! The last

thing Pat wanted was to spend any more time in the same room as him but she was damned if she was going to creep away leaving him in possession of the office. She also knew that if she was going to get anywhere in this job, she had to learn to work with this man. 'Maeve O'Connor rang in with her new address,' she told him.

Terry said nothing but she thought some of his tenseness relaxed just a little.

'She's gone into the local youth hostel and is trying to find another job. Not going to be easy without references from the Ealhams.' She tossed the notebook back on to the desk.

'She's lucky to get away with not being prosecuted,' he said neutrally.

'Do you think she really did steal those pearls?'

'Do you?' he turned the question.

Unfair, Pat thought, she'd asked first, but, again, she restrained herself. 'She had everything to lose. A good job in luxurious surroundings, not to mention a cosy relationship with the master of the house.'

'That was never mentioned!' Terry's hands came out of his pockets.

'You haven't read the transcript of my report properly,' Pat said calmly.

He looked at her blankly.

'The bit that says when the guv asked her if she and the boy were alone on the nursery floor at night-time, she answered, "You could say that, yeah."'

'And you interpret that as meaning she was having an affair with Basil Ealham?' His scorn was patent.

'Don't you?'

'Isn't there a son? I'd have thought he'd be the one.'

Pat smoothed her skirt along her thighs. 'Not when

you add it to her comment that Val Douglas was a stuck-up cow who thought she had Basil Ealham where she wanted.'

He pounced quickly. 'That isn't in the report.'

'It isn't?' Pat was startled. She was sure it had all gone in. And William had checked it. 'Let's see.'

It took a little time to find the right report and Terry didn't help. He remained where he was as Pat finally unearthed and quickly scanned it. 'You're right,' she said in disgust.

'Keep up the good work.' He patted her on the shoulder in a maddeningly condescending way and sauntered out of the CID room.

Furiously Pat started to amend the report. Anger seethed through her. Not only had Terry not told her what he thought about the nanny, he'd found her out in a slip. Unacknowledged even to herself was the fact that William had checked her report and not noticed the omission.

Keen to get on top of the remaining staff statements, Pat stayed late that night and was in early the next morning.

They were a turgid lot, full of irrelevant data. The only interesting thing about them was the way that, together, they built up a picture of a happy company and if the company was on the financial skids, rumour hadn't yet started amongst the staff.

She'd reached the last but one as Terry walked in.

'Spent the night here, did you?' he asked and for once his tone was almost friendly.

She didn't notice. Her attention was entirely focused on the statement she was reading. 'Have you seen this?'

she asked excitedly, not caring that it was Terry she was showing it to instead of William.

He took the report and she watched him read it, a smile of anticipation on her face.

'When did this come in?' he asked.

'Must have been last night, it was waiting with several others to be entered this morning.'

'I think we should follow it up now,' Terry said. 'Come on.'

Pat didn't question his decision or feel they should wait for William's arrival. She grabbed her jacket and followed him.

Heidi Walker lived in a council house several miles from the Eat Well Foods factory.

'Basil Ealham's office isn't far away,' Pat said as she drove them over.

For a moment Terry was silent, then he said, 'Perhaps the guv could be right about Ealham's involvement in this case.'

Pat felt it must have taken something for him to say this. 'I wonder how reliable a witness Heidi Walker is?' she offered.

'We shall see,' he said and she felt that some sort of truce had been signed between them.

They parked behind an A-registered Ford Escort that looked in astonishingly good condition for its age. The little garden was neat, the windows sparkling and the door freshly painted in a smart navy blue. The brass fittings shone with that brightness that only comes from regular cleaning. 'Bought from the council?' murmured Pat.

The woman who opened the door was large, like a cottage loaf, with a comfortable bosom, big hips and a generous head of fair hair, done up in a loose but neat heap on the top of her head. Her kind, placid face looked polite enquiry at the two detectives.

'DI Pitman and DS James,' said Terry, flashing his warrant card. Pat showed hers as well. 'We want to talk to you about your statement on Eat Well Foods.'

'Ach, so, it's the fire,' Heidi said with a strong continental accent. 'Come in, I put coffee on, yes?'

'That would be great,' Pat said, reminded that she hadn't had any breakfast.

Heidi showed them into a neat front room and took herself off to the kitchen.

'Need your caffeine fix, sergeant?' asked Terry, peering at photographs on the mantelpiece. But, again, the sneering note was, for the moment, absent from his voice.

'Jump starts me into the day,' Pat said cheerfully, admiring a drawn-threadwork cloth on the coffee table that stood in front of a well upholstered three-piece suite. It only took a few minutes before Heidi was back with a jug of what smelt like real coffee and a plate of small pastries that could only have been home-made. 'Now I don't go to factory, I have time to bake,' she said, putting the tray on the coffee table and giving them a big smile as she poured out the strong, black liquid.

Pat took an almond slice and bit into it, releasing a shower of pastry crumbs. It was the most delicious thing she had ever tasted, with a real almond flavour and fresh raspberry jam. Terry was already reaching for another.

Heidi beamed at them. 'Is good, yes? At home I am pastry chef.' She handed each of them a minute square of linen which unfolded into a small napkin, also edged in drawn-thread work.

'Where is home?' Pat asked.

'Austria, near Zell-am-See. Is big lake, not far from mountains. I meet my James when he on holiday there. I come here twenty years ago. I like it here but miss mountains. When you grow up with them, hard to forget, no?'

The coffee was as good as the almond slices. Pat drank hers with deep appreciation. 'I'm sure,' she said. 'Now, you've given a statement to the police about your work with Eat Well Foods.'

'Is something wrong?' For the first time a frown appeared on Heidi's face. 'I say something wrong?'

'No, Mrs Walker,' Terry leaned forward, his hand hovering over the pastries. 'We just want to clarify one or two things.' As though not realizing what he was doing, he transferred another almond slice to his plate.

'My English is not good,' she said cheerfully.

'Your English is as good as your baking,' Pat assured her, which brought another beaming smile to the woman's face. 'It's about the time you saw the night-watchman, Gerry Aherne, in a cafe when you were shopping. Can you go through it again?'

'Tell you again?' Heidi said, her cheerfulness undiminished.

'Just so we are in the picture,' Terry said.

'OK, no problem. I was in town, I leave early that day, look for special present for my husband, is birthday soon, you know? And there is craft market with cafe. I think perhaps I find piece of glass my husband like.' Heidi glanced over at a small table that carried a collection of modern glass paperweights. 'He collect,' she said.

'But nothing good there. I just go when I see sitting at table in cafe Gerry.'

'How well did you know Mr Aherne?' Pat asked. 'I understand he hadn't been working at the factory long.'

Heidi nodded vigorously. 'We both join company at same time, is connection, yes? He very friendly. Walk round factory in afternoon, talk workers. I know he live tiny apartment in back. I bring him once cake; sachertorte, but my recipe.' She grinned at them, 'My husband, he say sachertorte to die for.'

'So you got on well with Gerry Aherne,' Terry said.

'Yes, I like talk, hear him explain Ireland. Beautiful place he say. Perhaps James and I visit.'

'So when you saw the nightwatchman in this cafe, you thought you'd join him?' suggested Pat.

Heidi's light blue eyes widened and she leaned forward, confidentially. 'I think, yes. But then I see he with other man. Other man have back to me, he talking to Gerry, stabbing finger at him.' She poked her own finger towards Pat in an aggressive way. 'Then Gerry grab his hand,' she brought her hand down with a jerk on to the coffee table, making the tray rattle. 'Gerry very, very,' she searched for the right word.

Pat longed to prompt her but knew that would be fatal. In the other chair she could feel Terry equally intent on the woman.

'Gerry very powerful,' Heidi said at last. 'Dominant? Is right? Is correct?'

'Could be,' Pat assured her. 'So Gerry didn't see you?' The report hadn't covered this point.

'But, yes!' said Heidi instantly. 'He see me. I think I look too much at them. He see me and he shake head.'

She demonstrated, gazing at Pat and making the tiniest possible movement of her head.

'So the other man at the table with him didn't see?' asked Terry.

'So, yes!' agreed Heidi. 'I know Gerry not like him to know I there. So I go,' she added with an air of finality.

'You didn't tell the police who interviewed you this,' Terry said. 'All you told them was you saw Mr Aherne and another man in the cafe and they appeared to be arguing.'

Heidi shrugged. 'Not always I understand what people ask,' she said. 'And sometimes people not understand what I say.'

Terry glanced at Pat and she knew they were both thinking that the police officer who'd questioned Heidi Walker needed to brush up his interviewing techniques.

'And did you mention this occasion to Mr Aherne afterwards?' asked Pat.

'Yes, of course! Very strange, mysterious, I think. So, next day, I take biscuits to Gerry after work finish and I ask.'

'And how did he react?' asked Terry. 'I mean,' he said as she looked blankly at him, 'was Mr Aherne annoyed or angry?'

'Angry? Why angry? It happen, I there.'

'So, he wasn't angry,' Pat soothed her. 'What did he say?'

'He say sorry not talk with me yesterday. Big business, he say, and do so.' Heidi laid her right forefinger against the side of her nose and looked knowing.

'Business,' repeated Terry. 'You're sure he said business?'

'Sure I sure.' Heidi looked injured.

'Did he say anything else?' Pat asked.

Heidi shook her head.

'You saw Gerry Aherne and this man last Tuesday, that's right?' Terry asked.

Heidi nodded.

'On the Wednesday afternoon you spoke to Mr Aherne and he told you it had been big business.'

Again Heidi nodded.

'And the Wednesday night the factory caught fire,' he said, more to himself than anybody else.

Heidi looked frightened. 'You think man in cafe start fire?'

Terry didn't answer. 'You recognized the man you saw in the cafe?'

'No,' said Heidi unexpectedly.

'But you said—' Pat interposed.

Terry held up his hand, stopping her. 'Tell us what you said to the police.'

Heidi looked flustered for the first time. 'They say do I know who Gerry saw at cafe. I say yes.'

'Then you did know,' Terry said, exasperated.

'No, not then. Police, they ask me, what he look like. So I tell, tall, fair hair. And they say, do I know who he is. And I say, yes, I do not know name but I see him with Mrs Douglas Thursday morning, after fire.' That was where the statement had ended.

Pat again saw Basil Ealham arriving in his Rolls Royce as all the women were giving their names and addresses to Val Douglas's secretary. Saw the large man put his arm around her shoulder, his fair hair gleaming in the chilly morning sun.

'Basil Ealham,' she breathed to Heidi.

Heidi looked back at her in surprise. 'No, not Mr Ealham.'

Pat and Terry stared at her in astonishment. The answer had seemed so obvious to both of them.

'Mr Ealham, I know,' Heidi said agitatedly. 'Mrs Douglas bring him round factory, he talk with us. This man I not see in office. But he there Thursday morning.'

'Paul Robins,' said Pat suddenly. 'Of course, the PR man!'

Why on earth, she wondered, could that smooth looking chap have needed to meet the nightwatchman in a tucked away cafe? The natural habitat for both would surely have been a bar or pub. And had Paul Robins tried to threaten Gerry Aherne?

Chapter Seventeen

The Hon. Mrs Cynthia Beauchamp lived in a four-storey terrace mansion just off Eaton Square. The door was opened by a maid and Darina taken up to a first-floor drawing room.

'How nice to meet you,' her hostess said, coming forward.

Darina judged the Hon. Cynthia Beauchamp to be in her forties. She was lithe figured and blonde haired, with a face that looked as though it just might have had an extremely skilful lift, the golden skin was so nicely taut and the area round the bright blue eyes so unlined.

'It's very good of you to see me,' Darina murmured. Then decided that a bit of name dropping wouldn't come amiss here. 'You're almost neighbours with my husband's uncle and aunt, Lord and Lady Doubleday.' She left the sentence hanging.

Cynthia's face lightened. 'Oh, dear Geoffrey and Honor, we know them well! So, you're related?'

'William's father is Geoffrey's brother.'

'His uncle! Well, isn't that nice!' Darina was waved to a chair. The drawing room had an interior designer's touch without being oppressively over decorated. 'I feel I know you already. Now,' the blue eyes looked at her thoughtfully, 'your husband is the policeman, yes?'

'Yes,' Darina agreed.

'Recently promoted, I believe.' So Cynthia Beauchamp not only knew the Doubledays well, she actually listened to what other people told her. Darina's expectations of this visit rose a little. 'You must be very proud.'

Darina agreed she was.

'And no wonder, then, that you have taken to investigation as well. Are you a private detective?' The blue eyes were inquisitive.

'No, not at all,' Darina said quickly. 'Only I have been involved in several cases and Jemima has asked me if I could help in trying to find Rory's father.'

'Ah, yes, Rory's father. Well, before we get down to that, can I offer you some coffee?' A tray was all ready, the coffee in a smart vacuum flask, the cream and sugar in silver containers, the cups and saucers fine porcelain.

'Now,' Cynthia said, handing a cup of coffee to Darina. 'How can I help? I was just devastated when little Sophie disappeared,' she continued without a pause. 'And then when she died, well,' she spread out her hands in a helpless gesture. 'And Basil was just broken by it all.' Cynthia sat down and ran a hand through her blonde curls. She'd shed any hint of artifice and looked genuinely moved.

'I understand it was you who suggested it would be a good idea for Sophie to have a season?'

Cynthia drank some of her coffee. 'I'd met her several times at Basil's house and she was such a sweet girl but lost, no idea what to do. She wasn't a modern miss, she needed a husband and a family to devote herself to. And I had such a ball when I came out,' she added with a faint smile.

Yes, Darina could see this confident woman as an

equally confident but fresh young girl conquering the young men she met as much by her personality as her looks. She wondered what had happened to her husband.

'Of course, it was long past the days when one was presented to the Queen but, even so, there were all these parties and my father gave a wonderful ball at Manston, our country seat.'

'And did you meet your husband then?'

'Oh, Charlie! Yes.' Again that little smile of reminiscence. 'Mummy was so pleased! Even then she could see he was going all the way. Background, breeding and a terrific sense of the money markets.'

'So it worked out well?' Darina probed.

Cynthia's frank eyes met hers. 'For the first twenty years, yes. Then he got careless and I found out what was going on. Women I might have managed to ignore; after all, a man needs his little pleasures and one can't expect to keep the flame alight for ever, can one? But when I found out there were boys, well,' a small toss of the head tried to dismiss the knowledge, 'that was too much.' Cynthia put down her drink and lit a cigarette. 'I mean, there were the children to consider. Anyway, I came out of it all right, kept the house,' her gaze encompassed the elegant room, 'and an income to go with it. But, well, it's lonely.' Again that frank gaze met Darina's. 'Still, one has one's friends.'

'And you met Basil Ealham?'

'As you say, I met Basil Ealham.' A sardonic note entered Cynthia's voice.

It must have seemed meant. The lonely, attractive socialite and Basil, ever ambitious, ever magnetic, ever one to need lovely ladies. And with the vulnerable, shy, motherless Sophie.

'What sort of arrangement did you come to over Sophie?'

A trace of hauteur entered the bright blue eyes. 'Arrangement?'

'I'm sorry,' Darina stumbled, aware of her error, 'I mean, did she come and stay with you here?'

'Ah, I see what you mean.' The touch of frost melted away. 'Yes, for part of the time. My own daughter, Tiggy, was her age and I took them around together.'

Darina saw immediately what a convenient arrangement this must have been for the Hon. Cynthia Beauchamp. Basil would surely have contributed handsomely to expenses.

'You must have got to know Sophie well.'

'Indeed I did. Such a loving little girl. She and Tiggy got on so well together.'

This was the first Darina had heard of Sophie having a close friend her own age. 'Didn't Tiggy have any idea where Sophie might have gone after she left her brother's?'

'Oh, she was so upset. Do you want to talk to her yourself? She's upstairs.'

It sounded as though Tiggy hadn't found a husband during her season.

Darina said she would find that very helpful and Cynthia rang a bell then despatched the maid to bring down her daughter.

When Tiggy arrived, it was with a tiny baby with a puckered mouth giving forth weak, plaintive cries.

'My first grandson,' Cynthia said reverently. 'George, five weeks old!'

Darina dutifully admired him while thinking she preferred babies a little older, like Rory.

'He's hungry,' Tiggy announced. 'I'll feed him while we talk.'

Tiggy was a big girl with her mother's open manner, lots of naturally fair hair worn loose and a cheerful face. She sat down in a corner of the sofa, unbuttoned the big blue shirt she was wearing over jeans, revealing heavy breasts in a nursing bra, and soon had the baby contentedly sucking, watching his determined feeding with an expression of such tenderness Darina suddenly felt a pang of real envy.

'We're talking about Sophie Ealham,' Cynthia said.

Tiggy looked up immediately. 'Oh, poor Sophie! When I think how she never saw her baby, I can't bear it.'

'Jemima wants to find out who his father is,' Darina told her.

Tiggy made a small face. 'Jemima, eh! Pity she didn't care a bit more while Sophie was alive.'

Darina looked expectantly at her, 'You mean Sophie didn't feel she could confide in her?'

'Sophie couldn't confide in any of her family,' Tiggy said roundly, hitching little George up closer to her breast. A tiny hand waved briefly before he settled again. 'Her eldest brother, Job, lived in some rarefied world of his own, Jemima was too involved in her own activities and as for Jasper!'

'What about him? I thought he was very close to her.'

'Did you never wonder why all their names start with J except for Sophie's?' asked Tiggy.

'No,' said Darina, wondering now why it had never

occurred to her. Cynthia said nothing but her eyes watched her daughter.

'Apparently Jasper told her one day that his father wasn't hers!'

Darina remembered the story about the gardener and the pool house. Had Julie Ealham become pregnant and had Basil then accepted Sophie as his own? 'Poor Sophie,' Darina said.

'Poor Basil,' Cynthia said roundly. 'I knew,' she told her daughter. 'Basil told me. He said his wife had had a very brief affair with someone totally unsuitable and had confessed all to him and, "thrown herself on his mercy", I seem to remember was the phrase used.' Her mouth looked as though she'd sucked on a lemon. 'Basil said he'd felt he had to forgive her and assume total responsibility for Sophie.' She fiddled with a gold bracelet for a moment then added, 'He said it wasn't difficult, she was such a lovely child.'

No doubt it had suited Basil to have something over his wife and remaining married to her meant he could enjoy other women without having to make any commitment, thought Darina cynically. No doubt Jasper had put two and two together as he grew up.

'Sophie said to me that she wouldn't believe it at first and that she really went for Jasper. But apparently he told her it was quite easy to prove, it just needed a blood test and asked her if she'd like to have one done.'

'What a bastard,' murmured Cynthia.

'Well, that convinced her but she didn't feel she could trust Jasper after that,' said Tiggy.

'How dreadful,' Darina said. 'They were both so fond of each other. I spent a holiday with the Ealhams in Italy once and Jasper was the one who looked after Sophie, she was only about five at the time.'

'I think she adored him,' Tiggy agreed. 'But he made her feel she wasn't part of the family and she couldn't take that.'

'Oh, poor Sophie,' said Cynthia, visibly distressed. 'Basil really loved her. In fact,' she glanced down at her drink, her eyes hooded, 'well, I felt quite jealous at times.' She gave a self-deprecating laugh and lifted her cup.

'Did you see her after she moved to her elder brother's?' Darina asked Tiggy.

She shook her head. 'Afraid not. My father was working in New York on a special assignment and after the dance that Sophie and I shared, I went out there. That's where I met Angus and after that, well, everything else went out the window.'

'Angus is Tiggy's husband,' Cynthia explained, a trifle unnecessarily. 'He's in futures. Works terribly hard.'

'Never home before eight or nine o'clock,' said Tiggy gloomily. 'George is going to grow up with a stranger for a father. We live in Clapham and it takes ages for Angus to get home so Mummy thought we might like to stay with her while I got used to having George. At least Angus gets here before I've fallen asleep.'

'My husband's always late home as well,' Darina commiserated with her. 'Everyone seems to work so hard these days. But, back to Sophie,' she said hastily.

'Oh, yah, Sophie. Well, as I said, I went off to America and by the time I came back, Sophie had, well, disappeared.'

'Do you know of any friends she could have gone to or got help from?'

Tiggy shook her head. 'Like I told Mummy at the time, Soph was hopeless making friends. She never chattered like the rest of us, just was, you know? Either sat or stood so quietly half the time you forgot she was there.'

'But you became friends with her?'

'Oh, yah. Well, she was staying here, wasn't she? And she had a good eye for fashion,' Tiggy said with sudden enthusiasm. 'We'd go shopping for clothes and she always knew what was going to suit me.' She looked down at the open sides of the blue shirt. 'Can't wait to get out of this sort of thing but it's no use dressing up at the moment, the milk leaks out or George is sick on me. Anyway, I can't fit into anything good. Come on lad,' she gave the baby a little shake, 'don't go to sleep on the job. He takes for ever,' she said to Darina. 'I have to keep reminding him what he's supposed to be doing. At nighttime we both go to sleep together,' she giggled.

'So you have no idea where she could have gone to?' Darina was beginnning to despair of keeping the conversation on target.

Tiggy looked regretful. 'I'm sorry, I really can't think. I told Mummy and Basil when I got back that, as far as I knew, Sophie didn't have any other friends. Come on, little one,' she caressed George's minute nose with one finger. His creased face creased some more and he began sucking again.

'Have you met Rory?' Darina asked Cynthia.

She nodded. 'Once. By the time he was born, Basil and I had parted.' She looked down at her hands, lying in her expensively clad lap, then smiled. 'I couldn't take his possessiveness any longer.'

'Mummy! You told me you found out he was seeing someone else,' protested Tiggy.

Cynthia looked daggers but rallied. 'There was that, too. One does like to have a monopoly on one's man. Anyway, he did ring me and ask if I'd like to see Sophie's child and of course I went. I thought Rory seemed a dear little boy. Have some more coffee.'

Darina handed over her cup, little George went on quietly sucking and his mother and grandmother gazed at him in mutual adoration. 'Can I just get Sophie's movements straight in my mind,' she said. 'She stayed here until the season ended, that would have been August?'

'Not exactly,' Cynthia said. 'We had a dance in early July and then Sophie went back to her father. Before that she divided her time between us and Blackboys. It depended on whether there were parties and balls in London to go to. For Ascot and Henley, Tiggy and I would drive down to Blackboys and pick up Sophie. Basil usually arranged a driver. Once or twice we spent the night there.'

'I never really liked that,' Tiggy said suddenly.

'Didn't you, sweet?' her mother said in astonishment. 'Why?'

'I couldn't stand Basil.' Tiggy sounded uncomfortable.

'You never said.'

'No, well, there wasn't much point. You were dotty over him.'

'I was not "dotty over him",' Cynthia protested roundly.

'Yes you were. Sliced bread wasn't in it. Actually, that was one of the reasons I went to the States. Of course I wanted to see Daddy but I really couldn't bear the sight of you and Basil together.'

'Sweetie!' Cynthia gazed at her daughter in amazement.

'I was never so relieved as when I came back and found that you weren't together any more. Except I was upset about Sophie. If it hadn't been for that, it would all have been perfect,' she added sorrowfully.

'Why didn't you like Basil?' Darina asked as her mother seemed silenced.

'Oh, I don't know. I was so young,' Tiggy said with all the maturity of her new-found motherhood. She couldn't be more than about twenty-two. 'I didn't like the way he looked at me,' she said after a moment's thought. 'What was it you called certain young men you didn't like me going around with?' she asked her mother. 'NTS?'

'NST,' her mother said, reviving. 'Not Safe in Taxis.'

'Well, he had that sort of look.'

'Good heavens,' Cynthia said faintly.

'And his hand would linger on my shoulder. And when I danced with him at our ball, he held me much too tight. It was, well, it was really embarrassing.'

'Sweetie, you should have told me.' Tiggy looked at her mother and after a moment Cynthia added, 'Well, I see your problem. But I'm really sorry, darling. What a shit the man was. Thank heavens I never married him.'

'You wouldn't have, would you?' Tiggy was appalled.

'Perhaps not,' Cynthia agreed but there was a lingering trace of regret in her voice. Darina reckoned it had been a near thing. Perhaps if Sophie hadn't disappeared, who knew?

There wasn't anything more Cynthia or Tiggy could tell Darina that was of any use but she stayed a little longer, finishing her drink and admiring the tiny

George. Then she took her leave, thanking them both sincerely for all they'd told her.

Cynthia showed Darina out herself. 'I do hope you manage to find Rory's father,' she said. 'I told Basil at the time he should do everything in his power to find out who he was. But I don't think he took my advice, perhaps because of who Sophie's father had been. I mean, he may have thought blood had spoken and the truth would be more of a burden to Rory than ignorance.'

As Darina walked back along the King's Road to her house, she thought that this offered a more reasonable explanation for Basil doing nothing about Rory's father than anything else she could think of. It didn't make her task any easier, though.

Her next move must be to talk to Paul Robins.

Darina looked at her watch. If the traffic wasn't too bad, she should be able to arrive at his office just before lunch, which might mean she could persuade him to have something to eat with her. It was always easier to get people to talk over food.

Chapter Eighteen

Paul Robins didn't start Thursday in a temper but he certainly ended it in one. What his secretary called 'one of his paddies'.

When, early in the morning, he actually managed to get hold of Val he really thought that this might be his day. 'At last,' he said jovially.

'Sorry, Paul,' she said, sounding remote, almost as though she was attending to something else while talking to him, 'I have been busy.'

Oh, yes, sure. Busy with Basil!

'There really has been a lot to see to,' she went on, sounding tired.

Instantly, he'd felt compassion. She'd been hit hard by the fire and its aftermath. He remembered the shadows under her eyes that awful morning. Had he really not seen her since then? 'You should let me take more of the burden,' he told her tenderly. 'Come out to lunch. I'll bring a draft press release on your new arrangements.'

'Paul, that's sweet of you but I really haven't time. Fax it to me.'

'We need to talk,' he began to get upset. 'Discuss what else is needed to reassure all your customers. Public relations is more than press releases, you know.'

'We've got things well in hand, Paul. Shaz is sending out a letter to all our major accounts. Thank heavens for a freelance accountant, he had all their details.'

'But,' he pressed her, 'what about your end buyers? They aren't going to get a letter.'

'Paul, I haven't time for this, you know I'm off to that conference this evening.'

Ah, yes, the conference! To think that it had been his idea. Good for her image, he'd said. Underline her authority in the field of food intolerances and make useful contacts. The first thing he'd said after the fire was that she mustn't think of cancelling her paper. Now it was an excuse not to see him. Val had no right to treat him this way. 'I'll drive you to the airport,' he offered.

'That's kind of you, Paul, but Basil's going to take me.'

Burning jealousy filled Paul's breast. 'He seems to monopolize all of your time these days,' he said resentfully. He knew exactly what the situation was, at least he thought he did, but the amount of time she spent with that big bag of wind still got to him. He wondered that she'd even bothered to ring him from the scene of the fire. If Basil had been able to stay with her, she probably wouldn't have.

'Oh, Paul, don't go all hurt pride on me,' Val snapped. 'You don't seem to understand what I'm up against.'

Once he would have melted and apologized for upsetting her. 'Of course I do,' he snapped back. 'And you're not the only person to have business troubles. Keeping a PR company going over the last few years hasn't been easy.'

'Paul, I've got to go now,' she sounded very tired. 'Fax me that release.' The line went dead.

For some time he just sat there, staring at the phone

and trying to get to grips with the various emotions that seethed within him like molten iron in a crucible, red hot and very dangerous.

He got Rachel, his secretary, to fax the draft release through to Val, then he attacked paper work with furious energy.

Halfway through the morning Rachel buzzed through. 'The police are here and want to speak to you,' she said, all excited.

Oh God, he thought, another weary trawl through his connections with Eat Well Foods and where he was on Wednesday night last week. How many people could produce evidence they were in bed at four o'clock in the morning if they hadn't got a partner and wouldn't it be suspicious if they could?

'Send them in,' he said.

Instead of the two uniformed constables who'd interviewed him before, it was a man and a woman in plain clothes. After a moment, Paul recognized the girl as having been with the chief inspector at the factory on the morning of the fire.

'DI Pitman and WDS James,' said the man and Paul's depression deepened. He'd met men with that sneering look in their eyes before.

'All these initials,' he said in a jolly tone, just to show he wasn't in the least fazed by their appearance. 'What do they mean?'

'Detective Inspector and Woman Detective Sergeant,' the girl said helpfully as they put away their warrant cards.

'An inspector and a sergeant, aren't I the lucky one!' Watch it, he said to himself, you're coming on much too

strong. 'How about a cup of coffee? We offer nice biscuits with it.'

'No, thank you,' said the sergeant. 'We've just had
some.'

Paul told his secretary not to put calls through. Then
he waved his visitors towards his sitting area, a wide,
curving white leather sofa behind a round glass table
and a couple of white leather armchairs.

The two detectives edged round the table and
lowered themselves on to the squishy leather with care.
He took one of the chairs. 'How can I help you?'

'We'd like to hear about your relationship with
the nightwatchman, Gerry Aherne,' the inspector said
abruptly.

Somehow Paul had known that was what they were
there for.

'Aherne? We exchanged the odd word once when I
called at the Eat Well Foods office one evening, that's
hardly a relationship,' he said judiciously. 'It was a shock
to hear of his death,' he added, for once sounding
sincere.

'We understand you met him in a cafe near here a
couple of days before he died,' Pat James said in her
quiet way.

How the hell did they know that? The only people
who ever went into that craft market were tourists, that
was why he'd chosen it. How it kept going, he didn't
know, there never seemed to be many customers.

'Oh, of course. I came across him in town and it
seemed only right to offer him a cup of coffee.' He dismissed the occasion as hardly worthy of attention.

'Surely a drink would have been more acceptable?'

said Inspector Pitman, his eyes firmly fixed on Paul's face.

'I dare say but coffee was what I offered,' Paul said sharply.

'And what did you discuss?' the girl asked.

'I really can't remember. Nothing of moment. Probably the weather,' Paul said helpfully.

'Our witness says you were arguing,' Pitman challenged him.

Who in the name of everything unholy could it have been? How much did they see? Paul felt sweat breaking out on his forehead. He went and opened a window, letting in the noise of the high-street traffic. 'Never know what the weather's going to do at the moment,' he said cheerfully. 'Let me know if you can't cope with the racket.' The two officers looked at him as though they usually worked in the middle of the M1.

'We'll manage,' said the girl, Sergeant James. 'What were you arguing with Aherne about?'

'Threatening him, the witness said,' added Pitman, his eyes boring into Paul's.

'Threatening? Oh, that's an exaggeration,' Paul said, too quickly.

'Really?' Pitman raised an eyebrow. 'Perhaps you'd like to give us the unexaggerated version.'

Paul found his hands playing with the heavy perspex cigarette box that stood on the glass table. He took out a cigarette and fished in his pocket for the gold Dunhill lighter Val had given him. Then offered the box to the police. Neither admitted to smoking.

'Well, let's see how anybody could think I was threatening that poor man,' he said easily, drawing nicotine laden smoke into his lungs. 'What were we talking about?' He paused, his brain working overtime. 'We started with how he was getting on with the company. I mean, nightwatchman, it's not the greatest of jobs.' He sounded indulgently compassionate. There was no reaction from either of the officers. 'Anyway, I was asking Gerry how he was getting on with the job and, yes,' he said as though light had suddenly dawned, which in a way it had, 'that's when your witness, whoever it is,' and he'd give a good deal to know who, 'must have seen us. Because I was trying to impress upon him the importance of security and I may well have overdone it.' He could see himself now, so angry he could hardly speak, spitting out words across the table, jabbing his finger in Aherne's face. But if the police knew what he'd said, they'd hardly be trying to get it out of him, would they?

He gave a little laugh and hoped his nervousness wasn't coming through. 'Perhaps if you didn't know what I was saying, it might have looked a little threatening. But, of course, Aherne knew it wasn't.'

Pat flicked a few pages back in her notebook. 'Our witness spoke with Mr Aherne the following day and asked him what it had been about.'

Who the hell could it have been? Aherne knew hardly anyone apart from the workers at Eat Well Foods and his damn daughter. Was it her? Well, Aherne wouldn't have told the truth, no matter who it had been. 'And what did he say?'

'Apparently he said it had been "big business",' Pat flicked the pages back again.

So that was it? Paul relaxed a little. 'Well, I suppose to him it might well have been. I mean, he'd been out of work for a long time, hadn't he?'

'According to the Irish police, Gerry Aherne has served a term for blackmail,' said the inspector.

Paul's heart almost stopped. 'Blackmail?' It came out as a squeak. 'Get a life, officer. What could Gerry Aherne possibly have to blackmail *me* about?'

'It's an interesting question,' agreed Pitman, continuing to hold Paul with his intense stare. 'Why don't you tell us.'

Paul stubbed out his cigarette and made a play of lighting another. 'Gerry Aherne could have nothing over me.'

'He was blackmailing someone,' Pat James said, her voice soft but positive. 'Regular amounts of cash have been paid into his bank account. Large amounts.'

'Well, they weren't from me, I can tell you that.' Paul was on sure ground here. 'I wish I knew where to get large amounts of cash from! You can check my accounts and my bank statement any time.'

'So maybe you decided to kill the man instead,' Pitman said with quiet menace.

Paul took another drag on his cigarette. 'No,' he said positively. 'I did not kill Gerry Aherne and I did not start that fire. For God's sake,' he added passionately, 'that's the last thing I'd do! Eat Well Foods are my main client. Not only that, I've got money invested in the firm.'

'Have you indeed?' Both police officers looked at him with interest. 'There's no trace of your investment in the company.'

At first all Paul felt was confusion. 'It was a personal arrangement between Mrs Douglas and myself.'

'You mean you made her a loan?' suggested the little sergeant.

'Covered by shares in the company.' A slow anger

began to burn in him. Of course there must be a record of his investment. He remembered Val's lovely face lit by such gratitude it had taken his breath away. He'd enjoyed doing something for someone he loved. Done it with a recklessness and generosity that had made him feel like a god with the power to change lives. 'My father died and left me some money just as Val, Mrs Douglas, was trying to set up her company. I was going to handle the public relations and I had, I have, complete confidence in her.'

'How much was your investment?' asked the sergeant.

They'd stopped being polite, he noticed automatically. No 'sirs' now.

'One hundred thousand pounds.' He could hear despair in his voice. How could he have been so unbusinesslike not to insist on a share certificate? He'd written out a cheque and the money had disappeared from his account into Val's. How easy it had been for her! She'd told him he now owned thirty-three per cent of the company and he'd believed her.

'Have you ever been paid a dividend?' Sergeant James asked.

'Well, it's a new company, any money that's been made has been ploughed back, invested in expansion, you know? It made more sense for my consultancy to be paid a generous fee.' That was how Val had put it. And it really had seemed sensible.

'You probably signed a private agreement,' Sergeant James suggested in a kind way.

'Oh, yes, I did,' he said eagerly. How could he have forgotten the official looking piece of paper she'd produced, laughing at such formality between them. He hadn't bothered to read it, just scribbled his signature before removing her clothes, very slowly, garment by garment.

For a moment Paul felt relief. He shouldn't have doubted for a moment. But the burning sensation wouldn't go away.

'I'd like to go back to your meeting in the cafe,' the inspector said smoothly.

For the next thirty minutes he took Paul through his account of this again and again. Looking for discrepancies, of course. Paul had to concentrate very hard, which enabled him to convert his anger over the share situation they'd revealed into adrenalin that took him through the ordeal.

He didn't know if the officers had got what they came for but they looked as though they had plenty to think about as they left his office.

He shut the door behind them, lit another cigarette and tried to get Val on the telephone. Unavailable, he was told. He left a message for her to ring but there was no one who was so good at making herself unavailable when she wanted as Val.

Was she with Basil? The thought was acid in his stomach. Why the hell had he gone along with her on her involvement with the man? All right, if Ealham acquired the company, they would both be sitting pretty financially speaking. But what made Val think she had to offer herself as well as her company? Did she enjoy keeping the two of them on her little string? And how much longer could she keep Basil from knowing about their relationship?

Paul stubbed out his cigarette and immediately lit another one as he wondered whether Val was now just playing him along rather than Basil. She couldn't dump him, he'd ask for his money back and she couldn't afford repayment, he knew that. Why couldn't she reel Basil in? If only Val would stop arguing with him over the way the business was to be run, she could have sold him the company long before this, Paul was sure of it.

Nobody knew better than he how rational she could make any proposition sound, however dodgy it might prove to cool analysis. There was the time she'd had that idea for providing special meals for food intolerant passengers on British Airways. By the time she'd finished working on him, he'd been convinced all he had to do was knock on BA's door. Until he'd tried it.

He still squirmed as he remembered how quickly he'd been seen off by the airline.

Round and round went the thoughts whilst he smoked cigarette after cigarette.

He made one more attempt to get hold of Val. He left another message almost choking with anger. Just wait until he got hold of her! Then he remembered she was off that evening to the conference and that Basil was taking her to the airport.

No, Paul decided. Basil wasn't. He would.

Having made this decision he began to feel a little better. He checked the time, a quarter to one. He wasn't in any mood for lunch but a drink would be welcome. He started towards his drink cabinet just as Rachel buzzed through and said there was a Darina Lisle in reception wondering if she could have a word with him.

For a moment the name meant nothing, then he remembered Val telling him about the talented cook she'd asked to work on baby-food recipes for the range she wanted to launch. That bloody Basil wanted to launch!

'Tell her to come in,' he said. She probably wanted to discuss public relations possibilities for the new line. He remembered seeing her once on television. She'd come over very well and maybe he could persuade her to hire him for a personal publicity campaign. Paul rose, smoothed his hair into place and adjusted the set of his jacket.

She was a stunning girl, he thought as she came in, even better looking in the flesh than on the small screen. Blonde hair had always been one of his weaknesses. Val had been blonde when he first met her. When she'd gone back to her natural dark brown, saying the upkeep was more than she could afford, he'd told her it was a great mistake. It was soon after that she'd met Basil, who apparently preferred brunettes.

'Mr Robins, this is very kind of you.' Darina held out her hand to him.

It was a warm, dry hand that made him aware just how sweaty his was. 'I understand you are doing great things with baby food,' he said in an effort to get their meeting off to a comfortable start.

She looked a little startled. 'Oh, yes, of course,' she said. 'Val will have told you. I hope I can produce some good ideas.'

'I'm sure you will. Won't you sit down?' he asked her courteously.

'Thanks, but I wondered if I could offer you lunch,' she produced a most attractive smile.

Paul was taken aback, he was usually the one who offered a meal. Always because he wanted something.

What did she want? 'Lunch is a delightful idea,' he murmured. 'Do you have somewhere in mind?'

She shook her head. 'I was hoping you could suggest a place.'

'Why not? After all, this is my territory. Come with me.' He led the way out. 'Be back later,' he told Rachel on the way out.

'There's a very nice place just on the edge of town, by the river,' he said, opening the door to the car park. 'Do you mind if I drive you there?'

She appeared delighted by the suggestion and he enjoyed helping her into the low slung Porsche that was his pride and joy.

He didn't bother with small talk and she seemed content to sit quietly as he wove skilfully through the traffic until they reached a well-preserved beamed and thatched building that sat tranquilly by the river.

It was another Indian summer day and Darina enthusiastically endorsed his suggestion they sit outside.

'The food has something of a reputation,' he assured her as menus were brought and he ordered a whisky for himself and a mineral water for her.

'I'm driving,' she explained. Well, so was he but one whisky wasn't going to harm.

'Looks great,' she said, her eyes skimming the dishes on offer. 'What will you have?'

Which reminded him with a start that it was her lunch. What was this all about?

They both chose fresh scallops with grilled red peppers to start, followed by steak for him and a leek tart for her. 'And to drink?' she asked.

'Uh, I think just a glass of the house red,' he said. He

could always have another whisky back in the office if he needed it.

The garden sloped down to the river. A couple of dinghies lay on the grass in a far corner. 'I love the sound of water lapping banks, don't you?' said Darina while they waited for their food.

He nodded. 'My home is on the river, not far from here.' He'd had to pay a premium for the location but it had been worth it. With the way property was rising at the moment, it was going to prove an excellent investment. Suddenly he couldn't wait for her to orchestrate their discussion. 'This is delightful, but I'm sure you haven't asked me out so we can look at moving water.'

Darina fixed him with an open gaze and said, 'I've been asked by Jemima Ealham to look into where her sister, Sophie, spent the last few months of her life. I've spoken to Nicola and Job Ealham and apparently you visited her while she was staying with them.'

Paul was so astonished that for a moment he couldn't speak. A range of emotions ran through him ending with a wave of nostalgia. He could see Sophie now, her small, trusting face with those marvellous brown eyes, hear the slightly breathy way she had of speaking that made him feel so strong and powerful. 'Yes,' he said slowly, 'I did.'

'Did you know her well?'

'I met Sophie when her father came to see Eat Well Foods. Basil Ealham had met Val at some function or other and thought her business sounded interesting.' Paul pushed away the memory of Val's excitement, how she'd impressed upon him that this man could be important to the company.

'And Sophie came too?' Darina asked and he realized he'd stopped speaking.

'I took her round the factory.' He smiled reminiscently. 'She seemed very interested, said it was just like their kitchen at home only multiplied. And she really enjoyed the sampling session at the end.'

'Did she like cooking?'

Paul shrugged. 'Never knew. Given her background, I thought it highly unlikely she knew one end of a rolling pin from the other.' He grinned at Darina, who smiled back at him.

'So you got on well together.'

'Famously.' What Paul didn't say was that the way Sophie had hung on his words had done his soul good. Particularly as he'd disliked her father on sight and he was quite sure the great Basil wouldn't approve of any relationship between the two of them. 'I took her out for a drink after that and to a couple of gigs I thought she'd enjoy. She liked up-beat music, you know?' Again, Paul failed to mention what a refreshing change taking a young, innocent girl around had been from the heady sophistication of a liaison with an older woman.

'Did she mention any friends?'

Paul thought briefly. 'Nah, I don't think she had any. Just a minute, there was one, Wiggy, was it? Some such silly name.'

'Tiggy Beauchamp was the girl she came out with.'

'Of course! Though I don't think Sophie was too impressed with her season.' He had a quick mental picture of Sophie in a skimpy, very short dress, putting her heart and soul into dancing with him at a disco, then flopping down with a Coke and saying, 'I haven't had so much fun since, well, since I don't know when.' Her brightness had faded as she spoke.

'Did she let you know she was moving to her brother's?'

'Look, what is this?' he protested. 'You're sounding just like the police.'

'Oh, I'm sorry,' Darina looked distressed. 'I just want to find out all I can about Sophie.'

He capitulated, he could never resist women when they looked at him like that. 'Well, yes, she did.'

'So, she considered you a friend,' Darina said, her gaze sharp. 'Did she tell you why she was leaving home?'

Paul shook his head. He was suddenly conscious he hadn't asked Sophie many questions. She had been such a restful little thing and had always been so interested in him. The idea she'd thought him a friend was unbearably poignant. 'She said something about helping her brother with his family. It seemed, well, rather natural.' He looked at Darina then burst out with, 'Her father was hardly a sympathetic man!'

'Did Sophie tell you that?'

'No,' he admitted. 'But she seemed very much in awe of him. It was always, "my father wouldn't like this," or "my father always says."'

'Did she tell you she was thinking of leaving her brother's?'

'No,' he said positively. 'It was a shock to hear she'd disappeared.'

'How did you hear?'

'Val told me. She and Basil were seeing something of each other.' He swallowed as he remembered his chagrin at the time. He had a swift vision of Val in his bed, gloriously relaxed, running a finger down his spine and telling him, her voice all sultry, how Basil's precious younger daughter seemed to have disappeared. 'The poor man's distraught,' she'd said. 'I think he needs comforting so don't expect to see too much of me for a bit.' He could date the decline of his relationship with Val from that point.

'Did you ever think you might be Rory's father?'

Paul's mind reeled. 'Hey,' he said urgently. 'Don't go getting the idea that just because I took the girl out for a drink or two we made it to bed!'

'You're saying you never made love to Sophie Ealham?'

'Damn right I am!'

Chapter Nineteen

Back at Paul's office, Darina got out of the Porsche as elegantly as she could and said goodbye.

She started to walk back to her car, thinking about what she'd learned that morning.

Sophie had been a sweet girl who hadn't been too bright in the brain department but not backward. Darina was now certain of this. Cynthia Beauchamp would never have brought her out if she had been. Given maturity and confidence, Darina was sure she would have grown into the sort of person everyone wanted as a friend, sympathetic and intuitive, who would always spare the time to listen.

She'd obviously had more of a relationship with Paul Robins than anybody else had realized. Had it gone further than Paul claimed?

Martin, too, had obviously been attracted to Sophie. Darina thought she must have been the kind of girl who made any man feel better about himself, more attractive, more intelligent, and maybe nicer.

Everyone was hungry for approbation, everyone needed to feel better about themselves. Darina left the question of Sophie for a moment and asked herself if she was making William feel good about himself? And if not, was there a gap there for someone else to fill? A certain WDS perhaps? Darina had no very clear idea of how a police station operated but she was sure there'd be plenty of opportunity for a small, curvy, intelligent female sergeant to stroke her boss's ego.

Darina reached her car and told herself that jealousy was demeaning, degrading and had a nasty tendency to make things worse. Her job was to make sure William wanted to come home each night.

Then she sat in the driving seat and forced herself back to considering the mystery of Sophie's disappearance.

There were really several mysteries here. First, what had caused Sophie to leave Blackboys and go and live with Job and his family. Job seemed to think it was because Basil was pressuring her to act as hostess for him. But Tiggy had suggested she was upset at finding out he wasn't actually her father.

Was it true? Just because Jasper believed it was didn't prove anything.

It did make sense, though.

Quite apart from the detail of her name, Sophie had inherited nothing of Basil's blazing personality. Each of the other children had a cutting edge, even Jasper, that Sophie seemed to have lacked. Then there had been her mother's deep unhappiness. Darina had seen that herself. The fact that she hadn't left Basil did suggest he'd had some sort of hold on her.

The second mystery was why Sophie had left what seemed to have been a happy haven with Job and Nicola. Could either Paul or Martin have had anything to do with her disappearance? Darina could imagine the effect a passionate pass, for instance, could have on a sensitive girl but surely a word to Nicola or Job could have sorted things out and made sure she wasn't troubled again? No, it sounded much more as though Sophie had felt threatened. What by? Rape?

The word had come from nowhere and now reverberated in Darina's mind. Had Sophie been so sensitive she hadn't felt she could turn to her relations after such a violation? Perhaps she'd thought she mightn't be believed. Especially if it had been a family friend that had been responsible.

But Darina found it difficult to imagine the gentle Martin capable of rape. Paul, though, whilst on the surface coming over as someone rather weak, might just be the sort of man who, when insulted or cornered, could wind himself up into the sort of rage that precipitated rape.

But while Martin had been very tense during their talk in the embankment gardens, Paul had appeared relaxed. Darina was almost certain that Martin knew something he hadn't told her and that Paul had been completely open, about Sophie at any rate.

How strange both conversations should have taken place by the same river. But so much narrower and more attractive flowing by the restaurant than its dirty, if stately, progress through London.

Lastly there was the mystery of who Rory's father was. Poor Sophie, the result of one unfortunate affair giving birth as the result of another. For surely, whatever had happened it must have been unfortunate.

Jemima had stated that Rory was six weeks premature. Which meant that he had to have been conceived after Sophie left Job and Nicola. But what if he'd been only four week's premature, or even less? That would make it possible Sophie was already pregnant when she left Battersea and that Paul, for instance, could be Rory's father.

Rory had blond hair and blue eyes. Sophie's eyes and hair had both been brown. Paul had fair hair and blue eyes, less intense in colour than Rory's but perhaps the boy's would fade as he grew older. Paul was tall and Sophie had been short. What about Rory? You could tell from the length of a child's foot how tall he was likely to end up. Darina wished she had noticed the boy's feet. She looked at her watch. Nearly half past two. Could she call at Blackboys and check? It was so near. But if Jemima was at the office and a strange nanny was in charge, would Darina be allowed to see Rory and his gorgeous grin?

Forgetting that she didn't want anything to do with small children and refusing to acknowledge that a look at Rory's feet wasn't going to prove a thing, Darina let in the clutch and set off.

As she left the town behind, Darina could see autumn had well and truly arrived. Red hips and haws jewelled the hedgerows and the newly ploughed fields resembled dark brown corduroy. The late sun would soon be gone.

When she reached Blackboys, it was Jemima who opened the door. 'Oh, it's you!' she said, sounding both surprised and pleased. 'Thank God! Everything's total chaos here. The new nanny's just left, Dad's off on a business trip, Mrs Starr says it's not her job to look after Rory and you can't trust Jasper. Rory's furious because his lunch is late and I'm going out of my mind.'

She led the way through to the kitchen. Her feet were bare and she was wearing expensive looking designer jeans with a T-shirt.

Rory was in his high chair, banging the tray with a spoon and screaming, tears squeezing themselves out of screwed-up eyes, his cheeks flushed with temper.

At the other end of the table stood a stolid looking Mrs Starr, ignoring Rory as she fussed about making a cake, her lips firmly pressed together, an obstinate expression on her face. But her eyes were watchful.

'Oh, heavens,' groaned a harassed Jemima. 'Leave him for one minute and he thinks the world's come to an end.'

'Gah!' shrieked Rory, waving the spoon. 'Gah, gah, gah, raaaham!'

'OK, OK, OK!' Jemima went to the fridge and got out a small strawberry fromage frais. On a discarded plate Darina could see the remains of a fish finger. No gourmet baby foods in this house!

'Mrs Starr, are you sure you couldn't, just for a few days?' pleaded Jemima, sitting down beside the high chair and starting to push pink goo with astonishing efficiency down a now silent child who reached forward like a starving fledgling.

'Couldn't take the responsibility, miss,' Mrs Starr said firmly, carefully folding flour into a fruit-cake mixture.

'Well, do you think you could make us some coffee?' Jemima said, sounding at the end of her tether.

'Soon as I've got this in the oven, miss.' Mrs Starr gave the cake mixture a few more turns and reached for the prepared cake tin.

'I'll do it,' said Darina and filled the kettle.

Mrs Starr evened out the mixture, wrapped the tin with several layers of newspaper, secured them with string, placed the tin in a roasting pan lined with more paper, popped several layers of tin foil over the top and carefully placed the shrouded mixture into the oven. Then she got out two cups and saucers and started preparing the coffee tray, her lips firmly pressed together.

'Right, that's it,' announced Jemima as Rory gulped down the last of his dessert. 'It's rest time for you, my lad.' She hauled him up out of his high chair. 'Come upstairs with us,' she said to Darina. 'Take the coffee into the library, Mrs Starr, we'll have it there.'

Rory's room on the second floor was out of some fantasy child's kingdom. Murals from nursery rhymes decorated all the walls, there were silver stars on a blue ceiling, his cot was full of soft toys and a mobile of planes, space craft and shooting stars idly circled above.

When Rory realized he was being put into his cot, he howled, large tears sparkling on cheeks red with rage. Jemima tried to lay him down. He fought back and stood, screaming, clutching the top rail of the cot.

'You know you're tired,' Jemima told him coldly. 'What you need is a good sleep. Come on,' she said to Darina. 'As soon as we leave, he'll settle down.'

But Rory's outrage followed them down the stairs. In the library a tray of coffee stood on a low table. 'Heavens, I need this!' Jemima poured out the cups and handed one to Darina, then flopped into a chair. 'Christ, I must look a mess,' she muttered, pushing her short hair back from her face. 'This thing's got ketchup on it!' she pulled the T-shirt away from her chest in disgust, then levered herself swiftly up and walked with quick, jerky strides across to the window. 'I don't know what to do,' she said, sounding near to tears.

'Tell me about it,' Darina invited.

Jemima half sat on the narrow windowsill, her

hands gripping the wood, the knuckles white. 'I was nearly killed today,' she announced.

'What do you mean?' Darina couldn't be too alarmed, it was typical of the dramatic statements Jemima liked to make.

'I was crossing the road with Rory in his push chair and a car shot out of nowhere and nearly mowed us down!'

'Good heavens! Weren't you watching?'

'Of course I was! It was deliberate I tell you.' Jemima was near to tears. 'Dad says I've got to look after Rory while he's away, that we can't get another nanny until he gets back. I know what it is, he doesn't trust me to get the right girl. It's too much, Darina!'

'He trusts you to look after him,' Darina pointed out.

But Jemima wasn't listening. 'I'm not a nanny and I can't look after that boy night and day. And now this! I tell you, someone's after me.'

'It sounds like an accident,' Darina said comfortingly.

Jemima turned back to the window and started tapping it with her nail, staring at the leaves blowing down from the trees. 'I can't stay here and look after Rory, I've got to go, I've got to!' she repeated desperately. Then she swung round again, her face suddenly illuminated. 'Darina, this is your opportunity! Val told us yesterday that you're working on baby-food recipes for her. You take Rory and test your ideas. It's perfect!'

Oh, no, it wasn't! 'I don't know anything about babies,' Darina protested, listening to the screams that still floated down from upstairs. 'And what on earth would your father say?'

'Oh, he'd think it was a great idea! Anyway, he's all

excited about marrying Val. You know they announced their engagement last night?'

'Really?' Darina was startled, she hadn't thought Val would succumb to the lure of financial security. Then she told herself not to be cynical, after all, Val herself had said how attracted she was to Basil.

Jemima nodded. 'You better believe it. We had a family dinner here last night, champagne and the works. Val's daughter, Sally, came, all giggles and sucking up to Dad. He was thrilled, all over her as well as Val,' she said in disgust.

'Wasn't Val pretty pleased as well?'

'Oh, you know her, cool and contained. What Dad sees in her beats me.'

Darina remembered the hysterical woman in the kitchen. 'Jasper could tell you different,' she said.

'What do you mean? Jasper didn't say anything last night.'

So, he'd kept quiet about Val's loss of control. Darina warmed towards him. 'Well, why not get Val to look after Rory? After all, she'll have to after they get married, won't she?'

Jemima waved an impatient hand. 'She's going abroad tonight. Some conference or other.' She came back and flung herself into the chair again, her face pale and tense. 'Darina, you've got to. I'm frightened. Someone's after me. Leaving Rory with me means he's in danger too.'

Darina had never seen Jemima in such a state. There was a febrile excitement about her and her whole body was tense with some suppressed emotion. Was she really frightened for her life? Darina couldn't believe the traffic incident had been anything more than a near accident, after all, who could wish her dead? But Jemima didn't operate by the laws of logic.

Jemima leaned forward, hugging her upper arms, 'Please say you'll take Rory, Darina, please! Each for the other and never to rat, remember?'

Just suppose for a moment that the car had nearly run Jemima and Rory down deliberately. Just suppose that Darina's enquiries had frightened someone into trying to remove Jemima. Could she ever forgive herself if a second attack was successful? And Jemima did have a point about using Rory as a guinea pig for her baby-food ideas. A faint frisson of excitement ran through her as she thought of having the child all to herself. 'How long would it be for?' she asked cautiously.

'Oh, darling, that's wonderful, I knew I could count on you.' Jemima was instantly ecstatic, over the moon in her relief. 'Come upstairs and I'll get his things together, the sooner you take him over the better. He can sleep in the car.'

'Hang on a minute,' Darina protested. 'You do realize I won't be able to do any more poking around into where Sophie went and who could be his father while I have him with me, don't you?'

'Oh, you can still do that,' Jemima said airily. 'He plays perfectly happily by himself while you're on the phone and if you want to go out, you can take him with you.'

She made it all sound so simple!

'You'll have to tell me exactly what Rory's daily regime is, when he eats, when he has rests and goes to bed, when he should be taken out, all that.' Darina had only the dimmest idea of what an eighteen-month-old baby's life should be.

'Sure, Maeve wrote everything down for the next nanny and I made sure that stupid cow didn't take the instructions with her.'

It obviously took someone of character to remain in the Ealham employ for any length of time and Darina's respect for both Maeve and Mrs Starr increased.

Wondering if she was being a complete idiot, Darina followed Jemima up to the nursery, where Rory's screams had died down to a steady grizzle.

All Jemima seemed to think was necessary for her to take with the child was a packet of disposable nappies, some baby wipes and a change of clothes.

Darina had other ideas. 'How long before you get back from wherever it is you're going?'

'Only a few days. And if I'm not back by then, Dad will be.'

'Two days, that's my limit. After that you'd better have some other arrangement in place. Right, now I'll need far more clothes than that, and what about his cot? And his favourite toys? And that list Maeve made out?'

'Surely he can sleep in a bed?' Jemima argued. 'He's quite a big boy now.'

'Exactly,' Darina said grimly. 'If he's not in a cot, he'll be everywhere, I can't possibly leave his door closed. And what about a buggy? I can't carry him everywhere.'

'Big strong girl like you,' Jemima grumbled. But Darina refused to be deflected and finally Jemima agreed.

'What about a playpen?' Darina asked as Rory followed them down the stairs, negotiating the treads with confident agility. No longer forced to rest, he seemed to have recovered his temper and the angelic smile shone out.

264

'Oh, he doesn't like a playpen and Maeve said he was really too old for one.'

Darina sighed.

It took a good half hour to get everything together Darina felt she needed to take with her. Finally she and Jemima loaded everything into the back of the large Volvo station-wagon that was more used to coping with quantities of food than baby impedimenta.

'You'll need his car seat.' Jemima shot off round the house and came back carrying a padded plastic shell. She showed Darina how to fix it on the seat of her Volvo and together they strapped Rory in. 'One more thing.' Jemima was off again, back into the house.

Darina and Rory were left looking at each other. Rory had a most peculiar expression on his face. Darina, panicking, felt he was summing up the situation.

Jemima returned. 'If he gets very grizzly, try him with some of these.' She dropped several little boxes of raisins into Darina's hand. 'He loves them.'

Fruits of the sun, she thought, just the thing, concentrated sweetness and vitamins. 'You'd better tell me where you're going.'

Jemima shook her head. 'I don't even know myself. Look, you've got my mobile number and I've got yours so we can keep in touch. I promise you it will be all right. And you'll enjoy looking after Rory, he's a poppet.'

'If that's the case, why aren't you taking him with you?' Darina shot back.

'Darling, look what a performance it is.' Jemima gave a meaningful glance at the loaded back of the car. Now that it had all been organized, she seemed to have forgotten that she was frightened.

'Don't let anyone know you've got him,' Jemima said suddenly.

'I thought it was yourself you were frightened for. Who on earth do you think would try to harm him?' Darina didn't like this at all.

'I don't know, darling. But Dad's got pots of money, someone could be trying to kidnap him.' It was the first thing she'd said that made any sense.

Jemima reached up and hugged Darina. 'You're the greatest, really you are. I won't forget this.' Then she stuck her head through the open window and gave her nephew a kiss. 'Bye, Rory, be a good boy now. Gotta go,' she said and vanished.

Darina got into the car and looked at Rory. 'It's you and me now, kiddo. Whadya think?'

His eyelids drooped and a moment later he was asleep.

Thank the Lord, Darina thought and drove home very carefully.

Chapter Twenty

'And so you're convinced that Gerry Aherne was trying to blackmail Paul Robins?' William said. He'd returned in the mid-afternoon from a meeting with Superintendent Roger Marks to find Terry Pitman and Pat James waiting to tell him the results of the interviews they'd carried out that morning.

'Right, guv,' agreed Terry.

'And what's your opinion, sergeant?' William turned to Pat. She was looking particularly attractive that day, in a cinnamon coloured two-piece of some sort with a bright coral coloured scarf at her neck. It was peculiarly soothing the way he knew he could turn to her and not get a spiky response.

Still, since this case had come along, the team had at last begun working together, forgetting to feel aggrieved at being asked to pull their finger out.

'Yes, I think Aherne probably was,' Pat said quietly.

That was a surprise, somehow William hadn't expected Pat to back her colleague. In fact he was amazed they were still speaking to each other.

'I don't think, though, that Robins clocked him one,' Pat continued and gave Terry the sort of glance that said they'd disagreed strongly on this.

'Honestly, guv,' said Terry quickly, 'the bloke's got

all the motivation. First off, Aherne's threatening the existence of the firm. One word to Ealham his girlfriend has an arrangement with Robins and he takes his money elsewhere. Second off, if that happens, he loses not only his girlfriend but his money as well. His PR company will be looking pretty sick too; by his own admission Eat Well Foods is his major client!'

'All that could be said to go for the Douglas woman as well,' Pat said quietly. She looked at William. 'Ealham told you they both took sleeping pills. How far is it from Blackboys to the industrial estate? At that time of night, twenty minutes, no more. Allowing time to slosh around some petrol and strike a match, say an hour round journey. Neither of them can alibi the other.'

'The story Robins tells of investing money in her firm without shares or any formal acknowledgement certainly puts her into a rather different light,' William said slowly, remembering the charming woman they had interviewed. He would not have thought her capable of such devious behaviour. 'But we only have Robins's word that he did, indeed, invest his money in the firm.'

'If he was lying, he's a fantastic actor, guv,' said Terry.

Pat nodded as though she agreed with this. 'But if he isn't, and I doubt it myself, what a cool lady Douglas is. Talk about butter, ice cream would remain frozen in her mouth.'

William could only agree with her. 'Right,' he said. 'Terry, look into the bank accounts of both Robins and Douglas. See if you can match any outgoings with the monies that have been paid into Aherne's account. And see if you can find any trace of the money Robins claims he invested with Eat Well Foods. I can't see any justification at the moment for looking into Ealham's accounts, we'll encounter considerable opposition and I have no doubt that his cash drawings could easily hide any payments to Aherne. But we have a classic triangle here: Douglas, Ealham and Robins. Any of them could have an excellent reason for silencing a blackmailer. Sergeant, you and I will visit Douglas again.' He looked at his watch, half past four. 'She's off to some international conference tonight or tomorrow. Ring her now and say we need to speak to her immediately. Call her mobile number.'

Pat went off to phone, returning in a few minutes. 'She's at her flat, guv, packing for her trip. She says she could see us now if it's really urgent. Very helpful she sounded.'

Val Douglas would, William thought. That lady had managed to get where she was today by giving the impression of sweet co-operation. Inside, he was beginning to suspect, she was hard as tungsten.

There were one or two other details he had to attend to before they could leave, though, and by the time he and Pat set off, it was nearly five o'clock.

'How are you getting along with Terry?' he asked as Pat drove them to Val Douglas's flat.

'We're speaking,' Pat said without expression.

'He's a good detective,' William said, 'but tact is not one of his strong points.'

'Tact? He acts like a giant hedgehog determined to push people out of his path, all spikes and shove,' Pat said bitterly. 'He's the type who believes women are only good for two things and I'm not going to spell them out.'

'Most of it's due to his background,' William said after

a brief pause for thought. He didn't approve of revealing personal facts about officers but in this case he was certain it was the right thing to do. 'What I'm going to tell you is in confidence, I don't want it spread around the station.'

'Right, guv,' Pat said eagerly.

'Terry's mother abandoned him and his two younger brothers when he was six years old. His father took to drink, couldn't keep things together and the two younger boys ended up in care. Terry remained with the father. I believe there were a couple of failed relationships with other women but basically he was brought up without a mother by an alcoholic.'

Pat was silent for several minutes. 'It explains a lot,' she said finally. 'Thanks for telling me, guv. I shan't let it get around.'

He thought he could rely on her.

Then she said, 'By the way, guv, I missed a detail in my report on our interview with the nanny.'

William listened to her in dismay as she revealed the slip. How could he have failed to spot it? He'd always prided himself on his memory. Almost as bad was the fact that Pat revealed Terry Pitman was aware he'd missed something.

He spent the rest of the journey fuming in silence.

'This is it, guv.' Pat pulled up outside a respectable looking but by no means luxurious block of flats. Built in the thirties, William decided. The expanse of lawn around the block was more generous than would have been allowed in modern times but it needed cutting and weeds were growing out of the low wall running alongside the pavement.

According to the list in the foyer, Val Douglas lived on the top floor. A creaky lift took them up.

As they came out, they could hear two voices raised in argument, one male, one female. Then a front door opened and a very angry Basil Ealham emerged. 'You're a bitch, you know that? I'm not going to accept this!' Then he saw William. 'My God, what do you want now?' he shot at him, strode over to the lift and pressed the button. The doors opened immediately, he entered, the doors closed and he was gone.

Left standing in the doorway was Val Douglas, her hair mussed and lipstick smeared. She looked very upset as she stared at William. 'I'd forgotten you were coming,' she said abruptly. 'You'd better come in. I warn you, I haven't got long.' She went back inside the flat.

William suddenly became aware that the door of the next flat was slightly ajar. As he looked, a bright eye met his. Then the door slowly closed with a slight click.

He followed Pat through a small hall and into Val Douglas's living room.

This was square, without distinguishing features and furnished with more taste than cash. It looked as though redecoration had been needed for so long its owner had given up even thinking about it.

Val waved the two police officers towards a small sofa and a button back chair. She took the only armchair. She didn't offer them refreshment but sat biting her lip.

'A lover's tiff?' William offered.

Her eyes looked as though she'd been crying. 'None of your business.'

'If it affects the Eat Well Foods company I'm afraid it probably is,' he said calmly.

'My God, you want your pound of flesh, don't you?'

she said and sighed. 'I suppose everyone will know soon enough. I've broken off my engagement to Basil.'

'We didn't know you were engaged,' Pat said quietly.

She switched her gaze to the sergeant. 'Oh, yes, it happened yesterday. We had an official dinner last night. All the family, well, not quite all. My daughter Sally came,' her voice softened for an instant. 'She was really pleased I'd, as she puts it, found happiness. My other daughter is in Australia. Then we had Jemima and Jasper. Basil rang Job and Nicola but they declined the invitation. However, he said they sent their good wishes.' Her voice now was sardonic, almost sarcastic. 'We managed without them. Dom Perignon, Beluga Caviar, fillet of venison (so much more recherche than beef, my dear), and souffle Rothschild with real gold leaf. It was quite a meal.'

She made it sound as though the trappings had been more important than the reason for the celebration. Had she wanted a quiet evening a deux with her fiance? Had the family not proved as welcoming to the news as she'd hoped? The change in her voice as she'd mentioned Basil's children had been almost dramatic.

William had spoken to each of them and each had confirmed that Val had spent the night of the fire at Blackboys. Jemima had come over as intelligent, not particularly in favour of her father's liaison, as she'd termed it, but acknowledging she had little say in the matter. She'd said her father and Val had been in bed by the time she herself had returned around one thirty in the morning.

Jasper had been equally frank and told them he was merely living at home until he could afford to set up his own establishment. 'This rather spoils you for

272

the starving artist in a garret syndrome,' he'd said, encompassing the comforts of Blackboys with a wave of his hand. 'But as soon as my first substantial advance comes through, I'll be off. The old man can do what he likes.' Then he'd added, 'So, to answer your question, I was out until about eleven thirty Wednesday evening. No one was around when I got back. I went to bed and knew nothing more until morning.' It had all been said with an insouciance that suggested nothing his father did really mattered to him. So neither Jemima nor Jasper had actually seen Val but there was no good reason to doubt she and Basil hadn't been in bed as they claimed and were there when the call about the fire had come through.

'So you had a family celebration last night,' Pat said to Val. 'What went wrong today?'

'Oh, that was nothing,' she said with a fine attempt at lightness. 'By the time I get back on Monday, it'll all have blown over.'

William cleared his throat. 'Paul Robins has stated he invested one hundred thousand pounds in your company. Is that true?'

He'd expected her to deny all knowledge. Instead she slowly nodded. 'Yes, when I was first organizing the factory.'

'But we haven't found his name in the list of shareholders,' said Pat sharply.

'I used a nominee name,' Val said easily.

Pat leafed back through her book and read out a list of some six names. The last was Kate Douglas Ltd.

Val nodded. 'That's my elder daughter. Her shares and Paul's were invested together as a company. It was a tax move suggested by the accountant I had at the time.' Her gaze was limpid, full of candour.

Pat looked again at her notebook. 'The list of shareholder names for Kate Douglas Ltd does not contain that of Paul Robins,' she told Val.

Val looked fleetingly disturbed. 'It doesn't? I know Paul signed the right documents. Oh, dear, it's so long ago, at least three years. You'll have to ask my accountant about it, he handled all the ins and outs. He always has such good ideas for saving tax – within the law of course,' she added, sending them a glance from under her eyelids that William could only call coy.

'Perhaps you'll give me his name?' Pat raised her pencil.

Val went over to the desk and let down the front. Behind all looked neatly arranged, documents in the little niches, some papers on the base. She picked up an address book and leafed through it, then looked at William with wide eyes. 'I'm sorry, I've just remembered, he moved and I had his new address in the office. It's probably gone in the fire. That damned fire!'

'Just give us his name, I'm sure we can track him down,' he said steadily.

'Piers Maurice,' she said quickly. 'And Shaz, my secretary, knows where he is, she can give you the details tomorrow.'

What was the woman doing? Trying to cover up a devious plot to embezzle Robins's money, or revealing herself as someone who had little idea of accountancy? Whichever, it was interesting and suggested that Paul Robins had been speaking the truth.

'I'd like to return to the night of the fire in Eat Well

Foods,' William said. 'You say you spent both the evening and the night with Basil Ealham?'

She nodded. 'As I told you, I arrived at Blackboys about eight o'clock. Originally I had other plans. But Basil returned from abroad early and I cancelled them after he rang me at lunchtime.' She picked at the crease of her smart jeans. 'We had a quiet supper together, talked about plans for a new baby-food line for my company then went to bed about midnight.' She looked up at William. 'And that was it until my mobile rang at about five o'clock in the morning.'

'You slept in a double bed?' he asked.

She nodded again.

'Did you take a sleeping pill?'

Her eyes were suddenly alert, as if she saw where the questions were leading. 'Yes, I was very tired.'

'The phone woke you?'

'No, Basil did.'

'Then he's a fairly light sleeper?' William suggested.

A momentary hesitation before she nodded.

'But that night he says he took a sleeping pill as well.'

She shrugged. 'If that's what he says, then he did. Perhaps his aren't as strong as mine.'

'So if Mr Ealham left the bed while you were sleeping, you wouldn't be aware of the fact?' It was almost a statement.

'No,' she whispered, her eyes huge. 'Are you suggesting Basil set fire to my factory?' She plucked nervously again at her jeans.

'We're just investigating possibilities,' William told her.

'Well, even if I was sleeping deeply, I'm sure I would have known if he'd left the house!' She said it with an air of bravado.

The confidence with which she'd faced his questioning a week earlier seemed to have vanished. Because she'd had a row with Basil? And just which one of them had broken off the engagement?

'How long are you going to be away?' asked William abruptly.

'Away?' she repeated as though not quite understanding what he was saying. 'Oh, of course, the conference! I'll be back on Monday. I have to get ready,' she said abruptly. 'I have a taxi coming to take me to the airport.'

'You weren't expecting Mr Ealham to take you?' William asked, surprised.

'No, his plane leaves from Heathrow, mine from Gatwick.'

'We'd like to know where you can be contacted,' he said.

'Of course.' She went to the desk again. 'This has got all the details.' She handed William a leaflet promoting an international conference on food intolerances. 'I just hope you can find who was responsible for poor Gerry's death before I return.' Her voice was clipped, her mind obviously now on catching her plane.

Was he wise, letting her leave the country like this? But William knew he'd already decided that there was little risk. She would come back all right.

'What did you think, sergeant?' he asked as Pat drove them back to the station.

'That was a very different woman from the one we saw before.'

'Which one do you think broke the engagement and do you think they'll be getting together again?'

'Oh, it was her!' Pat was positive. 'He wouldn't have been nearly so angry if he'd called it off. He was a man who'd been thwarted and he didn't like it one bit. As to whether it will all be on again, that was a very angry man we saw. But she no doubt knows him better than we do.'

'That's true,' said William. 'But I'd say it'll be some time before he calms down.'

At the station, he left Pat writing up her notes and said he'd see her tomorrow. He knew she'd hoped he'd ask her out for a drink but he was exhausted. All he wanted was to get home and have Darina provide him with one of her delicious little meals, a glass of wine and an early night.

The hall seemed remarkably cluttered as he opened the front door. Before he could work out why, he heard a child crying. A very angry child. The noise came from the spare room next to his and Darina's. 'What the hell?' he said, taking the stairs two at a time.

The bed had been pushed aside and a cot faced the doorway.

A small child stood grasping the cot rail and crying noisily. The moment he realized he had an audience he raised the pitch of his voice, creasing his hot, flushed face into a mask of thwarted passion. The noise echoed round William's brain, preventing thought.

'Oh, darling, you're back!' said Darina from behind him.

'What on earth's going on?'

'I'm babysitting Rory for a couple of days. I can't get him to settle at all, I thought this might help.' She held up a cassette player. 'I haven't got any nursery rhymes but maybe this will do the trick.' She plugged the little machine in, set it near the cot and pressed a button. Mendelssohn's *Hebrides Overture* filled the room.

Rory continued to howl.

'I can't stand this,' William said abruptly. He picked the child up.

Rory stopped crying but his body shook as he continued to take deep, hiccuping breaths. He leant his head against William's chest. William sat down on the bed and held him gently.

'Is that a good idea?' Darina asked anxiously. 'Won't he just start crying again when you put him down?'

'We can't have him screaming away like that. Let's take him downstairs.'

'I don't really know what's best,' Darina said, sounding most unlike her normally decided self. 'I thought first he wasn't ready to go down, he slept in the car coming back. So I took him out and played with him. Twice. But each time I put him back, the screaming started again. I thought maybe if I left him he'd go off. But it just got worse. I don't think he's ever left Blackboys before.'

'Poor boy,' William said, liking the feel of the child in his arms. Rory had quietened right down now and was gazing fascinated at the cassette player. 'Let's go and have something to eat, shall we?' He rose and carried the boy downstairs.

The table in the kitchen was laid for two. 'Can you get us some wine? I daren't put him down,' he said as he settled himself in his usual place with the boy on his lap.

But Rory insisted on being lowered to the ground, then went straight for a cardboard box beside the fridge that appeared to contain a variety of toys. He pulled out several cars, a bag of building blocks and a bright yellow plastic telephone.

'He doesn't seem to be sleepy at all,' William remarked, watching as Rory made the telephone ring, again and again. 'What on earth are you doing babysitting?' he added after a moment. 'I thought you didn't like children.'

Darina poured out two glasses of wine then put on a pan of water and brought some prepared runner beans out of the fridge. 'I never said I didn't like children,' she protested, pushing her long hair back behind her ears. 'I just said I didn't want them yet. And every minute Rory's here, confirms that. He takes over totally.'

William watched Rory abandon the telephone, pick up a large motor car and bring it to him, knocking it hard on his knees.

'He wants you to wind it up,' Darina explained, heating a sauce on the stove. 'He's used to having every wish immediately gratified.'

'OK, lad, here you go.' William wound the key, set the car on the floor and watched it zoom off towards the kitchen door. Rory scampered after it, clapping his hands with glee.

It took four goes of that before Darina was able to place plates of hot ham with an orange sauce and the runner beans on the table.

'No, darling,' said Darina to Rory as he banged his car against William's knee again. 'You play with your bricks.' She started building a tower with the blocks, then left it to sit down and have her supper.

Rory proceeded to make clear that he wanted his car wound up again.

Somehow they managed to eat their supper and keep Rory amused.

William found the whole story of why Darina had brought the boy home quite odd. 'But Basil Ealham can afford to employ any number of nannies,' he said when she'd finished. 'So why doesn't he?'

'He's off on a business trip somewhere, doesn't know Jemima's gone away.' Darina sounded as doubtful as he was over the situation.

'That's another thing. Why on earth should she think someone's out to get her? Come on, darling, there's something here you're not telling me.'

He then listened with increasing incredulity as she told him how Jemima had hired her to find out who Rory's father was. Darina was mixed up in his murder case and she hadn't told him anything about it. William felt all his tiredness and frustration with their lack of progress build up in his chest like steam in an engine.

'So, instead of devoting yourself to your career, which is the reason you've given me for not starting a family, you're following futile leads in a way that threatens an official murder investigation,' he said coldly.

Rory looked up from the edifice he was building on the floor and started to cry. Darina picked him up and sat him on her lap, where he grizzled and fidgeted. 'I knew you'd object, that's why I didn't tell you.' She removed a long hank of cream coloured hair from Rory's little fist. 'I couldn't see that it had anything to do with your case. And you wouldn't discuss anything with me.' Darina sounded as angry as William felt. 'Ever since you started this job you've come home late, tired and ill-tempered. Why on earth shouldn't I try and find out something about Sophie's life before she died? It can't have anything to do with the fire in Val Douglas's factory, even if Paul Robins was involved with her.'

The name struck through the fog which was growing around William's anger and threatened to break his control.

'What do you mean? Are you saying Paul Robins was involved with Sophie Ealham?'

'Only that he took her out,' Darina said in a low voice as she reached down for one of Rory's toys to try to distract him. 'They met when Basil took her along on his first visit to Eat Well Foods.'

'You found this out and never told me?' William couldn't believe it.

'I haven't had a chance. I only spoke to him today.'

Rory looked from one to other of them and started crying again.

'Doesn't he ever sleep?' William asked furiously.

Chapter Twenty-One

Darina was wakened by the alarm. Her arm groped for the button and for a moment she lay there in the silence and wondered why it should feel so blessed.

Then she remembered. They'd gone to bed not speaking to each other. No sooner had Darina managed to drift off than Rory had started up.

'Oh, for Christ's sake,' William had said.

Darina had lain still and hoped Rory would go back to sleep. William had drawn the duvet over his ears.

After a few minutes Darina had slipped out of bed and gone through to Rory. He was sitting up in his cot, his face flushed and tear streaked, smelling. She got him up and changed him, wrinkling her nose as she removed the dirty nappy and wiped his bottom. 'Poor boy,' she said as his crying died down to the odd snivel. 'You must have been so uncomfortable.' She re-poppered his sleeping suit and picked him up. He felt warm and alive and his blue eyes looked back at her with interest. 'Time for beddy-bies,' she said and laid him in the cot again bracing herself for more cries. For a moment he looked unblinkingly up at her, then his eyelids dropped and he was asleep.

Darina stood there for several minutes looking at the long lashes that brushed perfect skin, the little hands closing and unclosing themselves like pale sea anemones beside his small, beautifully formed ears. Life starts with such simple demands, she thought: love, food, sleep and cleanliness equal happiness. Then, suddenly, it's all complicated. What happens?

Look at her, she thought miserably. Her life was in a complete mess and her relationship with William rapidly deteriorating. Soon they wouldn't be speaking to each other and she had this terrible feeling little Pat James was consoling him down at the station. Her food writing was getting nowhere and ideas were drying up. This investigation into Rory's parentage was annoying William and getting nowhere. Every time she thought she might have something, it slipped through her fingers. She was finding it more and more difficult to concentrate on getting behind what facts she had because she was worrying about her life and William's, not Sophie's. At the moment if the answer to the question of who Rory's father was burst in front of her three times lifesize, she doubted she could recognize it.

Wearily she went back to bed, to find William scratching his leg in his sleep. She gently took his hand away, found the tube of cream on his bedside table and carefully rubbed a little into the red and angry patch on the hairy flesh. Then lay down and closed her eyes.

It had seemed no more than minutes before Rory woke her again. This time William flung back the bedclothes and stomped off to the spare room. A few minutes later the crying had stopped and he was back. 'I put on the music, he seems to like that,' he said, slipping back into bed – and starting to scratch his leg again.

'Darling, do go and see that homoeopathic doctor, please?'

She could feel him stiffen beside her. 'How the hell do you think with a murder investigation on, I can find time to go and see a quack,' he ground out.

'It might help you, really!'

He turned away from her, humped up under the duvet and said nothing. But he had stopped scratching.

The next time Rory started, Darina was awake and next door in an instant and this time she took him back to bed with her. Now here he was, his little body lying between herself and William, still asleep.

'It seems very quiet, Rory not awake yet?' William groaned beside her.

'Look,' she said and showed him the baby.

William looked. 'You little monster,' he said. 'So that's what disturbed nights are all about.'

'He didn't seem to disturb you very much,' Darina said.

'No,' he admitted. 'After I turned on his music that time I never heard a thing. Tired, I suppose. Just shows . . .' His voice trailed off.

'Shows what?'

'How sometimes you don't know whether someone's in the bed with you or not,' he said without further explanation.

Rory woke just as William was leaving the house.

Darina was amazed at how long it took her to get a small child up, changed and fed. By the end of the process, coming on top of her disturbed night, she felt like a piece of linen after a day in the tropics, crumpled, flagging and not fit for use.

She consulted the piece of paper, written in a large,

unformed hand, that detailed Rory's regime. At some stage in the morning, it said, Rory would need a rest. So would she! Useless to imagine she could do any work.

It was another fine early autumn day.

The question was, should she abandon the search for Rory's father in the face of William's opposition.

No, she couldn't see how it could cut across his investigation into the food factory fire.

Darina went and found a jacket for Rory, fastened him into his car seat, put the baby buggy in the boot and set off for Ladbroke Grove. As she'd hoped, he had a sleep on the way there. She found somewhere to park, worked out how to open the buggy, then unfastened his seat belt. He opened his eyes and gave her his best grin, waving his arms and talking excitedly in his own special language.

Darina fastened him into the buggy and set off.

It was amazing how having a baby along made everything both so much easier and took so much more time.

Everyone wanted to talk to Rory. And he played up to his audience like a pro, smiling, clapping his hands and wanting to stroke dogs. Shopkeepers, assistants, restaurateurs, they all loved him. Which meant they wanted to give him a sweet, or a biscuit, anything. Darina had to work at persuading them to look at Sophie's photograph. She slipped the offerings into her pocket, 'for later', dreading a return of his tantrums of the previous evening.

But he seemed to have settled down. Nothing disturbed his temper. Half-way through the morning he even fell asleep again, his head on one side, his arms flopping as she manoeuvred the buggy up and down pavements and steps, into and out of shops.

Darina had no more luck that morning than she'd had before. No one she spoke to could remember seeing Sophie. She began to feel sorry for police who had to conduct house-to-house inquiries and longed for someone, anyone, to say they recognized the girl in the photograph. Was this exercise going to be a complete waste of time?

Lunchtime neared.

There wasn't much more of this part of Ladbroke Grove to cover. Darina found herself outside a small restaurant that offered reasonably priced French food, made a quick decision and entered.

'Do you mind babies?' she asked the young girl who came forward.

'*Mais, non!*' she said. 'He is so beautiful.' Nobody else was in the restaurant yet and the girl fussed over settling Rory into a high chair she produced from the back. Darina wondered just how many restaurants there were in London that would welcome a child so whole-heartedly.

She looked at the menu. Lamb and herb sausages, she was assured, were made in house, and served with julienne of courgette and carrot. Darina reckoned Rory could eat all that and ordered an adult- and a child-sized portion.

The sausages were delicious. Darina cut one into tiny pieces with the courgette and carrot and Rory ate his with gusto. Then she considered dessert. All the experts said it wasn't good to give small children food with a high sugar content. Which meant a chocolate terrine with a coffee creme anglaise had to be turned down. Likewise the raspberry sorbet. But they did have some fresh strawberries. Darina ordered a portion and mashed up a little with cream for Rory, which went down well. Darina ate the rest of the strawberries herself without cream. Babies might need fat, she definitely didn't.

As they ate, she talked to Rory. 'The seasoning of the sausage is really excellent,' she told him. 'Can you tell exactly what's in there?' He looked back at her with wide eyes and she was sure he shook his head. 'Not sure I can,' she said delightedly. 'But I think there's definitely some onion and parsley, a little fresh coriander and just a hint of tarragon. Ah, I see you agree with me.' Rory chuckled at her and opened his mouth for more.

Altogether Darina found she was enjoying herself hugely. While they ate, the restaurant filled up around them and Rory drew interested looks. No Prada bag or Gucci belt would have drawn such attention.

When the waitress brought her bill, Darina showed her the snapshot of Sophie.

'I'm sorry, I work here only short time. I ask for you.' She disappeared out to the back.

'He come soon,' she told Darina a few minutes later.

'Soon' proved an optimistic forecast. Normally she wouldn't have minded waiting but keeping Rory amused proved more and more difficult as he got bored with being in the high chair. She tried letting him get down and wander about but a couple of businessmen were far from amused when he pulled at one of their trousered legs. She rescued him with many apologies, took Rory back to the table, sat him on her lap and offered him the cruets to play with. Then let him go through her handbag. Just as the entire contents had been placed on the table and she was thinking she'd have to give up, a middle-aged man in a checked shirt and jeans came to the table. A large hand placed the snapshot on the table in front of Darina. 'This girl not work here,' he said and his accent was also French, 'but maybe I see her. Why you want to know?'

So used was Darina to receiving a negative response to her enquiries, for a moment she failed to take in what he'd said. Then it sank in.

'This is her son,' she said eagerly as the man ruffled Rory's hair. 'She was called Sophie. Unfortunately, she died giving birth and I'm trying to find out where she was living and working before that. It was somewhere round here,' she added.

The man ran a thick finger down Rory's cheek. 'Beautiful boy.'

'She ate in here, did she?'

'Maybe.' He picked up the snapshot again and studied it, glancing at Rory as though to detect a likeness.

Something was holding him back from telling her more.

'Was she with anyone?'

'Yes,' he said, almost reluctantly.

'A man?'

No hesitation now. 'Of course.' His look said for a girl as lovely as Sophie not to have been with a man would have been against nature.

'Young, middle-aged, old?'

The Frenchman gave her a self-deprecating smile, 'I say he not old, he about my age.' He twinkled at her. Then it was as though he'd come to a decision. 'He often in here. Sometimes with wife. But two, three times with this girl.' He tapped the snapshot.

'Do you know his name?'

Again the hesitation. 'No, mademoiselle, no, I do not.'

That was nonsense, of course he knew the man's name. But if he was a regular customer, the restaurateur probably wouldn't want to tell her.

She decided to try her luck. 'Monsieur Price will be very glad you are so discreet,' she said.

He was very still for the briefest of moments. Then, 'Mademoiselle, I do not say it is Monsieur Price.'

'No, I understand,' she assured him with a big smile. 'Come, Rory, we've got to go. The meal was delicious,' she added, setting the boy on the floor.

The *patron* came and helped her sort out the levers of the buggy. In no time Rory was settled back in his seat and Darina was on her way.

Back in her car, Darina got out her mobile and rang Martin Price. 'I've got to see you again,' she told him without ceremony.

'There's nothing more I can tell you,' he protested.

'I think there is. I've just had lunch at *La Bonne Auberge* just off Ladbroke Grove.'

There was a long silence. Then a tired voice said, 'All right, where do you want to meet?'

'The embankment gardens where we walked.' She looked at her watch. 'In three quarters of an hour.'

'I've got a meeting,' he said.

'Cancel,' she said shortly. 'It can't wait. Of course, I could always call on your wife,' she added as he started to protest.

She felt a heel but what else was she to do? She

couldn't possibly meet him after work, who'd look after Rory? By then he'd be needing to be bathed and have his supper. And she needed to wrap up this investigation so she could get out of William's hair.

Martin Price made up his mind. 'All right, but make it in an hour,' he said.

'OK,' she agreed and rang off before he could think of any more conditions.

It wasn't difficult to find a free parking meter on the embankment.

Rory had fallen asleep during the drive from Ladbroke Grove, the motion of the car seemed to be a great soporific, and he hardly woke as Darina manoeuvred him out of his seat and into the buggy. Strapped into place, he surveyed the world through half-closed eyes as she pushed him along the pavement towards the gardens. She was getting quite used now to avoiding hazards such as shopping baskets and briefcases, all liable to knock the side of the buggy or attract Rory's curious attention.

By the time they reached the gardens, Rory was awake and looking around him with interest. 'Dog!' he said suddenly. Darina was sure it was 'dog' and not his favourite 'da'. He pointed to a perky little szchitzu with a pink bow holding up the long hair on its head, the rest of its coat cut short for summer wear.

Darina got Rory out of the buggy and held him by the hand as he set off towards the little dog. Its owner appeared to be a well-dressed middle-aged woman. 'Come on, Puzzle,' she said, yanking on a long lead, as Rory lurched towards the dog with happy cries.

'Can he say hello?' asked Darina.

After a moment's pause, the woman smiled and

stopped, allowing Rory to pat the small animal, who frisked enchantingly and tried to lick his face. Rory, backed away with excited squeals, then came forward again, his hands outstretched.

Suddenly someone shouted out, 'Hey, isn't that your buggy?'

Darina turned, to see a couple of teenagers in jeans, baggy T-shirts and shaved heads moving off with Rory's chariot.

'Stop!' she cried. 'That's mine!' Then she scooped up Rory and dashed after them.

The two boys gathered speed, heading for the exit next to the Savoy Hotel. Normally fast, Darina found herself hampered by having to carry Rory. She made up for her lack of speed by shouting at the top of her voice, 'Stop! Thief!' in a time-honoured manner. Heads turned as she charged past but nobody seemed willing to help. In her arms Rory started to cry. She clutched him tighter and tried to run faster.

Then, just as she thought they'd get away, a burly man coming in the opposite direction grabbed at the buggy. 'Not yours,' he said and wrenched it away, holding it in front of him like a combined shield and weapon.

For a moment the youngsters hesitated, assessing the possibilities.

He hefted the buggy challengingly, his shoulders broad under his bright blue anorak, his bony face threatening. 'Don't mix with us, mister,' one cried and they darted off.

'Oh, thank you,' Darina gasped. 'I only took my eye off it for a moment. I never realized . . !' She collapsed on to a bench with Rory and tried to soothe him.

'Can't afford to take your eye off anything these days,' the man grunted. 'All right, are you?'

'Yes, thanks,' she said, then saw Martin approaching. 'Here's my friend!'

The man looked at Martin with an uncertain expression. And Darina had to admit that with his creased face, narrow shoulders and grey suit he looked the sort of ineffectual man who'd be useless in a crisis. 'OK, if you're sure you're all right, I'll be off,' her rescuer said and left, walking with firm steps, hands in pockets.

Martin hadn't noticed anything. 'Sorry I'm late,' he said, sounding as out of breath as she was. 'Damn phone wouldn't stop ringing.'

'Not to worry,' she said and set a wriggling Rory on the ground. She felt she knew how Jemima had got into such a state. What if those youngsters had wanted to snatch Rory instead of just his buggy?

Martin sat himself down with a small sigh and watched the boy set off in the direction of some pigeons. They fluttered off and settled again a little way away. Rory followed. Darina went and grabbed his hand. The buggy incident had thoroughly unsettled her. 'You'll never catch them,' she said as she led him back to the bench. She sat down, took a ball from her bag and threw it very gently towards him. 'I need one of those retractable dog leads,' she told Martin.

He looked at the fair-haired boy. 'Is he yours?' he asked.

Rory pounced on the ball with delight and staggered forward with it to Darina. 'Can't you guess who he is?' she said.

Martin took the ball from her and Rory fixed his big blue eyes on him and moved away, excitedly clapping his hands together, waiting for him to throw it. But Martin just sat looking at the child. 'Sophie's,' he said and it wasn't a question. 'Sophie's son.'

'Yes,' said Darina.

Rory ran forward and grabbed at the ball, chattering away. Then he tried to throw it. The ball dropped more or less at his feet.

Darina scooped him up, sat him on her lap and felt in the pocket of her jacket for one of the tiny boxes of raisins Jemima had given her.

Martin's attention was on the child, the deep pouches under his eyes prominent as he stared at him. 'I knew, of course, that she'd had him before she died.'

'Poor Sophie,' said Darina, feeling the solid round-ness of Rory, now for once still as he explored how to open the little box. 'Did you know she was pregnant?'

'I, well, yes I did,' he confessed, his eyes never leaving the boy. 'Though you could hardly tell, not even towards the end. She was so small and wore these loose clothes. It wasn't until . . .' His voice died away.

'Until you made love to her,' Darina said softly. Her panic had subsided now and she was beginning to feel the end of her quest was in sight.

Martin's hooded lids dropped over his eyes and he said nothing.

'Why don't you tell me from the beginning,' sug-gested Darina. Rory had now managed to open the box and was delicately fishing out the raisins one by one and popping them in his mouth. 'Did you find her some-where to live after she left Job and Nicola's?'

Martin stared at a discarded snack-bar wrapper on the dusty ground. His hands were loosely clasped between his legs and for the first time Darina noticed he

293

wore a signet ring. There was a long pause. At last he heaved a great sigh and said, 'I suppose I knew it would all come out at some stage. I just hope Eleanor doesn't have to know.'

'Your wife?'

He nodded. 'Over the last year or so, things have been so much better between us.'

Darina wondered what his wife was like. All she could remember hearing about her was that she'd blamed Martin for the death of their son.

He raised his narrow shoulders, gave another big sigh then said, 'I was as surprised as everybody else when Sophie disappeared.'

'But you were in love with her,' Darina stated, now sure of her ground.

'It crept up on me,' he said in wonder. 'I didn't realize until I ran into her one evening in Ladbroke Grove, about four months after she'd disappeared. I'd gone out to get some wine, some friends had just rung and announced their arrival and we didn't have any. I was on my way back when she literally bumped into me. She'd been buying some food at a little supermarket that stays open late. A bag burst and oranges scattered on the pavement. I helped her pick them up then suddenly recognized her. It was such a wonderful surprise! And she seemed pleased to see me.' The depressed lines of his face lifted for a moment.

'She must have known you lived round there.' Rory finished eating his raisins and laid his head against Darina's chest. The feel of the weight against her breast was oddly satisfying, she tightened her grip around him slightly as he closed his eyes.

Martin nodded. 'When she was with Job and Nicola, I

took her to the Portobello Road market once. I thought it might amuse her. And then I drove her around North Kensington and showed her the Grand Union Canal. I also pointed out my street – but I didn't show her which was my house. I, well, I thought she might get the wrong idea. Anyway, as I gave her back the oranges, I asked her what she was doing and she suddenly panicked and got all upset. Thought I was going to tell her family.'

'What did you do?'

'Promised her I wouldn't and persuaded her to come and have a drink with me in a nearby pub.'

Darina had a sudden vision of his wife waiting at home, the friends arriving, and Martin sitting in the pub with Sophie and the wine.

'What did she tell you?'

Martin ran his hands down his well pressed trouser legs. 'She wasn't very coherent. She kept on asking me to promise I wouldn't tell anyone where she was. I swore I wouldn't and after a bit she calmed down. I tried to get her to tell me where she was living but she got all upset again, so I backed off. But I got her to agree to have lunch with me the following Saturday.'

'What about your wife?' Darina asked. 'Didn't she want to know what you were up to?' She couldn't imagine William suddenly taking off at lunchtime for a date with another girl. But then, she thought suddenly, how many Saturdays recently had he worked? If he'd taken someone out to lunch, she'd never know! It was an unsettling thought.

'That was when things were at their worst between us. When Eleanor returned from her mother's she told me she couldn't see we had any future. I'd persuaded her to stay and try for a bit longer. But it wasn't working.

I need hardly say when I got back that night, the frost practically sent me into cold storage. No, at that time Eleanor didn't care what I did.' He mulled that over for a little.

'So what happened next?'

'We met for lunch and Sophie seemed really happy to have someone to talk to.'

Rory was now asleep and Darina slightly shifted him into a more comfortable position on her lap, then studied Martin's lined face, noting the brown eyes and the long ears. Rory didn't look like him at all but, then, genes were funny things. Maybe they could skip a generation or two.

'Look, you don't want to know about Sophie and me, what you need is where she was living and who she was living with,' Martin said rapidly, turning towards her. 'You want to know who Rory's father is.'

Darina was startled. 'But aren't you his father?'

'Me?' Martin gave a short laugh. 'My dear, if only I was!'

Chapter Twenty-Two

'I had mumps just before I met Eleanor. Destroyed my ability to father children.'

'But,' stammered Darina, 'your son?' She floundered, the puzzle Sophie had left eluding her once more.

'Wasn't mine.' Martin stared at the ground again. 'That was half the trouble. After I'd recovered and the doctor had told me the worst, I was very upset. A mutual friend introduced Eleanor and I poured it all out on our first date. She was very sympathetic. Later she told me she was pregnant by some man she had no intention of marrying and asked if I'd like to be its father in every way other than biological. It seemed a gift from the gods. I mean, Eleanor was intelligent, attractive and everything I thought I wanted in a wife, and she could give me a child. We married a few weeks later. When Charles was born I was over the moon. Until that terrible accident.' He paused and twisted his hands together. 'That's not true, actually, things had started going wrong before that. I found out afterwards that Charles's real father had reappeared and Eleanor felt I didn't really match up to him. He mightn't have been husband material but he was sinfully attractive. That was her phrase, sinfully attractive. I, well, I was reliable. Until I allowed Charles to get run over.' He put his face in his hands, grinding the heels into his deepset eyes. 'God, I've relived those moments so often. If only we'd left home five minutes earlier, if only I hadn't gone back for my library tickets, if only I'd had a tighter grasp on his hand. But, there it was, we were on that particular piece of pavement at that particular moment in time. He saw a friend over the other side of the road, pulled free and ran straight under a speeding car. I shall hear the screech of those brakes in nightmares until the end of my life. And Eleanor told me I hadn't cared, that because Charles wasn't my son, I'd let him be run over. For months it was like living with an iceberg. Then her mother had the accident and Eleanor had to go to her; I thought it would give her a chance to get away and perhaps remember the good times we'd had together; instead she concentrated on all the bad.'

There was nothing Darina could say. She sat with Rory's warm weight against her and let Martin wrestle with his demons.

'Anyway,' he said heavily, 'that's all in the past now. But I wanted you to know why Sophie was like, well, a fine shower of rain on parched earth, if you can forgive a florid analogy.'

'I think it's rather good,' Darina said gently. She could see exactly how the gentle, loving, undemanding Sophie had been what tormented Martin had needed at that time.

'That first lunch we had, Sophie told me she was working in some record shop down Notting Hill Gate.' Right to the south of Notting Hill! Darina knew she would never have managed to work her way down there. 'And that she was living just round the corner from where we ran into each other. She told me,' there was remembered pain in his voice, 'she told me she was living with a young man who'd befriended her.'

'Befriended her?'

'She didn't tell me how then, just that he'd offered her somewhere to live. She wanted to know how things were going between Eleanor and me and I poured everything out. She was so warm, so sympathetic. As sympathetic as Eleanor had been when I first met her. By the end of lunch Sophie seemed quite relaxed and she gave me her telephone number. She said she was working the following weekend but perhaps we could have a drink one evening. And then Eleanor walked out saying she wanted to give her failed love affair another chance. After that, well, Sophie was the only bright spot in my life. I suggested she come round one Saturday night, said I'd cook for her.' He gave Darina a ghost of a smile. 'I'm not much good in the kitchen, I went to Marks and Sparks and bought everything ready made. They're very good,' he said anxiously, as though fearing she'd contradict him.

'I'm sure Sophie thought it was wonderful not having to cook,' Darina assured him. She remembered what Jemima had said about Sophie being half-starved. Had the only times she'd eaten been with Martin?

'When eventually I saw where she was living, I wondered how she could stick it.' He looked at Darina. 'Sophie stayed the night with me. She just asked if I'd like her to, as though it was the most natural thing in the world. And it was as if I'd been invited into a warm and brightly lit room after being condemned to hang around outside in the cold. I wanted her to move in with me but she said she couldn't leave Noah.'

'Noah?'

'The boy who'd befriended her. That was the night she told me what had happened after she'd left her brother's. We were in bed together and I think she felt safe in a way she hadn't for a long time.'

To be in bed with another woman's husband and to feel safe! What had Sophie been running away from? 'So why did she leave?'

Martin moved uncomfortably on the seat. 'She wouldn't tell me. "I couldn't stay, I couldn't," she kept saying. She got terribly upset. I held her and told her it didn't matter. She was so small and slight in my arms. Eleanor is quite tall,' he glanced at Darina, 'a little like you.'

Darina decided this was a compliment.

'Sophie said when she left Job and Nicola her only thought was that I might be able to help. She managed to get to Ladbroke Grove and then realized that she didn't know which my house was. She walked up and down my road, hoping I might come along. But then she remembered that I was Job's friend and would probably tell him where she was. She couldn't think of anyone she could trust, she said. She didn't have much money and was sure if she used her credit cards, her father would be able to trace her.'

'She wasn't altogether stupid, then,' Darina said. She tried to imagine how hopeless Sophie must have felt, alone and with nowhere to go.

'Sophie wasn't stupid,' Martin said with sudden passion. 'I told you that before. She was very sensitive and not very bright but she wasn't stupid.' He thought about this, then said again, 'No, not stupid. But that night she said she thought that life was no longer worth living. So she went and found her way to the canal. She was going to jump in. "I thought I wouldn't have to worry any more," she said and told me her mother had committed suicide. Apparently Sophie had always thought it was her fault. I think she felt committing suicide herself would somehow wipe out her sense of guilt.'

'Oh, poor girl!' Once again Darina tried to imagine what had happened to drive her to this desperate state. 'What happened to stop her?'

'She met Noah. Heaven only knows what he was doing there, probably buying drugs. He asked her if she'd got a light, typical of Noah.' Martin's voice was angry. 'Goes to buy a joint without having a match! When she said she hadn't any, he asked her what was wrong, said he could see something was and he'd like to help. Apparently they were the first friendly words she'd heard all day and made her burst into tears. Noah got the story out of her and, I'll say this for him, he got a grip on things. He took her to his hovel and looked after her. Gave her one of his joints, calmed her down, then found her something to eat. After that, she said, things didn't seem quite so awful and so she stayed with him.'

He made Sophie sound like an autumn leaf, blown by the wind, first one way, then another, entirely at the mercy of events.

'And she found a job.'

Martin nodded. 'Apparently it had been very difficult without any qualifications or experience but this shop needed part-time help. It was hard work being on her feet all the time but she liked being useful, she knew quite a lot about pop records and it was exciting earning money. I think most of it went on drugs for Noah, though. Food never seemed to feature much in her life.'

Poor little rich girl, Darina thought. 'When did you realize she was pregnant?' she asked.

Martin looked bleak. 'That first night I slept with her. I could remember exactly how Eleanor's body had looked and felt in the early stages.'

Darina glanced down at the sleeping Rory, at the curve of his fair eyelashes, the rosebud mouth. 'Was she sleeping with Noah as well?'

'Yes,' he said, his mouth drooping.

'My,' Darina commented.

'I know,' Martin said despairingly. 'She said we both needed her and it seemed natural.' That word again.

'Presumably if she was spending nights away, Noah knew about you?'

'She told him straight away, she said lies never got anyone anywhere.'

Had that been a reference to the way she'd been deceived over her parentage? 'Did you meet him?'

'Yes,' Martin said in a low voice. 'After she refused to move in with me, I insisted. I wanted to know who she was involved with.'

'What was he like?'

Martin shrugged helplessly. 'What can I say? He's a drop-out, a druggie. He lives for the moment and in total chaos. He has one of these charity housing flats, the rent's very low but even that he finds difficulty keeping up with. Sophie must have been a real godsend. There she was, working away and he just sat around smoking pot and snorting cocaine and no doubt trying anything else he could lay his hands on. Sophie said he earned money every now and then but it can't have been much.' He looked down at his hands, turning them around as though he'd never seen them before. 'I got angry with her when I realized she was pregnant. I hadn't met Noah then but she'd told me enough to know that he'd be a hopeless father. I said some pretty unforgivable things and she just sat in the middle of the bed, looking at the tiny curve of her stomach between her bony hips and wept. The tears just ran down her cheeks. So I held her and promised that everything would be all right.'

But everything hadn't been all right. 'What did you do?'

'I asked her to marry me!' Martin almost shouted out the words. Several people looked round but that was all. Darina could see what an ordinary group they must appear. A man and his wife and their child, probably fighting about some dreary domestic detail, or the fact that the man was out of work, for why else would he be sitting on a bench by the embankment on a weekday afternoon?

'I begged and pleaded with her. I told her my marriage was over, that Eleanor wasn't going to return. And she gave me this wistful little smile and said I might think I wanted to marry her but it wouldn't work. Then, quite suddenly, she cheered up and said I wasn't to worry, she'd manage things.'

How could he not have told Sophie's family? Darina wondered. Or at the very least helped her change her lifestyle. Then decided that Martin was someone who found it difficult to accept responsibility. 'According to Jemima, Sophie wasn't getting proper ante-natal care. Do you know if she was going to a clinic?'

Martin ran a hand impatiently through his thinning hair. 'She said she'd been to a doctor but he'd asked so many questions and wanted her to have a blood test. It seemed to worry her that. I tried to explain how it was all routine but she got upset, said giving birth was a completely natural process and that she'd got a book from the library! I didn't like to worry her and I thought there was plenty of time to get her used to the fact she needed medical attention, so I left it.'

'Didn't your wife, Eleanor, tell you how regularly she went to the clinic when she was having her baby?' asked Darina, amazed at his attitude.

'Well,' Martin ducked his head, avoiding her eyes, 'she kept all the details very private. She made it sound as though pregnancy was something men had nothing to do with. And I wasn't the father so I didn't think I had any right to pry. After all,' he added more strongly, 'I was working all day, how was I to know how often she went?'

Darina gave up.

'Anyway,' Martin continue, 'every time I asked how she was, Sophie said she was all right, everything was under control. I had to go away on business to the Far East for nearly a month. When I got back, I was horrified; her hands and feet were so swollen. I'd given her a ring and it was buried in flesh. I had to take her to a jeweller to have it cut off. I asked her what on earth she'd been doing and she burst into tears and told me unless I stopped going on at her, she'd leave. I was terrified I'd lose her again and I didn't know what to do.' He looked distracted. 'I was sure she needed a doctor. Eventually I took her back to Noah's. Then I contacted my own doctor and persuaded him to call on her with me the following night. But she wasn't there. Noah said he'd thought she was with me. The doctor said we'd wasted his time and went off in a huff. I didn't know what to do. I rang Noah the following day, still no news. He didn't even seem worried, said she'd come back when she was ready!' Martin's voice expressed his disgust at this attitude. 'Then, just as I was getting ready to phone the police and the hospitals, Job rang and said Sophie had died. I was devastated.' He buried his face in his hands again.

Darina held Rory tight and shivered.

Martin dropped his hands and sat back. He seemed exhausted. 'It was ages since I'd seen Job. They knew about Eleanor leaving, of course, and Nicola kept asking me round but I made excuses. I didn't feel I could face them, not when I knew where Sophie was.'

Darina said nothing. She found it almost impossible to understand how he could have failed the girl in the way he had.

'And did you tell Noah?' she asked, expecting to hear he hadn't.

'Yes, I went round there. Told him everything. Except, I said the baby had died. I couldn't stand the thought of someone like Noah being involved with Sophie's baby,' Martin burst out. Darina looked down at the happily sleeping Rory in her arms. 'Would you want him to have a drug addict for a father? Much better that he should think himself an orphan, brought up with all the advantages the Ealhams could give him.'

'They didn't do Sophie much good,' Darina told him ruefully.

Martin looked intently at her, his face more like a bloodhound's than ever. 'But aren't they a better alternative than some sleazy flat in Ladbroke Grove?'

'And you're sure Noah is Rory's father?'

He nodded vigorously. 'The timing fits. Job told me Rory was premature. And I knew Sophie, she couldn't have been sleeping with anyone else. No, Noah's his father, God help him.'

Darina felt depressed. She had the answer but it wasn't going to help. 'Couldn't Rory know who his father is and be protected from him at the same time?'

'What if Noah went to the courts and insisted on custody? You know what the law is like, it's giving all sorts of rights to the father these days.'

'Can I have Noah's last name and his address?'

A mulish look came over Martin's face and for a moment she thought he was going to refuse. She looked at him challengingly and, true to form, he caved in, brought out a small notebook and gave her the details.

Darina managed to find paper and pencil in her bag without waking Rory and wrote them down. Then she drew the buggy towards her and gently lowered the still-sleeping child in. 'When did your wife return?' she asked as she did up the straps.

'About a year ago,' he said. 'She just turned up, said it hadn't worked with the chap she'd gone off with, that she was sorry she'd been so rotten to me over Charlie's death and could we please try again.'

'You must have been very pleased.' What a wimp the man was, let anyone trample all over him!

'The best thing of all was she agreed to try artificial insemination. Now she's six months pregnant.' Martin's face was transformed, the depressed, hangdog look gone. 'I shall have a child after all.' He looked warily at her. 'You see why I'm so anxious Eleanor shouldn't hear anything about this?'

'You mean, you haven't told her about Sophie?' Darina was shocked.

'She thinks I was faithful while she was away,' he muttered.

'Well, I shan't tell her but these things have a way of getting out,' Darina said. 'Remember what Sophie said, lies never get you anywhere?'

He looked unconvinced.

Big drops of rain began to fall. 'Oh, dear,' Darina said, 'I'd better run.' She started pushing the buggy fast towards Westminster Bridge. Martin kept pace beside her. 'You promise you won't tell I knew where Sophie was and everything?' he repeated.

'If I can keep you out of it, I will,' she told him. The drops were turning into real rain and she started running.

Chapter Twenty-Three

Back home Rory demanded Darina's full attention.

She was giving him broccoli with minced ham in a cream sauce for supper. She reckoned she'd worked things out rather well. The ham was left over from the previous evening's supper and she'd worked out the baby food recipe while waiting for William to come home.

Which was as well because it proved no easy task to mince ham, make a white sauce and cook broccoli with Rory proclaiming how hungry he was. She gave him a bread stick, sat him on the kitchen floor with his toys and got down to preparing his evening meal.

It was the hardest cooking she'd ever done. Rory was everywhere. Opening kitchen cupboards, taking out bowls and plates and banging them together. Rubber bands linking handles together solved that one, much to Rory's disgust. The floor became a minefield, littered with the toys. If she turned her attention too whole-heartedly to what she was doing, Rory was out of the kitchen, through the hall and into the drawing room, with all its little knick-knacks. He proved astonishingly adept at opening doors and finally Darina had to lock the drawing-room door, which meant Rory went for the stairs instead. And every time she had to interrupt her cooking, it meant she had to wash her hands again before returning to the stove.

It didn't take long to convince Darina that the only way to produce food for Rory was while he slept. Gourmet convenience baby food suddenly seemed highly desirable.

Finally she was able to leave the prepared food in a cool place and take him up for a bath. That was fun.

She'd found a baby bubble bath in the supermarket the previous day and he splashed happily while she washed him, hair and all. Then dried him in a big, warm, fluffy towel, playing peek-a-boo. It was amazing how such simple games could give so much pleasure to them both! Then it was time for a clean nappy, the sleeping suit and a cardigan so he wouldn't get cold.

Finally Darina reheated a portion of the ham and broccoli in the microwave, then had to wait until it cooled sufficiently before she could anxiously offer up the first mouthful.

Rory looked at the loaded spoonful suspiciously, his head on one side. Then opened his mouth, accepted the portion, swallowed it – and opened up for more.

Darina glowed with success and put a big tick on the recipe, now spattered with grease and bits of broccoli.

How well, she wondered, would it take to mass production? The broccoli could have a tendency to go to mush but with careful cooking and folding in on a batch principle, it should work. But if it was made with a huge machine paddling it all together, she reckoned it might taste all right but the texture would be nothing. Who was going to win out over the production method – Val or Basil?

And if it was Val, with no preservatives, the

distribution would have to be handled very carefully. It would surely add to the cost. Still, wonderful for mothers to know they were giving their children food as pure as if they'd made it themselves. Darina could now understand the charms of fish fingers.

Rory finished the ham and Darina got out one of the fruit fromage frais without extra sugar she'd so carefully chosen, and fed that to Rory. Then she looked at the E numbers on the carton. Surely pure, plain yoghurt with some fruit puree added would be better for him? Something else for Val to produce, perhaps. Finally Darina heated up a bottle of milk and gave it into his eager hands while she gathered up the toys from the floor.

Boy, did babies take up time! Three hours had elapsed since they'd got back home from the embankment. And she was utterly exhausted. Jemima's claim that Rory spent so much time sleeping Darina would be able to do everything she wanted was nonsense. Darina wondered how much Jemima had had to do with him.

Then wondered why she hadn't heard from her. She'd expected a call Thursday evening. Then that there'd be a message on her answering machine when she'd returned after her meeting with Martin. Nothing. Her mobile hadn't rung either. Darina picked up the kitchen receiver and checked the line was working. Then she rang Jemima's mobile number, only to be told that the machine wasn't switched on. Well, it was a vote of confidence, showed she wasn't worried about her nephew, but it was odd, Darina thought.

By the time William got back, late as usual, Darina had got Rory asleep and, with the help of a glass of wine, gathered herself together. She braced herself as she heard the front door open, not sure she had the energy to deal with a husband who had been as difficult as William the previous evening.

'How's the lad?' was William's first question.

'Sleeping,' said Darina with heartfelt gratitude.

'I'll just go and check on him,' he said, putting down his briefcase and disappearing upstairs.

It was a little time before he came down and she saw he'd changed into jeans and a sweatshirt. She gave him a glass of wine as he sat down at the kitchen table, laid for their supper. 'We're having baby food,' she told him, summoning her reserves of cheerfulness. 'Gourmet variety – ham and broccoli.'

'Ham,' William said, then he looked at his drink. 'I think I'll have mineral water,' he said sliding his glass over to Darina. 'You drink this.' Then he pushed away his plate, 'I always said nursery food was my favourite but I think I'll give this a miss. Make myself a couple of boiled eggs.' He went over to the stove and put on a small saucepan of water on to heat.

Darina felt her temper begin to rise. Was he rejecting her food as well as her? 'William,' she started in a dangerous voice.

'I went to see your man this afternoon,' he said before she could get further.

'My man?'

'The homoeopathic doctor.'

Darina stared at him, not able to believe what she was hearing. 'Darling! How did you find the time?'

'It isn't my time you should be asking about, it's his. I felt so dreadful last night I thought anything was worth trying and rang as soon as I got into the station this morning. Only to hear that his first appointment was six

311

weeks away! I gave the receptionist a great sob story about being responsible for the nation's safety and how I couldn't do that in my state of health and she wasn't moved at all.' He shook his head and lowered two eggs into the boiling water. 'But after lunch she rang and said the doctor had just had a cancellation and could I make it by three? I put everything off and went over.'

'My,' Darina said. This was extraordinary! And worrying, William must have been feeling really awful. 'What did he say?'

'He thinks your instinct is probably right, especially when I told him I'd had a full physical from the medics only last month and they'd given me a clean bill of health.'

'What did you tell him your symptoms were?'

'Extreme tiredness, headaches, a general feeling of not being able to cope and the leg rash.'

'Darling, I didn't realize it was as bad as that!'

'I didn't want you to,' he told her frankly.

'But we should share things. No wonder you've been so crabby! Promise me you'll let me know if it gets as bad again?'

He gave her one of his old smiles and Darina realized just how much she'd missed them. 'Promise,' he said.

'Did he test you and find out what you shouldn't be eating?'

'Ah,' he said, gazing at his watch. 'What he's done is to put me on something called an elimination diet. If I feel better after a few days, and he warned me I could feel worse before that happens, then I'm probably eating something my system finds difficult to cope with.'

'What do you have to cut out?'

'Quite a lot, I'm afraid. All preserved meats, like that ham, and sausages, which is going to be a serious deprivation; all dairy products, especially cheese. When the doctor discovered how much I like it, he said it could be a major source of the trouble. All smoked and shell fish, all cereals, yeast, some oils, all citrus fruit and tomatoes, coffee and tea, and, alas, alcohol. There could be one or two other things, I've got all the details in my briefcase.'

'That's a hell of a list,' Darina said slowly. 'Val only mentioned wheat and dairy products.'

'After my system's cleansed and I feel really good, we start adding ingredients back, one at a time, to see if I get a reaction. Eventually, we find out what it is that's causing the trouble.'

'And do you believe it's going to work?' Darina found it hard to accept that her normally sceptic husband was willingly submitting himself to this regime.

'If it's going to help me feel able to cope again, I don't mind what I do,' he said simply, took his eggs out of the water and brought them over to the table.

'You'd better give me the list and let me work out how to feed you.'

'And is there something I can make a packed lunch out of for tomorrow that won't contain any no-noes? If I'm passing up Rory's gourmet dinner tonight, I don't want to upset the regime tomorrow.'

'That means you're working again.' It wasn't a question.

'Afraid so. We've got to get this case wrapped up.'

Got to get the case wrapped up or got to get together with Sergeant James? And if the latter, what could Darina do about it?

*

The next morning Darina checked William's list of allowables. While he fed Rory, she cooked a breast of chicken in olive oil for his lunch then sliced and mixed it with a chopped ripe pear, runner beans and grilled red peppers, all tossed in a little vinaigrette dressing.

William checked what she was doing while spooning soggy cereal into Rory and eating two apples and a banana for his own breakfast. 'The doc suggested rice is good to start the day on,' he told her. 'If it's brown, of course. You eat that all up, boy. Grow up nice and strong, be an athlete.' He threw a punch at Rory's midriff, pulling it back before it connected. Rory thought that was a great joke and then grabbed at the spoon, showering William with milk and bits of cereal.

William took it back. 'We can't have that, what will the team think if I come in spattered with your breakfast?'

'The team?' wondered Darina. That was new. She decided to take advantage of the change in atmosphere.

'I forgot to tell you last night, I've discovered who his father is.'

William turned and stared at her. 'You have? Good work! Who is it?'

Darina told him of her conversation with Martin. 'All I've got to do now is get hold of this Noah Whitstable person and I can report to Jemima.' She glanced at the telephone. 'I'll have another go at her mobile this morning, she'll be so pleased.'

But would she be? Darina had to agree with Martin that Noah didn't sound an ideal dad for Rory.

'If he's still at that address. Sounds an unreliable sort

of person to me,' William commented, brushing down his suit.

'He's listed in this year's phone book, I checked when I got back last night. I have a feeling it's all going to fall into place now. Here's your lunch,' Darina handed over the plastic box together with an apple and a bottle of mineral water.

'Great, one way or another I'm going to get to the bottom of this food intolerance thing as well as the arson case.' He gave both Darina and Rory a kiss and left, leaving Darina hoping his optimism wasn't misplaced in either direction.

From then on she didn't have a moment to relax. There was Rory to keep amused while she cleared up, did the minimum of housework and then sat down with William's list to try and plan meals and getting to grips with thinking how a seemingly innocuous diet could slowly poison one over the years.

Then it was time for Rory's rest and for Darina to attack more gourmet baby food recipes. Working as fast as her catering experience had trained her, she prepared chicken with courgettes and corn, hoping Rory would like the colour of the corn as well as its sweetness; pork with potato, leek and grilled red peppers; smoked haddock with rice and carrot; and lamb with couscous and parsnip. When she'd finished, she stood looking at the results with satisfaction. They all tasted excellent and the textures were interesting. Darina also reckoned the balance of protein, fats and vitamins would be good, too. It just remained to see what Rory thought. She put the various bowls of mixtures to cool in a sink filled with ice cubes.

Before she went upstairs to collect Rory, she tried

Noah Whitstable's number. No reply. Then she rang Jemima's mobile again – the machine was still switched off. Had she forgotten to take a battery charger with her? It seemed unlikely, Jemima had always been wedded to the phone. Anyway, if she had, wouldn't she have rung on an ordinary phone to check on Rory?

Darina tried not to feel uneasy as she set off with Rory for a walk in Chelsea Hospital grounds. There could be any number of reasons why Jemima hadn't been in touch. She stopped worrying as heavy rain started again and she had to dash back.

Lunch was another triumph as Rory eagerly demolished the chicken and corn dish. Then Darina wondered if he would have eaten baked beans with exactly the same gusto. Did it really matter what you gave small children as long as the nutritional factors were right and they ate it? She wished Rory could talk, could tell her what he really thought. But he couldn't so she had to be content that he'd appeared to appreciate the dish. Until proved otherwise, she would remain convinced it was important to educate the palate from an early age.

She put Rory down for his nap then took the chance to try and call both Noah and Jemima. Still no joy. She caught up on her mail and tried to get down to some work but no sooner had she managed to get started than Rory woke and it was playtime.

Followed by bath time, supper time and, at last, bedtime. The previous night Darina had only been woken once. She hoped this meant that tonight Rory would sleep all the way through. She went downstairs, poured herself a drink, collapsed into a chair and wondered how mothers ever managed to cope.

Perhaps it was like trench warfare; you just got used

to it. Maybe after a while you couldn't imagine any other sort of life.

If it wasn't that Rory was such an enchanting child, so good-humoured and with such a wonderful smile, so openly loving, so intelligent and so obviously happy to be with her, Darina would have been desperate.

She had one more go on the telephone. And this time Noah's phone was answered by a female voice with an Australian accent. Noah, she said, was away for the weekend but would probably be back on Monday. Cheered by this, Darina dialled Jemima again. No luck there. She rang Blackboys. An answering machine. She left a message for Basil to ring when he got back.

Worry niggled away at Darina. Two days, Jemima had said, was all Darina had to look after Rory for. Two days were now up and Jemima hadn't been in contact.

'I don't understand it,' she said to William when he got back.

'She doesn't sound the most reliable of girls.'

Darina dished up wild mushroom risotto while he laid the table. 'She really seemed frightened on Thursday, said she was sure someone had tried to run her down.'

'Any evidence?' asked William calmly, arranging cutlery.

'Only what she said.'

'Hysterical, was she?'

'Not hysterical, exactly.' Darina brought over the dish of risotto. 'It was as though she couldn't bear to be where she was any longer than she absolutely had to. She practically pushed me and Rory out of the door. I'd have said she was genuinely frightened. Whether it was justified or not is, of course, a different matter. I still think it's odd that she isn't anxious about Rory.'

'Why? She knows he's being well looked after.' He paused then added, 'He's a great child, I only wish we could see more of him.'

Darina wasn't going to get involved in another discussion about starting a family. 'It's all ready,' she said. 'Is the table?'

The risotto was made with brown rice and was accompanied by salad. It was followed by a home-made mango sorbet that was as creamy as ice cream. 'Not bad,' said William. 'I don't mind following a diet if this is what I get.'

'Are you feeling any different?'

'Yes, worse,' he said cheerfully. 'I've got the most terrible headache. Withdrawal symptoms, I was warned.'

'Poor you. But I suppose you could look on it as encouraging, shows that something's happening.'

'Unless I'm just developing a propensity for migraines!'

'How's the case going?'

'Stickily,' he said, looking depressed. 'Nothing seems to be breaking for us. One or two interesting developments, though. Forensic think they've identified a heavy rolling pin amongst various bits of charred wood in the factory and Val Douglas's secretary says there was a new one, a sample sent in by a kitchen equipment company, sitting on her desk that night, waiting for a test run.'

'You mean that's what could have been used to kill the nightwatchman?'

'Well, knock him out anyway.'

'You mean he was left to die in the fire?'

William nodded unhappily, 'The autopsy says he died from asphyxiation not the wound in his head.'

'That's awful! Anything else?'

'I don't know but Maeve O'Connor, Rory's ex-nanny, rang us yesterday and said she had something to tell us and would drop by. But she hasn't. If only I'd been the one to speak to her! I'd have told her to remain where she was and sent a car. As it was, by the time I got the message, she'd gone out somewhere and we haven't been able to contact her again.'

'Do you think it could be important, whatever it is?'

William finished his glass of apple juice. 'Heaven knows! I'd have thought if it was, she'd have told us when Pat and I interviewed her but she's a funny little thing and was very upset about her father.'

'Probably still is. Give her a day or so and she'll be back in touch.'

'I just hope you're right.' William got up and started stacking the supper plates together.

Darina left William clearing up and had another go at ringing Jemima. Once again she got the message that the mobile was switched off. She tried Blackboys again. This time Jasper answered.

'Hi,' Darina said. 'Do you know where Jemima is?'

He didn't.

'Is your father there?'

'He's away until Tuesday, I think. What's up? Won't the son and heir do?' he added flippantly.

Darina nearly reminded him that Job was the heir. 'Not unless you want to take over Rory,' she said instead, then remembered that Jemima had said she couldn't trust Jasper with him.

'You mean, *you've* got Rory?' he said, astonished. 'I

319

thought Jemima had taken him with her. Dad will go berserk,' he added with a note of satisfaction in his voice.

'I'm quite able to look after Rory,' Darina said with dignity.

'Frustrated mothering instincts?'

'Nothing of the sort. He's the guinea-pig for Val's gourmet baby-food line.'

'Dad won't like that, either.' Jasper appeared to delight in needling her.

'Why ever not?'

'He's got some hot-shot experts working on it.'

'Is it his company or Val's?' Darina asked pointedly.

'Depends which one you talk to,' Jasper shot back. 'And we all know who holds the money bags. If you take my advice, you won't invest too much time working on any ideas you may have come up with.'

Darina felt dismay. Then wondered just how much Jasper knew about things anyway. As far as she knew, he had nothing to do with his father's business and certainly nothing to do with Val's. 'Thank you for your advice,' she said smoothly.

'No trouble,' he returned equally smoothly. 'Now, why don't I come and collect Rory from you?'

'I'm enjoying having him and he was given into my care by Jemima,' Darina said carefully. 'Do you know when she will be back?' she asked.

'I'm not my sister's keeper,' he said carelessly.

'So you don't know where she went?'

'No idea. Look, I'm the boy's uncle, I do think I should be looking after him.'

Darina thought about happy-go-lucky Jasper coping with food times, bedtimes, play times. 'I can't agree, Jasper,' she said firmly. 'And I know Basil would want him to stay here.' That seemed to take care of that. But her worry over Jemima's whereabouts remained. She couldn't forget how tense Jemima had been and her relief when she'd realized Darina was prepared to take care of Rory so she herself could get away. Get away from what or whom?

Darina spent an uneasy evening turning over possibilities as William worked on his case notes. It didn't seem either of them had come to any satisfactory conclusion before it was time for bed.

Once again Rory woke them during the night and this time it was William who went in and set the cassette player going. In the morning, Darina brought Rory and his bottle of milk into bed with them while William got breakfast. Hers was croissants and coffee, his was cold mushroom risotto and hot apple juice. 'I stirred it with a cinnamon stick,' he said proudly. 'Makes all the difference.'

'How's the headache?'

He groaned. 'Don't ask!'

There followed a pleasant hour with Darina and William fielding clocks, ornaments, books and pencils as Rory explored the bedside tables, finally allowing him to hang on to an antique paperweight of polished black stone. This Rory threw on to the duvet and then the floor with increasing enthusiasm.

'You look after him,' Darina said after a while, 'I'm getting up.'

Yesterday's rain hadn't let up, which meant they couldn't take Rory out. William played with him while Darina cooked lunch, changing her planned cauliflower cheese to accompany the half shoulder of lamb to cauliflower cooked with cumin. She slipped slivers of garlic underneath the meat skin and wondered what could replace the apricot creme caramel she'd planned for pudding. She couldn't even soak the dried apricots in orange juice for a compote. Pastry of any sort was out as well. As was chocolate. She sighed. Well, fruit was better for them anyway.

Just as she started feeding Rory his meal, the telephone rang. Darina snatched it up, convinced it had to be Jemima at last.

It was for William.

His face grew dark as he listened. 'I see,' he said at last. 'You've sent for the SOCO team and the pathologist, of course?'

The Scenes of Crime Officers were required for a wide range of felonies but a pathologist surely meant a fatality. Darina felt herself go cold.

William put down the phone. 'I'm sorry, darling, I've got to go. A body has been discovered by the lock gates, on the very edge of my patch, damn it!' He paused then said carefully, 'It's a woman, they think she's been in the river several days.'

Darina felt sick. 'A lock? It wouldn't be downstream of Blackboys by any chance?'

'Now look, darling, Blackboys is quite a way from where she's been found. There's absolutely no reason to think it's your friend, Jemima.'

'No, of course not,' Darina said without conviction.

Chapter Twenty-Four

Pat James had gone into the office on Sunday morning with a feeling of expectation. Being on call offered opportunities.

If she wasn't interrupted by any new criminal activity, she could work through the computer entries on the arson case and just maybe uncover a trail that would lead to the killer of the nightwatchman.

But no sooner had she flashed up the first entry than the door opened and in came the last person she wanted to see.

'All quiet on the manor front, then?' asked Terry in a horribly jocular way.

He was dressed in his usual uniform of jeans and a leather blouson, except that under the jacket was a T-shirt sporting a psychedelic print rather than his more normal open-necked checked shirt.

'Unable to keep away, then?' she retorted.

He strolled over to his desk. 'Left my Raybans.'

She looked at the greyness of the day outside. 'Of course, couldn't be expected to slay the girls without your Raybans,' she muttered to herself.

'You said something?' he asked pleasantly.

'Off somewhere exciting?' She matched his conversational tone.

'Just down the pub.' He put the glasses in the top pocket of his jacket and strolled over to where she sat. 'Anything interesting, sergeant?'

'Nothing that sticks out, sir.' She enjoyed calling him sir rather than the more intimate guv.

'Since I'm here, might as well have a coffee and run an eye over the case myself,' he said, shrugging his shoulders out of the jacket and draping it round a chair. 'Fancy one yourself?'

Pat sighed. It was obvious he was as keen to make the vital breakthrough as she was. And that the office was no longer her own. 'Just had one,' she said repressively. Did he think he could get round her by switching on the electric kettle?

Equipped with a cup of instant, Terry sat himself at another VDU and started tapping keys, whistling through his teeth is a way Pat found immensely provocative.

Just as she thought she couldn't stand it any longer, her phone rang.

She listened, then said, 'Right, I'm on my way,' put back the receiver and picked up her jacket.

'Trouble?' Terry looked up, his hazel eyes bright, his thin face alert.

'Lock-keeper's reported a body in the river,' Pat said reluctantly. The last thing she wanted was to be accompanied by Terry. 'No need for you to disturb yourself, sir.'

'I'm sure you're more than capable of handling the initial stages, sergeant,' Terry said, getting up and grabbing his jacket. 'But I think I'll come along for the ride.'

There was nothing she could do.

'Know the way?' he asked as she got into the car in furious silence.

Over the last couple of weeks she'd spent every one of the few precious spare moments she'd had in studying the area covered by the station.

'Yup,' she said shortly and started the engine.

'If you turn right at the lights, I'll show you a back route that's much quicker,' Terry said.

He would, he just would insist on showing off, she thought as she flicked the indicator switch and pulled into the centre of the road. But it was, she had to admit as she cruised along a residential street, a nifty little way. One that maybe she would have worked out if she'd taken a good look at the map before they'd started.

The lock normally attracted quite a few visitors on the weekend and the tourist season wasn't quite over. Despite the fact that it had only just stopped raining, there were a number of cars outside the pub that stood next to the lock-keeper's house and a crowd of people blocked the view of the river.

'Bloody voyeurs,' said Terry.

They worked their way through the crowd of people.

A constable had cordoned off an area of river bank next to the lock with blue and white crime-scene tape and was now trying to keep the curious back. More people crowded the decks, craning their necks, trying to see what was causing the hold up.

'DI Pitman and WDS James, constable,' said Terry, flashing his warrant card. 'Show us the rabbit.' Pat winced.

'It's here, sir,' the constable said stolidly and turned to lead them down the short stretch of grass between the tape and the river, but not before Pat had seen the expression on his middle-aged, craggy face. It made her forget Terry's crassness and try to turn her mind into a blank. This had to be a nasty one.

'By rights, she should have gone over the weir,' the constable said. 'But *Fun Days*, that boat there,' he indicated a powerful and expensive-looking cruiser drawn into the side of the river as though waiting for the lock, 'well, it got too far over, saw the weir and swung sharply over to this side. The body must have been coming down at the time. With all the rain we've had, the current's pretty strong.'

Yes, the river was flowing fast, past the willows lining both the banks that were edged with humbler houses than the mansions that lay further upriver but desirable all the same. For the river was like a private road, one that was sheltered from the dreariness and overcrowding of so much of the densely developed area it ran through as it gathered strength on its way into London and out to the sea.

Terry hid Pat's view of the body. The stillness of his shoulders, the rigidity of the set of his head, betrayed shock. Then he replaced his Raybans and stepped aside without a comment.

Forcing herself to take several slow, deep breaths, Pat looked at the corpse lying on the path beside an upturned boat. Then she gasped, closed her eyes and hung on to her sanity before opening them again slowly, aware of Terry's silent presence beside her.

This was not a body so much as a piece of mangled flesh. The screws of the boat had torn into the head and shoulders, mincing the features into nothingness, ripping off the ears, chewing up the shoulders. Blood streaked the loose fragments of skin and muscle and splinters of bare bone. There were no eyes, no nose, only a rictus for a mouth and cracked bones where once had been a jaw. Wet strands of dark hair adhered to what was left of the scalp but even they couldn't make the head look human. The lower arms and hands of the corpse, though, had been left untouched. Yet they also looked unnatural, bloated and blanched by immersion in the water.

Pat's stomach gave a sickening lurch. She counted slowly, thinking of nothing, and gradually it settled.

'Spoiled their Pimms, it did,' the constable said, with a jerk of his head towards the boat. 'The woman saw it first, apparently, and screamed at her husband to cut the engine. Which he did. Too late, of course. But, then, it would have been too late anyway. Reckon she's been dead several days.'

Pat could see into the cabin of the cruiser moored at the side of the river. A woman was crying helplessly, her arms wrapped around herself. The man stood staring out of the cabin's wide window, his hands jammed into his trouser pockets. Each of the figures looked intensely alone.

'Have you got their names, constable?' Terry asked. There was an oddly detached note to his voice as though, he, too, couldn't come to terms with the sight they'd been presented with.

'Yes, sir.'

'And sent for the SOCO team and the pathologist?'

'Yes, sir.'

'And no doubt the guvnor will be here soon?'

The sick feeling in Pat's stomach suddenly intensified as she realized that part of her resentment at Terry's presence had been because if he hadn't shown up, she would have had the pleasure of working with William alone, just the two of them. The two of them and the Soco squad, the pathologist, the uniform branch and probably the Superintendent as well. What a cosy little duo that would have been!

But they would have been a team within a team. Now Terry would be part of it, too.

'Haven't seen many worse sights than that,' Terry said casually to her. 'And I don't know many officers who could have taken it the way you've done.'

She wanted to make some flip remark back, instead tears threatened and she had to turn away for a moment. 'Line of duty, isn't that what it's about?' she muttered.

A police van drew up and several white-clad technicians came over carrying screens.

'Thank God,' said Terry. 'Now we can get a bit of privacy. Give us a shout if the pathologist or the chief arrives,' he told the constable.

By the time William arrived on the scene, Pat and Terry had interviewed the badly shocked couple on board *Fun Days* but learned little more that could be added to the constable's brief statement.

They negotiated the narrow plank that linked boat to shore and went to join their chief.

'Glad I haven't had my lunch,' was his brief comment. 'Don't suppose I'll have much of an appetite for the rest of today. Pity, Darina's preparing one of her specials, roast lamb with home-made red currant jelly. Ah well!' He gave them both a grin that said, ghastly as the job was, they had to retain a sense of proportion.

Suddenly Pat saw how ridiculous she was being. This was a man who hadn't been married much more than a year. Who'd been crazy about his wife ever since Pat had known him. What on earth had she been thinking of?

'Any sign of the pathologist yet?' William continued.

'He's another one being dragged away from someone's speciality, guv,' Terry said with an answering grin. 'Lunching with the wife's relations, apparently. He said he'll be with us about three thirty, didn't think the delay would matter.'

'He's right, of course,' said William absently. He looked again at the pathetic remains. 'No sign of any identity, I suppose?'

Terry shook his head. 'The constable went through her pockets, but nothing.'

'Any record of a missing person who might fit the description?'

It had been Pat who had put together such details as were available: woman, about five foot eight inches tall, short brown hair, unmarried or at least wearing no rings, dressed in blue designer jeans, a silk shirt and a leather waistcoat. It wasn't much to go on but it at least suggested the dead woman had had a lifestyle of quality.

'No,' she said in a voice that sounded odd to her ears.

William looked at her sharply. 'You all right, sergeant?'

'Yup.' Pat pulled herself together. Terry's glee if she fell apart now was not to be borne.

'Better go and see if the lock-keeper can give us any guidance on where the body floated down from.'

There followed a long, long afternoon of frustrating activity.

The lock-keeper could only suggest that the body had been caught upriver by a tree root or reeds, then been dislodged by the increased current caused by the heavy rains. 'Can't have come far without someone seeing it, though,' had been his comment. 'The bad weather's cut down on the number of craft on the river but you'd have thought someone would 'ave seen 'er if she'd come far.'

Cold, wet and depressed, Pat and Terry finally finished their inquiries at the lock.

By eight o'clock the body had been inspected by the pathologist and removed. Post-mortem would be carried out the following morning. The SOCO technicians had finished their investigations. 'Nothing more they can do,' William told Pat and Terry. 'That's the devil with water, it washes so much away. But they're satisfied the incident occurred just as the *Fun Days* owners claim.'

He turned and looked upriver. Twilight had deepened into night and a fine rain was falling. Light splashed out from the pub and the lock-keeper's cottage and from the little houses by the river. Beyond, from where the corpse must have come, all was dark. 'How far is Blackboys?' William asked Terry.

'Blackboys?' Terry sounded disconcerted. 'I dunno, let's see, 'bout two miles, something like that, guv. You're not suggesting the corpse can have had anything to do with *Blackboys*?'

'Darina's worried about Jemima Ealham. She says the girl went away last Thursday for a couple of days and she hasn't been able to contact her since.'

Pat remembered the chic girl who'd accused the nanny of stealing her pearls. A little madam, she'd thought at the time. Someone used to luxury and getting her own way. 'The clothes could certainly be hers,' she said doubtfully. It was difficult to tie in that terrible piece of ripped flesh and bone with the self-possessed

Jemima Ealham but, she found, by no means impossible. 'The jeans are really expensive.' They'd had the
make advertised on the metal buttons and she'd seen
them, or an almost identical pair, featured in a fashion
magazine.

'Might be an idea if the two of you paid a call on
Blackboys. It's unlikely our unfortunate corpse is that of
Jemima Ealham but we can't afford to ignore the possi-
bility. I'll see you at the station later.'

'Waste of time, this, if you ask me,' Terry muttered to
Pat as he followed her to the car. 'Why should anyone
want to kill the silly bitch?'

Pat's feelings entirely, but she wasn't going to
question William's judgement. 'Stranger things have
happened,' she murmured, opening the car door and
slipping into the driver's seat, glad to be out of the rain,
now getting heavier by the minute.

She had to think as she switched on the engine how
to get to Blackboys from where they were. But after a
moment the route slipped into place in her mind and
she started driving confidently.

No alternative suggestions as to the way came from
Terry and they reached the drive of the big house in
little more than fifteen minutes.

'It'd be less by river,' Terry said as they drew up.

It seemed as though all the lights had been turned on
in the house. No curtains were drawn and rectangles of
golden light beamed out of the big windows. Chandeliers
could be seen in a couple of rooms. As Terry rang the
doorbell, the insistent beat of rock music could be
heard.

There was no response. 'Someone's in all right,' said

Terry; he grasped the big brass door knocker and beat authoritatively on it. Before he'd finished, the door was opened, almost causing him to stumble as the knocker was wrenched out of his hand.

There stood the handsome young man Pat had glimpsed on her last visit. Jasper, the son.

'Yes?' he enquired.

His fair hair was tousled, a cigarette held casually in his hand.

Terry and Pat flashed their warrant cards.

'My goodness,' said Jasper gaily, standing back from the door. 'The police again and on such a nasty night, too! Not to mention it being Sunday. Well, you'd better come in.'

The music was louder now, pouring down the stairs from somewhere up above as they walked into the brightly lit marble-floored hall. Pat wondered if someone waited for Jasper's return.

Jasper took them into the library where Pat and William had interviewed Val Douglas. Here too, all the lights were on but the room was chilly. Pat wondered whether she would ever feel warm again.

Jasper made no move to light the fire that stood ready in the hearth but waved courteously towards the leather seating. 'And what can I do to help the processes of justice this evening?'

'Well, it's your sister, Jemima, we'd like to speak to, actually,' said Pat.

'Jemima? Oho, what's the dear girl been up to?'

'It's not that she's done anything,' Pat said patiently. Terry appeared to be happy to leave things to her for the moment. 'We'd just like to be reassured as to her whereabouts.'

'Reassured?' Jasper shot back. 'You make that sound very unsettling.' There'd been a subtle change in his attitude. The flip, self-confident young man was suddenly uncertain. He came and sat next to Pat. 'Why don't you level with me? What's with my sister?'

'The thing of it is,' Pat said slowly, 'Darina Lisle is worried that she hasn't been in touch and this afternoon the body of a woman answering to your sister's description was found just down river from here.'

His face grew quite pale. 'Jemima, drowned? Don't be absurd, of course she can't be drowned. She's just gone off for a few days. She's like that. Does things on the spur of the moment. She'll be back any time now.'

'Well, when she does reappear, could you please ask her to telephone us?' Terry said, getting to his feet.

Jasper stubbed out his cigarette. 'You bet!' Then he looked down at his feet. 'You wouldn't like me to have a look at this person, I suppose?' he said quietly. 'Just to make sure it isn't my sister?'

'I'm afraid identification isn't possible,' Pat said gently. 'The body has been very battered about the head.'

That got to him. He took another cigarette from a box on the desk, and lit it with hands that shook. After a deep drag he said, 'That's awful!'

Pat liked the uncertain youngster he now was much better than the cavalier young man who'd opened the door to them.

'Look, I'll try and track down Dad, he'll know what to do.'

'Let us know if you hear anything,' Pat repeated as they left.

She switched the heater full on as they drove away leaving a clearly shaken Jasper standing in the doorway.

'Fat lot of good that did,' grumbled Terry as they went down the drive. 'We're definitely no nearer identifying the poor bitch.'

'You know,' said Pat, changing down as they approached the wrought iron gates and the road, 'Jemima Ealham isn't the only missing girl we know of.'

Terry looked at her. 'You're thinking of that Irish bint? The nanny who stole the pearls?'

'Who was accused of stealing the pearls,' Pat corrected him. 'Yes. We had that message on Friday to say that she was coming in to tell us something but she's never appeared.'

'Probably found something better to do,' Terry said.

Pat turned out of the gates and increased her speed. 'The clothes on the corpse were far too good to be hers but why don't we drop by that hostel she's staying at and see what gives?'

Terry thought for a moment. Then said, 'Well, it's not far out of our way.'

At the hostel, they were told that Maeve O'Connor had gone out on Friday and hadn't been seen since. 'They don't always let us know if they're taking a trip somewhere,' a comfortable looking woman in her forties said. 'She's paid up until the end of next week.'

'Are her things in her room?' Pat asked.

'We'll go and see, shall we?'

The room was small and shared with another girl who received the police inquiries with profound disinterest. 'I dunno,' she said. 'Hardly spoke to her. There's things in that cupboard, though.' She pointed to one of a pair of narrow wardrobes that stood side by side between the beds.

Pat flipped through the few garments that were hanging there. 'These are very good quality,' she said.

'Yeah, she said the daughter of the house gave them to her, cast-offs, she said. I should be so lucky with cast-offs.'

Pat looked at a smart pair of trousers and silently agreed.

Chapter Twenty-Five

By the time William returned home on Sunday evening, Darina was at the end of her tether.

Rory had been fractious all day. It was as though he'd picked up the vibes from her. Only at lunchtime had he been amenable, wolfing down the smoked haddock with his usual ardour. But afterwards he hadn't wanted his rest. Even music had failed to calm him and at length Darina had taken him downstairs to play. But he'd thrown his toys around, demanding attention, then hitting at her. By the time supper and bedtime were reached, both of them were exhausted. Rory had finally fallen asleep sitting on the sofa beside her with his bottle of milk. She carried him up to his cot and settled him down with a sigh of thankfulness.

William rang from the station and said it had been impossible to identify the corpse. She asked for a description. 'I know it sounds as though it could be her,' William said hurriedly down the line, 'but there's nothing that says it is.'

Perfectly true but it didn't help. Nor did the fact that Jemima's mobile was still not switched on.

When William finally walked through the door, Darina rushed at him. 'I have no more information,' he said wearily.

She dragged her mind back from Jemima. 'You look exhausted,' she said. 'Have you had anything to eat? I've got some soup ready and there's cold lamb.'

'That'd be nice. Pat and Terry produced fish and chips. By the time I'd picked the flesh out of the batter, it wasn't enough to keep a kitten happy. One thing that might cheer you is that the nanny's gone missing as well and she also fits the dead woman's description. But, look, I've been thinking about what you said, Jemima being frightened and suggesting your investigation into Rory's background might have disturbed something.'

'She didn't exactly say that,' Darina said carefully.

'So tell me what she did say and who you've told you're looking for Rory's father.'

Darina felt as if her heart were made of lead. Surely nothing she'd done could have threatened Jemima? 'Job Ealham and his wife, the PR chap, Paul Robins, Job's friend Martin Price and Cynthia Beauchamp, an old friend of Basil's. I don't think any of them would have told anybody else, I stressed it was confidential. Look, I'll tell you everything we discussed but then you fill me in on what's going on with your fire investigation.' And I'll count the number of times you mention Pat James, she thought to herself.

At the end of their joint exchange of information, William admitted he couldn't identify any threat to Jemima and Darina hadn't heard one mention of the female sergeant. Was that a good or a bad sign? she wondered as they went up to bed.

She found it difficult to sleep.

In the morning William came up as Darina was heating Rory's milk. 'I'll let you know as soon as we find out anything, promise.'

'Aren't you having anything for breakfast? I did some rice for you last night and there's lots of fruit.'

William hesitated then said, 'It's the autopsy this morning.'

Darina stared at him, her face white. There was nothing that could be said.

After William had left, Darina took Rory back upstairs with her and sat him on her bed with his bottle while she tried Jemima's mobile again. Still switched off. While she dressed she tried to tell herself it meant nothing. She looked at Rory, holding his bottle in his chubby little hands, dragging greedily on the nipple, squinting at her to check on what she was doing. It seemed she could hardly remember a time when she didn't have a small boy to take care of.

What did he think of losing Maeve, his surrogate mother, and of being handed over to someone he hardly knew? Jemima was right, Darina told herself finishing dressing. He needs a proper father.

She scooped Rory up from the bed. 'You can have an egg,' she told him, going downstairs.

At nine o'clock, with Rory fed and dressed and playing with a car, she rang Noah again.

The same Australian voice answered. 'Yeah, he's here. It was you rang before, wasn't it? Half a mo and I'll get him for you.'

'Noah,' came another voice, male and soft.

Darina asked if it would be convenient if she came round that morning.

'Guess so,' the soft voice said. 'But what's it about?'

'Do you remember Sophie Ealham?'

'Sophie? Sure. Why do you want to talk about her?' She heard something at the back of his voice, a little slippy note as though he wasn't really comfortable with the thought of Sophie Ealham.

'I can't explain over the telephone, that's why I want to come round,' she told him.

Finally he agreed.

She put Rory in his car seat, confident he'd go to sleep once she started driving. He looked up at her with eager eyes. 'Da!' he said, waving his hands excitedly. 'Da, da, da!'

'Yes, we're going to take a little ride to meet your daddy,' she told him as she fastened the straps and seat belt.

That seemed a good idea to Rory, he clapped his hands together and gave her his big grin and for once he didn't go to sleep as she drove up towards Ladbroke Grove again.

Noah Whitstable's insignificant door was located between a newsagent's and a launderette and was badly in need of a paint job. Darina rang the bell and waited with Rory in her arms.

After a little she heard footsteps coming downstairs, then the door opened and there was Noah Whitstable.

He was tall, with wheat fair hair and a pleasant, rather weak face. It was impossible to tell what colour his eyes were, so dilated were the pupils. He hadn't shaved and a fair stubble that had nothing of the designer about it covered his lower face. He was dressed in shabby jeans, the material on the knees so pale it was almost white, and a T-shirt with a washed-out design. Both shirt and jeans looked clean. His feet were bare, the big toes splayed as though unused to being confined in shoes. Standing a step up from the pavement level, he was sufficiently tall to be able to look down on Darina.

When he saw Rory, his face lit up. 'Hey, man,' he said, flicking a finger against the little cheek. 'Who've we got here, then?'

Well, at least he liked children.

'Can we come in?' Darina asked.

'Sure, come upstairs.' He turned and led the way up uncarpeted wooden treads.

The tiny landing offered a couple of doors, one of which stood open.

Because the room had very little furniture, it seemed larger than it was. A stove and sink were in one corner, a battered table with two chairs in another. A low table stood in front of two huge cushions covered with some sort of Indian material. A bronze joss-stick holder held two expired sticks. The faint smell of incense fought with cooking spices to create an atmosphere that was warm and slightly mysterious.

Sitting on one of the cushions was a small girl with spiky hair a lurid shade of lime, a broad face and lively eyes. There was a nasty looking bruise on her left cheek. She was wearing denim dungarees over a skimpy white T-shirt and flip-flops. Her toenails were painted lime green to match her hair. She jumped up when Darina entered and came across bouncing off her flip-flops like a little kangaroo.

'Hey, isn't that the most gorgeous tyke you ever saw?' said the Australian accent that had answered the phone. 'You're heaven, you are,' she told Rory. 'Isn't he heaven, Noah? Can I hold him?' She held out her arms and Rory gave her his big grin, chuckled, then buried his head in Darina's shoulder.

That acceptance of her as his protector made Darina

feel wonderful. 'He's a little shy,' she told the girl, 'let him get used to you.'

'What's his name?' She didn't seem at all upset as she gently stroked the thick fair hair.

'Rory, and I'm Darina.'

'I'm Laurel,' she said. 'Would you like something?'

'Coffee would be nice.'

'We don't drink coffee,' Laurel said cheerfully. 'Not good for the system. We've got roasted barley or camomile tea.'

Darina opted for the latter.

Noah moved over to the little kitchen area and busied himself with putting a kettle to heat on the gas. Darina was struck by how little equipment there was. No electric kettle, no gadgets on the small working surfaces, only a couple of cupboards to hold everything that preparing, cooking and eating food called for. There was, however, a small fridge.

'Rory's Sophie's baby, isn't he?' Noah said as he switched on the gas. 'I knew that frigging Martin was lying to me.' The viciousness in his voice took Darina by surprise. He banged a fist down on the edge of the sink, making her jump. 'Sodding bastard.' His accent, which had seemed well educated on the doorstep, now sounded rougher, nearer to south London than Knightsbridge.

'Noah,' said Laurel in a warning voice. 'He can't hurt you.'

The muscles under his T-shirt knotted as his hands clenched on to the sink's edge, making him look unexpectedly powerful. Then, just as suddenly as it had come, the violent mood passed. He opened the cupboard above the sink and took out three earthenware mugs. 'That sod was always jealous of Sophie and me.' He had a way of talking that jerked along, like a car that had grit in its petrol. He leant back against the sink. His jeans hung so loosely on his lean frame Darina wondered if they'd been bought from some street market or from a second-hand shop. Everything about the place said its inhabitants survived on very little money. Yet there was none of the squalor Martin had led her to expect. All was clean and neatly organized.

Darina folded herself down on to one of the cushions. 'If you didn't believe him, why didn't you find out what had happened for yourself?'

Noah scratched his head. 'Didn't seem I could.' No trace now of the emotion that had racked him.

'Didn't Sophie tell you anything about herself?'

Laurel sat beside Darina and started to play with Rory, running fingers up his jersey and on to his nose. He leant back against Darina and chuckled at her.

Noah busied himself with getting out herbal tea bags. He seemed all elbows and hands with his legs in almost constant motion. 'Sophie, well, she didn't talk 'bout her family.'

'Noah doesn't like to talk about his background.' Laurel lifted an uncomplaining Rory on to her lap. 'My father deserted us and my mum says the less she sees of us the better, me and my brothers have ruined her life, if it hadn't been for us, she could have gone off and done something, that's what she says,' she told Darina with great good humour. 'So I reckon if someone doesn't talk about their family it's usually with good reason. Makes sense to forget and all that. That right, Noah?'

He nodded and looked relieved to have been spoken for. The kettle boiled. He made the teas and brought them over, placing Darina and Laurel's mugs on the low table.

Laurel clucked, opened a small drawer in the table, brought out raffia mats and put one under each of the mugs. 'He's hopeless,' she told Darina. 'Before I came here, you wouldn't believe what the place looked like.' She wrinkled her nose.

'Stuff it, Laurel,' Noah said amiably. 'Making me sound like some sort of berk.'

'Reckon you've always needed a woman to keep you straight,' she said without malice. 'Reckon without that Sophie girl you were getting in a right old mess until I came along.'

'How did you meet Sophie?' Darina asked, cautiously sipping the tea, then relaxing as she realized it was a good quality camomile, fragrant and soothing with no dusty aftertaste.

Noah went and leant against the windowsill, holding his mug in both hands. Yesterday's rain had gone and a watery sun was shining, making a halo of his fair hair. 'Met her by the canal,' he muttered into his tea.

'Martin says she tried to throw herself in it. Is that true?'

He ducked his head again. 'Maybe,' he murmured.

'Do you know why?'

He shrugged his shoulders. 'Like I said, she didn't like talking about her family.'

'So it was something to do with them?' Darina coaxed him.

Noah put his mug on the table, walked over to the other side of the room, inspected the poster of some pop group that hung on the wall, flicked at a small tear in one of its curling sides, then turned and leant against the wall. 'Dunno, really,' he said. 'I told her it was stupid to throw her life away. She said she didn't have a home so I said she could come here.'

Darina tried to picture a desperate Sophie, so desperate she'd wanted to end everything, being offered a lodging by this taciturn young man.

'So she came back with you that night?'

'Yeah, and, like, it seemed sort of all right.'

'You mean, she cleaned the place up,' Laurel said suddenly, glancing up from playing horsey-horsey with Rory. 'And cooked. Jammy for you,' she added approvingly.

'I wasn't no good at cooking,' Noah muttered.

'You liked her,' said Darina. 'And she liked you?'

'Yeah, well, as I said, it seemed sort of all right.'

Yes, Darina could see how to Sophie it must have done. Someone who placed no intellectual demands on her, who made her feel wanted and important, who'd told her it was stupid to throw her life away and then showed her something she could do with it.

'What did you think when she suddenly disappeared?' she asked.

Noah took a flat tin out of his back pocket and slid down the wall. He opened the tin, took out a pack of cigarette papers and some weed and started rolling what looked to Darina like a joint. He glanced up at her and his eyes were the dark pools she'd seen when he opened the door. 'Thought she'd legged it,' he said briefly.

'Had you had an argument?'

He looked down at his hands, skilfully rolling the paper round its shredded contents.

Darina waited.

Laurel was showing Rory how the bronze incense

344

holder could be rolled across the table and hauling him back from lunging after it.

Noah finished preparing his joint, found a match book in his pocket and lit it. He took a long drag, laid his head back against the wall and closed his eyes. Smoke eventually floated down his nose and the sweet, curious smell invaded the room. 'I couldn't stand that she didn't visit the clinic,' he said finally, his eyes still closed.

'You mean the ante-natal clinic?'

'Yeah! I mean, you're pregnant, right? So you want everything for the baby to be right, don't yer?'

'Why wouldn't Sophie go for check-ups?'

Noah took another drag then wrapped his arms around his knees, the dark emptiness of his eyes looking across the room at the window. 'Don't know,' he said. 'Just wouldn't. Said it was a natural process.'

'Did you try to get her to go?' Darina tried to imagine the two of them in this small flat, Sophie insisting she didn't need medical help and this drop-out but strangely sensible young man trying to persuade her she did. And Martin in the background, offering her glimpses of the sort of life she'd known before.

'Her ankles and wrists had no right to swell like that. I told her.' Noah was getting angry again. For a moment Darina thought he was going to hit the floor but instead he took an even deeper drag on his joint. 'So we had this row,' he said, his eyes closed again, his head once more back against the wall. 'I didn't mean to hit her but some-times, well, sometimes things get too much for me.'

Laurel was still holding Rory but she was looking at Noah, her expression watchful.

'I don't think I hurt her much. And she came back that night and the next. And I thought things was all right. Then she didn't and I reckoned I'd blown it after all and she'd gone to that other fellow.' His face looked bitter. 'Then Martin frigging Price comes round and tells me she's dead. And the baby.'

He looked at Darina, his expression curiously blank. 'Why'd he have to tell me that, eh? Why? Weren't it bad enough Soph had died?'

'Would you have been able to look after him?' she asked. 'A new born baby without a mother?'

'Why should I 'ave to look after 'im?'

Darina felt baffled. 'He's your son, isn't he?'

Laurel's head with its spiky green hair turned towards Noah. 'Hey, mate, you never told me you'd had a son!' She sounded injured.

'Why should I?' he ground out.

'I thought we'd told each other everything!' Laurel was dismayed.

'We have,' he said truculently. 'Don't you trust me?'

'What do you mean?'

'Are you going to believe what this, this woman says rather than me?'

'You mean . . .'

'Yeah. That boy *isn't* mine.'

Chapter Twenty-Six

'He isn't your child?' Darina felt as though she was in a lift which had suddenly dropped a great many floors. 'Are you sure?'

'Course I'm sure. She was pregnant when she came 'ere.'

'But,' said Darina. 'But,' she repeated. 'Jemima, that's Sophie's elder sister, she says that Rory was born at least six weeks premature and that means Sophie didn't become pregnant until, well, until she started living with you.'

Noah looked at her scornfully. 'So what makes you believe what this Jemima says?'

What, indeed? Had Jemima been deceiving her? Or had Jemima herself been deceived? She'd repeated what her father had told her.

Suddenly the whole landscape of Sophie's last year of life shifted for Darina and she realized that her investigation had got her nowhere. The truth about Rory's conception didn't lie here.

'Let me make sure I've got this right,' Darina said at last. 'Sophie told you she was pregnant when you first met her?'

'Yeah, she told me, oh, 'bout three weeks after we met. Didn't say much, just cried.'

'And even knowing she was pregnant, Sophie had wanted to kill herself?' Darina couldn't believe it. It went against everything she'd found out about the girl.

Noah took a deep drag on his cigarette and let the smoke emerge gently through his nose. 'That's what I said to her after she told me.' He looked around the small room. 'She'd been desperate before she come here, she said.'

Desperate? When she had two homes she could have gone to? Not to mention Lady Beauchamp's. But Tiggy was abroad and Cynthia Beauchamp would have undoubtedly told Basil Ealham his daughter was with her. Darina thought of the powerful, short-fused man who Sophie looked on as father. Was she really so terrified of him? But it had to be that relationship that lay at the heart of why she'd disappeared. A terrible possibility began to dawn on Darina.

Noah offered his cigarette to Laurel but she shook her head. 'Not while the boy's here, Noah,' she said, sounding shocked.

'The boy, yeah,' he said and carefully pinched the smouldering end of the joint, then placed the fag end in his tin box and returned it to his back trouser pocket. 'She didn't *know* she was pregnant, she was afraid she was,' he said, enunciating his words carefully, sounding once again well educated. 'Like I said, she wouldn't go to the doctor, not after that one time. Said everything was OK, said native women didn't need doctors. She seemed almost terrified.' He winced.

'Did she tell you who the father was?' Darina asked, holding her breath.

'Nah, she was too afraid,' he said in disgust. 'If I'd ever met him, he'd have known all about it!' He drummed the fingers of his right hand on his knee. 'I bopped that ponce Price one when he tried to interfere between us.' He laughed, a high unsteady whinny. 'Right prat he looked. Must've had a real shiner to show everyone!'

Martin hadn't said he'd had an actual set to with Noah. Had he been ashamed at being bested by a hippy? Or had there been some other reason for his reticence? Darina only had his word that he was sterile. She felt now that she couldn't trust anything anyone had told her.

'Did she ever tell you that she was illegitimate?'

'You kidding me?' Noah looked genuinely startled. He got up and moved jerkily over to the window and stood looking out, his right fingers beating an irregular pattern on his leg.

'She found out just before she left home to go and live with her brother and sister-in-law.'

'She never said nothing like that. Seems to me you been listening to the wrong people.' Noah appeared to lose interest.

Rory staggered across the room, opened the cupboard by the stove and started taking out cleaning stuff.

Noah let out a roar and kicked the door to. 'Bugger off,' he said to Rory, who started crying.

Laurel dashed across and picked him up. 'You bastard,' she said to Noah, 'pick on someone your own size.'

'Like you, eh,' he said and swung the back of his hand at her. But she ducked and scuttled out of range.

Noah looked at her, a tic flickering his left eyelid. For a moment Darina thought he was going to fling himself after Laurel. Instead, 'Gotta see someone,' he muttered, opened a jar at the back of the sink, removed some money and left the room.

'That's right, fuck off,' Laurel called after him. She went and looked in the jar and cursed. Then she brought a whimpering Rory back to the low table. 'Let's see what we can find here, shall we?' she said to him and reached beneath one of the cushions to drag out a magazine. 'Look at the pretty pictures.' She flicked over the pages. Rory plumped a finger down on a photograph of a horse and made a noise that might have been a whinny.

'Where's he gone?' Darina asked.

Laurel tossed her head, her face defiant. 'To get a fix. He's taken this week's rent and the housekeeping money, everything I earned last week. My next job doesn't start until Wednesday.'

'What do you do?'

'I'm a freelance butcher.'

'A butcher?' Darina was amazed, and then cross with herself for being amazed. Why shouldn't a girl be a butcher? 'Where did you train?'

'Back in Tazzy, Tasmania. I know I look little but I'm strong.' Laurel squared her shoulders as though to demonstrate.

'I'll believe you,' Darina said, looking at the bruise on her cheek.

'I didn't duck fast enough that time.' Laurel fingered the greeny-black contusion ruefully. 'Usually I can see them coming. Noah's a lovely guy. It's just his habit.'

'The drugs, you mean?'

'The pot calms him down but with the smack, well, you don't know what he'll do.'

'Does he work at all?'

'Oh, yeah, now and then. He's real intelligent, could

do anything.' Laurel said this with pride. 'He's always getting odd jobs around. Drove an old guy up to New-castle on Saturday with overnight stay and train fare paid back. Course, he dossed down and hitched, doubled his pay.'

'So he should be able to pay the rent?'

Laurel shook her head regretfully. 'Owed too many people. And to think I was the one made him pay them back! Or some of them.'

'Noah's lucky to have you.'

Her face broke into a sad grin, 'You said it! He knows it too. When he's himself. And, like I said, then he's a lovely guy. We have some really great times together. It's just you can't trust what he says. He could win Olympic Gold in the lying game.'

Darina remembered how quickly Noah had turned from being a charmer to lashing out. 'Has he told you anything about Sophie?'

Rory picked up the magazine and flapped it exper-imentally. Darina rescued it and shoved it back beneath the cushion.

'Not much,' Laurel admitted. 'I didn't want to hear. I mean, what girl wants to be told about the previous love in her boyfriend's life?'

'So Noah loved Sophie?'

'Sure!'

'I thought maybe she just made him comfortable, earned the money and all that.'

'Like me, you mean?' Laurel said sardonically. 'Actu-ally, he loves me in his own way, too. And I'm better for him than Sophie, I don't depend on him like she did. That sort of girl always needs a man in her life.'

Had Sophie? There'd always been one there,

sometimes more than one. First Jasper and her father, then her elder brother, then Noah and Martin. In the end, none of them had been able to help.

'My strength is that I can always leave and Noah knows it,' Laurel declared pugnaciously. 'I'm not hooked on him.'

Darina wondered how far that was true.

All the way back to her house, Darina thought about what Noah had said.

Sophie had suspected she was pregnant when she left Battersea. So what Basil had told Jemima was, at best, misleading. Rory wasn't a premature baby at all. The fact that he'd been so small was because Sophie hadn't been eating properly and had neglected herself. That chimed in with what Martin had said. Oh, if only Martin could have told her family where she was! Or at the very least bullied her into going to a doctor.

But according to Job, Sophie had left home because her father bullied her. Everyone Darina had spoken to had said how sensitive Sophie was and how she dissolved into tears whenever she thought she was being got at. Darina herself could remember how shy she was at five. Perhaps Martin had good reason for respecting her wishes.

How happy had Sophie been living with Noah? He seemed very unstable. Laurel said he could be great. Darina wondered just what 'great' meant. From what Noah said, Sophie had found someone even more dysfunctional than herself and discovered a role in looking after him. But Laurel claimed you couldn't rely on anything Noah told you and his sudden loss of control had been shocking. As shocking as Val's had been. How often did people lose their tempers with children? How often had Noah lost control with Sophie?

According to Martin, he'd offered her an escape route.

But then her family would have known where she was.

Was that the reason she hadn't gone to him? But what was it she'd said? That even though he thought he wanted to marry her it wouldn't work? Why not? Because she wasn't in love with him?

Sophie obviously had her own moral code. Darina thought that rather than being weak as everyone seemed to think, Sophie had had an amazing inner strength.

She'd been very upset on hearing Basil wasn't her father. Well, that was natural. Judging by Martin, 'natural' was a word that meant a lot to Sophie. She had found it natural to move in with her brother and sister-in-law when she didn't want to live at home any more. It was natural to give comfort when it was needed even if it involved sleeping with two men whilst bearing another man's child. It was not natural to move in with someone just to make your life more comfortable. What had been so unnatural she had had to move out of her brother's house?

Darina was very much afraid that she knew.

Stopped at traffic lights, Darina looked at Rory through the rear view mirror. He was chuckling to himself, then saw a dog in the car next door. 'Dog!' he shouted gleefully, 'dog!' He banged on the window pane. The dog barked at him and he laughed even more. Nothing shy or retiring there.

Much as she wanted to, Darina could see no resemblance to Noah or Martin or Paul Robins. But, thought Darina, she herself was nothing like her petite, chic mother.

Her mother! The lights went green and Darina shot away in a panic. She had completely forgotten that her mother was coming today. Might even have arrived!

Darina raced home through the traffic, her thoughts in a jumble. Likenesses and non-likenesses to parents, what she was going to do if her mother had arrived before she got home, and whether William had identified the body from the river. Her certainty that it was Jemima's had been constantly at the back of her mind, an aching tension that threatened to break through everything else.

But at least she reached home before her mother.

First thing was to check the answermachine. No messages. Darina felt relief. Fears could be dissipated, facts could not.

Clutching Rory by the hand, Darina found a couple of late roses in the tiny courtyard. She put them on her mother's dressing table in the back bedroom and thanked heaven she kept the beds made up, a house in Chelsea meant chums ringing up at any time for a night's lodging. She switched on the electric blanket and then put Rory in his cot.

Rory didn't like this.

Darina took him out of his cot and wondered whether pandering to his wishes was bad training for later. The doorbell rang, she put Rory back and ran downstairs, ignoring his screams of protest.

'Darling!' said Ann Stocks. She stood on the doorstep dressed in an elegant chocolate-brown suit with a silk blouse. The soft neckline flattered her neck and the cream lightened her pretty face. 'What on earth is that noise? I know it's a long time since I've seen you but you can't, surely, have managed to produce a child?' She tilted her face to receive Darina's kiss.

'I'm babysitting, Ma. Where's your car? Let me get your case.'

Ann's little BMW was not far away. Somehow she always managed to find parking near to where she wanted. Darina hefted a large suitcase out of the boot.

'I know what you're thinking, darling, but I really didn't know what to bring and when you've got the car, it doesn't matter, does it?' Ann retrieved a couple of jackets and a fur-collared coat from the back seat. 'Now tell me all about this child you're babysitting.'

'You'll love him,' Darina said, hauling the case back to the house. And I've got the most marvellous nursery food for us all to lunch on. However did you manage to get this in the car?

'The gardener, darling. Lunch sounds heavenly. Nursery food was always your father's favourite. Not that I was any good in the kitchen, as you know. Don't you think you should do something about that baby?'

But Rory's cries were lessening. 'He'll be asleep in a few minutes, he needs a rest. Do you want to go up to your room now?'

'Oh, I think a drink first, don't you? It's nearly twelve after all.'

In the short hour before Rory woke again, Darina got her mother a pre-lunch gin and tonic and heard all about what was happening with her bridge, the village feuds, the change of ownership in the local shop, the new restaurant that had just locally opened and the dreadful things a great friend had said to her.

Ann appeared in great form. Eighteen months earlier her second husband had died after a short but very happy marriage. Darina decided that she had now adapted once again to widowhood.

'Now, darling, tell me all about you. That's what I've come here to hear.' Ann sat back in the small armchair that was her favourite and looked about her. 'I'm so glad your tenants didn't do too much damage, this is such a pretty room. You know, if you didn't want to live here yourselves, you could let it for far more than they were paying. I don't care how nice they were, you were robbing yourself.'

Darina opened her mouth to say that she and William were very happy here themselves when the first cry came from upstairs.

Her mother fell instantly for Rory. 'What a delightful child,' she said.

Rory opened his big blue eyes and reached for her pearls. 'Gah!' he said, twisting the string.

'Naughty, naughty,' Ann said, laughing, and gently removed the pearls. 'Let's find something else for you to play with, shall we?' She reached into her lizard-skin handbag, detached the pearl and gold chain from her glasses and dandled that. Rory went for it in a big way. Darina looked on in astonishment. She had never seen her mother take any interest in babies before.

Soon they were all sitting down to minced lamb with parsnip and peas. 'Darling, he's gorgeous, just like you were as a baby.'

'I bet I wasn't as handsome,' said Darina.

'You were the most beautiful baby in the world. And

your father adored you. I was almost jealous!' Ann pouted prettily.

Darina knew there was no way even a baby could have displaced Ann in her husband's affections. 'I must have been a great trial,' she said. 'Babies seem very demanding.'

'I loved every minute of you. I don't suppose I was a very good mother, far too selfish, and you were so much more intelligent than me, but you were a joy.'

Ann sounded as though she meant it. Darina looked at her and thought how amazing life could be. Here she was, over thirty and it was the first time she felt truly loved by her mother.

Chapter Twenty-Seven

By the time William arrived at the morgue, everything was ready. The green-overalled pathologist was already examining the dreadful remains. Still dressed in her damp clothes, the unknown woman lay on a stainless steel table with a channel running round its edge. The smell of formalin mixed with decay with undertones of river debris floated towards William, the disturbing odours filling the pores of his skin.

Leaning against the wall beside the door, as though reluctant to move away from an escape route, was Terry Pitman, his thin face set into knife-like lines.

The pathologist nodded to his team and the police officers. 'Hope everyone had a good breakfast,' he said cheerfully. 'Bacon and eggs really sets a man up for the day.'

William could have told the last pathologist he'd worked with that he was a sadist and just to get on with the job but Peter Ross was an unknown quantity.

'All you cutters of cadavers are the same, not happy unless we're ready to puke,' he growled out. 'And you may well have your wish before this job's over.'

Ross looked at him as though for the first time. 'Not a pretty sight, is she?' he said jovially, adjusting the overhanging microphone. 'But you'll be OK, and Tel there never flinches.'

William saw Terry stir slightly and knew he had no more confidence in himself than William did.

'Right, we'll make a start,' said Peter Ross.

The curiously remote process of removing the layers of a dead person never failed to upset William.

Because he didn't know the identity of the victim, it should have been easier to watch but nibbling away at the edges of his consciousness was Darina's conviction that this was her friend, Jemima Ealham. But more likely was the chance that this was the body of Maeve O'Connor. Killed because she knew something she was going to tell police?

But maybe this wasn't murder. Maybe it was an accident or suicide. And maybe it wasn't either Jemima Ealham or Maeve O'Connor.

William's headache seemed worse than ever and he found it almost impossible to think straight.

The dry, disinterested voice of the pathologist had started to dictate his findings.

'Rigor mortis no longer present. Body has been in the water at least two days.' He turned over the woman's clenched hand. 'Cadaveric spasm of the right hand.' Then glanced at William and Terry and added, 'Often a drowning person will grab at whatever's to hand. You can find stones, water weeds, branches, all sorts of things when you undo the fingers.' Gently but firmly he was doing that as he spoke. 'Well, well, well,' he murmured. 'Look what we have here.' He beckoned to William, who came forward and was given a small circle of metal with a notched cross band. A moment's inspection revealed it to be a button.

Screwing up his eyes, William tried to read the lettering impressed into the metal. 'US Issue' he finally made out. Fishing out a small plastic evidence bag from his pocket, he slipped the button inside. It could mean something or nothing.

'Cadaveric spasm?' he asked.

'Usually a sure indication of death by drowning,' said the pathologist, watching his assistants take scrapings from under the fingernails of both hands. 'The victim panics, clutches at anything that can save him then movement is arrested by a sudden stopping of the heart. The shock of sudden immersion into cold water can lead to reflex cardiac arrest. Doesn't always happen, of course.'

'When it does, does it mean the victim doesn't breathe in water?' asked Terry, coming forward also.

'If it happens instantly, the classic signs of death by drowning are not present,' agreed Peter Ross. 'Then handfuls of pond weed or reeds can be indicators that the victim was alive when immersion took place.'

'But this isn't such an indicator,' murmured William, still inspecting the button.

'No. She almost certainly grabbed it just before death, though.'

'And it doesn't belong to any of her clothes?'

The pathologist examined the outer garments carefully. 'Not that I can see.'

William had a sudden vision of the dead woman struggling with an attacker, perhaps starting to lose consciousness and clutching at her assailant's coat, ripping off the button in the process. Would her attacker have realized it had gone?

The pathologist picked up the right hand again,

looked at it closely, then studied the left. 'Flesh swollen by immersion in water but we should be able to obtain fingerprints for you.'

The autopsy proceeded with the detailed examination of the clothed body, then the removal of the dead woman's garments. 'Pants intact without visible staining,' the dry voice said. 'Doesn't look as if any attack was sexual unless the assailant found himself with an unexpected corpse on his hands and decided to dump it as quickly and unobtrusively as possible.'

Finally the body lay naked on the examination table.

William wondered if it was his imagination or was the disturbingly complex aroma of the mortuary actually growing stronger? Or was it just the headache that seemed to be increasing in intensity? He allowed medical terms to float by him but found his attention became focused on the terribly bruised and damaged neck area. 'Any chance she could have been strangled before being dumped in the river?' he asked abruptly.

The pathologist paused with a sigh of heavy resignation. 'Now, now, chief inspector, you should know better than that.' Then he relented. 'This was the area I was about to turn to.' He turned his steely gaze on to the ruined neck. 'It's difficult to be certain, water immersion always plays the devil with blood, but if you want my expert opinion,' he paused meaningfully.

What else could he want, William thought with exasperation but said, 'I'd be most grateful.'

'Well, putting it in layman's terms and considering the boat injuries occurred a couple of days after immersion, I think the likelihood she was strangled is strong. I shall be most surprised if we find signs of anoxia in the air passages or lungs.'

'Which would only be there if the death was by drowning?'

'Quite, chief inspector.'

Well, a likelihood of death by strangulation wasn't hard evidence but at least it gave them something to work on. Photography of the wounds proceeded before the gut wrenching business of stripping what was left of the scalp from the remains of the skull before it was opened up with an electric saw.

At the end of the autopsy, William, his sensibilities anaesthetized by all he'd experienced, summed up the particular points he'd caught during the mentally bruising process. 'So, you found no signs of anoxia either in the air passages or the lungs and you consider death occurred before immersion in the river. And your expert opinion is that the victim was over twenty-five but no older than the early forties.'

The pathologist sucked his teeth for a moment. 'The skull and teeth are so badly damaged it's hard to be sure of either limit but it's a good guestimate,' he said finally. 'Sorry I can't narrow it any further.'

'And the victim has been in the water two to three days.'

'Certainly at least two days. Water slows up the disappearance of rigor mortis but, as I said at the beginning, the body shows no sign of it now. And not longer than four days, the decomposition gases had not begun to swell the body.'

William felt thankful for minute mercies.

'You'll get my full report as soon as it's been typed up. Good to meet you chief inspector, I look forward to our future collaboration.'

'Quite.' William found it impossible to sound enthusiastic.

'That age thing,' said Terry after he'd taken a deep breath of the clear air outside the mortuary. 'Twenty-five to forty means the nanny is well in the frame. She was twenty-seven.'

And Jemima Ealham was the same age as Darina, early thirties.

Back at the station CID room, Pat James was on the telephone. The moment William and Terry entered, she waved compulsively at them. 'Right,' she said to her caller. 'Right, got that. Look, the chief inspector has just returned to the office, I'll have a word with him and ring you back, OK?'

She put down the phone, her eyes snapping with excitement. 'You'll never guess who that was.' Then recollected herself. 'Sorry, guv. It was Paul Robins. He went to the airport to meet Val Douglas this morning from her international conference but she wasn't on the plane. When he got back to the office, the organizer had been on the line. Apparently Robins was their liaison chap. Val Douglas never turned up at the conference! They rang her home number all weekend but no answer. As soon as he'd had the call, Robins went over to her flat to see if she was ill. No sign of her. He rang Basil Ealham's offices. He's abroad and she hasn't been seen. He rang one of her daughters but she hasn't spoken to her since the middle of last week. So then he rang here to see if we knew of any accident.'

William and Terry looked at each other. 'How old would you say Mrs Douglas was?' William asked Pat.

'Thirty-eight, forty?'

'Within the frame, definitely, guv,' said Terry.

'Where is Robins now?'

'Still at Mrs Douglas's flat, he said he'd stay there until I rang him back.'

'Right, we'll take the clothes over and see if he can identify them and we'll have another look at her place. Sergeant, ring the mortuary, stop them sending the clothes to forensic's and then collect them and meet me at the Douglas flat.'

Pat reached for her coat.

'We need to check whether she showed up for her flight and instigate a house-to-house for any sightings of her that evening. Also to check with her secretary, see if she knows anything about her movements or can throw light on unexpected appointments or callers. You know what's needed, inspector.' William threw the words at Terry like a golfer hitting balls on a driving range.

'Right, guv, leave it to me.'

As he rang Val Douglas's bell, William saw the door of the next flat open a crack.

Paul Robins flung open Val's door, his face drawn. 'What do you think has happened?' he asked immediately. 'Val would never have just walked out on a conference like that.' He led the way into the living room, collapsed into one of the small armchairs and put his head in his hands. 'I'm distraught,' he said unnecessarily.

The room looked smaller and shabbier than it had the previous week. Because Val Douglas was no longer drawing the eye with her dynamism and dark good looks?

'Would you like a cup of tea?' William asked.

Paul shook his head violently. 'I couldn't drink a thing. It's the not knowing that's so awful. I promised to ring Sally the moment I knew anything.'

William looked at the telephone, a red light glowed on the answering machine. 'Have you checked the messages?'

Paul looked up. 'Oh my God, no! Why didn't I think of that?' He made to get up but William was before him.

'Hi, Mum! Sorry to have missed you,' said a fresh young female voice. 'Just wanted to wish you good luck with the conference. Look forward to hearing all about it when you get back.'

There were a number of clicks and then a Dutch accent asked if Mrs Douglas could contact the Conference Organizer as soon as possible and gave an international number. More clicks. A repeat of the same message. Then a call from the desk sergeant at a nearby police station that asked Mrs Douglas to contact them, they'd found what seemed to be a case of hers.

Almost before the message ended, William was dialling the number that had been given and talking to the duty sergeant.

'The case was found in a ditch in a back lane not far from the river yesterday afternoon,' William told Paul when he'd finished. 'Some honest soul thought it must have fallen off a roof rack and took it to their local station. The police opened it and found clothes, personal possessions and what seem to be Mrs Douglas's conference papers. They had her name and address on.'

'Oh, God,' groaned Paul. He levered himself up and

walked over to the window. 'What can have happened to her?'

The doorbell rang. William opened it to Pat, who carried several transparent plastic bags.

He took them into the living room. 'Would you please look at these, sir, and tell me if you recognize any of them?'

Paul looked nervously at the bags, then took the one containing the waistcoat, handling it as though it could be infectious. 'Where has it come from?'

'Have you seen it before?' William repeated patiently.

Paul gazed at the still damp leather through the plastic, turning the bag this way and that to get the best view.

Finally he said, 'I can't be sure but it's like one Val wears.'

Suddenly he thrust it back at William. 'What's happened to her? You know something, I'm sure you do. Why don't you tell me?'

William jerked his head at Pat, indicating the kitchen. She took the hint.

'Sit down, Mr Robins,' he said gently.

Paul slowly lowered himself into a chair.

William put the bags on a table and sat opposite him. 'The body of a woman was pulled out of the river yesterday. She was wearing those clothes,' he indicated the bags. 'With what you have told us and the discovery of Mrs Douglas's suitcase, it is beginning to look as though it could be her.'

Paul gazed at him. Sweat began to bead his brow. He tried to speak several times, finally he managed, 'You want me to identify her?'

'I'm sorry, that won't be possible. The body is damaged beyond recognition.'

'Beyond recognition?' Paul brought the words out slowly. Then, 'Basil!' he shouted. 'I knew it! He's done her in!'

'Why do you suggest that?'

'Because he couldn't stand being stood up! My God, the man's ego is higher than the Empire State.' Paul walked rapidly to the window and back again to stand in front of William, balancing on the balls of his feet like a boxer ready to launch the first blow. 'I'll do him! I will!'

Pat brought in a tray of tea. William hastily removed the garment bags so she could put it down on the table.

'How do you know Mrs Douglas broke off her engagement to Mr Ealham?' William asked.

Paul flung himself back into the armchair and ignored the tea Pat placed beside him. 'God,' he groaned. 'If only I'd been earlier!'

Pat gave William a cup then sat down with one herself. He looked at his tea, the delicate of aroma of Darjeeling reached his nostrils. William's head pounded with pain and he longed to sip the fragrant liquid. He reached for the cup. Then withdrew his hand. What was the point of only doing half the job? If he didn't feel any better in a couple of days, though, he was going to give up this stupid diet.

'OK,' said Paul. 'Here's the full story. Thursday evening I was desperate. Val hadn't responded to any of my calls and I was terrified she was going to announce her engagement to that man.'

'Why?' interposed William quietly.

'Why?' Paul looked at him startled. 'Ever since the fire everything about Val this last week has suggested that she was deciding to marry Basil Ealham. Staying at Blackboys, working from his offices, closing me out of her life! But I thought she'd wait until she got back from Europe. I knew Basil was supposed to take her to the airport but I thought if I arrived early enough, I could persuade her to let me take her.'

'She told you Basil Ealham was taking her to the airport?' asked Pat, catching William's eye.

Paul nodded. Then seemed to realize something wasn't quite as he'd thought. 'You mean, he wasn't going to?'

'She told us he was catching a plane from Gatwick and hers went from Heathrow.'

Paul looked at William with bitter eyes. 'The bitch!' Then he frowned. 'But he collected her anyway.'

'You saw Basil Ealham pick up Mrs Douglas?' asked William carefully.

'I missed them by that,' Paul clicked his middle finger and thumb together. 'I should have been there in good time but, would you believe it, I had a puncture. I never have punctures! You wouldn't believe how fast I tried to mend it. But I didn't know where anything was and then the nuts were impossible to move, I had to stand on the spanner, can you believe that?' He was disgusted. 'And when I at last got here, it was to see Mr Mighty's Roller disappearing in the distance! I was gutted!' He flung himself back in the chair and raised his eyes to the ceiling.

'What time was this? asked William.

'Six twenty-two! I can tell you to the last minute, my eyes were on the clock all the way after I'd mended that puncture. I've never driven so fast through traffic before!'

Six twenty-two, thought William. He and Pat had left just before quarter to six. There'd been no trace of Basil's Rolls Royce then. Had he come back for Val Douglas?

'But there I was, watching them both drive away from me. I'd thought it was my last chance, swooping down, carrying her off and swaying her with my eloquence.' He fixed William with a wild eye. 'You don't know how eloquent I can be with Val. That's how . . . well, that's another part of the story.'

William made a mental note not to forget to follow this up. 'Are you sure it was Mr Ealham's Rolls Royce?'

Paul nodded vigorously. 'I wouldn't forget that number plate: BE1; Be First, what monumental cheek!'

'What did you do then?'

'Went back to my flat and got plastered. I haven't been that drunk since my college days.' He rubbed his forehead. 'I spent Friday in an alcoholic haze with the mother of all hangovers. I switched off the phone, locked the door and gave myself up to blinding self-pity.' He paused but neither William nor Pat said anything.

'Anyway, I finally pulled myself together and by this morning I'd returned to a state approaching normality. On my desk as I get in is a note of my office answer-machine messages from my secretary. The first one is from Val, obviously rung in before Basil arrived.'

Pat put down her cup of tea and reached for her notebook.

'She'd said she wanted me to know she'd finished with Basil and could I meet her at the airport on Monday. I knew her flight, of course, I'd done all the arranging, and I reckoned I could just make it in time. And I did, but she wasn't on the flight. At first I thought she'd changed it because I hadn't rung her in Holland. I tell you, marble-plinthed bronze horses weren't as high as the one Val could get on when she reckoned you'd failed her in any way.' He looked moodily at his trouser leg and flicked a piece of fluff away. 'I rang her here and left a message, it'll be on there if you play it to the end.' He flicked his gaze towards the answermachine. 'Then I went back to the office and my secretary tells me the Conference Organizer has been on the line asking if Val's all right and wanting to know why she never turned up. That's when I started to get really worried. I rang Sally, Blackboys and Basil's office and then came over here to see if she'd collapsed on the way to the airport and been brought back. But everything was just as you see it and no Val. It wasn't much of a hope anyway and by the time I rang you lot, I was out of my mind. And now you tell me she was in the river all the time!' He ended on a sort of wail.

Pat refilled his cup, put in two spoons of sugar and gave it a good stir. 'Drink that,' she commanded.

Paul raised the tea obediently to his lips. Then put it down again without drinking. 'It can't be her in the river.' He sounded as though hysteria would break out at any moment.

William said, 'When you were talking about how eloquent you could be with Mrs Douglas, you told us that that was how, then broke off and said that was another part of the story. What did you mean?'

'Eloquent?' Paul looked puzzled. 'Oh,' he added, his face clearing, 'I remember.' Then he paused and flicked again at his trousers. 'Look,' he said in a man-to-man manner, 'I'm going to level with you. I told your sergeant over here,' he glanced at Pat, 'Aherne wasn't blackmailing me. Well, he tried it on.'

William felt a sense of excitement. The case was beginning to unravel, he could sense it.

'The thing was, shortly after Aherne started working as nightwatchman, I called on Val one evening. I knew she wanted to make sure of Ealham's money, the company was going to go to the wall if someone didn't inject some cash and I was all for it, my money was involved as well. But she was distancing herself from me.'

'You mean you and she were an item before that?' interposed Pat.

'An item? You bet we were,' he said with sudden energy. 'We didn't broadcast it around, Val didn't think it would be good for business, but in private, we could have made all the headlines, that's how big an item we were.'

It sounded as though Val pushed the sexual button whenever she wanted something, William thought.

'Anyway, I was getting really frustrated. I rang and said I wanted her to check a press release. When I arrived I sent Aherne out to buy some cigarettes and gave him some money to have a drink at the same time. I thought that would get rid of him for at least half an hour or so. How was I to know he'd sneak back?' he complained, his voice a whine.

'You mean your eloquence got through to Mrs Douglas?' William asked.

Paul gave a reminiscent smile, 'And how!' Then distress washed over him again. 'But it was only that one evening. And then Aherne made me meet him in that wretched cafe and told me he was Ealham's spy. But that he wouldn't tell him what he'd seen as long as I coughed up three hundred a week. Three hundred! Well, I tore him off a strip, I can tell you!'

'And did he back down?' William asked.

'Well, no.' Paul plucked at the crease in his trousers. 'I, well, I decided I'd pay him for a week or two and see how things went.'

'But you didn't make any payments,' William suggested calmly.

'Well, I was going to, but then there was the fire, you see.' Paul stumbled to a stop, looking miserable. 'I didn't have to tell you any of this,' he said aggressively.

'So why are you telling us?'

'Don't you see, Ealham distrusted Val, that's obvious. If he found out she'd been double-dealing, he would, well,' he shuddered graphically. 'The man's a monster. Only a monster would set a spy on the woman he loved!'

'We shall need you to give a statement at the station,' William said expressionlessly. 'We'll let you know when.'

'But what about Val, are you really saying she's dead?'

'I think it looks almost certain that she is,' William said slowly. 'Fingerprints from the corpse and from here should confirm it.'

'Oh God,' Paul said.

'I'd like the sergeant here to go with you to your home, Mr Robins, and look through your wardrobe.'

Paul swallowed nervously. 'Don't you need a search warrant for that?'

'We can always get one,' William assured him. 'Co-operation on your part, though, will greatly assist our inquiries.'

Another nervous swallow. 'In that case, I'll be happy.'

'The sergeant will be with you in a minute,' William said and took Pat outside. 'You know what we need?'

'To check whether any of his clothes have a button missing matching the one the victim was clutching. Also if they bear signs of having been near a river or damage sustained during a possible struggle.'

'And check for signs of spilt petrol as well. I don't like it that he claims she rang and said she'd broken with Basil Ealham when she told us it was nothing more than a tiff. Either she's an even more devious woman than we realized or he's setting up an alibi. Watch him like a hawk.'

Pat nodded. 'I wouldn't put anything past the Douglas woman, though, guv. She could just have been hedging all her bets.'

William nodded. 'We need some sort of evidence. Before you go, get a SOCO team over here, I want this place gone over with the same sort of care they'd give the love of their lives. I'll let them in. I'm going to have a word with whoever it is next door takes such a keen interest in their neighbour.' He went back into the living room and got Paul Robins's key off him.

A brass knob on the next door flat shone brilliantly at William as he rang the bell. There was a long pause. Then came the sound of shuffling feet. The door was slowly opened a crack and the same eye he'd seen the other night looked at him. 'Yes?' It was a croak more than a word.

William flashed his warrant card. 'DCI Pigram, I wonder if I could have a word?' It was impossible to know whether the owner of the eye was male or female.

A delighted cackle. 'That's what they say on *The Bill*!' The door closed and he heard the sound of a chain being drawn. The door opened again, wide this time. The peeping Tom was a woman. She looked in her seventies with a frizz of iron-grey hair, a deeply lined face, large, bright grey eyes, a hook of a nose, thin mouth, emaciated figure in an elegant emerald green two-piece, what must once have been sensational legs, and feet in slippers.

'I'll take another look at that warrant card, the way you flashed it at me it could be anything.' William handed it over and she carefully scrutinized the identifying photograph. Finally she handed it back and motioned him in. 'Molly Cummings. To what do I owe the pleasure, then, chief inspector?'

Her living room was the same size as Val Douglas's, furnished with what looked like the remnants of a more gracious life. There was a less than appetizing smell and William saw a foil dish of some supermarket cottage pie steaming gently on a table by the window. The aroma combined with the influence of the autopsy and his splitting headache to make him feel faintly sick.

'I'm sorry, I've interrupted your lunch.'

'No matter.' The woman picked up dish and fork, there was no plate. 'It can go back in the oven. Like a coffee, would you?'

William refused politely. She disappeared and he turned to look out of the window. It was screened with a net curtain. It was fine enough to conceal from her neighbours that Molly Cummings spent the day in an upright armchair monitoring their activities but coarse enough to offer a perfect view.

Molly Cummings reappeared and sat down. 'Pull up a seat and tell me what you want,' she ordered, waving her hand at another chair.

William obeyed, seating himself so he could see her full face. Her eyes were sharp and malicious, as was the slight smile on her face. She wore a wedding ring on her left hand.

'Mrs Cummings, I'm anxious to know whether you saw anything of your neighbour, Mrs Douglas, after my sergeant and I left here last Thursday evening.'

She looked down at her slippers, set her feet toes to toes. 'I'm a nosy old parker,' she said looking up again. 'As you know. A bit of a bitch too, I expect, but there's not much that's interesting in my life.'

William said nothing.

'Other people are my hobby. Take Mrs Douglas. Goes away for days on end. Has at least two steady boy-friends, which of them does she stay with, I wonder? Both tall and both fair headed but what a difference! She controls one and the other controls her. How much does each know about the other, eh?' Amused, sardonic, Molly Cummings was enjoying herself. 'And some-thing's up. She hasn't been here since Thursday but the pet arrived at least an hour ago. And I don't suppose he's been sitting in there doing nothing, do you?'

'Mrs Cummings, did you see anything of Mrs Douglas Thursday evening?'

She looked a little piqued. 'I was leading up to that, young man. Quite an evening that was! First the macho man. And such a row they had! Always knew she was too wilful for that one. Then you and that woman arrive. Then everything's quiet for a little. But just as I settle with my supper, I hear her come out and the lift arrive. It pings as the doors open, you probably noticed.'

'Did you see her get in?'

She shook her head. 'Stayed in my chair.' William

could imagine her with fork poised. Wondering whether she'd reach the door in time to see anything, then deciding it wasn't worth a try.

'But I saw her come out down below. She was carrying a case.' Molly seemed delighted to have an audience for her nosiness. 'She sat down on the wall, as though waiting for someone. It's a very convenient height for sitting on, that wall. I sometimes take a little breather there on my way back from shopping.' William looked through the curtain. The wall was some two feet in height and finished off with a slight pillar either side of the path that led up to the flats.

'Did you see what the case looked like?'

'One of those smallish things on wheels with a handle, you see all the stewardesses using them in airports.' She looked impishly at him. 'Quite a traveller I was in the old days. If I had the cash I'd be off tomorrow even now.'

'I can believe it,' William assured her gravely. 'Did you see what colour it was?'

'No,' she said reluctantly.

'Never mind, you've given us a most helpful description. Now, you said she sat on the wall, what happened then?'

'She stayed there for about ten minutes and kept looking at her watch. Waiting for someone to collect her, I thought. And he's late. Then I saw a Rolls Royce draw up. He had to double park, no hope of a place after six o'clock here. The passenger window slid down and the driver bent forward, I could just see his fair head. Macho man, all right. He didn't always use the Rolls, sometimes it was a Volvo, but that night I reckoned he'd put his best foot forward. Because he had ground to make up, hadn't he? I mean, walking out like that and then being late collecting her.'

'And what time exactly was this?'

'Six fifteen. I know because I listened to the news headlines as I heated my fish pie.'

Six fifteen was about an hour after he and Pat had arrived. Plenty of time for Basil to have gone home, decide he'd take Val to the airport after all and get out his best car. It all fitted in with what Paul Robins had told them. 'And Mrs Douglas got in the Rolls?'

'Not at first she didn't.' Molly was making the most of her story. 'Came to the car, stuck her head through the window and stood there arguing with him.'

William looked at the distance between a car double parked in the road and this third floor window. 'How could you tell she was arguing?'

'What else would she have been doing?' Molly gave a cackle. 'And he must have sweet talked her because after a little she takes her head back, goes and picks up her case, puts it in the boot, then gets in and off the car glides.'

Something about this scenario struck William as odd. 'The driver didn't get out of the car at all? Didn't help her with her luggage?'

'Macho man doesn't have many manners.' Another cackle. 'And the car was beginning to cause a hold up.'

'Well, thank you, Mrs Cummings, you've been most helpful.'

'Just a minute, young man, don't you want to hear the rest?'

'Rest?'

'Two minutes after macho man whisks wilful lady off, a taxi arrives. Has to double park again. Driver gets out, walks up the path, waits around for a few minutes, then comes up to the third floor and rings Mrs Douglas's bell. I know she's not there so I think only fair if I tell him she's gone.' She gave William a malicious grin. 'Was he cross! Said he'd only been fifteen minutes late, and she should have waited for him. Can't wait when you've a plane to catch, I told him.'

'How did you know she had a plane to catch?'

'I didn't but he needed to realize you can't keep clients hanging about. In my day nobody kept me waiting.'

William would have bet money on it.

Molly Cummings had nothing else useful to add. William asked if she'd mind coming down to the station to make a statement.

'If you send a car for me.' She looked unexpectedly skittish.

William promised.

He let himself back into the Douglas flat, now empty, and played the telephone message tape right through. Paul Robins's call was there but nothing else of interest.

He put on a pair of plastic gloves and looked quickly through the desk. Nothing interesting came to light. He drew a blank in the bedroom as well. While he worked he mentally sifted through Molly Cummings' evidence.

A visit to Blackboys seemed called for. Robins had said Basil Ealham was still away. It would be interesting to see if Rolls Royce BE1 was there and if he could find any trace of a jacket with a missing metal button. And if young Jasper was home, William could reassure him that the corpse from the river now seemed highly unlikely to be his sister. Which reminded him. William took out his mobile and tried to call Darina. But all he got was the answermachine. Eventually the SOCO team arrived and William left them in possession.

The garage block at Blackboys was at the side of the house, set nicely back and shielded by massive shrubs.

William parked his car in front of the garage. Each of the four doors was open and he could see the Rolls Royce, its cream paint gleaming, its number plate bold. Beside it were two Volvos, one large family car, the other a smaller, sportier model. The fourth space was empty.

William went up to the house.

The door was opened by the housekeeper. William showed her his warrant card and asked to come in.

'Oh, it's not Jemima, is it? Her who you found in the river? Jasper told me,' she said as William raised an enquiring eyebrow.

'I'm happy to say it now looks as though the body we found was not Miss Ealham's.'

The look of relief on her face was heartwarming. 'Thank heavens, I must tell Mr Ealham immediately.' She moved in the direction of the library.

William went after her. 'I understood he was still away.'

'He came back this morning. Jasper rang him last night.' Mrs Starr moved again in the direction of the library. Once again William detained her. 'Can you tell me, please, do you recognize this button?' He fished the small plastic evidence bag out of his pocket.

She took and studied it. 'Why, that's off Mr Ealham's hunting waistcoat.'

'Hunting waistcoat?'

'Well, it's what he calls it.' She gave him an amused glance. 'More like a photographer's vest it is, lots of pockets. It usually hangs with the outdoor clothes, through here.' She took him through a door that opened on to a corridor. At the end a glass panelled door led into the garden. Beside it a row of hooks held a variety of jackets and coats. Mrs Starr shuffled amongst them and produced a khaki, many-pocketed safari type waistcoat.

William compared the buttons with the one in the plastic bag. It was a perfect match. He took hold of the garment. 'Thank you. Now I'll go and reassure Mr Ealham about his daughter,' he said.

Chapter Twenty-Eight

Darina drove to Blackboys with her mind in a turmoil. Beside her, her mother turned to play peek-a-boo with a delighted Rory, who for once showed no signs of falling asleep in the car.

The telephone had rung just as they were finishing lunch.

'Basil Ealham. I understand you have my grandson,' he said abruptly, no grace notes of greeting. 'Good of you to help but I'd like him returned now.' No would it be convenient, or can I come and collect him!

'Have you heard from Jemima?' Darina had to assume the fact he hadn't mentioned her disappearance yet must mean something.

'I gather she's taken off somewhere,' the autocratic voice said. 'She'll turn up, she always does.' The certainty in his voice was immensely comforting. But the Basils of this world always think they can order everything the way they want; until they discover some things are beyond even their power. 'You'll bring Rory back?' It was only just a question.

'Certainly,' said Darina. 'Once he's finished his lunch.' She didn't want Basil Ealham to think he could order her about the same way he did everyone else.

'Right.' Darina had been left with the tone buzzing in her ear.

'I've got to take Rory back,' she'd said to her mother. 'I'm sorry, you've only just arrived and I abandon you.'

'I'll come with you, darling. Help to keep baby amused.' Ann made a funny face at Rory and he screwed up his eyes and chortled with delight, the spoon he was trying to feed himself with waving in a highly dangerous manner.

'Are you sure?' asked Darina, dismayed. Everything told her this was not a good idea.

'I remember that house and Basil Ealham, I can't wait to see both again,' her mother insisted.

Darina faced facts. There was no way Lady Stocks was going to be deprived of this treat.

She pulled up in front of Blackboys and noted with relief that hers was the only car standing on the forecourt. She wasn't in the mood to cope with police, Val Douglas or anybody else today.

She opened the door for her mother then unfastened Rory from his seat. Remembering the amount of time it had taken the two of them to stack the car with all his bits and pieces, Darina decided Basil was going to help take them out.

Ann Stocks gazed up at the façade of the house. 'Oh, I do so remember this. Such a lovely place I thought, then I saw what they'd done to the inside.'

'I think you'll approve now, Ma.' Darina lifted Rory out of the car, carried him chattering excitedly to the front door and rang the bell.

Rory insisted on being put down.

The door was opened by a man in his mid-thirties.

Darina gazed at him in awe. This had to be the most

magnetic male she'd met in a long time. Dark hair flopped over a face that was too irregular to be called handsome but was nevertheless devastatingly attractive with its dark, dancing eyes, slightly crooked nose and wry mouth. He had a lean, contained body clad in well cut jeans, an equally well cut checked shirt and a puffa waistcoat. He could have stepped out of some American tobacco ad.

'Hi,' he said amiably.

Darina collected her scattered wits. 'Hi, I mean, hello. I've brought Rory back. I'm Darina Lisle and this is my mother, Lady Stocks.'

'Ann Stocks,' her mother said firmly with the smile that had been known to weaken the knees of the most intractable male. 'How nice to meet you, Mr, er?' She put her head on one side in pretty enquiry and proferred her hand.

How, Darina wondered in despair, had she managed to miss out on acquiring even some of her mother's brightly honed social graces?

He took her hand, 'Titus Masterson.' Then looked down at Rory, who had suddenly turned a little shy and stood clutching at Darina's hand. 'You must be Rory.'

Rory stuck his thumb in his mouth and nodded.

'Titus!' Darina said, light dawning. 'Is Jemima with you?'

He nodded. 'We've been snowboarding in the Trossachs.'

'I'm sorry?' It was all too much for Darina.

'Snowboarding, darling, such a healthy activity,' Ann Stocks said. 'Can we come in? Basil is expecting us.'

Titus stepped back with fluid grace. 'I've lost my

manners, I do apologize.' His accent had just a trace of the transatlantic.

In the big hall, Rory lost his shyness and suddenly took off in the direction of the library.

'Hey, son,' said Titus, going after him. 'I wouldn't go in there.'

Too late. Rory had already yanked on the door's handle and pushed it open. 'Dah!' he shouted, 'dah!' and ran across the room.

Titus, Darina and her mother all followed.

Basil was sitting behind his desk, his face a mask of anger. In front of him stood Jemima dressed in jeans, T-shirt and trainers, her short hair windswept, her thumbs stuck belligerently in her hip pockets.

'Oh, Jemima,' said Darina with heartfelt relief. 'I've been so worried about you.'

'You see!' Basil grated out as he bent down to lift an excited Rory on to his knee.

'I'm over thirty, a grown woman, I don't have to leave an itinerary every time I take off,' Jemima insisted.

'But you seemed so frightened,' Darina burst out. 'When I couldn't get hold of you, I didn't know what to think.'

Jemima looked slightly shamefaced. 'I did ham it up a bit. Titus had rung me, you see.' She glanced at him with a look that didn't seem able to pull itself free. 'And asked me to go away with him. I couldn't say no, he mightn't have asked me again. And I knew you wanted to develop the baby-food recipes so I thought you'd like looking after him. Were you really worried about me?'

Darina was very angry. 'I was. Particularly when that body was found . . .'

should be involved with, do you?' she said
er. 'Why don't we leave it to the police and
"

Basil's voice was a whiplash. Any veneer
ion had been peeled away. 'I want you as
vant there to be no doubt, absolutely no
out this.'

l at him for a long moment. He stared back
in dignity and charm of manner faced raw
f my presence can assist in any way,' she
and sat down again.

d to William, 'Well?' he barked.

d to you a scenario that required investi-
n said, his voice rough but steady. 'Your
firm is public knowledge. Your only alibi
vas Mrs Douglas, who admitted she took a
Ve have received evidence that Mr Aherne
by you to spy on Mrs Douglas and you
nown about the spare rooms that could
into accommodation for him, thereby
nstant presence at the factory.'

ry still. 'That is pure supposition. What is
he gave a savage emphasis to the word,
d Gerry Aherne as a spy? You can have
an's dead.'

t for you, isn't it?' William said quietly.
y, a picture of contained control, nicely
h Basil's flamboyant style. But Darina
uscle that twitched at the side of his jaw
he didn't feel nearly as assured as he

ou tell me why I should want to murder
ake, I was engaged to her!' For a fleeting

'Body?' Jemima asked. 'What do you mean, body?'

'The corpse of a woman was pulled from the river yesterday. For a while it seemed as though it might be yours,' William said, coming forward from where he'd been standing by a window. 'I rang you,' he said to Darina. 'But you must have left. There's a message on your answering machine.'

'William, how nice,' said his mother-in-law, giving him another of her full voltage smiles.

'I didn't see your car,' Darina said.

'It's by the garage, behind the shrubs,' he said. He seemed to be clutching some sort of khaki garment.

Jemima reached an arm back towards Titus with a smile the like of which Darina had never seen her give before. He slipped an arm round her shoulders.

'And how nice to see you again, Basil,' Ann Stocks said, moving on to offer him her hand. 'It's been a long time.'

He looked at her blankly for a moment then smiled. Darina was reminded of rhymes about tigers. 'Ann Lisle, how delightful.'

'Stocks, now. I was widowed and remarried.'

'Lucky man,' he said, holding her hand in his.

Ann twinkled at him. 'You always were a most charming man,' she said. 'Unfortunately, Geoffrey died also but not before we had a most happy time together.' She sat herself down on one of the sofas.

'What's happening?' Darina whispered to William. 'What are you doing here? It can't be official, surely?'

'Strangely enough, it is,' he said repressively. 'But my investigation appears to have been hijacked.' He moved over to the desk. 'Mr Ealham, can we continue our conversation somewhere quiet or would you prefer to come down to the station?' His voice was steel, his manner composed and Darina felt very proud of him. She went and sat beside her mother.

Basil removed his glasses from Rory's grasp. 'Carry on, chief inspector.'

William made no move and remained silent. Basil swept the others with a look that was hard to read. 'The body that wasn't Jemima's appears to be that of Val Douglas.'

Darina gasped. Jemima clutched at Titus's sleeve.

'And the police are accusing me of her murder.' Basil's voice was strained but steady.

'Dad!' Jemima screamed and ran to his side. 'Dad, they can't do that.'

Basil lowered Rory to the floor and ignored his daughter. 'You can have no evidence that will stand up in court,' he said to William.

'I have yet to accuse you of murder,' William said quietly. 'All I said was we have two witnesses who saw you and your car collect Mrs Douglas from her home on Thursday night. She has not been seen alive since.'

'You saw me leave her flat after she'd broken off our engagement. She can't have failed to tell you that. That was the last time I saw her.'

'Our witnesses say you came back later,' William said quietly.

Rory roared for attention, dancing up and down, and stretching up his arms to Basil.

Darina rose but was beaten by Jasper, who came into the library at high speed and dashed across the floor. 'There, there, little man! All is well, Jass is here.' He picked the boy up, swinging him high above his blond head. Rory's cries gave way to screams of delight.

Jasper lowered a[...] still chortling. 'Wha[...] 'My sister returned [...] more unto his lovin[...] who else?' He looke[...] black holes.

'I'm Darina's m[...] belongs to your sist[...] society hostess.

'Jasper, sit dow[...] 'Everyone, sit dow[...] matter to this impe[...]

Darina looked [...] perched on an arm[...]

Rory tugged at [...] the floor, he then [...] though she'd beer[...] life, sat on the so[...] her lap.

William looke[...] shoulders and wa[...]

The only pe[...] Jasper, who lean[...] shelves and radia[...]

'Now,' said B[...] taking a board m[...] Jemima's arriva[...] fire to the prem[...] to acquire the co[...] the nightwatchm[...] to spy on Mrs D[...] mail me. Do I ha[...]

Ann Stocks [...]

something w[...] to her daugh[...] Basil's family[...]

'Sit dowr[...] of sophistica[...] witnesses. I [...] doubt at all a[...]

Ann stare[...] at her. Patrici[...] power. 'Well, [...] said gracefull[...]

Basil turn[...]

'I suggest [...] gation,' Willia[...] interest in th[...] for that night [...] sleeping pill. [...] was employe[...] would have [...] be converted[...] ensuring his c[...]

Basil sat v[...] this evidence, [...] 'that I employ[...] no proof, the r[...]

'Convenie.[...] He stood easi[...] contrasting w[...] could see the [...] and knew tha[...] looked.

'And can y[...] Val? For God's [...]

second his face crumpled, then his expression regained its cool composure.

'An engagement she broke the night she was killed, sending you from her in a rage.'

Basil laughed. 'Rage? Is that what you call it? You haven't been around me long if you call that a rage. All right, I was pissed off, I'll give you that. Wouldn't you be? You've just given a woman a twenty thousand pound ring and she throws it back in your face. It allows you to be something less than sweetness and light, right? But she'd have come round. By the time I'd returned, she'd have forgotten all about, what was it she called it?' He turned his eyes to the ceiling, one hand negligently tapping the desk as he sought the right phrase. It was an impressive performance. 'Ah yes, my "sacrifice of quality to the gods of mammon". That was it.' He glared at them. 'She already knew where extravagant production methods were taking her.'

Suddenly he stabbed the air with his finger, pointing it at William, and thrust his face forward, his expression cold and mean. 'How did this witness,' a sardonic note lit the word, 'claim I collected Val from her flat?'

William took a step forward, he was losing patience, Darina could tell. 'She recognized the car and you driving it. Look . . .'

Darina knew he was going to insist the rest of the interview was conducted down at the station, where Basil wouldn't be able to play to an audience. Instead Basil interrupted him. 'And this was at what time?'

'About six twenty,' said William grimly.

'And what was the car that your so-called witness saw?'

'Your Rolls Royce, cream with registration number BE1.'

Jemima stirred. 'But, Dad.'

'Quiet, please,' Basil said. 'I'll deal with this.' He turned back to William. 'First I'll ask you how I could have been picking up Val at six twenty when that was just about the time I was checking into my flight at Gatwick? I imagine the airline's computer records will confirm that. If not, the valet service that collected my car on arrival will certainly be able to – AND confirm that it wasn't a Rolls Royce I was driving but a Volvo estate.'

He'd wanted this, Darina recognized. He'd wanted to humiliate William in front of them all. But if he thought this meant William would give up, he was badly mistaken.

'Sock it to them, Dad,' Jasper said. 'You tell 'em.' He smiled beatifically at his father.

'And we'll tell them that you and Val decided at your celebration dinner you couldn't take her to the airport,' Jemima said, looking belligerently at William from the safety of Titus's arm. 'The timing's were all wrong. She made a joke of it, said it was a fine fiance that couldn't see his girl off to her conference.' She spoke steadily but her eyes were worried.

'You tell them, girl,' agreed Jasper. He thrust his hands into his pockets and started a tuneless humming. He had the happy, unthinking expression of someone who'd removed himself from day-to-day concerns and was inhabiting a world free from pain and sorrow and problems such as writing the great English novel, or even one that proved publishable, or coping with life without his father's backing. Darina realized he was stoned and an idea occurred to her. She slid Rory to the ground and whispered, 'Go see Uncle Jasper.'

The boy set off in his wayward walk, covering the short distance between them in a moment. He wrapped his arms around Jasper's legs and raised his face. 'Dah!' he said peremptorily. Jasper bent down and picked him up.

'Jasper, give Rory to me,' Basil commanded.

'He's fine with me, Dad,' Jasper said, in that same carefree tone.

Basil rose. His complacency had vanished. He strode over and took Rory from his son.

And now Darina was quite certain she was right. The resemblance was startling. And since they'd arrived at Blackboys, other details had clicked into place. Including the reason for Basil's wanting William to rehearse what evidence he had for accusing him of arson and two murders. And the answer was shocking.

'Did you know that Jemima asked me to investigate Rory's parentage?' she asked Basil conversationally as he returned to his desk with the boy.

William gave her the sort of look that should be patented under 'to kill'. She ignored it.

Basil's face darkened. 'What's this?' he rapped out at Jemima.

Some of her composure vanished but she faced her father. 'Dad, Rory has to have a proper parent. You wouldn't do anything about it so I had to.' Her look was pure challenge.

'There's no point,' Basil ground out. 'The trail's dead. I knew that at the time he was born.'

'What you knew,' Darina said calmly, 'was who Rory's father actually was.'

Jemima turned and stared at her. 'You mean, you've found out?'

When Darina said nothing, she moved urgently towards her. 'I hired you, you've got to tell me.'

Darina reached into her pocket and brought out Jemima's cheque. 'I'm returning this.' She handed the folded slip of paper to a disbelieving Jemima, then addressed Basil. It was one of the few times she appreciated her height. 'I can't really blame you, you wanted to protect both Rory and Jasper, didn't you?' She felt very, very sad. 'Over the last few years, it wasn't Jasper who looked after Sophie; it was Sophie, who everyone has kept telling me couldn't cope with life, who looked after him. Until his need for her became too much. Did she tell you why she had to leave home? Or did you assume like the rest of your family that you were asking too much of her?'

The colour had left Basil's face, leaving it an unhealthy grey. He hugged a half-asleep Rory to his chest. 'God damn you,' he grated.

'No!' shouted Jemima. 'I don't believe you.'

William looked at Darina with a dawning comprehension.

Jemima rushed at Jasper and grabbed his arms, shaking him. 'Tell me she's lying, Jass! You couldn't have done that, you couldn't!'

Titus went and pulled her away from her brother. 'Hush, angel, you've got me now, nothing matters any more.' She turned and buried her face in his chest.

Jasper clutched nervously at the bookshelves behind him and threw a glance of appeal at his father. 'Dad,' he started uncertainly.

'Shut up,' Basil said tersely.

'You've always protected Jasper,' Darina told Basil, flicking her hair back over her ears, watching his eyes move uneasily over her. 'After his mother died, you really tried to be there for him, and for Sophie, and they worshipped you. But I don't suppose Val understood your relationship, did she? Did you realize she distrusted him? And that he didn't like her any more than she did him? What was it you said to her on the phone when I was here for lunch that day? "You know Jasper never joins us"? Something like that. He couldn't stand the sight of her. And when you became engaged and had that family evening, he took that as a sign the comfortable life here with you and his son was over.'

Jasper was still leaning against the bookshelves but his insouciance had gone. Darina remembered the young boy she had shared that Italian holiday with, so anxious to entertain and be loved, so secure with Sophie, the one person who never asked him awkward questions, who never made a demand he couldn't fulfil. Behind her she could sense William's tense concentration.

'Dad?' Jasper pleaded uneasily. 'You tell them, Dad. We belong together. You, me and Rory. You loved Sophie, too. That Douglas bitch can't have meant anything to you. It was her business you were interested in, wasn't it? I thought, if she didn't have it, if it was burned down, then you'd lose interest. It wasn't my fault that chap suddenly appeared.'

They were all looking at him now, dawning horror on their faces as what he was saying gradually made sense to them. Except for Ann Stocks, whose expression was deeply puzzled.

'Jasper, shut up!' Basil said with every bit of his

393

considerable authority. He might as well have saved his breath.

'But then you went and got engaged!' Jasper sounded bewildered. 'Why did you do that? Sophie wouldn't have liked her and I couldn't have her looking after Rory, you must see that?' he said beseechingly. He and Basil might have been alone in the room for all the attention he paid to the others. 'When I turned up the other night, she didn't want to come with me at first. Said she was waiting for a taxi. But it didn't take long to persuade her I could take her to the airport instead. Or to drive down to the river and do what had to be done. She was easy meat!' Then his face suddenly crumpled. 'I miss Sophie! She told me it wasn't right to love her, but I had to, I had to!' He brought up his arm and wiped his eyes with his sleeve.

William held out the garment he'd been clutching. 'Is this yours?' he asked.

Jasper looked at it and smiled. 'The hunter's waistcoat,' he said. 'Dad says it's his and Jemima wears it but actually it's mine.' Automatically he slipped it on, the khaki twill settling neatly round his shoulders. He played with one of the metal buttons, then looked startled as it came off in his hand.

'Jasper Ealham,' said William, sounding very official, 'I'm arresting you for the murder of Gerry Aherne and Val Douglas. You do not have to say anything . . .'

Darina sighed as the caution unwound its formal phrases, but Jasper appeared incapable of taking anything in.

'I must ask you to accompany me to the station,' William ended.

Basil stood up. He'd aged twenty years since Darina

'Body?' Jemima asked. 'What do you mean, body?'

'The corpse of a woman was pulled from the river yesterday. For a while it seemed as though it might be yours,' William said, coming forward from where he'd been standing by a window. 'I rang you,' he said to Darina. 'But you must have left. There's a message on your answering machine.'

'William, how nice,' said his mother-in-law, giving him another of her full voltage smiles.

'I didn't see your car,' Darina said.

'It's by the garage, behind the shrubs,' he said. He seemed to be clutching some sort of khaki garment.

Jemima reached an arm back towards Titus with a smile the like of which Darina had never seen her give before. He slipped an arm round her shoulders.

'And how nice to see you again, Basil,' Ann Stocks said, moving on to offer him her hand. 'It's been a long time.'

He looked at her blankly for a moment then smiled. Darina was reminded of rhymes about tigers. 'Ann Lisle, how delightful.'

'Stocks, now. I was widowed and remarried.'

'Lucky man,' he said, holding her hand in his.

Ann twinkled at him. 'You always were a most charming man,' she said. 'Unfortunately, Geoffrey died also but not before we had a most happy time together.' She sat herself down on one of the sofas.

'What's happening?' Darina whispered to William. 'What are you doing here? It can't be official, surely?'

'Strangely enough, it is,' he said repressively. 'But my investigation appears to have been hijacked.' He moved over to the desk. 'Mr Ealham, can we continue our conversation somewhere quiet or would you prefer to come

385

down to the station?' His voice was steel, his manner composed and Darina felt very proud of him. She went and sat beside her mother.

Basil removed his glasses from Rory's grasp. 'Carry on, chief inspector.'

William made no move and remained silent. Basil swept the others with a look that was hard to read. 'The body that wasn't Jemima's appears to be that of Val Douglas.'

Darina gasped. Jemima clutched at Titus's sleeve.

'And the police are accusing me of her murder.' Basil's voice was strained but steady.

'Dad!' Jemima screamed and ran to his side. 'Dad, they can't do that.'

Basil lowered Rory to the floor and ignored his daughter. 'You can have no evidence that will stand up in court,' he said to William.

'I have yet to accuse you of murder,' William said quietly. 'All I said was we have two witnesses who saw you and your car collect Mrs Douglas from her home on Thursday night. She has not been seen alive since.'

'You saw me leave her flat after she'd broken off our engagement. She can't have failed to tell you that. That was the last time I saw her.'

'Our witnesses say you came back later,' William said quietly.

Rory roared for attention, dancing up and down, and stretching up his arms to Basil.

Darina rose but was beaten by Jasper, who came into the library at high speed and dashed across the floor. 'There, there, little man! All is well, Jass is here.' He picked the boy up, swinging him high above his blond head. Rory's cries gave way to screams of delight.

Jasper lowered and held him against his chest, Rory still chortling. 'What a holy circle!' Jasper exclaimed. 'My sister returned from the grave, Rory delivered once more unto his loving family, dear Darina, the police, and who else?' He looked at Ann Stocks and Titus, his eyes black holes.

'I'm Darina's mother and this young man, I believe, belongs to your sister,' Ann said with all the aplomb of a society hostess.

'Jasper, sit down,' Basil said with weary authority. 'Everyone, sit down while I explain the facts of the matter to this impertinent inspector.'

Darina looked at William, who said nothing. She perched on an arm of a sofa by way of compromise.

Rory tugged at Jasper. He was lowered reluctantly to the floor, he then made a bee line for Darina. She felt as though she'd been given the biggest compliment of her life, sat on the sofa properly and gathered him up on her lap.

William looked very annoyed. Then he shrugged his shoulders and waited as Jemima and Titus also sat.

The only people left standing were William and Jasper, who leaned his wide shoulders against the book-shelves and radiated good humour.

'Now,' said Basil, with the authority of a chairman taking a board meeting. 'Before we had the pleasure of Jemima's arrival, inspector, you were suggesting I set fire to the premises of Eat Well Foods because I wanted to acquire the company free of debt. And that I clubbed the nightwatchman to death because I had engaged him to spy on Mrs Douglas and he was now trying to black-mail me. Do I have it aright?'

Ann Stocks stood up. 'Darling, I don't think this is

something we should be involved with, do you?' she said to her daughter. 'Why don't we leave it to the police and Basil's family?'

'Sit down.' Basil's voice was a whiplash. Any veneer of sophistication had been peeled away. 'I want you as witnesses. I want there to be no doubt, absolutely no doubt at all about this.'

Ann stared at him for a long moment. He stared back at her. Patrician dignity and charm of manner faced raw power. 'Well, if my presence can assist in any way,' she said gracefully and sat down again.

Basil turned to William, 'Well?' he barked.

'I suggested to you a scenario that required investigation,' William said, his voice rough but steady. 'Your interest in the firm is public knowledge. Your only alibi for that night was Mrs Douglas, who admitted she took a sleeping pill. We have received evidence that Mr Aherne was employed by you to spy on Mrs Douglas and you would have known about the spare rooms that could be converted into accommodation for him, thereby ensuring his constant presence at the factory.'

Basil sat very still. 'That is pure supposition. What is this evidence,' he gave a savage emphasis to the word, 'that I employed Gerry Aherne as a spy? You can have no proof, the man's dead.'

'Convenient for you, isn't it?' William said quietly. He stood easily, a picture of contained control, nicely contrasting with Basil's flamboyant style. But Darina could see the muscle that twitched at the side of his jaw and knew that he didn't feel nearly as assured as he looked.

'And can you tell me why I should want to murder Val? For God's sake, I was engaged to her!' For a fleeting second his face crumpled, then his expression regained its cool composure.

'An engagement she broke the night she was killed, sending you from her in a rage.'

Basil laughed. 'Rage? Is that what you call it? You haven't been around me long if you call that a rage. All right, I was pissed off, I'll give you that. Wouldn't you be? You've just given a woman a twenty thousand pound ring and she throws it back in your face. It allows you to be something less than sweetness and light, right? But she'd have come round. By the time I'd returned, she'd have forgotten all about, what was it she called it?' He turned his eyes to the ceiling, one hand negligently tapping the desk as he sought the right phrase. It was an impressive performance. 'Ah yes, my "sacrifice of quality to the gods of mammon". That was it.' He glared at them. 'She already knew where extravagant production methods were taking her.'

Suddenly he stabbed the air with his finger, pointing it at William, and thrust his face forward, his expression cold and mean. 'How did this witness,' a sardonic note lit the word, 'claim I collected Val from her flat?'

William took a step forward, he was losing patience, Darina could tell. 'She recognized the car and you driving it. Look . . .'

Darina knew he was going to insist the rest of the interview was conducted down at the station, where Basil wouldn't be able to play to an audience. Instead Basil interrupted him. 'And this was at what time?'

'About six twenty,' said William grimly.

'And what was the car that your so-called witness saw?'

'Your Rolls Royce, cream with registration number BE1.'

Jemima stirred. 'But, Dad.'

'Quiet, please,' Basil said. 'I'll deal with this.' He turned back to William. 'First I'll ask you how I could have been picking up Val at six twenty when that was just about the time I was checking into my flight at Gatwick? I imagine the airline's computer records will confirm that. If not, the valet service that collected my car on arrival will certainly be able to – AND confirm that it wasn't a Rolls Royce I was driving but a Volvo estate.'

He'd wanted this, Darina recognized. He'd wanted to humiliate William in front of them all. But if he thought this meant William would give up, he was badly mistaken.

'Sock it to them, Dad,' Jasper said. 'You tell 'em.' He smiled beatifically at his father.

'And we'll tell them that you and Val decided at your celebration dinner you couldn't take her to the airport,' Jemima said, looking belligerently at William from the safety of Titus's arm. 'The timing's were all wrong. She made a joke of it, said it was a fine fiance that couldn't see his girl off to her conference.' She spoke steadily but her eyes were worried.

'You tell them, girl,' agreed Jasper. He thrust his hands into his pockets and started a tuneless humming. He had the happy, unthinking expression of someone who'd removed himself from day-to-day concerns and was inhabiting a world free from pain and sorrow and problems such as writing the great English novel, or even one that proved publishable, or coping with life without his father's backing. Darina realized he was stoned and an idea occurred to her. She slid Rory to the ground and whispered, 'Go see Uncle Jasper.'

The boy set off in his wayward walk, covering the short distance between them in a moment. He wrapped his arms around Jasper's legs and raised his face. 'Dah!' he said peremptorily. Jasper bent down and picked him up.

'Jasper, give Rory to me,' Basil commanded.

'He's fine with me, Dad,' Jasper said, in that same carefree tone.

Basil rose. His complacency had vanished. He strode over and took Rory from his son.

And now Darina was quite certain she was right. The resemblance was startling. And since they'd arrived at Blackboys, other details had clicked into place. Including the reason for Basil's wanting William to rehearse what evidence he had for accusing him of arson and two murders. And the answer was shocking.

'Did you know that Jemima asked me to investigate Rory's parentage?' she asked Basil conversationally as he returned to his desk with the boy.

William gave her the sort of look that should be patented under 'to kill'. She ignored it.

Basil's face darkened. 'What's this?' he rapped out at Jemima.

Some of her composure vanished but she faced her father. 'Dad, Rory has to have a proper parent. You wouldn't do anything about it so I had to.' Her look was pure challenge.

'There's no point,' Basil ground out. 'The trail's dead. I knew that at the time he was born.'

'What you knew,' Darina said calmly, 'was who Rory's father actually was.'

Jemima turned and stared at her. 'You mean, you've found out?'

When Darina said nothing, she moved urgently towards her. 'I hired you, you've got to tell me.'

Darina reached into her pocket and brought out Jemima's cheque. 'I'm returning this.' She handed the folded slip of paper to a disbelieving Jemima, then addressed Basil. It was one of the few times she appreciated her height. 'I can't really blame you, you wanted to protect both Rory and Jasper, didn't you?' She felt very, very sad. 'Over the last few years, it wasn't Jasper who looked after Sophie; it was Sophie, who everyone has kept telling me couldn't cope with life, who looked after him. Until his need for her became too much. Did she tell you why she had to leave home? Or did you assume like the rest of your family that you were asking too much of her?'

The colour had left Basil's face, leaving it an unhealthy grey. He hugged a half-asleep Rory to his chest. 'God damn you,' he grated.

'No!' shouted Jemima. 'I don't believe you.'

William looked at Darina with a dawning comprehension.

Jemima rushed at Jasper and grabbed his arms, shaking him. 'Tell me she's lying, Jass! You couldn't have done that, you couldn't!'

Titus went and pulled her away from her brother. 'Hush, angel, you've got me now, nothing matters any more.' She turned and buried her face in his chest.

Jasper clutched nervously at the bookshelves behind him and threw a glance of appeal at his father. 'Dad,' he started uncertainly.

'Shut up,' Basil said tersely.

'You've always protected Jasper,' Darina told Basil, flicking her hair back over her ears, watching his eyes move uneasily over her. 'After his mother died, you really tried to be there for him, and for Sophie, and they worshipped you. But I don't suppose Val understood your relationship, did she? Did you realize she distrusted him? And that he didn't like her any more than she did him? What was it you said to her on the phone when I was here for lunch that day? "You know Jasper never joins us"? Something like that. He couldn't stand the sight of her. And when you became engaged and had that family evening, he took that as a sign the comfortable life here with you and his son was over.'

Jasper was still leaning against the bookshelves but his insouciance had gone. Darina remembered the young boy she had shared that Italian holiday with, so anxious to entertain and be loved, so secure with Sophie, the one person who never asked him awkward questions, who never made a demand he couldn't fulfil. Behind her she could sense William's tense concentration.

'Dad?' Jasper pleaded uneasily. 'You tell them, Dad. We belong together. You, me and Rory. You loved Sophie, too. That Douglas bitch can't have meant anything to you. It was her business you were interested in, wasn't it? I thought, if she didn't have it, if it was burned down, then you'd lose interest. It wasn't my fault that chap suddenly appeared.'

They were all looking at him now, dawning horror on their faces as what he was saying gradually made sense to them. Except for Ann Stocks, whose expression was deeply puzzled.

'Jasper, shut up!' Basil said with every bit of his

considerable authority. He might as well have saved his breath.

'But then you went and got engaged!' Jasper sounded bewildered. 'Why did you do that? Sophie wouldn't have liked her and I couldn't have her looking after Rory, you must see that?' he said beseechingly. He and Basil might have been alone in the room for all the attention he paid to the others. 'When I turned up the other night, she didn't want to come with me at first. Said she was waiting for a taxi. But it didn't take long to persuade her I could take her to the airport instead. Or to drive down to the river and do what had to be done. She was easy meat!' Then his face suddenly crumpled. 'I miss Sophie! She told me it wasn't right to love her, but I had to, I had to!' He brought up his arm and wiped his eyes with his sleeve.

William held out the garment he'd been clutching. 'Is this yours?' he asked.

Jasper looked at it and smiled. 'The hunter's waist-coat,' he said. 'Dad says it's his and Jemima wears it but actually it's mine.' Automatically he slipped it on, the khaki twill settling neatly round his shoulders. He played with one of the metal buttons, then looked startled as it came off in his hand.

'Jasper Ealham,' said William, sounding very official, 'I'm arresting you for the murder of Gerry Aherne and Val Douglas. You do not have to say anything . . .'

Darina sighed as the caution unwound its formal phrases, but Jasper appeared incapable of taking anything in.

'I must ask you to accompany me to the station,' William ended.

Basil stood up. He'd aged twenty years since Darina

and Ann had entered the room. 'Can't you see he's in no fit state to be questioned?' he ground out.

Rory put his arms around his grandfather's neck and looked as though he was about to burst into tears. 'I must insist on my lawyer being present.' Basil reached for the telephone.

'Jasper!' shrieked Jemima, clutching at Titus. 'Say something! Tell them you didn't do it!'

Titus turned her so her head was buried in his chest and held her tightly.

Darina walked over to the desk and lifted Rory out of Basil's arms. 'We'll take him upstairs,' she said to her mother.

They left the library.

Chapter Twenty-Nine

As they started across the hall, Rory started to cry. Darina felt him warm and solid against her as they climbed the stairs. 'You can stay with him in the nursery while I get his things upstairs,' she told her mother. 'That is, if you don't mind?'

'It's such a relief to get out of there,' Ann said. 'That poor boy, did he really do all those dreadful things?'

Darina nodded, hefting the heavy child more comfortably on her hip, 'I think so. Once Sophie had died, Rory and Basil were his whole world. But Val threatened to destroy it.'

They reached the second floor and Darina opened the nursery door. Then nearly dropped Rory in surprise. 'Good heavens,' she said.

Maeve O'Connor stood there in a pair of smart jeans and a silk shirt.

She took the still crying boy from Darina, sat down in the rocking chair and hushed him. 'What's all the fuss that's going on downstairs?' she asked. 'Mrs Starr said there was a heap of people in the library and not to disturb them. So I came up here until they all left. Is Basil, Mr Ealham,' she corrected herself, 'by himself now?'

Darina shook her head. 'I'm afraid not.' She waved

her mother to a chair by the table in the window and took one of the others herself. 'Where've you been? The police thought you might be dead.'

'Stupid they are!' Maeve said contemptuously.

'Apparently you rang and said you had something to tell them, then disappeared.'

'I only went over to Ireland, to tell Mam about my da's death. I didn't want her to hear it from someone else. And to tell her about being accused of taking Miss High and Mighty's stinking pearls.' She rocked gently. Rory was calming down now. 'And Mam said to come back here and tell Mr Ealham it was nothing to do with me. And didn't he know it, anyway? The money he gave me!'

'I think it was Jasper put the pearls in your drawer,' Darina said.

Maeve didn't seem surprised at this suggestion. 'He was jealous of me and the boy. He wanted himself to be the only one in his life. He's strange that one, going out at all hours, and taking God knows what. Smoking a bit of pot's all right but he's into all sorts of other things too. He went out the other night in the wee small hours and came back looking as though he'd seen a whole host of ghosts.'

'Was that the night Mrs Douglas's factory was burned down?' asked Darina.

Maeve nodded and held Rory a little more closely. 'The boy woke in the night. I was holding him by the window and saw Jasper coming in round the back. Must have been after three. And I'd heard him come in earlier about eleven. Couldn't think where he'd been.'

'Is that what you were going to tell the police?'

'I didn't know what to do,' she suddenly burst out. 'I

knew it would make trouble for him – and that meant trouble for Basil, I mean Mr Ealham. I thought and thought about it, turned it round and round in me mind, I did. And finally I thought, I had to tell them. After all, Da died, didn't he? I thought Jasper must have been somewhere else entirely, but, then, he mightn't.' She stopped abruptly. Tears gathered in her eyes and silently ran down her face. Awkwardly she freed an arm from holding the boy and wiped them away.

'Did he?' she looked fiercely at Darina.

'I'm afraid it appears he did set fire to the factory,' she said quietly and went and took Rory from the girl.

'Ah, the bugger!' Maeve wrapped her arms around herself and rocked faster and faster.

'Jasper is Rory's father.'

'The Lord save us,' said Maeve in a whisper and Darina knew she was being serious. Maeve looked at Rory, now dropping off to sleep in Darina's lap. 'Mam said I should come back for his sake. No child should lose his mother, she said, and that's what I am to him, a mother. A child has an appetite for love, Mam says, that needs feeding as much as his tummy does.'

'We all need that,' Ann murmured. 'Well, darling, what about all that stuff in your car? Do you think this nice child can give us a hand?'

'I've been looking after Rory for the last few days,' Darina explained to Maeve. 'I've got his cot and a heap of things, plus a whole shelf of pots of convenience gourmet food that you can put in the freezer.'

Maeve looked at her dully, then rose. 'We'd better get them up, then.'

Twenty minutes later, with Darina and Maeve doing

the shifting while Ann held the sleeping boy, they had everything out of the car.

'So that's that,' said Darina as they placed Rory in the re-assembled cot. 'We'd better leave now. Good luck with Mr Ealham.'

'Oh, I know how to play him,' Maeve said. She seemed to have absorbed the shock of hearing about Jasper. She stood by the cot looking at Rory, her expression a mixture of love and streetwise savvy.

'I think we should say goodbye to Basil,' said Ann when they reached the hall. She knocked on the library door and entered.

It was more than Darina felt capable of but she followed her mother into the room.

William and Jasper had gone. Jemima was quietly crying on the sofa. Titus sat beside her, looking as though he'd rather be somewhere else. Basil was talking on the telephone.

He finished the call as Ann and Darina entered.

'Basil, I'm sorry, really I am,' Ann said. 'Don't blame Darina, though, she only did what she had to.'

He pulled a hand down his face, stretching the skin. He closed his eyes for a moment and stood up. For a second Darina thought he was going to lay into her, then he sighed deeply and said simply, 'I should have realized just how unstable Jasper was. If only Sophie had told me!'

'You didn't know?' Darina asked.

He glanced down at his hands. 'She said something that made me realize it was better to keep them apart, that was why I was happy for her to go to Job and Nicola. I thought a few months there would sort everything out. I didn't realize, though, how far it had gone. I told

Jasper better not to visit her. That I'd cut his allowance and turn him out if he didn't let her make her own life. I thought that'd mean he'd leave her alone. If only she'd told me! God, Val dead, I can't believe it. And Gerry Aherne.'

For the first time since she'd known him, Darina was able to feel a certain sympathy for Basil. He had bitter days ahead.

'Sophie knew how close you were to Jasper,' Jemima said angrily. 'He has always been able to do exactly what he wanted as far as you are concerned. When she first said she couldn't stay here, you should have kicked him out.'

He looked infinitely sad, 'But he was my son and she was, well, someone else's child.'

Jemima gasped and Darina realized that she had been in such a state the last time they'd met, she hadn't been able to tell her this. 'Not yours!' Jemima said to Basil. 'But you never said!' Then looked at him suspiciously. 'How did Jasper know?'

'He saw your mother and Sophie's father together one time. He was too young to understand then but later he put things together,' Basil said wearily. 'He asked me and I, well, I had to confirm it.'

'I still think you should have turned out Jasper instead of letting Sophie leave,' Jemima said mutinously, sitting on the sofa with her head held high. She rose and walked with swift, jerky steps towards the windows. 'I can't bear to think of it. Jasper going round there, forcing her to do what he wanted. Sophie must have been a soft touch, she would have hated to hurt him. And no wonder she couldn't tell anybody about it, it would have destroyed Jasper.' She swung round and confronted Basil again. 'Didn't you ask him if he'd been with her when she disappeared?'

Basil rubbed wearily at his face. 'Of course I did! And he told me.' He looked incredibly tired. 'He's always told me the truth. He said he'd visited her several times at Job's, twice when she was on her own and then hadn't been able to control himself. He said she cried every time but let him. And she never breathed a word to me.' He pulled his skin again, as though he had to find a new look to face the world. 'I tried everything to find her. When the man I'd hired couldn't find any trace of her and we heard she hadn't applied for benefit, I really did think she'd done away with herself. I didn't realize she was pregnant but when I saw Rory, I knew he must be Jasper's son. The only thing I could do for Sophie then was to give Rory a good home and hide the truth.' He looked hopelessly at Jemima. 'But you had to go and find it out.'

'You should have told me, Dad,' she said belligerently. 'It's no use trying to hide things like that.'

'Anyway, it wasn't Jemima who set fire to that factory and murdered your friend,' Titus chipped in. 'Come on, darling, let's get going.'

She turned to him in astonishment. 'Go? What do you mean? Surely you can see I can't leave Dad now?'

It seemed to Darina that Basil looked at his daughter with new eyes but Jemima's attention was all on Titus.

He shifted his feet a little uneasily, looked first at Jemima, then at her father. He seemed to be calculating various odds. Then, 'Well, I suppose we can stay for a while,' he said smoothly.

'A while? Dad's going to need me in the business, aren't you?' she said to Basil. 'You won't need to duplicate what I do any more. I'll be your right hand. And then I'll be your left as well.'

She looked very earnest. She went up and stood beside her father. 'We'll see Jasper through this, we'll be all right.'

Titus looked out of the window and Darina wondered if he was already thinking about the next Colorado River he'd go after.

'Jemima, we're going now but I'll be in touch,' she said. 'Believe me, if I'd known where this was going to lead, I'd never have started. Oh, just one thing, was it really true that you were nearly run over?'

Jemima looked slightly shamefaced, but only slightly. 'Well, it might have been a tiny bit of an exaggeration. I was desperate for you to take Rory, you see.' So she could go to Titus.

'Never, never do that again,' Darina said sternly.

'Oh, I won't,' her friend said blithely. 'Everything's going to be all right now. Dad's really going to need me.' She didn't even look towards the young man who stood gazing out of the window. But Basil held out his hand towards her.

'Now, darling,' said Ann when they were on their way back to Chelsea, 'I think you'd better tell me the whole story.'

'Poor little Rory,' she said when Darina had finished. 'What is to become of him?'

'Maybe Maeve will prove a steadying influence.'

'If Basil can keep his hands off her!' Ann said tartly.

'Mother! You saw what a state he's in.'

'That's not going to last long. The man's always

rutted like a stag. I remember a party your father and I went to at Blackboys, dreadful people and the food was too pretentious for words, some fashionable caterer had provided it, the champagne was excellent, though. Anyway, half-way through the evening Basil said he wanted to show me his prize orchids, took me into the conservatory and I practically had to fight him off. I made sure we didn't accept any more invitations.'

'You never told me that!'

'Well, darling, Jemima was your friend.'

'Was that before or after I went to Italy with them?'

'Oh, after, darling. I'd never have let you go otherwise. Anyway, it wouldn't surprise me if Basil had a lech for Sophie himself and that's why he wasn't sorry she wanted to leave home. Which I suppose could say something for him.'

If they hadn't reached home at that point, Darina would have argued about this. But by the time she'd found somewhere to park the car and they'd got in the house, she was beginning to wonder if her mother mightn't have a point.

'I think we need a cup of tea,' Darina said, going through to the kitchen.

'Oh, yes, how lovely. I'll get some cups out, shall I?'

Darina always used mugs but said nothing. There was something wrong with the kitchen and she tried to work out what it was as she filled the kettle.

'You'll miss that little boy,' her mother said, taking out the Spode porcelain tea set that had been her wedding present to them from the back of a cupboard. That was it – no Rory! It was all horribly neat, empty and quiet.

*

Darina expected William to be late. It was a surprise, therefore, when he walked in shortly after seven thirty as she and her mother were having a drink in the drawing room.

'Now I can say properly how pleased I am to see you,' said Ann, holding up her face for his kiss. 'You were splendid this afternoon.'

'I agree, darling,' said Darina, giving him a warm embrace. 'I'm sorry if I seemed to take over at one point, but it was all clear to me and I couldn't see any other way to get it over to you.'

'You were a good catalyst,' he said, his hand lingering on the back of her neck. 'Hey, isn't that Rory's?'

Darina looked where he was pointing; a small car had crashed into the skirting board. She picked up the toy and held it in her hand for a moment before placing it on a side table. She waited for William to say how quiet the house was without Rory.

'At least we'll be able to have a full night's sleep now,' he said cheerfully, sitting in his chair. 'As you're up, darling, can you get me a drink?'

Just about to pour William a whisky, Darina remembered his diet and gave him a glass of mineral water with ice instead. 'Have you finished interviewing Jasper already?'

'Haven't even started,' he said ruefully. 'The Ealham solicitor turned up immediately after we reached the station and insisted Jasper was seen by a doctor. Who gave him a sedative. Result, we won't be able to speak to him until tomorrow. Thanks,' he added, holding up the glass she'd given him in a mock salute.

'Are you going to be able to make a case against him?'

'We've got a SOCO team going through his quarters

and over the Rolls. Preliminary reports suggest they've found a pair of trainers with gravel in their soles that could match the gravel outside the broken factory window, and jeans and a sweatshirt splashed with petrol. There are female hairs in the Rolls that could be Val Douglas's, and Jasper's prints are all over it. Both of them had ample access to the car so it mightn't mean anything but for the fact that, according to the commissionaire at the Ealham offices, the Rolls had a complete valet clean last Thursday. Basil never used it at all that day, it was driven back to the house by an employee, who left it in the garage around five o'clock without, he said, a speck of dust on it. He even polished the steering wheel and car door as he got out. The only prints on the wheel are Jasper's, so the case is building up.'

'My, what a lot you've managed to achieve,' Darina said admiringly, then told him what Maeve had told her about seeing Jasper leaving and entering the house in the small hours of the morning the factory had been set on fire.

'Well,' William said, 'it's all circumstantial so far but we should be able to make it stick. However, I fear it may be a case of diminished responsibility.'

'Does that mean Broadmoor?' Ann asked.

William nodded. 'Probably.'

'Have you any doubts about his guilt?' Darina asked.

'What, after he more or less confessed everything to us all? Not that that would stick in a court of law. But, no, it all fits too neatly.'

'How is he?'

'Beginning to come down off his high.'

'Your team must be pleased the case is sewn up,

not to mention Superintendent Roger Marks,' Darina grinned at her husband, for once not resenting the influence the super had on his life.

'Cock-a-hoop. Two murders solved in one day. It's even put Operation Chippendale in the shade.'

'And will Sergeant Pat James become a permanent member of your team?' Darina found herself asking.

'That's up to Roger. I hope so, against all the odds and after a sticky start, she and Terry Pitman seem to have hit it off.' He seemed so pleased with this fact, Darina released a breath she hadn't realized she'd been holding.

'When did you put everything together?' William asked her curiously.

'Only very gradually, I'm afraid. Rory's resemblance to both Basil and Jasper is striking and at first I thought Basil was the father. This morning I met Noah Whitstable, an out-and-out no hoper who's just about managing at the moment because he's living with a very competent Australian girl. It was clear Sophie had looked after Noah just the way Laurel was doing now. Heaven only knows why, he knocks her about and is as likely to shout at her as thank her. She seems to like being needed. And I think it was the same with Sophie.

'Anyway, there we were in the library and Jasper came in, his eyes dilated just like Noah's, obviously under the influence of some drug, and I suddenly realized that he was probably as unreliable and maybe potentially violent as Noah and that Sophie could have slipped into a relationship with Noah because he reminded her so much of her brother. So then all sorts of things fell into place.

'You see, as I gradually learned more about Sophie, the thing that puzzled me was that everyone claimed she couldn't cope with pressure from Basil. But her sister-in-law told me she spoke regularly to him on the telephone and never seemed upset by any of their conversatons. It didn't seem to add up. If, however, she was happy for everyone to think that it was Basil she couldn't live with, but that the real reason was something else entirely, it all made some sort of sense.'

'She sounds quite a remarkable girl,' said Ann.

'I think she was. It was such a tragedy she couldn't bring herself to go to the doctor or the clinic when she was pregnant.'

'Why didn't she?'

'I think it was because she was afraid they would discover the baby she was carrying was Jasper's. He had told her blood tests could identify your father and she took that to mean if she had a blood test, the truth would out.'

'Even I know it's not as simple as that!' exclaimed Ann.

'Everyone was right that poor Sophie wasn't very intelligent, at least, not in that way,' Darina said sorrowfully.

'And you worked all that out without an ounce of solid evidence,' her husband said with grave admiration. 'Would that we could conduct our investigations like that.'

Darina threw a cushion at him. 'Well, now you and your team can beaver away at producing hard evidence to make a case. It's up to you to see that justice can be done.'

William ignored this. 'I say, that's the most wonderful smell. I do hope it's supper, I didn't get any lunch and I'm starving.'

'Roast lamb with red rice from the Camargue, broccoli and carrots, followed by pears poached with cinnamon and served with a sheep's milk and vanilla sauce thickened with cornflour. All allowed on your diet. How's the headache?' Darina asked anxiously.

William paused, as though he needed to think about it. 'Do you know,' he said in surprise, 'it's gone! I feel great, really, really great.' He gave her a beaming smile and rose. 'In fact, I'll have some more mineral water, I haven't felt this good in years.'

'What have you been doing?' asked Ann curiously. Then, after the diet had been explained to her, 'Heavens! Are you condemned to this extraordinary regime for the rest of your life?'

'No,' William assured her. 'Soon we'll be able to identify what's been causing the problem.'

'Well, that's a relief. I just hope you won't have to cut out anything you really like.'

'Probably cheese,' he said gloomily. 'But it's worth it if I can go on feeling like this.' He stretched his arms out, 'Anyone want to go dancing? I might just be able to keep going all night.'

'I've got other plans for tonight,' Darina said with a smile.